Praise for these bestselling authors:

"Thoroughly satisfying…
[Tess] Gerritsen has morphed into a dependable
suspense novelist whose growing popularity
is keeping pace with her ever-finer writing skills."
—*Publishers Weekly*

"Gerritsen fans know by now what to expect
from her: a fascinating story with a gripping plot
and believably human characters."
—*Booklist*

"Tess Gerritsen knows how to keep readers
on the edge of their seats."
—*Romantic Times*

"New author **Debra Webb** delivers
an entertaining adventure, laced with breathtaking
mystery and sensual romance…a sure winner!"
—*Rendezvous*

"Debra Webb's fast-paced thriller
will make you shiver in passion and fear."
—*Romantic Times* on *Personal Protector*

TESS GERRITSEN

is an accomplished woman with an interesting story. Once a practicing physician, she has chosen, instead, to write full-time. A woman of many talents, she even plays fiddle in a band! Tess has cowritten *Adrift*, a CBS screenplay, and has several other screenplays optioned by HBO. Having lived in Hawaii, she now resides in Camden, Maine, with her physician husband and two sons.

DEBRA WEBB

was born in Scottsboro, Alabama, to parents who taught her that anything is possible if you want it badly enough. She began writing at age nine. Eventually, she met and married the man of her dreams, and tried some other occupations, including selling vacuum cleaners, and working in a factory, a day-care center, a hospital and a department store. When her husband joined the military, they moved to Berlin, Germany, and Debra became a secretary in the commanding general's office. By 1985, they were back in the States, and finally moved to Tennessee, to a small town where everyone knows everyone else. With the support of her daughters, Debra took up writing again, looking to mystery and movies for inspiration. In 1998, her dream of writing for Harlequin came true. Now multipublished, Debra writes spine-tingling romantic suspense for Harlequin Intrigue and heartfelt love stories for Harlequin American Romance.

TESS GERRITSEN

DEBRA WEBB

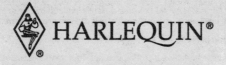

Double Impact

♦ HARLEQUIN®

TORONTO • NEW YORK • LONDON
AMSTERDAM • PARIS • SYDNEY • HAMBURG
STOCKHOLM • ATHENS • TOKYO • MILAN • MADRID
PRAGUE • WARSAW • BUDAPEST • AUCKLAND

ISBN 0-373-83583-3

DOUBLE IMPACT

Copyright © 2003 by Harlequin Books S.A.

The publisher acknowledges the copyright holders of the individual works as follows:

NEVER SAY DIE
Copyright © 1992 by Tess Gerritsen

NO WAY BACK
Copyright © 2003 by Debra Webb

This edition published by arrangement with Harlequin Books S.A.

® and TM are trademarks of the publisher. Trademarks indicated with ® are registered in the United States Patent and Trademark Office, the Canadian Trade Marks Office and in other countries.

Visit us at www.eHarlequin.com

Printed in U.S.A.

CONTENTS

NEVER SAY DIE
Tess Gerritsen

PROLOGUE

1970
Laos–North Vietnam border

THIRTY MILES OUT of Muong Sam, they saw the first tracers slash the sky.

Pilot William "Wild Bill" Maitland felt the DeHavilland Twin Otter buck like a filly as they took a hit somewhere back in the fuselage. He pulled into a climb, instinctively opting for the safety of altitude. As the misty mountains dropped away beneath them, a new round of tracers streaked past, splattering the cockpit with flak.

"Damn it, Kozy. You're bad luck," Maitland muttered to his copilot. "Seems like every time we go up together, I taste lead."

Kozlowski went right on chomping his wad of bubble gum. "What's to worry?" he drawled, nodding at the shattered windshield. "Missed ya by at least two inches."

"Try one inch."

"Big difference."

"One extra inch can make a *hell* of a lot of difference."

Kozy laughed and looked out the window. "Yeah, that's what my wife tells me."

The door to the cockpit swung open. Valdez, the cargo kicker, his shoulders bulky with a parachute pack, stuck his head in. "What the hell's goin' on any—" He froze as another tracer spiraled past.

"Got us some mighty big mosquitoes out there," Koz-lowski said and blew a huge pink bubble.

"What was that?" asked Valdez. "AK-47?"

"Looks more like .57-millimeter," said Maitland.

"They didn't say nothin' about no .57s. What kind of briefing did we get, anyway?"

Kozlowski shrugged. "Only the best your tax dollars can buy."

"How's our 'cargo' holding up?" Maitland asked. "Pants still dry?"

Valdez leaned forward and confided, "Man, we got us one weird passenger back there."

"So what's new?" Kozlowski said.

"I mean, this one's *really* strange. Got flak flyin' all 'round and he doesn't bat an eye. Just sits there like he's floatin' on some lily pond. You should see the medallion he's got 'round his neck. Gotta weigh at least a kilo."

"Come on," said Kozlowski.

"I'm tellin' you, Kozy, he's got a kilo of gold hangin' around that fat little neck of his. Who is he?"

"Some Lao VIP," said Maitland.

"That all they told you?"

"I'm just the delivery boy. Don't need to know any more than that." Maitland leveled the DeHavilland off at eight thousand feet. Glancing back through the open cock-pit doorway, he caught sight of their lone passenger sitting placidly among the jumble of supply crates. In the dim cabin, the Lao's face gleamed like burnished mahogany. His eyes were closed, and his lips were moving silently. In prayer? wondered Maitland. Yes, the man was definitely one of their more interesting cargoes.

Not that Maitland hadn't carried strange passengers be-fore. In his ten years with Air America, he'd transported German shepherds and generals, gibbons and girlfriends.

And he'd fly them anywhere they had to go. If hell had a landing strip, he liked to say, he'd take them there—as long as they had a ticket. Anything, anytime, anywhere, was the rule at Air America.

"Song Ma River," said Kozlowski, glancing down through the fingers of mist at the lush jungle floor. "Lot of cover. If they got any more .57s in place, we're gonna have us a hard landing."

"Gonna be a hard landing anyhow," said Maitland, taking stock of the velvety green ridges on either side of them. The valley was narrow; he'd have to swoop in fast and low. It was a hellishly short landing strip, nothing but a pin scratch in the jungle, and there was always the chance of an unreported gun emplacement. But the orders were to drop the Lao VIP, whoever he was, just inside North Vietnamese territory. No return pickup had been scheduled; it sounded to Maitland like a one-way trip to oblivion.

"Heading down in a minute," he called over his shoulder to Valdez. "Get the passenger ready. He's gonna have to hit the ground running."

"He says that crate goes with him."

"What? I didn't hear anything about a crate."

"They loaded it on at the last minute. Right after we took on supplies for Nam Tha. Pretty heavy sucker. I might need some help."

Kozlowski resignedly unbuckled his seatbelt. "Okay," he said with a sigh. "But remember, I don't get paid for kickin' crates."

Maitland laughed. "What the hell *do* you get paid for?"

"Oh, lots of things," Kozlowski said lazily, ducking past Valdez and through the cockpit door. "Eatin'. Sleepin'. Tellin' dirty jokes—"

His last words were cut off by a deafening blast that shattered Maitland's eardrums. The explosion sent Kozlowski—or what was left of Kozlowski—flying backward into the cockpit. Blood spattered the control panel, obscuring the altimeter dial. But Maitland didn't need the altimeter to tell him they were going down fast.

"Kozy!" screamed Valdez, staring down at the remains of the copilot. "*Kozy!*"

His words were almost lost in the howling maelstrom of wind. The DeHavilland shuddered, a wounded bird fighting to stay aloft. Maitland, wrestling with the controls, knew immediately that he'd lost hydraulics. The best he could hope for was a belly flop on the jungle canopy.

He glanced back to survey the damage and saw, through a swirling cloud of debris, the bloodied body of the Lao passenger, thrown against the crates. He also saw sunlight shining through oddly twisted steel, glimpsed blue sky and clouds where the cargo door should have been. What the hell? Had the blast come from *inside* the plane?

He screamed to Valdez, "Bail out!"

The cargo kicker didn't respond; he was still staring in horror at Kozlowski.

Maitland gave him a shove. "Get the hell *out* of here!"

Valdez at last reacted. He stumbled out of the cockpit and into the morass of broken crates and rent metal. At the gaping cargo door he paused. "Maitland?" he yelled over the wind's shriek.

Their gazes met, and in that split second, they knew. They both knew. It was the last time they'd see each other alive.

"I'll be out!" Maitland shouted. "*Go!*"

Valdez backed up a few steps. Then he launched himself out the cargo door.

Maitland didn't glance back to see if Valdez's parachute had opened; he had other things to worry about.

The plane was sputtering into a dive.

Even as he reached for his harness release, he knew his luck had run out. He had neither the time nor the altitude to struggle into his parachute. He'd never believed in wearing one anyway. Strapping it on was like admitting you didn't trust your skill as a pilot, and Maitland knew—everyone knew—that he was the best.

Calmly he refastened his harness and grasped the controls. Through the shattered cockpit window he watched the jungle floor, lush and green and heartwrenchingly beautiful, swoop up to meet him. Somehow he'd always known it would end this way: the wind whistling through his crippled plane, the ground rushing toward him, his hands gripping the controls. This time he wouldn't be walking away....

It was startling, this sudden recognition of his own mortality. An astonishing thought. *I'm going to die.*

And astonishment was exactly what he felt as the DeHavilland sliced into the treetops.

Vientiane, Laos

AT 1900 HOURS THE REPORT came in that Air America Flight 5078 had vanished.

In the Operations Room of the U.S. Army Liaison, Colonel Joseph Kistner and his colleagues from Central and Defense Intelligence greeted the news with shocked silence. Had their operation, so carefully conceived, so vital to U.S. interests, met with disaster?

Colonel Kistner immediately demanded confirmation.

The command at Air America provided the details. Flight 5078, due in Nam Tha at 1500 hours, had never arrived. A search of the presumed flight path—carried on until darkness intervened—had revealed no sign of wreckage. But flak had been reported heavy near the border, and

.57-millimeter gun emplacements were noted just out of Muong Sam. To make things worse, the terrain was mountainous, the weather unpredictable and the number of alternative nonhostile landing strips limited.

It was a reasonable assumption that Flight 5078 had been shot down.

Grim acceptance settled on the faces of the men gathered around the table. Their brightest hope had just perished aboard a doomed plane. They looked at Kistner and awaited his decision.

"Resume the search at daybreak," he said.

"That'd be throwing away live men after dead," said the CIA officer. "Come on, gentlemen. We all know that crew's gone."

Cold-blooded bastard, thought Kistner. But as always, he was right. The colonel gathered together his papers and rose to his feet. "It's not the men we're searching for," he said. "It's the wreckage. I want it located."

"And then what?"

Kistner snapped his briefcase shut. "We melt it."

The CIA officer nodded in agreement. No one argued the point. The operation had met with disaster. There was nothing more to be done.

Except destroy the evidence.

CHAPTER ONE

Present
Bangkok, Thailand

GENERAL JOE KISTNER did not sweat, a fact that utterly amazed Willy Jane Maitland, since she herself seemed to be sweating through her sensible cotton underwear, through her sleeveless chambray blouse, all the way through her wrinkled twill skirt. Kistner looked like the sort of man who ought to be sweating rivers in this heat. He had a fiercely ruddy complexion, bulldog jowls, a nose marbled with spidery red veins, and a neck so thick, it strained to burst free of his crisp military collar. *Every inch the blunt, straight-talking, tough old soldier,* she thought. *Except for the eyes. They're uneasy. Evasive.*

Those eyes, a pale, chilling blue, were now gazing across the veranda. In the distance the lush Thai hills seemed to steam in the afternoon heat. "You're on a fool's errand, Miss Maitland," he said. "It's been twenty years. Surely you agree your father is dead."

"My mother's never accepted it. She needs a body to bury, General."

Kistner sighed. "Of course. The wives. It's always the wives. There were so many widows, one tends to forget—"

"*She* hasn't forgotten."

"I'm not sure what I can tell you. What I ought to tell

you." He turned to her, his pale eyes targeting her face.
"And really, Miss Maitland, what purpose does this serve?
Except to satisfy your curiosity?"

That irritated her. It made her mission seem trivial, and
there were few things Willy resented more than being
made to feel insignificant. Especially by a puffed up, flat-
topped warmonger. Rank didn't impress her, certainly not
after all the military stuffed shirts she'd met in the past
few months. They'd all expressed their sympathy, told her
they couldn't help her and proceeded to brush off her questions. But Willy wasn't a woman to be stonewalled. She'd
chip away at their silence until they'd either answer her or
kick her out.

Lately, it seemed, she'd been kicked out of quite a few
offices.

"This matter is for the Casualty Resolution Committee," said Kistner. "They're the proper channel to go—"

"They say they can't help me."

"Neither can I."

"We both know you can."

There was a pause. Softly, he asked, "Do we?"

She leaned forward, intent on claiming the advantage.
"I've done my homework, General. I've written letters,
talked to dozens of people—everyone who had anything
to do with that last mission. And whenever I mention Laos
or Air America or Flight 5078, your name keeps popping
up."

He gave her a faint smile. "How nice to be remembered."

"I heard you were the military attaché in Vientiane.
That your office commissioned my father's last flight. And
that you personally ordered that final mission."

"Where did you hear *that* rumor?"

"My contacts at Air America. Dad's old buddies. I'd call them a reliable source."

Kistner didn't respond at first. He was studying her as carefully as he would a battle plan. "I may have issued such an order," he conceded.

"Meaning you don't remember?"

"Meaning it's something I'm not at liberty to discuss. This is classified information. What happened in Laos is an extremely sensitive topic."

"We're not discussing military secrets here. The war's been over for fifteen years!"

Kistner fell silent, surprised by her vehemence. Given her unassuming size, it was especially startling. Obviously Willy Maitland, who stood five-two, tops, in her bare feet, could be as scrappy as any six-foot marine, and she wasn't afraid to fight. From the minute she'd walked onto his veranda, her shoulders squared, her jaw angled stubbornly, he'd known this was not a woman to be ignored. She reminded him of that old Eisenhower chestnut, "It's not the size of the dog in the fight but the size of the fight in the dog." Three wars, fought in Japan, Korea and Nam, had taught Kistner never to underestimate the enemy.

He wasn't about to underestimate Wild Bill Maitland's daughter, either.

He shifted his gaze across the wide veranda to the brilliant green mountains. In a wrought-iron birdcage, a macaw screeched out a defiant protest.

At last Kistner began to speak. "Flight 5078 took off from Vientiane with a crew of three—your father, a cargo kicker and a copilot. Sometime during the flight, they diverted across North Vietnamese territory, where we assume they were shot down by enemy fire. Only the cargo kicker, Luis Valdez, managed to bail out. He was immediately captured by the North Vietnamese. Your father was never found.''

''That doesn't mean he's dead. Valdez survived—''

''I'd hardly call the man's outcome 'survival.' ''

They paused, a momentary silence for the man who'd endured five years as a POW, only to be shattered by his return to civilization. Luis Valdez had returned home on a Saturday and shot himself on Sunday.

''You left something out, General,'' said Willy. ''I've heard there was a passenger....''

''Oh. Yes,'' said Kistner, not missing a beat. ''I'd forgotten.''

''Who was he?''

Kistner shrugged. ''A Lao. His name's not important.''

''Was he with Intelligence?''

''That information, Miss Maitland, is classified.'' He looked away, a gesture that told her the subject of the Lao was definitely off-limits. ''After the plane went down,'' he continued, ''we mounted a search. But the ground fire was hot. And it became clear that if anyone *had* survived, they'd be in enemy hands.''

''So you left them there.''

''We don't believe in throwing lives away, Miss Maitland. That's what a rescue operation would've been. Throwing live men after dead.''

Yes, she could see his reasoning. He was a military tactician, not given to sentimentality. Even now, he sat ramrod straight in his chair, his eyes calmly surveying the verdant hills surrounding his villa, as though eternally in search of some enemy.

''We never found the crash site,'' he continued. ''But that jungle could swallow up anything. All that mist and smoke hanging over the valleys. The trees so thick, the ground never sees the light of day. But you'll get a feeling for it yourself soon enough. When are you leaving for Saigon?''

''Tomorrow morning.''

''And the Vietnamese have agreed to discuss this matter?''

''I didn't tell them my reason for coming. I was afraid I might not get the visa.''

''A wise move. They aren't fond of controversy. What *did* you tell them?''

''That I'm a plain old tourist.'' She shook her head and laughed. ''I'm on the deluxe private tour. Six cities in two weeks.''

''That's what one has to do in Asia. You don't confront the issues. You dance around them.'' He looked at his watch, a clear signal that the interview had come to an end.

They rose to their feet. As they shook hands, she felt him give her one last, appraising look. His grip was brisk and matter-of-fact, exactly what she expected from an old war dog.

''Good luck, Miss Maitland,'' he said with a nod of dismissal. ''I hope you find what you're looking for.''

He turned to look off at the mountains. That's when she noticed for the first time that tiny beads of sweat were glistening like diamonds on his forehead.

GENERAL KISTNER WATCHED as the woman, escorted by a servant, walked back toward the house. He was uneasy. He remembered Wild Bill Maitland only too clearly, and the daughter was very much like him. There would be trouble.

He went to the tea table and rang a silver bell. The tinkling drifted across the expanse of veranda, and seconds later, Kistner's secretary appeared.

"Has Mr. Barnard arrived?" Kistner asked.

"He has been waiting for half an hour," the man replied.

"And Ms. Maitland's driver?"

"I sent him away, as you directed."

"Good." Kistner nodded. "Good."

"Shall I bring Mr. Barnard in to see you?"

"No. Tell him I'm canceling my appointments. Tomorrow's, as well."

The secretary frowned. "He will be quite annoyed."

"Yes, I imagine he will be," said Kistner as he turned and headed toward his office. "But that's his problem."

A THAI SERVANT IN A CRISP white jacket escorted Willy through an echoing, cathedral-like hall to the reception room. There he stopped and gave her a politely questioning look. "You wish me to call a car?" he asked.

"No, thank you. My driver will take me back."

The servant looked puzzled. "But your driver left some time ago."

"He couldn't have!" She glanced out the window in annoyance. "He was supposed to wait for—"

"Perhaps he is parked in the shade beyond the trees. I will go and look."

Through the French windows, Willy watched as the servant skipped gracefully down the steps to the road. The estate was vast and lushly planted; a car could very well be hidden in that jungle. Just beyond the driveway, a gardener clipped a hedge of jasmine. A neatly graveled path traced a route across the lawn to a tree-shaded garden of flowers and stone benches. And in the far distance, a fairy blue haze seemed to hang over the city of Bangkok.

The sound of a masculine throat being cleared caught her attention. She turned and for the first time noticed the man standing in a far corner of the reception room. He cocked his head in a casual acknowledgment of her presence. She caught a glimpse of a crooked grin, a stray lock of brown hair drooping over a tanned forehead. Then he turned his attention back to the antique tapestry on the wall.

Strange. He didn't look like the sort of man who'd be interested in moth-eaten embroidery. A patch of sweat had soaked through the back of his khaki shirt, and his sleeves were shoved up carelessly to his elbows. His trousers looked as if they'd been slept in for a week. A briefcase, stamped U.S. Army ID Lab, sat on the floor beside him, but he didn't strike her as the military type. There was certainly nothing disciplined about his posture. He'd seem more at home slouching at a bar somewhere instead of cooling his heels in General Kistner's marble reception room.

"Miss Maitland?"

The servant was back, shaking his head apologetically. "There must have been a misunderstanding. The gardener says your driver returned to the city."

"Oh, no." She looked out the window in frustration. "How do I get back to Bangkok?"

"Perhaps General Kistner's driver can take you back? He has gone up the road to make a delivery, but he should return very soon. If you wish, you can see the garden in the meantime."

"Yes. Yes, I suppose that'd be nice."

The servant, smiling proudly, opened the door. "It is a very famous garden. General Kistner is known for his collection of dendrobiums. You will find them at the end of the path, near the carp pond."

She stepped out into the steam bath of late afternoon and started down the gravel path. Except for the *clack-*

clack of the gardener's hedge clippers, the day was absolutely still. She headed toward a stand of trees. But halfway across the lawn she suddenly stopped and looked back at the house.

At first all she saw was sunlight glaring off the marble facade. Then she focused on the first floor and saw the figure of a man standing at one of the windows. The servant, perhaps?

Turning, she continued along the path. But every step of the way, she was acutely aware that someone was watching her.

GUY BARNARD STOOD AT THE French windows and observed the woman cross the lawn to the garden. He liked the way the sunlight seemed to dance in her clipped, honey-colored hair. He also liked the way she moved, the coltish swing of her walk. Methodically, his gaze slid down, over the sleeveless blouse and the skirt with its regrettably sensible hemline, taking in the essentials. Trim waist. Sweet hips. Nice calves. Nice ankles. Nice...

He reluctantly cut off that disturbing train of thought. This was not a good time to be distracted. Still, he couldn't help one last appreciative glance at the diminutive figure. Okay, so she was a touch on the scrawny side. But she had great legs. Definitely great legs.

Footsteps clipped across the marble floor. Guy turned and saw Kistner's secretary, an unsmiling Thai with a beardless face.

"Mr. Barnard?" said the secretary. "Our apologies for the delay. But an urgent matter has come up."

"Will he see me now?"

The secretary shifted uneasily. "I am afraid—"

"I've been waiting since three."

"Yes, I understand. But there is a problem. It seems General Kistner cannot meet with you as planned."

"May I remind you that I didn't request this meeting. General Kistner did."

"Yes, but—"

"I've taken time out of *my* busy schedule—" he took the liberty of exaggeration "—to drive all the way out here, and—"

"I understand, but—"

"At least tell me why he insisted on this appointment."

"You will have to ask him."

Guy, who up till now had kept his irritation in check, drew himself up straight. Though he wasn't a particularly tall man, he stood a full head taller than the secretary. "Is this how the general normally conducts business?"

The secretary merely shrugged. "I am sorry, Mr. Barnard. The change was entirely unexpected...." His gaze shifted momentarily and focused on something beyond the French windows.

Guy followed the man's gaze. Through the glass, he saw what the man was looking at: the woman with the honey-colored hair.

The secretary shuffled his feet, a signal that he had other duties to attend to. "I assure you, Mr. Barnard," he said, "if you call in a few days, we will arrange another appointment."

Guy snatched up his briefcase and headed for the door. "In a few days," he said, "I'll be in Saigon."

A whole afternoon wasted, he thought in disgust as he walked down the front steps. He swore again as he reached the empty driveway. His car was parked a good hundred yards away, in the shade of a poinciana tree. The driver was nowhere to be seen. Knowing Puapong, the man was probably off flirting with the gardener's daughter.

Resignedly Guy trudged toward the car. The sun was like a broiler, and waves of heat radiated from the gravel road. Halfway to the car, he happened to glance at the garden, and he spotted the honey-haired woman, sitting on a stone bench. She looked dejected. No wonder; it was a long drive back to town, and Lord only knew when her ride would turn up.

What the hell, he thought, starting toward her. He could use some company.

She seemed to be deep in thought; she didn't look up until he was standing right beside her.

"Hi there," he said.

She squinted up at him. "Hello." Her greeting was neutral, neither friendly nor unfriendly.

"Did I hear you needed a lift back to town?"

"I have one, thank you."

"It could be a long wait. And I'm heading there anyway." She didn't respond, so he added, "It's really no trouble."

She gave him a speculative look. She had silver-gray eyes, direct, unflinching; they seemed to stare right through him. No shrinking violet, this one. Glancing back at the house, she said, "Kistner's driver was going to take me...."

"I'm here. He isn't."

Again she gave him that look, a silent third degree. She must have decided he was okay, because she finally rose to her feet. "Thanks. I'd appreciate it."

Together they walked the graveled road to his car. As they approached, Guy noticed a back door was wide open and a pair of dirty brown feet poked out. His driver was sprawled across the seat like a corpse.

The woman halted, staring at the lifeless form. "Oh, my God. He's not—"

A blissful snore rumbled from the car.

"He's not," said Guy. "Hey. Puapong!" He banged on the car roof.

The man's answering rumble could have drowned out thunder.

"Hello, Sleeping Beauty!" Guy banged the car again. "You gonna wake up, or do I have to kiss you first?"

"What? What?" groaned a voice. Puapong stirred and opened one bloodshot eye. "Hey, boss. You back so soon?"

"Have a nice nap?" Guy asked pleasantly.

"Not bad."

Guy graciously gestured for Puapong to vacate the back seat. "Look, I hate to be a pest, but do you mind? I've offered this lady a ride."

Puapong crawled out, stumbled around sleepily to the driver's seat and sank behind the wheel. He shook his head a few times, then fished around on the floor for the car keys.

The woman was looking more and more dubious. "Are you sure he can drive?" she muttered under her breath.

"This man," said Guy, "has the reflexes of a cat. When he's sober."

"*Is* he sober?"

"Puapong! Are you sober?"

With injured pride, the driver asked, "Don't I look sober?"

"There's your answer," said Guy.

The woman sighed. "That makes me feel *so* much better." She glanced back longingly at the house. The Thai servant had appeared on the steps and was waving goodbye.

Guy motioned for the woman to climb in. "It's a long drive back to town."

She was silent as they drove down the winding mountain road. Though they both sat in the back seat, two feet apart at the most, she seemed a million miles away. She kept her gaze focused on the scenery.

"You were in with the general quite a while," he noted.

She nodded. "I had a lot of questions."

"You a reporter?"

"What?" She looked at him. "Oh, no. It was just…some old family business."

He waited for her to elaborate, but she turned back to the window.

"Must've been some pretty important family business," he said.

"Why do you say that?"

"Right after you left, he canceled all his appointments. Mine included."

"You didn't get in to see him?"

"Never got past the secretary. And Kistner's the one who asked to see *me*."

She frowned for a moment, obviously puzzled. Then she shrugged. "I'm sure I had nothing to do with it."

And I'm just as sure you did, he thought in sudden irritation. Lord, why was the woman making him so antsy? She was sitting perfectly still, but he got the distinct feeling a hurricane was churning in that pretty head. He'd decided that she *was* pretty after all, in a no-nonsense sort of way. She was smart not to use any makeup; it would only cheapen that girl-next-door face. He'd never before had any interest in the girl-next-door type. Maybe the girl down the street or across the tracks. But this one was different. She had eyes the color of smoke, a square jaw and a little boxer's nose, lightly dusted with freckles. She also had a mouth that, given the right situation, could be quite kissable.

Automatically he asked, "So how long will you be in Bangkok?"

"I've been here two days already. I'm leaving tomorrow."

Damn, he thought.

"For Saigon."

His chin snapped up in surprise. "Saigon?"

"Or Ho Chi Minh City. Whatever they call it these days."

"Now that's a coincidence," he said softly.

"What is?"

"In two days, *I'm* leaving for Saigon."

"Are you?" She glanced at the briefcase, stenciled with U.S. Army ID Lab, lying on the seat. "Government affairs?"

He nodded. "What about you?"

She looked straight ahead. "Family business."

"Right," he said, wondering what the hell business her family was in. "You ever been to Saigon?"

"Once. But I was only ten years old."

"Dad in the service?"

"Sort of." Her gaze stayed fixed on some faraway point ahead. "I don't remember too much of the city. Lot of dust and heat and cars. One big traffic jam. And the beautiful women..."

"It's changed a lot since then. Most of the cars are gone."

"And the beautiful women?"

He laughed. "Oh, they're still around. Along with the heat and dust. But everything else has changed." He was silent a moment. Then, almost as an afterthought, he added, "If you get stuck, I might be able to show you around."

She hesitated, obviously tempted by his invitation.

Come on, come on, take me up on it, he thought. Then he caught a glimpse of Puapong, grinning and winking wickedly at him in the rearview mirror.

He only hoped the woman hadn't noticed.

But Willy most certainly *had* seen Puapong's winks and grins and had instantly comprehended the meaning. *Here we go again,* she thought wearily. *Now he'll ask me if I want to have dinner and I'll say no I can't, and then he'll say, what about a drink? and I'll break down and say yes because he's such a damnably good-looking man....*

"Look, I happen to be free tonight," he said. "Would you like to have dinner?"

"I can't," she said, wondering who had written this tired script and how one ever broke out of it.

"Then how about a drink?" He shot her a half smile and she felt herself teetering at the edge of a very high cliff. The crazy part was, he really *wasn't* a handsome man at all. His nose was crooked, as if, after managing to get it broken, he hadn't bothered to set it back in place. His hair was in need of a barber or at least a comb. She guessed he was somewhere in his late thirties, though the years scarcely showed except around his eyes, where deep laugh lines creased the corners. No, she'd seen far better-looking men. Men who offered more than a sweaty one-night grope in a foreign hotel.

So why is this guy getting to me?

"Just a drink?" he offered again.

"Thanks," she said. "But no thanks."

To her relief, he didn't press the issue. He nodded, sat back and looked out the window. His fingers drummed the briefcase. The mindless rhythm drove her crazy. She tried to ignore him, just as he was trying to ignore her, but it was hopeless. He was too imposing a presence.

By the time they pulled up at the Oriental Hotel, she was ready to leap out of the car. She practically did.

"Thanks for the ride," she said, and slammed the door shut.

"Hey, wait!" called the man through the open window. "I never caught your name!"

"Willy."

"You have a last name?"

She turned and started up the hotel steps. "Maitland," she said over her shoulder.

"See you around, Willy Maitland!" the man yelled.

Not likely, she thought. But as she reached the lobby doors, she couldn't help glancing back and watching the car disappear around the corner. That's when she realized she didn't even know the man's name.

GUY SAT ON HIS BED in the Liberty Hotel and wondered what had compelled him to check into this dump. Nostalgia, maybe. Plus cheap government rates. He'd always stayed here on his trips to Bangkok, ever since the war, and he'd never seen the need for a change until now. Certainly the place held a lot of memories. He'd never forget those hot, lusty nights of 1973. He'd been a twenty-year-old private on R and R; she'd been a thirty-year-old army nurse. Darlene. Yeah, that was her name. The last he'd seen of her, she was a chain-smoking mother of three and about fifty pounds overweight. What a shame. The woman, like the hotel, had definitely gone downhill.

Maybe I have, too, he thought wearily as he stared out the dirty window at the streets of Bangkok. How he used to love this city, loved the days of wandering through the markets, where the colors were so bright they hurt the eyes; loved the nights of prowling the back streets of Pat Pong, where the music and the girls never quit. Nothing bothered him in those days—not the noise or the heat or the smells.

Not even the bullets. He'd felt immune, immortal. It was always the *other* guy who caught the bullet, the other guy who got shipped home in a box. And if you thought otherwise, if you worried too long and hard about your own mortality, you made a lousy soldier.

Eventually, he'd become a lousy soldier.

He was still astonished that he'd survived. It was something he'd never fully understand: the simple fact that he'd made it back alive.

Especially when he thought of all the other men on that transport plane out of Da Nang. Their ticket home, the magic bird that was supposed to deliver them from all the madness.

He still had the scars from the crash. He still harbored a mortal dread of flying.

He refused to think about that upcoming flight to Saigon. Air travel, unfortunately, was part of his job, and this was just one more plane he couldn't avoid.

He opened his briefcase, took out a stack of folders and lay down on the bed to read. The file he opened first was one of dozens he'd brought with him from Honolulu. Each contained a name, rank, serial number, photograph and a detailed history—as detailed as possible—of the circumstances of disappearance. This one was a naval airman, Lieutenant Commander Eugene Stoddard, last seen ejecting from his disabled bomber forty miles west of Hanoi. Included was a dental chart and an old X-ray report of an arm fracture sustained as a teenager. What the file left out were the nonessentials: the wife he'd left behind, the children, the questions.

There were always questions when a soldier was missing in action.

Guy skimmed the pages, made a few mental notes and reached for another file. These were the most likely cases, the men whose stories best matched the newest collection of remains. The Vietnamese government was turning over three sets, and Guy's job was to confirm the skeletons were non-Vietnamese and to give each one a name, rank and serial number. It wasn't a particularly pleasant job, but one that had to be done.

He set aside the second file and reached for the next.

This one didn't contain a photograph; it was a supplementary file, one he'd reluctantly added to his briefcase at the last minute. The cover was stamped Confidential, then, a year ago, restamped Declassified. He opened the file and frowned at the first page.

Code Name: Friar Tuck
Status: Open (Current as of 10/85)
File Contains: 1. Summary of Witness Reports
                    2. Possible Identities
                    3. Search Status

Friar Tuck. A legend known to every soldier who'd fought in Nam. During the war, Guy had assumed those tales of a rogue American pilot flying for the enemy were mere fantasy.

Then, a few weeks ago, he'd learned otherwise.

He'd been at his desk at the Army Lab when two men, representatives of an organization called the Ariel Group, had appeared in his office. "We have a proposition," they'd said. "We know you're visiting Nam soon, and we want you to look for a war criminal." The man they were seeking was Friar Tuck.

"You've got to be kidding." Guy had laughed. "I'm

not a military cop. And there's no such man. He's a fairy tale.''

In answer, they'd handed him a twenty-thousand-dollar check—"for expenses," they'd said. There'd be more to come if he brought the traitor back to justice.

"And if I don't want the job?" he'd asked.

"You can hardly refuse" was their answer. Then they'd told Guy exactly what they knew about him, about his past, the thing he'd done in the war. A brutal secret that could destroy him, a secret he'd kept hidden away behind a wall of fear and self-loathing. They told him exactly what he could expect if it came to light. The hard glare of publicity. The trial. The jail cell.

They had him cornered. He took the check and awaited the next contact.

The day before he left Honolulu, this file had arrived special delivery from Washington. Without looking at it, he'd slipped it into his briefcase.

Now he read it for the first time, pausing at the page listing possible identities. Several names he recognized from his stack of MIA files, and it struck him as unfair, this list. These men were missing in action and probably dead; to brand them as possible traitors was an insult to their memories.

One by one, he went over the names of those voiceless pilots suspected of treason. Halfway down the list, he stopped, focusing on the entry "William T. Maitland, pilot, Air America." Beside it was an asterisk and, below, the footnote: "Refer to File #M-70-4163, Defense Intelligence. (Classified.)"

William T. Maitland, he thought, trying to remember where he'd heard the name. Maitland, Maitland.

Then he thought of the woman at Kistner's villa, the little blonde with the magnificent legs. *I'm here on family* business, she'd said. For that she'd consulted General Joe Kistner, a man whose connections to Defense Intelligence were indisputable.

See you around, Willy Maitland.

It was too much of a coincidence. And yet...

He went back to the first page and reread the file on Friar Tuck, beginning to end. The section on Search Status he read twice. Then he rose from the bed and began to pace the room, considering his options. Not liking any of them.

He didn't believe in using people. But the stakes were sky-high, and they were deeply, intensely personal. *How many men have their own little secrets from the war?* he wondered. *Secrets we can't talk about? Secrets that could destroy us?*

He closed the file. The information in this folder wasn't enough; he needed the woman's help.

But am I cold-blooded enough to use her?

Can I afford not to? whispered the voice of necessity.

It was an awful decision to make. But he had no choice.

IT WAS 5:00 P.M., AND the Bong Bong Club was not yet in full swing. Up onstage, three women, bodies oiled and gleaming, writhed together like a trio of snakes. Music blared from an old stereo speaker, a relentlessly primitive beat that made the very darkness shudder.

From his favorite corner table, Siang watched the action, the men sipping drinks, the waitresses dangling after tips. Then he focused on the stage, on the girl in the middle. She was special. Lush hips, meaty thighs, a pink, carnivorous tongue. He couldn't define what it was about her eyes, but she had *that look.* The numeral 7 was pinned on her G-string. He would have to inquire later about number seven.

"Good afternoon, Mr. Siang."

Siang looked up to see the man standing in the shadows. It never failed to impress him, the size of that man. Even now, twenty years after their first meeting, Siang could not help feeling he was a child in the presence of this giant.

The man ordered a beer and sat down at the table. He watched the stage for a moment. "A new act?" he asked.

"The one in the middle is new."

"Ah, yes, very nice. Your type, is she?"

"I will have to find out." Siang took a sip of whiskey, his gaze never leaving the stage. "You said you had a job for me."

"A small matter."

"I hope that does not mean a small reward."

The man laughed softly. "No, no. Have I ever been less than generous?"

"What is the name?"

"A woman." The man slid a photograph onto the table. "Her name is Willy Maitland. Thirty-two years old. Five foot two, dark blond hair cut short, gray eyes. Staying at the Oriental Hotel."

"American?"

"Yes."

Siang paused. "An unusual request."

"There is some…urgency."

Ah. The price goes up, thought Siang. "Why?" he asked.

"She departs for Saigon tomorrow morning. That leaves you only tonight."

Siang nodded and looked back at the stage. He was pleased to see that the girl in the middle, number seven, was looking straight at him. "That should be time enough," he said.

WILLY MAITLAND WAS standing at the river's edge, staring down at the swirling water.

From across the dining terrace, Guy spotted her, a tiny figure leaning at the railing, her short hair fluffing in the wind. From the hunch of her shoulders, the determined focus of her gaze, he got the impression she wanted to be left alone. Stopping at the bar, he picked up a beer—Oranjeboom, a good Dutch brand he hadn't tasted in years. He stood there a moment, watching her, savoring the touch of the frosty bottle against his cheek.

She still hadn't moved. She just kept gazing down at the river, as though hypnotized by something she saw in the muddy depths. He moved across the terrace toward her, weaving past empty tables and chairs, and eased up beside her at the railing. He marveled at the way her hair seemed to reflect the red and gold sparks of sunset.

"Nice view," he said.

She glanced at him. One look, utterly uninterested, was all she gave him. Then she turned away.

He set his beer on the railing. "Thought I'd check back with you. See if you'd changed your mind about that drink."

She stared stubbornly at the water.

"I know how it is in a foreign city. No one to share your frustrations. I thought you might be feeling a little—"

"Give me a break," she said, and walked away.

He must be losing his touch, he thought. He snatched up his beer and followed her. Pointedly ignoring him, she strolled along the edge of the terrace, every so often flicking her hair off her face. She had a cute swing to her walk, just a little too frisky to be considered graceful.

"I think we should have dinner," he said, keeping pace. "And maybe a little conversation."

"About what?"

"Oh, we could start off with the weather. Move on to politics. Religion. My family, your family."

"I assume this is all leading up to something?"

"Well, yeah."

"Let me guess. An invitation to your room?"

"Is that what you think I'm trying to do?" he asked in a hurt voice. "Pick you up?"

"Aren't you?" she said. Then she turned and once again walked away.

This time he didn't follow her. He didn't see the point. Leaning back against the rail, he sipped his beer and watched her climb the steps to the dining terrace. There, she sat down at a table and retreated behind a menu. It was too late for tea and too early for supper. Except for a dozen boisterous Italians sitting at a nearby table, the terrace was empty. He lingered there a while, finishing off the beer, wondering what his next approach should be. Wondering if anything would work. She was a tough nut to crack, surprisingly fierce for a dame who barely came up to his shoulder. A mouse with teeth.

He needed another beer. And a new strategy. He'd think of it in a minute.

He headed up the steps, back to the bar. As he crossed the dining terrace, he couldn't help a backward glance at the woman. Those few seconds of inattention almost caused him to collide with a well-dressed Thai man moving in the opposite direction. Guy murmured an automatic apology. The other man didn't answer; he walked right on past, his gaze fixed on something ahead.

Guy took about two steps before some inner alarm went off in his head. It was pure instinct, the soldier's premonition of disaster. It had to do with the eyes of the man who'd just passed by.

He'd seen that look of deadly calm once before, in the

eyes of a Vietnamese. They had brushed shoulders as Guy was leaving a popular Da Nang nightclub. For a split second their gazes had locked. Even now, years later, Guy still remembered the chill he'd felt looking into that man's eyes. Two minutes later, as Guy had stood waiting in the street for his buddies, a bomb ripped apart the building. Seventeen Americans had been killed.

Now, with a growing sense of alarm, he watched the Thai stop and survey his surroundings. The man seemed to spot what he was looking for and headed toward the dining terrace. Only two of the tables were occupied. The Italians sat at one, Willy Maitland at the other. At the edge of the terrace, the Thai paused and reached into his jacket.

Reflexively, Guy took a few steps forward. Even before his eyes registered the danger, his body was already reacting. Something glittered in the man's hand, an object that caught the bloodred glare of sunset. Only then could Guy rationally acknowledge what his instincts had warned him was about to happen.

He screamed, "Willy! Watch out!"

Then he launched himself at the assassin.

CHAPTER TWO

AT THE SOUND of the man's shout, Willy lowered her menu and turned. To her amazement, she saw it was the crazy American, toppling chairs as he barreled across the cocktail lounge. What was that lunatic up to now?

In disbelief, she watched him shove past a waiter and fling himself at another man, a well-dressed Thai. The two bodies collided. At the same instant, she heard something hiss through the air, felt an unexpected flick of pain in her arm. She leapt up from her chair as the two men slammed to the ground near her feet.

At the next table, the Italians were also out of their chairs, pointing and shouting. The bodies on the ground rolled over and over, toppling tables, sending sugar bowls crashing to the stone terrace. Willy was lost in utter confusion. What was happening? Why was that idiot fighting with a Thai businessman?

Both men staggered to their feet. The Thai kicked high, his heel thudding squarely into the other man's belly. The American doubled over, groaned and landed with his back propped up against the terrace wall.

The Thai vanished.

By now the Italians were hysterical.

Willy scrambled through the fallen chairs and shattered crockery and crouched at the man's side. Already a bruise the size of a golf ball had swollen his cheek. Blood trickled alarmingly from his torn lip. "Are you all right?" she cried.

He touched his cheek and winced. "I've probably looked worse."

She glanced around at the toppled furniture. "Look at this mess! I hope you have a good explanation for— What are you doing?" she demanded as he suddenly gripped her arm. "Get your hands off me!"

"You're bleeding!"

"What?" She followed the direction of his gaze and saw that a shocking blotch of red soaked her sleeve. Droplets splattered to the flagstones.

Her reaction was immediate and visceral. She swayed dizzily and sat down smack on the ground, right beside him. Through a cottony haze, she felt her head being shoved down to her knees, heard her sleeve being ripped open. Hands probed gently at her arm.

"Easy," he murmured. "It's not bad. You'll need a few stitches, that's all. Just breathe slowly."

"Get your hands off me," she mumbled. But the instant she raised her head, the whole terrace seemed to swim. She caught a watery view of mass confusion. The Italians chattering and shaking their heads. The waiters staring openmouthed in horror. And the American watching her with a look of worry. She focused on his eyes. Dazed as she was, she registered the fact that those eyes were warm and steady.

By now the hotel manager, an effete Englishman wearing an immaculate suit and an appalled expression, had appeared. The waiters pointed accusingly at Guy. The manager kept clucking and shaking his head as he surveyed the damage.

"This is dreadful," he murmured. "This sort of behavior is simply not tolerated. Not on *my* terrace. Are you a guest? You're not?'' He turned to one of the waiters. ''Call the police. I want this man arrested.''

''Are you all blind?'' yelled Guy. ''Didn't any of you see he was trying to kill her?''

''What? What? Who?''

Guy poked around in the broken crockery and fished out the knife. ''Not your usual cutlery,'' he said, holding up the deadly looking weapon. The handle was ebony, inlaid with mother of pearl. The blade was razor sharp. ''This one's designed to be thrown.''

''Oh, rubbish,'' sputtered the Englishman.

''Take a look at her arm!''

The manager turned his gaze to Willy's blood-soaked sleeve. Horrified, he took a stumbling step back. ''Good God. I'll—I'll call a doctor.''

''Never mind,'' said Guy, sweeping Willy off the ground. ''It'll be faster if I take her straight to the hospital.''

Willy let herself be gathered into Guy's arms. She found his scent strangely reassuring, a distinctly male mingling of sweat and after-shave. As he carried her across the terrace, she caught a swirling view of shocked waiters and curious hotel guests.

''This is embarrassing,'' she complained. ''I'm all right. Put me down.''

''You'll faint.''

''I've never fainted in my life!''

''It's not a good time to start.'' He got her into a waiting taxi, where she curled up in the back seat like a wounded animal.

The emergency-room doctor didn't believe in anesthesia. Willy didn't believe in screaming. As the curved suture needle stabbed again and again into her arm, she clenched her teeth and longed to have the lunatic American hold her hand. If only she hadn't played tough and sent him out to the waiting area. Even now, as she fought back tears of pain, she refused to admit, even to herself, that she needed any man to hold her hand. Still, it would have been nice. It would have been wonderful.

And I still don't know his name.

The doctor, whom she suspected of harboring sadistic tendencies, took the final stitch, tied it off and snipped the silk thread. "You see?" he said cheerfully. "That wasn't so bad."

She felt like slugging him in the mouth and saying, *You see? That wasn't so bad, either.*

He dressed the wound with gauze and tape, then gave her a cheerful slap—on her wounded arm, of course—and sent her out into the waiting room.

He was still there, loitering by the reception desk. With all his bruises and cuts, he looked like a bum who'd wandered in off the street. But the look he gave her was warm and concerned. "How's the arm?" he asked.

Gingerly she touched her shoulder. "Doesn't this country believe in Novocaine?"

"Only for wimps," he observed. "Which you obviously aren't."

Outside, the night was steaming. There were no taxis available, so they hired a *tuk-tuk,* a motorcycle-powered rickshaw, driven by a toothless Thai.

"You never told me your name," she said over the roar of the engine.

"I didn't think you were interested."

"Is that my cue to get down on my knees and beg for an introduction?"

Grinning, he held out his hand. "Guy Barnard. Now do I get to hear what the Willy's short for?"

She shook his hand. "Wilone."

"Unusual. Nice."

"Short of Wilhelmina, it's as close as a daughter can get to being William Maitland, Jr."

He didn't comment, but she saw an odd flicker in his eyes, a look of sudden interest. She wondered why. The *tuk-tuk* puttered past a *klong,* its stagnant waters shimmering under the streetlights.

"Maitland," he said casually. "Now that's a name I seem to remember from the war. There was a pilot, a guy named Wild Bill Maitland. Flew for Air America. Any relation?"

She looked away. "Just my father."

"No kidding! You're Wild Bill Maitland's kid?"

"You've heard the stories about him, have you?"

"Who hasn't? He was a living legend. Right up there with Earthquake Magoon."

"That's about what he was to me, too," she muttered. "Nothing but a legend."

There was a pause in their exchange, and she wondered if Guy Barnard was shocked by the bitterness in her last statement. If so, he didn't show it.

"I never actually met your old man," he said. "But I saw him once, on the Da Nang airstrip. I was working ground crew."

"With Air America?"

"No. Army Air Cav." He sketched a careless salute. "Private First Class Barnard. You know, the real scum of the earth."

"I see you've come up in the world."

"Yeah." He laughed. "Anyway, your old man brought in a C-46, engine smoking, fuel zilch, fuselage so shot up you could almost see right through her. He sets her down on the tarmac, pretty as you please. Then he climbs out and checks out all the bullet holes. Any other pilot would've been down on his knees kissing the ground. But your dad, he just shrugs, goes over to a tree and takes a nap.'' Guy shook his head. ''Your old man was something else.''

''So everyone tells me.'' Willy shoved a hank of wind-blown hair off her face and wished he'd stop talking about her father. That's how it'd been, as far back as she could remember. When she was a child in Vientiane, at every dinner party, every cocktail gathering, the pilots would invariably trot out another Wild Bill story. They'd raise toasts to his nerves, his daring, his crazy humor, until she was ready to scream. All those stories only emphasized how unimportant she and her mother were in the scheme of her father's life.

Maybe that's why Guy Barnard was starting to annoy her.

But it was more than just his talk about Bill Maitland. In some odd, indefinable way, Guy reminded her too much of her father.

The *tuk-tuk* suddenly hit a bump in the road, throwing her against Guy's shoulder. Pain sliced through her arm and her whole body seemed to clench in a spasm.

He glanced at her, alarmed. ''Are you all right?''

''I'm—'' She bit her lip, fighting back tears. ''It's really starting to hurt.''

He yelled at the driver to slow down. Then he took Willy's hand and held it tightly. ''Just a little while longer. We're almost there....''

It was a long ride to the hotel.

Up in her room, Guy sat her down on the bed and gently stroked the hair off her face. ''Do you have any pain killers?''

''There's—there's some aspirin in the bathroom.'' She started to rise to her feet. ''I can get it.''

"No. You stay right where you are." He went into the bathroom, came back out with a glass of water and the bottle of aspirin. Even through her cloud of pain, she was intensely aware of him watching her, studying her as she swallowed the tablets. Yet she found his nearness strangely reassuring. When he turned and crossed the room, the sudden distance between them left her feeling abandoned.

She watched him rummage around in the tiny refrigerator. "What are you looking for?"

"Found it." He came back with a cocktail bottle of whiskey, which he uncapped and handed to her. "Liquid anesthesia. It's an old-fashioned remedy, but it works."

"I don't like whiskey."

"You don't have to like it. By definition, medicine's not supposed to taste good."

She managed a gulp. It burned all the way down her throat. "Thanks," she muttered. "I think."

He began to walk a slow circle, surveying the plush furnishings, the expansive view. Sliding glass doors opened onto a balcony. From the Chaophya River flowing just below came the growl of motorboats plying the waters. He wandered over to the nightstand, picked up a rambutan from the complimentary fruit basket and peeled off the prickly shell. "Nice room," he said, thoughtfully chewing the fruit. "Sure beats my dive—the Liberty Hotel. What do you do for a living, anyway?"

She took another sip of whiskey and coughed. "I'm a pilot."

"Just like your old man?"

"Not exactly. I fly for the paycheck, not the excitement. Not that the pay's great. No money in flying cargo."

"Can't be too bad if you're staying here."

"I'm not paying for this."

His eyebrows shot up. "Who is?"

"My mother."

"Generous of her."

His note of cynicism irritated her. What right did he have to insult her? Here he was, this battered vagabond, eating *her* fruit, enjoying *her* view. The *tuk-tuk* ride had tossed his hair in all directions, and his bruised eye was swollen practically shut. Why was she even putting up with this jerk?

He was watching her with curiosity. "So what else is Mama paying for?" he asked.

She looked him hard in the eye. "Her own funeral arrangements," she said, and was satisfied to see his smirk instantly vanish.

"What do you mean? Is your mother dead?"

"No, but she's dying." Willy gazed out the window at the lantern lights along the river's edge. For a moment they seemed to dance like fireflies in a watery haze. She swallowed; the lights came back into focus. "God," she sighed, wearily running her fingers through her hair. "What the hell am I doing here?"

"I take it this isn't a vacation."

"You got that right."

"What is it, then?"

"A wild-goose chase." She swallowed the rest of the whiskey and set the tiny bottle down on the nightstand. "But it's Mom's last wish. And you're always supposed to grant people their dying wish." She looked at Guy. "Aren't you?"

He sank into a chair, his gaze locked on her face. "You told me before that you were here on family business. Does it have to do with your father?"

She nodded.

"And that's why you saw Kistner today?"

"We were hoping—I was hoping—that he'd be able to fill us in about what happened to Dad."

"Why go to Kistner? Casualty resolution isn't his job."

"But Military Intelligence is. In 1970, Kistner was stationed in Laos. He was the one who commissioned my father's last flight. And after the plane went down, he directed the search. What there was of a search."

"And did Kistner tell you anything new?"

"Only what I expected to hear. That after twenty years, there's no point pursuing the matter. That my father's dead. And there's no way to recover his remains."

"It must've been tough hearing that. Knowing you've come all this way for nothing."

"It'll be hard on my mother."

"And not on you?"

"Not really." She rose from the bed and wandered out onto the balcony, where she stared down at the water. "You see, I don't give a damn about my father."

The night was heavy with the smells of the river. She knew Guy was watching her; she could feel his gaze on her back, could imagine the shocked expression on his face. Of course, he would be shocked; it was appalling, what she'd just said. But it was also the truth.

She sensed, more than heard, his approach. He came up beside her and leaned against the railing. The glow of the river lanterns threw his face into shadow.

She stared down at the shimmering water. "You don't know what it's like to be the daughter of a legend. All my life, people have told me how brave he was, what a hero he was. God, he must have loved the glory."

"A lot of men do."

"And a lot of women suffer for it."

"Did your mother suffer?"

She looked up at the sky. "My mother..." She shook

her head and laughed. "Let me tell you about my mother. She was a nightclub singer. All the best New York clubs. I went through her scrapbook, and I remember some reviewer wrote, 'Her voice spins a web that will trap any audience in its magic.' She was headed for the moon. Then she got married. She went from star billing to a—a footnote in some man's life. We lived in Vientiane for a few years. I remember what a trouper she was. She wanted so badly to go home, but there she was, scraping the store shelves for decent groceries. Laughing off the hand grenades. Dad got the glory. But she's the one who raised me." Willy looked at Guy. "That's how the world works. Isn't it?"

He didn't answer.

She turned her gaze back to the river. "After Dad's contract ended with Air America, we tried it for a while in San Francisco. He worked for a commuter airline. And Mom and I, well, we just enjoyed living in a town without mortars and grenades going off. But…" She sighed. "It didn't last. Dad got bored. I guess he missed the old adrenaline high. And the glory. So he went back."

"They got divorced?"

"He never asked for one. And Mom wouldn't hear of it anyway. She loved him." Willy's voice dropped. "She still loves him."

"He went back to Laos alone, huh?"

"Signed up for another two years. Guess he preferred the company of danger junkies. They were all like that, those A.A. pilots—all volunteers, not draftees—all of 'em laughing death in the face. I think flying was the only thing that gave them a rush, made them feel alive. Must've been the ultimate high for Dad. Dying."

"And here you are, over twenty years later."

"That's right. Here I am."

"Looking for a man you don't give a damn about. Why?"

"It's not me asking the questions. It's my mother. She's never wanted much. Not from me, not from anyone. But this was something she had to know."

"A dying wish."

Willy nodded. "That's the one nice thing about cancer. You get some time to tie up the loose ends. And my father is one hell of a big loose end."

"Kistner gave you the official verdict—your father's dead. Doesn't that tie things up?"

"Not after all the lies we've been told."

"Who's lied to you?"

She laughed. "Who hasn't? Believe me, we've made the rounds. We've talked to the Joint Casualty Resolution Committee. Defense Intelligence. The CIA. They all had the same advice—drop it."

"Maybe they have a point."

"Maybe they're hiding the truth."

"Which is?"

"That Dad survived the crash."

"What's your evidence?"

She studied Guy for a moment, wondering how much to tell him. Wondering why she'd already told him as much as she had. She knew nothing about him except that he had fast reflexes and a sense of humor. That his eyes were brown, and his grin distinctly crooked. And that, in his own rumpled way, he was the most attractive man she'd ever met.

That last thought was as jolting as a bolt of lightning on a clear summer's day. But he *was* attractive. There was nothing she could specifically point to that made him that way. Maybe it was his self-assurance, the confident way he carried himself. *Or maybe it's the damn whiskey,* she thought. That's why she was feeling so warm inside, why her knees felt as if they were about to buckle.

She gripped the steel railing. "My mother and I, we've had, well, *hints* that secrets have been kept from us."

"Anything concrete?"

"Would you call an eyewitness concrete?"

"Depends on the eyewitness."

"A Lao villager."

"He saw your father?"

"No, that's the whole point—he didn't."

"I'm confused."

"Right after the plane went down," she explained, "Dad's buddies printed up leaflets advertising a reward of two kilos of gold to anyone who brought in proof of the crash. The leaflets were dropped along the border and all over Pathet Lao territory. A few weeks later a villager came out of the jungle to claim the reward. He said he'd found the wreckage of a plane, that it had crashed just inside the Vietnam border. He described it right down to the number on the tail. And he swore there were only two bodies on board, one in the cargo hold, another in the cockpit. The plane had a crew of *three.*"

"What did the investigators say about that?"

"We didn't hear this from them. We learned about it only after the classified report got stuffed into our mailbox, with a note scribbled 'From a friend.' I think one of Dad's old Air America buddies got wind of a cover-up and decided to let the family know about it."

Guy was standing absolutely still, like a cat in the shadows. When he spoke, she could tell by his voice that he was very, very interested.

"What did your mother do then?" he asked.

"She pursued it, of course. She wouldn't give up. She hounded the CIA. Air America. She got nothing out of them. But she did get a few anonymous phone calls telling her to shut up.''

''Or?''

''Or she'd learn things about Dad she didn't want to know. Embarrassing things.''

''Other women? What?''

This was the part that made Willy angry. She could barely bring herself to talk about it. ''They implied—'' She let out a breath. ''They implied he was working for the other side. That he was a traitor.''

There was a pause. ''And you don't believe it,'' he said softly.

Her chin shot up. ''Hell, no, I don't believe it! Not a word. It was just their way to scare us off. To keep us from digging up the truth. It wasn't the only stunt they pulled. When we kept asking questions, they stopped release of Dad's back pay, which by then was somewhere in the tens of thousands. Anyway, we floundered around for a while, trying to get information. Then the war ended, and we thought we'd finally hear the answers. We watched the POWs come back. It was tough on Mom, seeing all those reunions on TV. Hearing Nixon talk about our brave men finally coming home. Because hers didn't. But we were surprised to hear of one man who did make it home— one of the crew members on Dad's plane.''

Guy straightened in surprise. ''Then there *was* a survivor?''

''Luis Valdez, the cargo kicker. He bailed out as the plane was going down. He was captured almost as soon as he hit the ground. Spent the next five years in a North Vietnamese prison camp.''

''Doesn't that explain the missing body? If Valdez bailed out—''

''There's more. The very day Valdez flew back to the

States, he called us. I answered the phone. I could hear he was scared. He'd been warned by Intelligence not to talk to anyone. But he thought he owed it to Dad to let us know what had happened. He told us there was a passenger on that flight, a Lao who was already dead when the plane went down. And that the body in the cockpit was probably Kozlowski, the copilot. That still leaves a missing body.''

"Your father.''

She nodded. "We went back to the CIA with this information. And you know what? They denied there was any passenger on that plane, Lao or otherwise. They said it carried only a shipment of aircraft parts.''

"What did Air America say?''

"They claim there's no record of any passenger.''

"But you had Valdez's testimony.''

She shook her head. "The day after he called, the day he was supposed to come see us, he shot himself in the head. Suicide. Or so the police report said.''

She could tell by his long silence that Guy was shocked. "How convenient,'' he murmured.

"For the first time in my life, I saw my mother scared. Not for herself, but for me. She was afraid of what might happen, what they might do. So she let the matter drop. Until…'' Willy paused.

"There was something else?''

She nodded. "About a year after Valdez died—I guess it was around '76—a funny thing happened to my mother's bank account. It picked up an extra fifteen thousand dollars. All the bank could tell her was that the deposit had been made in Bangkok. A year later, it happened again, this time, around ten thousand.''

"All that money, and she never found out where it came from?''

"No. All these years she's been trying to figure it out.

Wondering if one of Dad's buddies, or maybe Dad himself—'' Willy shook her head and sighed. "Anyway, a few months ago, she found out she had cancer. And suddenly it seemed very important to learn the truth. She's too sick to make this trip herself, so she asked me to come. And I'm hitting the same brick wall she hit twenty years ago."

"Maybe you haven't gone to the right people."

"Who *are* the right people?"

Quietly, Guy shifted toward her. "I have connections," he said softly. "I could find out for you."

Their hands brushed on the railing; Willy felt a delicious shock race through her whole arm. She pulled her hand away.

"What sort of connections?"

"Friends in the business."

"Exactly what *is* your business?"

"Body counts. Dog tags. I'm with the Army ID Lab."

"I see. You're in the military."

He laughed and leaned sideways against the railing. "No way. I bailed out after Nam. Went back to college, got a master's in stones and bones. That's physical anthropology, emphasis on Southeast Asia. Anyway, I worked a while in a museum, then found out the army paid better. So I hired on as a civilian contractor. I'm still sorting bones, only these have names, ranks and serial numbers."

"And that's why you're going to Vietnam?"

He nodded. "There are new sets of remains to pick up in Saigon and Hanoi."

Remains. Such a clinical word for what was once a human being.

"I know a few people," he said. "I might be able to help you."

"Why?"

"You've made me curious."

"Is that all it is? Curiosity?"

His next move startled her. He reached out and brushed back her short, tumbled hair. The brief contact of his fingers seemed to leave her whole neck sizzling. She froze, unable to react to this unexpectedly intimate contact.

"Maybe I'm just a nice guy," he whispered.

Oh, hell, he's going to kiss me, she thought. *He's going to kiss me and I'm going to let him, and what happens next is anyone's guess....*

She batted his hand away and took a panicked step back. "I don't believe in nice guys."

"Afraid of men?"

"I'm not afraid of men. But I don't trust them, either."

"Still," he said with an obvious note of laughter in his voice, "you let me into your room."

"Maybe it's time to let you out." She stalked across the room and yanked open the door. "Or are you going to be difficult?"

"Me?" To her surprise, he followed her to the door. "I'm never difficult."

"I'll bet."

"Besides, I can't hang around tonight. I've got more important business."

"Really."

"Really." He glanced at the lock on her door. "I see you've got a heavy-duty dead bolt. Use it. And take my advice—don't go out on the town tonight."

"Darn! That was next on my agenda."

"Oh, and in case you need me—" he turned and grinned at her from the doorway "—I'm staying at the Liberty Hotel. Call anytime."

She started to snap, *Don't hold your breath.* But before she could get out the words, he'd left.

She was staring at a closed door.

CHAPTER THREE

TOBIAS WOLFF swiveled his wheelchair around from the liquor cabinet and faced his old friend. "If I were you, Guy, I'd stay the hell out of it."

It had been five years since they'd last seen each other. Toby still looked as muscular as ever—at least from the waist up. Fifteen years' confinement to a wheelchair had bulked out those shoulders and arms. Still, the years had taken their inevitable toll. Toby was close to fifty now, and he looked it. His bushy hair, cut Beethoven style, was almost entirely gray. His face was puffy and sweating in the tropical heat. But the dark eyes were as sharp as ever.

"Take some advice from an old Company man," he said, handing Guy a glass of Scotch. "There's no such thing as a coincidental meeting. There are only planned encounters."

"Coincidence or not," said Guy, "Willy Maitland could be the break I've been waiting for."

"Or she could be nothing but trouble."

"What've I got to lose?"

"Your life?"

"Come on, Toby! You're the only one I can trust to give me a straight answer."

"It was a long time ago. I wasn't directly connected to the case."

"But you were in Vientiane when it happened. You must remember something about the Maitland file."

"Only what I heard in passing, none of it confirmed. Hell, it was like the Wild West out there. Rumors flying thicker'n the mosquitoes."

"But not as thick as you covert-action boys."

Toby shrugged. "We had a job to do. We did it."

"You remember who handled the Maitland case?"

"Had to be Mike Micklewait. I know he was the case officer who debriefed that villager—the one who came in for the reward."

"Did Micklewait think the man was on the level?"

"Probably not. I know the villager never got the reward."

"Why wasn't Maitland's family told about all this?"

"Hey, Maitland wasn't some poor dumb draftee. He was working for Air America. In other words, CIA. That's a job you don't talk about. Maitland knew the risks."

"The family deserved to hear about any new evidence." Guy thought about the surreptitious way Willy and her mother *had* learned of it.

Toby laughed. "There was a secret war going on, remember? We weren't even supposed to be in Laos. Keeping families informed was at the bottom of anyone's priority list."

"Was there some other reason it was hushed up? Something to do with the passenger?"

Toby's eyebrows shot up. "Where did you hear that rumor?"

"Willy Maitland. She heard there was a Lao on board. Everyone's denying his existence, so my guess is he was a very important person. Who was he?"

"I don't know." Toby wheeled around and looked out the open window of his apartment. From the darkness came the sounds and smells of the Bangkok streets. Meat sizzling on an open-air grill. Women laughing. The rumble of a *tuk-tuk*. "There was a hell of a lot going on back then. Things we never talked about. Things we were even ashamed to talk about. What with all the agents and counteragents and generals and soldiers of fortune, you could never really be sure who was running the place. Everyone was pulling strings, trying to get rich quick. I couldn't wait to get the hell out." He slapped the wheelchair in anger. "And this is where I end up. Great retirement." Sighing, he leaned back and stared out at the night. "Let it be, Guy," he said softly. "If you're right—if someone's out to hit Maitland's kid—then this is too hot to handle."

"Toby, that's the point! *Why* is the case so hot? Why, after all these years, would Maitland's brat be making them nervous? What do they think she'll find out?"

"Does she know what she's getting into?"

"I doubt it. Anyway, nothing'll stop this dame. She's a chip off the old block."

"Meaning she's trouble. How're you going to get her to work with you?"

"That's the part I haven't figured out yet."

"There's always the Romeo approach."

Guy grinned. "I'll keep it in mind."

In fact, that was precisely the tactic he'd been considering all evening. Not because he was so sure it would work, but because she was an attractive woman and he couldn't help wondering what she was really like under that tough-gal facade.

"Alternatively," Toby said, "you could try telling her the truth. That you're not after her. You're after the three million bounty."

"Two million."

"Two million, three million, what's the difference? It's a lot of dough."

"And I could use a lot of help," Guy said with quiet significance.

Toby sighed. "Okay," he said, at last wheeling around to look at him. "You want a name, I'll give you one. May or may not help you. Try Alain Gerard, a Frenchman, living these days in Saigon. He used to have close ties with the Company, knew all the crap going on in Vientiane."

"Ex-Company and living in Saigon? Why haven't the Vietnamese kicked him out?"

"He's useful to them. During the war he made his money exporting, shall we say, raw pharmaceuticals. Now he's turned humanitarian in his old age. U.S. trade embargoes cut the Viets off from Western markets. Gerard brings in medical supplies from France, antibiotics, X-ray film. In return, they let him stay in the country."

"Can I trust him?"

"He's ex-Company."

"Then I can't trust him."

Toby grunted. "You seem to trust me."

"You're different."

"That's only because I owe you, Barnard. Though I often think you should've left me to burn in that plane." Toby kneaded his senseless thighs. "No one has much use for half a man."

"Doesn't take legs to make a man, Toby."

"Ha. Tell that to Uncle Sam." Using his powerful arms, Toby shifted his weight in the chair. "When're you leaving for Saigon?"

"Tomorrow morning. I moved my flight up a few days." Guy's palms were already sweating at the thought of boarding that Air France plane. He tossed back a mind-numbing gulp of Scotch. "Wish I could take a boat instead."

Toby laughed. "You'd be the first boat person going *back* to Vietnam. Still scared to fly, huh?"

"White knuckles and all." He set his glass down and headed for the door. "Thanks for the drink. And the tip."

"I'll see what else I can do for you," Toby called after him. "I still might have a few contacts in-country. Maybe I can get 'em to watch over you. And the woman. By the way, is anyone keeping an eye on her tonight?"

"Some buddies of Puapong's. They won't let anyone near her. She should get to the airport in one piece."

"And what happens then?"

Guy paused in the doorway. "We'll be in Saigon. Things'll be safer there."

"In Saigon?" Toby shook his head. "Don't count on it."

THE CROWD AT THE Bong Bong Club had turned wild, the men drunkenly shouting and groping at the stage as the girls, dead-eyed, danced on. No one took notice of the two men huddled at a dark corner table.

"I am disappointed, Mr. Siang. You're a professional, or so I thought. I fully expected you to deliver. Yet the woman is still alive."

Stung by the insult, Siang felt his face tighten. He was not accustomed to failure—or to criticism. He was glad the darkness hid his burning cheeks as he set his glass of vodka down on the table. "I tell you, this could not be predicted. There was interference—a man—"

"Yes, an American, so I've been told. A Mr. Barnard."

Siang was startled. "You've learned his name?"

"I make it a point to know everything."

Siang touched his bruised face and winced. This Mr. Barnard certainly had a savage punch. If they ever crossed paths again, Siang would make him pay for this humiliation.

"The woman leaves for Saigon tomorrow," said the man.

"Tomorrow?" Siang shook his head. "That does not leave me enough time."

"You have tonight."

"Tonight? Impossible." Siang had, in fact, already spent the past four hours trying to get near the woman. But the desk clerk at the Oriental had stood watch like a guard dog over the passkeys, the hotel security officer refused to leave his post near the elevators, and a bellboy kept strolling up and down the hall. The woman had been untouchable. Siang had briefly considered climbing up the balcony, but his approach was hampered by two vagrants camped on the riverbank beneath her window. Though hostile-looking, the tramps had posed no real threat to a man like Siang, but he hadn't wanted to risk a foolish, potentially messy scene.

And now his professional reputation was at stake.

"The matter grows more urgent," said the man. "This must be done soon."

"But she leaves Bangkok tomorrow. I can make no guarantees."

"Then do it in Saigon. Whether you finish it here or there, *it has to be done*."

Siang was stunned. "Saigon? I cannot return—"

"We'll send you under Thai diplomatic cover. A cultural attaché, perhaps. I'll decide and arrange the entry papers accordingly."

"Vietnamese security is tight. I will not be able to bring in any—"

"The diplomatic pouch goes out twice a week. Next

drop is in three days. I'll see what weapons I can slip through. Until then, you'll have to improvise.''

Siang fell silent, wondering how it would feel to once again walk the streets of Saigon. And he wondered about Chantal. How many years had it been since he'd seen her? Did she still hate him for leaving her behind? Of course, she would; she never forgot a grudge. Somehow, he'd have to work his way back into her affections. He didn't think that would be too difficult. Life in the new Vietnam must be hard these days, especially for a woman. Chantal liked her comforts; for a few precious luxuries, she might do anything. Even sell her soul.

She was a woman he could understand.

He looked across the table. "There will be expenses."

The man nodded. "I can be generous. As you well know.''

Already Siang was making a mental list of what he'd need. Old clothes—frayed shirts and faded trousers—so he wouldn't stand out in a crowd. Cigarettes, soap and razor blades for bartering favors on the streets. And then he'd need a few special gifts for Chantal....

He nodded. The bargain was struck.

"One more thing," said the man as he rose to leave.

"Yes?"

"Other…parties seem to be involved. The Company, for instance. I wouldn't want to pull that particular tiger's tail. So keep bloodshed to a minimum. Only the woman dies. No one else.''

"I understand.''

After the man had left, Siang sat alone at the corner table, thinking. Remembering Saigon. Had it really been fifteen years? His last memories of the city were of panicked faces, of hands clawing frantically at a helicopter

door, of the roar of chopper blades and the swirl of dust
as the rooftops fell away.

Siang took a deep swallow of vodka and stood to leave.
Just then, whistles and applause rose from the crowd gathered around the dance stage. A lone girl stood brown and
naked in the spotlight. Around her waist was wrapped an
eight-foot boa constrictor. The girl seemed to shudder as
the snake slithered down between her thighs. The men
shouted their approval.

Siang grinned. Ah, the Bong Bong Club. Always something new.

Saigon

FROM THE ROOFTOP GARDEN of the Rex Hotel, Willy
watched the bicycles thronging the intersection of Le Loi
and Nguyen Hue. A collision seemed inevitable, only a
matter of time. Riders whisked through at breakneck
speed, blithely ignoring the single foolhardy pedestrian
inching fearfully across the street. Willy was so intent on
silently cheering the man on that she scarcely registered
the monotonous voice of her government escort.

"And tomorrow, we will take you by car to see the
National Palace, where the puppet government ruled in
luxury, then on to the Museum of History, where you will
learn about our struggles against the Chinese and the
French imperialists. The next day, you will see our lacquer
factory, where you can buy many beautiful gifts to bring
home. And then—"

"Mr. Ainh," Willy said with a sigh, turning at last to
her guide. "It all sounds very fascinating, this tour you've
planned. But have you looked into my other business?"

Ainh blinked. Though his frame was chopstick thin, he

had a cherubic face made owlish by his thick glasses. "Miss Maitland," he said in a hurt voice, "I have arranged a private car! And many wonderful meals."

"Yes, I appreciate that, but—"

"You are unhappy with your itinerary?"

"To be perfectly honest, I don't really care about a tour. I want to find out about my father."

"But you have paid for a tour! We must provide one."

"I paid for the tour to get a visa. Now that I'm here, I need to talk to the right people. You can arrange that for me, can't you?"

Ainh shifted nervously. "This is a…a complication. I do not know if I can…that is, it is not what I…" He drifted into helpless silence.

"Some months ago, I wrote to your foreign ministry about my father. They never wrote back. If you could arrange an appointment…"

"How many months ago did you write?"

"Six, at least."

"You are impatient. You cannot expect instant results."

She sighed. "Obviously not."

"Besides, you wrote the Foreign Ministry. I have nothing to do with them. I am with the Ministry of Tourism."

"And you folks don't communicate with each other, is that it?"

"They are in a different building."

"Then maybe—if it's not too much trouble—you could take me to their building?"

He looked at her bleakly. "But then who will take the tour?"

"Mr. Ainh," she said with gritted teeth, "*cancel* the tour."

Ainh looked like a man with a terrible headache. Willy almost felt sorry for him as she watched him retreat across the rooftop garden. She could imagine the bureaucratic quicksand he would have to wade through to honor her request. She'd already seen how the system operated—or, rather, how it didn't operate. That afternoon, at Ton Son Nhut Airport, it had taken three hours in the suffocating heat just to run the gauntlet of immigration officials.

A breeze swept the terrace, the first she'd felt all afternoon. Though she'd showered only an hour ago, her clothes were already soaked with sweat. Sinking into a chair, she gazed off at the skyline of Saigon, now painted a dusty gold in the sunset. Once, this must have been a glorious town of tree-lined boulevards and outdoor cafés where one could while away the afternoons sipping coffee.

But after its fall to the North, Saigon slid from the dizzy impudence of wealth to the resignation of poverty. The signs of decay were everywhere, from the chipped paint on the old French colonials to the skeletons of buildings left permanently unfinished. Even the Rex Hotel, luxurious by local standards, seemed to be fraying at the edges. The terrace stones were cracked. In the fish pond, three listless carp drifted like dead leaves. The rooftop swimming pool had bloomed an unhealthy shade of green. A lone Russian tourist sat on the side and dangled his legs in the murky water, as though weighing the risks of a swim.

It occurred to Willy that her immediate situation was every bit as murky as that water. The Vietnamese obviously believed in a proper channel for everything, and without Ainh's help, there was no way she could navigate *any* channel, proper or otherwise.

What then? she thought wearily. *I can't do this alone. I need help. I need a guide. I need—*

"Now *there's* a lady who looks down on her luck," said a voice.

She looked up to see Guy Barnard's tanned face framed

against the sunset. Her instant delight at seeing someone familiar—even *him*—only confirmed the utter depths of despair to which she'd sunk.

He flashed her a smile that could have charmed the habit off a nun. "Welcome to Saigon, capital of fallen dreams. How's it goin', kid?"

She sighed. "You need to ask?"

"Nope. I've been through it before, running around like a headless chicken, scrounging up seals of approval for every piddly scrap of paper. This country has got bureaucracy down to an art."

"I could live without the pep talk, thank you."

"Can I buy you a beer?"

She studied that smile of his, wondering what lay behind it. Suspecting the worst.

Seeing her weaken, he called for two beers, then dropped into a chair and regarded her with rumpled cheerfulness.

"I thought you weren't due in Saigon till Wednesday," she said.

"Change of plans."

"Pretty sudden, wasn't it?"

"Flexibility happens to be one of my virtues." He added, ruefully, "Maybe my only virtue."

The bartender brought over two frosty Heinekens. Guy waited until the man left before he spoke again.

"They brought in some new remains from Dak To," he said.

"MIAs?"

"That's what I have to find out. I knew I'd need a few extra days to examine the bones. Besides—" he took a gulp of beer "—I was getting bored in Bangkok."

"Sure."

"No, I mean it. I was ready for a change of scenery."

"You left the fleshpot of the East to come here and check out a few dead soldiers?"

"Believe it or not, I take my job seriously." He set the bottle down on the table. "Anyway, since I happen to be in town, maybe I could help you out. Since you probably need it."

Something about the way he looked at her, head cocked, teeth agleam in utter self-assurance, irritated her. "I'm doing okay," she said.

"Are you, now? So when's your first official meeting?"

"Things are being arranged."

"What sorts of things?"

"I don't know. Mr. Ainh's handling the details, and—"

"Mr. Ainh? You don't mean your *tour guide?*" He burst out laughing.

"Just why is that so funny?" she demanded.

"You're right," Guy said, swallowing his laughter. "It's not funny. It's pathetic. Do you want an advance look in my crystal ball? Because I can tell you exactly what's going to happen. First thing in the morning, your guide will show up with an apologetic look on his face."

"Why apologetic?"

"Because he'll tell you the ministry is closed for the day. After all, it's the grand and glorious holiday of July 18."

"Holiday? What holiday?"

"Never mind. He'll make something up. Then he'll ask if you wouldn't rather see the lacquer factory, where you can buy many beautiful gifts to bring home...."

Now she was laughing. Those were, in fact, Mr. Ainh's exact words.

"Then, the following day, he'll come up with some other reason you can't visit the ministry. Say, they're all sick with the swine flu or there's a critical shortage of pencil erasers. *But*—you can visit the National Palace!''

She stopped laughing. ''I think I'm beginning to get your point.''

''It's not that the man's deliberately sabotaging your plans. He simply knows how hopeless it is to untangle this bureaucracy. All he wants is to do his own little job, which is to be a tour guide and file innocuous reports about the nice lady tourist. Don't expect more from him. The poor guy isn't paid enough for what he already does.''

''I'm not helpless. I can always start knocking on a few doors myself.''

''Yeah, but *which* doors? And where are they hidden? And do you know the secret password?''

''Guy, you're making this country sound like a carnival funhouse.''

''*Fun* is not the operative word here.''

''What *is* the operative word?''

''*Chaos.*'' He pointed down at the street, where pedestrians and bicycles swarmed in mass anarchy. ''See that? That's how this government works. It's every man for himself. Ministries competing with ministries, provinces with provinces. Every minor official protecting his own turf. Everyone scared to move an inch without a nod from the powers that be.'' He shook his head. ''Not a system for the faint of heart.''

''That's one thing I've never been.''

''Wait till you've been sitting in some sweatbox of a 'reception' area for five hours. And your belly hurts from the bad water. And the closest bathroom is a hole in the—''

''I get the picture.''

''Do you?''

''What are you suggesting I do?''

Smiling, he sat back. "Hang around with me. I have a contact here and there. Not in the Foreign Ministry, I admit, but they might be able to help you."

He wants something, she thought. *What is it?* Though his gaze was unflinching, she sensed a new tension in his posture, saw in his eyes the anticipation rippling beneath the surface.

"You're being awfully helpful. Why?"

He shrugged. "Why not?"

"That's hardly an answer."

"Maybe at heart I'm still the Boy Scout helping old ladies cross the street. Maybe I'm a nice guy."

"Maybe you could tell me the truth."

"Have you always had this problem trusting men?"

"Yes, and don't change the subject."

For a moment, he didn't speak. He sat drumming his fingers against the beer bottle. "Okay," he admitted. "So I fibbed a little. I was never a Boy Scout. But I meant it about helping you out. The offer stands."

She didn't say a thing. For Guy, that silence, that look of skepticism, said it all. The woman didn't trust him. But why not, when he'd sounded his most sincere? He wondered what had made her so mistrustful. Too many hard knocks in life? Too many men who'd lied to her?

Well, watch out, baby, 'cause this one's no different, he thought with a twinge of self-disgust.

He just as quickly shook off the feeling. The stakes were too high to be developing a conscience. Especially at his age.

Now he'd have to tell another lie. He'd been lying a lot lately. It didn't get any easier.

"You're right," he said. "I'm not doing this out of the kindness of my heart."

She didn't look surprised. That annoyed him. "What do

you expect in return?'' she asked, her eyes hard on his.
"Money?'' She paused. "Sex?''

That last word, flung out so matter-of-factly, made his
belly do a tiny loop-the-loop. Not that he hadn't already
thought about that particular subject. He'd thought about
it a lot ever since he'd met her. And now that she was
sitting only a few feet away, watching him with those unyielding eyes, he was having trouble keeping certain images out of his head. Briefly he considered the possibility
of throwing a little sex into the deal, but he just as quickly
discarded the idea. He felt low enough as it was.

He calmly reached for the Heineken. The frostiness had
gone out of the bottle. "No,'' he said. "Sex isn't part of
the bargain.''

"I see.'' She bit her lip. "Then it's money.''

He gave a nod.

"I think you should know that I don't have any. Not
for you, anyway.''

"It's not *your* money I'm after.''

"Then whose?''

He paused, willing his expression to remain bland. His
voice dropped to a murmur. "Have you ever heard of the
Ariel Group?''

"Never.''

"Neither had I. Until two weeks ago, when I was contacted by two of their representatives. They're a veterans'
organization, dedicated to bringing our MIAs home—
alive. Even if it means launching a Rambo operation.''

"I see,'' she said, her lips tightening. "We're talking
about paramilitary kooks.''

"That's what I thought—at first. I was about to kick
'em out of my office when they pulled out a check—a
very generous one, I might add. Twenty thousand. For expenses, they said.''

"Expenses? What are they asking you to do?"

"A little moonlighting. They knew I was scheduled to fly in-country. They wanted me to conduct a small, private search for MIAs. But they aren't interested in skeletons and dog tags. They're after flesh and blood."

"Live ones? You don't really think there are any, do you?"

"They do. And they only have to produce one. A single living MIA to back up their claims. With the publicity that'd generate, Washington would be forced to take action."

He fell silent as the waiter came by to collect the empty beer bottles. Only when the man had left did Willy ask softly, "And where do I come in?"

"It's not you. It's your father. From what you've told me, there's a chance—a small one, to be sure—that he's still alive. If he is, I can help you find him. I can help you bring him home."

His words, uttered so quietly, so confidently, made Willy fall still. Guy could tell she was trying to read his face, trying to figure out what he wasn't telling her. And he wasn't telling her a lot.

"What do you get out of this?" she asked.

"You mean besides the pleasure of your company?"

"You said there was money involved. Since I'm not paying you, I assume someone else is. The Ariel Group? Are they offering you more than just expenses?"

"Move to the head of the class."

"How much?"

"For an honest to God live one? Two million."

"Two million *dollars?*"

He squeezed her hand, hard. "Keep it down, will you? This isn't exactly public information."

She dropped her voice to a whisper. "You're serious? Two million?"

"That's their offer. Now you think about *my* offer. Work with me, and we could both come out ahead. You'd get your father back. I'd pick up a nice little retirement fund. A win-win situation." He grinned, knowing he had her now. She'd be stupid to refuse. And Willy Maitland was definitely not stupid. "I think you'll agree," he said. "It's a match made in heaven."

"Or hell," she muttered darkly. She sat back and gave him a look of pure cast iron. "You're nothing but a bounty hunter."

"If that's what you want to call me."

"I could call you quite a few things. None of them flattering."

"Before you start calling me names, maybe you should think about your options. Which happen to be pretty limited. The way I see it, you can go it alone, which so far hasn't gotten you a helluva lot of mileage. Or—" he leaned forward and beamed her his most convincing smile "—you could work with me."

Her mouth tightened. "I don't work with mercenaries."

"What've you got against mercenaries?"

"Just a minor matter—principle."

"It's the money that bothers you, isn't it? The fact that I'm doing it for cash and not out of the goodness of my heart."

"This isn't some big-game hunt! We're talking about *men.* Men whose families have wiped out their savings to pay worthless little Rambos like you! I know those families. Some of them are still hanging in, twisting around on that one shred of hope. And you know as well as I do that those soldiers aren't sitting around in some POW camp, waiting to be rescued. They're *dead.*"

"You think *your* old man's alive."

"He's a different story."

"Right. And every one of those five hundred other MIAs could be another 'different story.'"

"*I* happen to have evidence!"

"But you don't have the smarts it takes to find him." Guy leaned forward, his gaze hard on hers. In the last light of sunset, her face seemed alight with fire, her cheeks glowing a beautiful dusky red. "If he's alive, you can't afford to screw up this chance. And you may get only one chance to find him. Because I'll tell you now, the Vietnamese won't let you back in the country for another deluxe tour. Admit it, Willy. You need me."

"No," she shot back. "You need *me*. Without my help, how are you going to cash in on your 'live one'?"

"How're *you* going to find him?"

She was the one leaning forward now, so close, he almost pulled back in surprise. "Don't underestimate me, sleazeball," she muttered.

"And don't overestimate yourself, Junior. It's not easy finding answers in this country. No one, nothing's ever what it seems here. A flicker in the eye, a break in the voice can mean all the difference in the world. You *need* a partner. And, hey, I'm not unreasonable. I'll even think about splitting the reward with you. Say, ten percent. That's money you never expected, just to let me—"

"I don't give a damn about the money!" She rose sharply to her feet. "Go get rich off someone else's old man." She spun around and walked away.

"Won't you even think about it?" he yelled.

She just kept marching away across the rooftop garden, oblivious to the curious glances aimed her way.

"Take it from me, Willy! You need me!"

A trio of Russian tourists, their faces ruddy from a few

rounds of vodka, glanced up as she passed. One of the men raised his glass in a drunken salute. ''Maybe you like Russian man better?'' he shouted.

She didn't even break her stride. But as she walked away, every guest on that rooftop heard her answer, which came floating back with disarming sweetness over her shoulder. ''Go to hellski.''

CHAPTER FOUR

GUY WATCHED HER storm away, her chambray skirt snapping smartly about those fabulous legs. Annoyed as he was, he couldn't help laughing when he heard that comeback to the Russian.

Go to hellski. He laughed harder. He was still laughing as he wandered over to the bar and called for another Heineken. The beer was so cold, it made his teeth ache.

"For a fellow who's just gotten the royal heave-ho," said a voice, obviously British, "you seem to be in high spirits."

Guy glanced at the portly gentleman hunched next to him at the bar. With those two tufts of hair on his bald head, he looked like a horned owl. China blue eyes twinkled beneath shaggy eyebrows.

Guy shrugged. "Win some, lose some."

"Sensible attitude. Considering the state of womanhood these days." The man hoisted a glass of Scotch to his lips. "But then, I could have predicted she'd be a no go."

"Sounds like an expert talking."

"No, I sat behind her on the plane. Listened to some oily Frenchman ooze his entire repertoire all over her. Smashing lines, I have to say, but she didn't fall for it." He squinted at Guy. "Weren't *you* on that flight out of Bangkok?"

Guy nodded. He didn't remember the man, but then, he'd spent the entire flight white-knuckling his armrest and

gulping down whiskey. Airplanes did that to him. Even
nice big 747s with nice French stewardesses. It never
failed to astonish him that the wings didn't fall off.

At the other end of the garden, the trio of Russians had
started to sing. Not, unfortunately, in the same key. Maybe
not even the same song. It was hard to tell.

"Never would've guessed it," the Englishman said,
glancing over at the Russians. "I still remember the Yanks
drinking at that very table. Never would've guessed there'd
be Russians sitting there one day."

"When were you here?"

"Sixty-eight to '75." He held out a pudgy hand in greeting. "Dodge Hamilton, *London Post.*"

"Guy Barnard. Ex-draftee." He shook the man's hand.
"Reporter, huh? You here on a story?"

"I was." Hamilton looked mournfully at his Scotch.
"But it's fallen through."

"What has? Your interviews?"

"No, the concept. I called it a sentimental journey. Visit
to old friends in Saigon. Or, rather, to one friend in particular." He took a swallow of Scotch. "But she's gone."

"Oh. A woman."

"That's right, a woman. Half the human race, but they
might as well be from Mars for all I understand the sex."
He slapped down the glass and motioned for another refill.
The bartender resignedly shoved the whole bottle of
Scotch over to Hamilton. "See, the story I had in mind
was the search for a lost love. You know, the sort of copy
that sells papers. My editor went wild about it." He poured
the Scotch, recklessly filling the glass to the brim. "Ha!
Lost love! I stopped by her old house today, over on Rue
Catinat. Or what used to be Rue Catinat. Found her brother
still living there. But it seems my old love ran away with
some new love. A sergeant. From Memphis, no less."

Guy shook his head in sympathy. "A woman has a right to change her mind."

"One day after I left the country?"

There wasn't much a man could say to that. But Guy couldn't blame the woman. He knew how it was in Saigon—the fear, the uncertainty. No one knowing if there'd be a slaughter and everyone expecting the worst. He'd seen the news photos of the city's fall, recognized the look of desperation on the faces of the Vietnamese scrambling aboard the last choppers out. No, he couldn't blame a woman for wanting to get out of the country, any way she could.

"You could still write about it," Guy pointed out. "Try a different angle. How one woman escaped the madness. The price of survival."

"My heart's not in it any longer." Hamilton gazed sadly around the rooftop. "Or in this town. I used to love it here! The noise, the smells. Even the whomp of the mortar rounds. But Saigon's changed. The spirit's flown out of it. The funny part is, this hotel looks exactly the same. I used to stand at this very bar and hear your generals whisper to each other, 'What the hell are we doing here?' I don't think they ever quite figured it out." He laughed and took another gulp of Scotch. "Memphis. Why would she want to go to Memphis?"

He was muttering to himself now, some private monologue about women causing all the world's miseries. An opinion with which Guy could almost agree. All he had to do was think about his own miserable love life and he, too, would get the sudden, blinding urge to get thoroughly soused.

Women. All the same. Yet, somehow, all different.

He thought about Willy Maitland. She talked tough, but

he could tell it was an act, that there was something soft, something vulnerable beneath that hard-as-nails surface. Hell, she was just a kid trying to live up to her old man's name, pretending she didn't need a man when she did. He had to admire her for that: her pride.

She was smart to turn down his offer. He wasn't sure he had the stomach to go through with it anyway. Let the Ariel Group tighten his noose. He'd lived with his skeletons long enough; maybe it was time to let them out of the closet.

I should just do my job, he thought. *Go to Hanoi, pick up a few dead soldiers, fly them home.*

And forget about Willy Maitland.

Then again...

He ordered another beer. Drank it while the debate raged on in his head. Thought about all the ways he could help her, about how much she needed *someone's* help. Considered doing it not because he was being forced into it, but because he wanted to. *Out of the goodness of my heart?* Now that was a new concept. No, he'd never been a Boy Scout. Something about those uniforms, about all that earnest goodliness and godliness, had struck him as faintly ridiculous. But here he was, Boy Scout Barnard, ready to offer his services, no strings attached.

Well, maybe a few strings. He couldn't help fantasizing about the possibilities. He thought of how it would be, taking her up to his room. Undressing her. Feeling her yield beneath him. He swallowed hard and reached automatically for the Heineken.

"No doubt about it," Hamilton muttered. "I tell you, it's all their fault."

"Hmm?" Guy turned. "Whose fault?"

"Women, of course. They cause more trouble than they're worth."

"You said it, pal." Guy sighed and lifted the beer to his lips. "You said it."

MEN. THEY CAUSE MORE trouble than they're worth, Willy thought as she viciously wound her alarm clock.

A bounty hunter. She should have guessed. Warning bells should have gone off in her head the minute he so generously offered his help. *Help.* What a laugh. She thought of all the solicitation letters she and her mother had received, all the mercenary groups who'd offered, for a few thousand dollars, to provide just such worthless help. There'd been the MIA Search Fund, the Men Alive Committee, Operation Chestnut—Let's Pull 'Em Out Of The Fire! had been *their* revolting slogan. How many grieving families had invested their hopes and savings on such futile dreams?

She stripped down to a tank top and flopped onto the bed. A decent night's sleep, she could tell, was another futile dream. The mattress was lumpy, and the pillow seemed to be stuffed with concrete. Not that it mattered. How could she get any rest with that damned disco music vibrating through the walls? At 8:00 the first driving drumbeats had announced the opening of Dance Night at the Rex Hotel. *Lord,* she thought, *what good is communism if it can't even stamp out disco?*

It occurred to her that, at that very minute, Guy Barnard was probably loitering downstairs in that dance hall, checking out the action. Sometimes she thought that was the real reason men started wars—it was an excuse to run away from home and check out the action.

What do I care if he's down there eyeing the ladies? The man's scum. He's not worth a second thought.

Still, she had to admit he had a certain tattered charm. Nice straight teeth and a dazzling smile and eyes that were brown as a wolf's. A woman could get in trouble for the sake of those eyes. *And heaven knows, I don't need that kind of trouble.*

Someone knocked on the door. She sat up straight and called out, "Who is it?"

"Room service."

"There must be a mistake. I didn't order anything."

There was no response. Sighing, she pulled on a robe and padded over to open the door.

Guy grinned at her from the darkness. "Well?" he inquired. "Have you thought about it?"

"Thought about what?" she snapped back.

"You and me. Working together."

She laughed in disbelief. "Either you're hard of hearing or I didn't make myself clear."

"That was two hours ago. I figured you might have changed your mind."

"I will *never* change my mind. Good *night.*" She slammed the door, shoved the bolt home and stepped back, seething.

There was a tapping on her window. She yanked the curtain aside and saw Guy smiling through the glass.

"Just one more question," he called.

"What?"

"Is that answer final?"

She jerked the curtain closed and stood there, waiting to see where he'd turn up next. Would he drop down from the ceiling? Pop up like a jack-in-the-box through the floor?

What was that rustling sound?

Glancing down sharply, she saw a piece of paper slide under the door. She snatched it up and read the scrawled message. "Call me if you need me."

Ha! she thought, ripping the note to pieces. "The day I need you is the day hell freezes over!" she yelled.

There was no answer. And she knew, without even looking, that he had already walked away.

CHANTAL GAZED AT THE bottle of champagne, the tins of caviar and foie gras, and the box of chocolates, and she licked her lips. Then she said, "How dare you show up after all these years."

Siang merely smiled. "You have lost your taste for champagne? What a pity. It seems I shall have to drink it all myself." He reached for the bottle. Slowly, he untwisted the wire. The flight from Bangkok had jostled the contents; the cork shot out, spilling pale gold bubbles all over the earthen floor. Chantal gave a little sob. She appeared ready to drop to her knees and lap up the precious liquid. He poured champagne into one of two fluted glasses he'd brought all the way from Bangkok. One could not, after all, drink champagne from a teacup. He took a sip and sighed happily. "Taittinger. Delightful."

"Taittinger?" she whispered.

He filled the second glass and set it on the rickety table in front of her. She kept staring at it, watching the bubbles spiral to the surface.

"I need help," he said.

She reached for the glass, put it to her trembling lips, tasted the rim, then the contents. He could almost see the bubbles sliding over her tongue, slipping down that fine, long throat. Even if the rest of her was sagging, she still had that beautiful throat, slender as a stalk of grass. A legacy from her Vietnamese mother. Her Asian half had held up over the years; the French half hadn't done so well. He could see the freckles, the fine lines tracing the corners of her greenish eyes.

She was no longer merely tasting the champagne; she was guzzling. Greedily, she drained the last drop from her glass and reached for the bottle.

He slid it out of her reach. "I said I need your help."

She wiped her chin with the back of her hand. "What kind of help?"

"Not much."

"Ha. That's what you always say."

"A pistol. Automatic. Plus several clips of ammunition."

"What if I don't have a pistol?"

"Then you will find me one."

She shook her head. "This is not the old days. You don't know what it's like here. Things are difficult." She paused, looking down at her slightly crepey hands. "Saigon is a hell."

"Even hell can be made comfortable. I can see to that."

She was silent. He could read her mind almost as easily as if her eyes were transparent. She gazed down at the treasures he'd brought from Bangkok. She swallowed, her mouth still tingling with the taste of champagne. At last she said, "The gun. What do you want it for?"

"A job."

"Vietnamese?"

"American. A woman."

A spark flickered in Chantal's eyes. Curiosity. Maybe jealousy. Her chin came up. "Your lover?"

He shook his head.

"Then why do you want her dead?"

He shrugged. "Business. My client has offered generous compensation. I will split it with you."

"The way you did before?" she shot back.

He shook his head apologetically. "Chantal, Chantal." He sighed. "You know I had no choice. It was the last flight out of Saigon.'' He touched her face; it had lost its former silkiness. That French blood again: it didn't hold up well under years of harsh sunlight. ''This time, I promise. You'll be paid.''

She sat there looking at him, looking at the champagne. ''What if it takes me time to find a gun?''

''Then I'll improvise. And I will need an assistant. Someone I can trust, someone discreet.'' He paused. ''Your cousin, is he still in need of money?''

Their gazes met. He gave her a slow, significant smile. Then he filled her glass with champagne.

''Open the caviar,'' she said.

''I NEED YOUR HELP,'' said Willy.

Guy, dazed and still half-asleep, stood in his doorway, blinking at the morning sunlight. He was uncombed, unshaven and wearing only a towel—a skimpy one at that. She tried to stay focused on his face, but her gaze kept dropping to his chest, to that mat of curly brown hair, to the scar knotting the upper abdomen.

He shook his head in disbelief. ''You couldn't have told me this last night? You had to wait till the crack of dawn?''

''Guy, it's eight o'clock.''

He yawned. ''No kidding.''

''Maybe you should try going to bed at a decent hour.''

''Who says I didn't?'' He leaned carelessly in the doorway and grinned. ''Maybe sleep didn't happen to be on my agenda.''

Dear God. Did he have a woman in his room? Automatically, Willy glanced past him into the darkened room. The bed was rumpled but unoccupied.

''Gotcha,'' he said, and laughed.

"I can see you're not going to be any help at all." She turned and walked away.

"Willy! Hey, come on." He caught her by the arm and pulled her around. "Did you mean it? About wanting my help?"

"Forget it. It was a lapse in judgment."

"Last night, hell had to freeze over before you'd come to me for help. But here you are. What made you change your mind?"

She didn't answer right off. She was too busy trying not to notice that his towel was slipping. To her relief, he snatched it together just in time and fastened it more securely around his hips.

At last she shook her head and sighed. "You were right. It's all going exactly as you said it would. No official will talk to me. No one'll answer my calls. They hear I'm coming and they all dive under their desks!"

"You could try a little patience. Wait another week."

"Next week's no good, either."

"Why?"

"Haven't you heard? It's Ho Chi Minh's birthday."

Guy looked heavenward. "How could I forget?"

"So what should I do?"

For a moment, he stood there thoughtfully rubbing his unshaven chin. Then he nodded. "Let's talk about it."

Back in his room, she sat uneasily on the edge of the bed while he dressed in the bathroom. The man was a restless sleeper, judging by the rumpled sheets. The blanket had been kicked off the bed entirely, the pillows punched into formless lumps by the headboard. Her gaze settled on the nightstand, where a stack of files lay. The top one was labeled Operation Friar Tuck. Declassified. Curious, she flipped open the cover.

"It's the way things work in this country," she heard

him say through the bathroom door. "If you want to get from point A to point B, you don't go in a straight line. You walk two steps to the left, two to the right, turn and walk backward."

"So what should I do now?"

"The two-step. Sideways." He came out, dressed and freshly shaved. Spotting the open file on the nightstand, he calmly closed the cover. "Sorry. Not for public view," he said, sliding the stack of folders into his briefcase. Then he turned to her. "Now. Tell me what else is going on."

"What do you mean?"

"I get the feeling there's something more. It's eight o'clock in the morning. You can't have battled the bureaucracy this early. What really made you change your mind about me?"

"Oh, I haven't changed my mind about *you.* You're still a mercenary." Her disgust seemed to hang in the air like a bad odor.

"But now you're willing to work with me. Why?"

She looked down at her lap and sighed. Reluctantly she opened her purse and pulled out a slip of paper. "I found this under my door this morning."

He unfolded the paper. In a spidery hand was written "Die Yankee." Just seeing those two words again made her angry. A few minutes ago, when she'd shown the message to Mr. Ainh, his only reaction was to shake his head in regret. At least Guy was an American; surely *he'd* share her sense of outrage.

He handed the note back to her. "So?"

"'*So?*'" She stared at him. "I get a death threat slipped under my door. The entire Vietnamese government hides at the mention of my name. Ainh practically *commands* me to tour his stupid lacquer factory. And that's all you can say? 'So?'"

Clucking sympathetically, he sat down beside her. *Why does he have to sit so close?* she thought. She tried to ignore the tingling in her leg as it brushed against his, struggled to sit perfectly straight though his weight on the mattress was making her sag toward him.

"First of all," he explained, "this isn't necessarily a personal death threat. It could be merely a political statement."

"Oh, is *that* all," she said blandly.

"And think of the lacquer factory as a visit to the dentist. You don't want to go, but everyone thinks you should. And as for the elusive Foreign Ministry, you wouldn't learn a thing from those bureaucrats anyway. Speaking of bureaucrats, where's your baby-sitter?"

"You mean Mr. Ainh?" She sighed. "Waiting for me in the lobby."

"You have to get rid of him."

"I wish."

"We can't have him around." Rising, Guy took her hand and pulled her to her feet. "Not where we're going."

"Where *are* we going?" she demanded, following him out the door.

"To see a friend. I think."

"Meaning he might not see us?"

"Meaning I can't be sure he's a friend."

She groaned as they stepped into the elevator. "Terrific."

Down in the lobby, they found Ainh by the desk, waiting to ambush her. "Miss Maitland!" he called. "Please, you must hurry. We have a very busy schedule today."

Willy glanced at Guy, who simply shrugged and looked off in another direction. Drat the man, he was leaving it up to her. "Mr. Ainh," she said, "about this little tour of the lacquer factory—"

"It will be quite fascinating! But they do not take dollars, so if you wish to exchange for dong, I can—"

"I'm afraid I don't feel up to it," she said flatly.

Ainh blinked in surprise. "You are ill?"

"Yes, I…" She suddenly noticed that Guy was shaking his head. "Uh, no, I'm not. I mean—"

"What she means," said Guy, "is that I offered to show her around. You know—" he winked at Ainh "—a little *personal* tour."

"P-personal?" Flushing, Ainh glanced at Willy. "But what about *my* tour? It is all arranged! The car, the sightseeing, a special lunch—"

"I tell you what, pal," said Guy, bending toward him conspiratorially. "Why don't *you* take the tour?"

"I have been on the tour," Ainh said glumly.

"Ah, but that was work, right? This time, why don't you take the day off, both you and the driver. Go see the sights of Saigon. And enjoy Ms. Maitland's lunch. After all, it's been paid for."

Ainh suddenly looked interested. "A free lunch?"

"And a beer." Guy slipped a few dollars into the man's breast pocket and patted the flap. "On me." He took Willy's arm and directed her across the lobby.

"But, Miss Maitland!" Ainh called out bleakly.

"Boy, what a blast you two guys're gonna have!" Guy sounded almost envious. "Air-conditioned car. Free lunch. No schedule to tie you down."

Ainh followed them outside, into a wall of morning heat so thick, it made Willy draw a breath of surprise. "Miss Maitland!" he said in desperation. "This is *not* the way it is supposed to be done!"

Guy turned and gave the man a solemn pat on the shoulder. "That, Mr. Ainh, is the whole idea."

They left the poor man standing alone on the steps, staring after them.

"What do you think he'll do?" whispered Willy.

"I think," said Guy, moving her along the crowded sidewalk, "he's going to enjoy a free lunch."

She glanced back and saw that Mr. Ainh had, indeed, disappeared into the hotel. She also noticed they were being followed. A street urchin, no more than twelve years old, caught up and danced around on the hot pavement.

"Lien-xo?" he chirped, dark eyes shining in a dirty face. They tried to ignore him, but the boy skipped along beside them, chattering all the way. His shirt hung in tatters; his feet were stained an apparently permanent brown. He pointed at Guy. *"Lien-xo?"*

"No, not Russian," said Guy. "Americanski."

The boy grinned. "Americanski? Yes?" He stuck out a smudgy hand and whooped. "Hello, Daddy!"

Resigned, Guy shook the boy's hand. "Yeah, it's nice to meet you too."

"Daddy rich?"

"Sorry. Daddy poor."

The boy laughed, obviously thinking that a grand joke. As Guy and Willy continued down the street, the boy hopped along at their side, shooing all the other urchins who had joined the procession. It was a tattered little parade marching through a sea of confusion. Bicycles whisked by, a multitude of wheels. And on the sidewalks, merchants squatted beside their meager collections of wares.

The boy tugged on Guy's arm. "Hey, Daddy. You got cigarette?"

"No," said Guy.

"Come on, Daddy. I do you favor, keep the beggars away."

"Oh, all right." Guy fished a pack of Marlboro cigarettes from his shirt pocket and handed the boy a cigarette.

"Guy, how could you?" Willy protested. "He's just a kid!"

"Oh, he's not going to smoke it," said Guy. "He'll trade it for something else. Like food. See?" He nodded at the boy, who was busy wrapping his treasure in a grimy piece of cloth. "That's why I always pack a few cartons when I come. They're handy when you need a favor." He turned and frowned up at one of the street signs. "Which, come to think of it, we do." He beckoned to the boy. "Hey, kid, what's your name?"

The boy shrugged.

"They must call you something."

"Other Americanski, he say I look like Oliver."

Guy laughed. "Probably meant Oliver Twist. Okay, Oliver. I got a deal for you. You do us a favor."

"Sure thing, Daddy."

"I'm looking for a street called Rue des Voiles. That's the old name, and it's not on the map. You know where it is?"

"Rue des Voiles? Rue des Voiles..." The boy scrunched up his face. "I think that one they call Binh Tan now. Why you want to go there? No stores, nothing to see."

Guy took out a thousand-dong note. "Just get us there."

The boy snapped up the money. "Okay, Daddy. You wait. Promise, you wait!" The boy trotted off down the street. At the corner, he glanced back and yelled again for good measure, "You wait!"

A minute later, he reappeared, trailed by a pair of bicycle-driven cyclos. "I find you the best. Very fast," said Oliver.

Guy and Willy stared in dismay at the two drivers. One

smiled back toothlessly; the other was wheezing like a freight train.

Guy shook his head. "Where on earth did he dig up these fossils?" he muttered.

Oliver pointed proudly to the two old men and grinned. "My uncles!"

A VOICE BEHIND THE DOOR said, "Go away."

"Mr. Gerard?" Guy called. There was no answer, but the man was surely lurking near the door; Willy could almost feel him crouched silently on the other side. Guy reached for the knocker fashioned after some grotesque face—either a horned lion or a goat with teeth—that hung on the door like a brass wart. He banged it a few times. "Mr. Gerard!"

Still no answer.

"It's important! We have to talk to you!"

"I said, go away!"

Willy muttered, "Do you suppose it's just possible he doesn't want to talk to us?"

"Oh, he'll talk to us." Guy banged on the door again. "The name's Guy Barnard!" he yelled. "I'm a friend of Toby Wolff."

The latch slid open. One pale eye peeped out through a crack in the door. The eye flicked back and forth, squinting first at Guy, then at Willy. The voice attached to the eye hissed, "Toby Wolff is an idiot."

"Toby Wolff is also calling in his chips."

The eye blinked. The door opened a fraction of an inch wider, the slit revealing a bald, crablike little man. "Well?" he snapped. "Are you just going to stand there?"

Inside, the house was dark as a cave, all the curtains drawn tightly over the windows. Guy and Willy followed the crustacean of a Frenchman down a narrow hallway. In the shadows, Gerard's outline was barely visible, but Willy could hear him just ahead of her, scuttling across the wood floor.

They emerged into what appeared to be a large sitting room. Slivers of light shimmered through worn curtains. In the suffocating darkness hulked vaguely discernible furniture.

"Sit, sit," ordered Gerard. Guy and Willy moved toward a couch, but Gerard snapped, "Not *there!* Can't you see that's a genuine Queen Anne?" He pointed at a pair of massive rosewood chairs. "Sit there." He settled into a brocade armchair by the window. With his arms crossed and his knobby knees jutting out at them, he looked like a disagreeable pile of bones. "So what does Toby want from me now?" he demanded.

"He said you could pass us some information."

Gerard snorted. "I am not in the business."

"You used to be."

"No longer. The stakes are too high."

Willy glanced thoughtfully around the room, noting in the shadows the soft gleam of ivory, the luster of fine old china. She suddenly realized they were surrounded by a treasure trove of antiques. Even the house was an antique, one of Saigon's lovely old French colonials, laced with climbing vines. By law it belonged to the state. She wondered what the Frenchman had done to keep such a home.

"It has been years since I had any business with the Company," said Gerard. "I know nothing that could possibly help you now."

"Maybe you do," said Guy. "We're here about an old matter. From the war."

Gerard laughed. "These people are perpetually at war!

Which enemy? The Chinese? The French? The Khmer Rouge?"

"You know which war," Guy said.

Gerard sat back. "*That* war is over."

"Not for some of us," said Willy.

The Frenchman turned to her. She felt him studying her, measuring her significance. She resented being appraised this way. Deliberately she returned his stare.

"What's the girl got to do with it?" Gerard demanded.

"She's here about her father. Missing in action since 1970."

Gerard shrugged. "My business is imports. I know nothing about missing soldiers."

"My father wasn't a soldier," said Willy. "He was a pilot for Air America."

"Wild Bill Maitland," Guy added.

The sudden silence in the room was thick enough to slice. After a long pause, Gerard said softly, "Air America."

Willy nodded. "You remember him?"

The Frenchman's knobby fingers began to tap the armrest. "I knew of them, the pilots. They carried goods for me on occasion. At a price."

"Goods?"

"Pharmaceuticals," said Guy.

Gerard slapped the armrest in irritation. "Come, Mr. Barnard, we both know what we're talking about! Opium. I don't deny it. There was a war going on, and there was money to be made. So I made it. Air America happened to provide the most reliable delivery service. The pilots never asked questions. They were good that way. I paid them what they were worth. In gold."

Again there was a silence. It took all Willy's courage to

ask the next question. "And my father? Was he one of the pilots you paid in gold?"

Alain Gerard shrugged. "Would it surprise you?"

Somehow, it wouldn't, but she tried to imagine what all those old family friends would say, the ones who'd thought her father a hero.

"He was one of the best," said Gerard.

She looked up. "The best?" She felt like laughing. "At what? Running drugs?"

"Flying. It was his calling."

"My father's calling," she said bitterly, "was to do whatever he wanted. With no thought for anyone else."

"Still," insisted Gerard, "he was one of the best."

"The day his plane went down…" said Guy. "Was he carrying something of yours?"

The Frenchman didn't answer. He fidgeted in his chair, then rose and went to the window, where he fussed prissily with the curtains.

"Gerard?" Guy prodded.

Gerard turned and looked at them. "Why are you here? What purpose do these questions serve?"

"I have to know what happened to him," said Willy.

Gerard turned to the window and peered out through a slit in the curtains. "Go home, Miss Maitland. Before you learn things you don't want to know."

"What things?"

"Unpleasant things."

"He was my father! I have a right—"

"A right?" Gerard laughed. "He was in a war zone! He knew the risks. He was just another man who did not come back alive."

"I want to know why. I want to know what he was doing in Laos."

"Since when does *anyone* know what they were really

doing in Laos?'' He moved around the room, covetously touching his precious treasures. "You cannot imagine the things that went on in those days. Our secret war. Laos was the country we didn't talk about. But we were all there. Russians, Chinese, Americans, French. Friends and enemies, packed into the same filthy bars of Vientiane. Good soldiers, all of us, out to make a living.'' He stopped and looked at Willy. "I still do not understand that war.''

"But you knew more than most,'' said Guy. "You were working with Intelligence.''

"I saw only part of the picture.''

"Toby Wolff suggested you took part in the crash investigation.''

"I had little to do with it.''

"Then who was in charge?''

"An American colonel by the name of Kistner.''

Willy looked up in surprise. "*Joseph* Kistner?''

"Since promoted to general,'' Guy noted softly.

Gerard nodded. "He called himself a military attaché.''

"Meaning he was really CIA.''

"Meaning any number of things. I was liaison for French Intelligence, and I was told only the minimum. That was the way the colonel worked, you see. For him, information was power. He shared very little of it.''

"What do you know about the crash?''

Gerard shrugged. "They called it 'a routine loss.' Hostile fire. A search was called at the insistence of the other pilots, but no survivors were found. After a day, Colonel Kistner put out the order to melt any wreckage. I don't know if the order was ever executed.''

Willy shook her head. "Melt?''

"That's jargon for destroy,'' explained Guy. "They do it whenever a plane goes down during a classified mission. To get rid of the evidence.''

"But my father wasn't flying a classified mission. It was a routine supply flight."

"They were *all* listed as routine supply flights," said Gerard.

"The cargo manifest listed aircraft parts," said Guy. "Not a reason to melt the plane. What was really on that flight?"

Gerard didn't answer.

"There was a passenger," Willy said. "They were carrying a passenger."

Gerard's gaze snapped toward her. "Who told you this?"

"Luis Valdez, Dad's cargo kicker. He bailed out as the plane went down."

"You spoke to this man Valdez?"

"It was only a short phone call, right after he was released from the POW camp."

"Then…he is still alive?"

She shook her head. "He shot himself the day after he got back to the States."

Gerard began to pace around the room again, touching each piece of furniture. He reminded her of a greedy gnome fingering his treasures.

"Who was the passenger, Gerard?" asked Guy.

Gerard picked up a lacquer box, set it back down again.

"Military? Intelligence? What?"

Gerard stopped pacing. "He was a phantom, Mr. Barnard."

"Meaning you don't know his name?"

"Oh, he had many names, many faces. A rumor always does. Some said he was a general. Or a prince. Or a drug lord." Turning, he stared out the curtain slit, a shriveled silhouette against the glow of light. "Whoever he was, he represented a threat to someone in a high place."

Someone in a high place. Willy thought of the intrigue that must have swirled in Vientiane, 1970. She thought of Air America and Defense Intelligence and the CIA. Who among all those players would have felt threatened by this one unnamed Lao?

"Who do *you* think he was, Mr. Gerard?" she asked.

The silhouette at the window shrugged. "It makes no difference now. He's dead. Everyone on that plane is dead."

"Maybe not all of them. My father—"

"Your father has not been seen in twenty years. And if I were you, I would leave well enough alone."

"But if he's alive—"

"If he's alive, he may not wish to be found." Gerard turned and looked at her, his expression hidden against the backglow of the window. "A man with a price on his head has good reason to stay dead."

CHAPTER FIVE

She stared at him. "A price? I don't understand."

"You mean no one has told you about the bounty?"

"Bounty for what?"

"For the arrest of Friar Tuck."

She fell instantly still. An image took shape in her mind: words typed on a file folder. *Operation Friar Tuck. Declassified.* She turned to Guy. "You know what he's talking about, don't you. Who's Friar Tuck?"

Guy's expression was unreadable, as if a mask had fallen over his face. "It's nothing but a story."

"But you had his file in your room."

"It's just a nickname for a renegade pilot. A legend—"

"Not just a legend," insisted Gerard. "He was a real man, a traitor. Intelligence does not offer two-million-dollar bounties for mere legends."

Willy's gaze shot back to Guy. She wondered how he had the nerve—the gall—to meet her eyes. *You knew,* she thought. *You bastard. All the time, you knew.* Rage had tightened her throat almost beyond speech.

She barely managed to force out her next question, which she directed at Alain Gerard. "You think this—this renegade pilot is my father?"

"Intelligence thought so."

"Based on what evidence? That he could fly planes? The fact that he's not here to defend himself?"

"Based on the timing, the circumstances. In July 1970,

William Maitland vanished from the face of the earth. In August of the same year, we heard the first reports of a foreign pilot flying for the enemy. Running weapons and gold.''

"But there were hundreds of foreign pilots in Laos! Friar Tuck could have been a Frenchman, a Russian, a—"

"This much we did know—he was American."

She raised her chin. "You're saying my father was a traitor."

"I am telling you this only because it's something you should know. If he's alive, this is the reason he may not want to be found. You think you are on some sort of rescue mission, Miss Maitland, but you may be sadly mistaken. Your father could go home to a jail cell."

In the silence that followed, she turned her gaze to Guy. He still hadn't said a word; that alone proved his guilt. *Who do you work for?* she wondered. *The CIA? The Ariel Group? Or your lying, miserable self?*

She couldn't stand the sight of him. Even being in the same room with him made her recoil in disgust.

She rose. "Thank you, Mr. Gerard. You've told me things I needed to hear. Things I didn't expect."

"Then you agree it's best you drop the matter?"

"I don't agree. You think my father's a traitor. Obviously you're not the only one who thinks so. But you're all wrong."

"And how will you prove it?" Gerard snorted. "Tell me, Miss Maitland, how will you perform this grand miracle after twenty years?"

She didn't have an answer. The truth was, she didn't know what her next move would be. All she knew was that she would have to do it alone.

Her spine was ramrod straight as she followed Gerard back down the hall. The whole time, she was intensely aware of Guy moving right behind her. *I knew I couldn't trust him,* she thought. *From the very beginning I knew it.*

No one said a word until they reached the front door. There Gerard paused. Quietly he said, "Mr. Barnard? You will relay a message to Toby Wolff?"

Guy nodded. "Certainly. What's the message?"

"Tell him he has just called in his last chip." Gerard opened the front door. Outside, the sunshine was blinding. "There will be no more from me."

SHE MADE IT SCARCELY FIVE steps before her rage burst through.

"You lied to me. You scum, you were *using* me!"

The look on his face was the only answer Willy needed. It was written there clearly; the acknowledgment, the guilt.

"You knew about Friar Tuck. About the bounty. You weren't after just any 'live one,' were you? You were after a particular man—my father!"

Guy gave a shrug as though, now that the truth was out, it hardly mattered.

"How was this 'deal' with me supposed to work?" she pressed on. "Tell me, I'm curious. Were you going to turn him in the instant we found him—and my part of the deal be damned? Or were you going to humor me awhile, give me a chance to get my father home, let him step off the plane and onto American soil before you had him arrested? What was the plan, Guy? What *was* it?"

"There was no plan."

"Come on. A man like you always has a plan."

He looked tired. Defeated. "There was no plan."

She stared straight up at him, her fists clenching, unclenching. "I bet you had plans for that two million dollars. I bet you knew exactly how you were going to spend it. Every penny. And all you had to do was put my father away. You bastard." She should have slugged him right then and there. Instead, she walked away.

"Sure, I could use two million bucks!" he yelled. "I could use a lot of things! But I didn't want to use *you!*"

She kept walking. It took him only a few quick strides to catch up to her.

"Willy. Dammit, will you listen?"

"To what? More of your lies?"

"No. The truth."

"The truth?" She laughed. "Since when have you bothered with the truth?"

He grabbed her arm and pulled her around to face him. "Since right now."

"Let me go."

"Not until you hear me out."

"Why should I believe anything you say?"

"Look, I admit it. I knew about Friar Tuck. About the reward. And—"

"And you knew my father was on their list."

"Yes."

"Then why didn't you tell me?"

"I would have. I was going to."

"It was all worked out from the beginning, wasn't it? Use me to track down my father."

"I thought about it. At first."

"Oh, you're low, Guy. You're really scraping bottom. Does money mean so much to you?"

"I wasn't doing it for the money. I didn't have a choice. They backed me into it."

"Who?"

"The Ariel Group. I told you—two weeks ago they showed up in my office. They knew I was headed back to Nam. What I didn't tell you was the real reason they wanted me to work for them. They weren't tracking MIAs. They were tracking an old war criminal."

"Friar Tuck."

He nodded. "I told them I wasn't interested. They offered me money. A lot of it. I got a little interested. Then they made me an offer I couldn't refuse."

"Ah," she said with disdain.

"Not money…" he protested.

"Then what's the payoff?"

He ran his hand through his hair and let out a tired breath. "Silence."

She frowned, not understanding. He didn't say a thing, but she could see in his eyes some deep, dark agony. "Then that's it," she finally whispered. "Blackmail. What do they have on you, Guy? What are you hiding?"

"It's not—" he swallowed "—something I can talk about."

"I see. It must be pretty damn shocking. Which is no big surprise, I guess. But it still doesn't justify what you tried to do to me." She turned and walked away in disgust.

The road shimmered in the midmorning heat. Guy was right on her heels, like a stray dog that refused to be left behind. And he wasn't the only stray following her. The slap of bare feet announced the reappearance of Oliver, who skipped along beside her, chirping, "You want cyclo ride? It is very hot day! A thousand dong—I get you ride!"

She heard the squeak of wheels, the wheeze of an out-of-breath driver. Now Oliver's uncles had joined the procession.

"Go away," she said. "I don't want a ride."

"Sun very hot, very strong today. Maybe you faint. Once I see Russian lady faint." Oliver shook his head at the memory. "It was very bad sight."

"Go *away!*"

Undaunted, Oliver turned to Guy. "How about you, Daddy?"

Guy slapped a few bills into Oliver's grubby hand. "There's a thousand. Now scram."

Oliver vanished. Unfortunately, Guy wasn't so easily brushed off. He followed Willy into the town marketplace, past stands piled high with melons and mangoes, past counters where freshly butchered meat gathered flies.

"I was going to tell you about your father," Guy said. "I just wasn't sure how you'd take it."

"I'm not afraid of the truth."

"Sure you are! You're trying to protect him. That's why you keep ignoring the evidence."

"He wasn't a traitor!"

"You still love him, don't you?"

She turned sharply and walked away. Guy was right beside her. "What's wrong?" he said. "Did I hit a nerve?"

"Why should I care about him? He walked out on us."

"And you still feel guilty about it."

"Guilty?" She stopped. "Me?"

"That's right. Somewhere in that little-girl head of yours, you still blame yourself for his leaving. Maybe you had a fight, the way kids and dads always do, and you said something you shouldn't have. But before you had the chance to make up, he took off. And his plane went down. And here you are, twenty years later, still trying to make it up to him."

"Practicing psychiatry without a license now?"

"It doesn't take a shrink to know what goes on in a kid's head. I was fourteen when *my* old man walked out. I never got over being abandoned, either. Now I worry about my own kid. And it hurts."

She stared at him, astonished. "You have a child?"

"In a manner of speaking." He looked down. "The boy's mother and I, we weren't married. It's not something I'm particularly proud of."

"Oh."

"Yeah."

You walked out on them, she thought. *Your father left you. You left your son. The world never changes.*

"He wasn't a traitor," she insisted, returning to the matter at hand. "He was a lot of things—irresponsible, careless, insensitive. But he wouldn't turn against his own country."

"But he's on that list of suspects. If he's not Friar Tuck himself, he's probably connected somehow. And it's got to be a dangerous link. That's why someone's trying to stop you. That's why you're hitting brick walls wherever you turn. That's why, with every step you take, you're being followed."

"What!" In reflex, she turned to scan the crowd.

"Don't be so obvious." Guy grabbed her arm and dragged her to a pharmacy window. "Man at two o'clock," he murmured, nodding at a reflection in the glass. "Blue shirt, black trousers."

"Are you sure?"

"Absolutely. I just don't know who he's working for."

"He looks Vietnamese."

"But he could be working for the Russians. Or the Chinese. They both have a stake in this country."

Even as she stared at the reflection, the man in the blue shirt melted into the crowd. She knew he was still lingering nearby; she could feel his gaze on her back.

"What do I do, Guy?" she whispered. "How do I get rid of him?"

"You can't. Just keep in mind he's there. That you're probably under constant surveillance. In fact, we seem to be under the surveillance of a whole damn army." At least a dozen faces were now reflected there, all of them crowded close and peering curiously at the two foreigners. In the back, a familiar figure kept bouncing up and down, waving at them in the glass.

"Hello, Daddy!" came a yell.

Guy sighed. "We can't even get rid of *him*."

Willy stared hard at Guy's reflection. And she thought, *But I can get rid of you.*

MAJOR NATHAN DONNELL OF the Casualty Resolution team had shocking red hair, a booming voice and a cigar that stank to high heaven. Guy didn't know which was worse—the stench of that cigar or the odor of decay emanating from the four skeletons on the table. Maybe that's why Nate smoked those rotten cigars; they masked the smell of death.

The skeletons, each labeled with an ID number, were laid out on separate tarps. Also on the table were four plastic bags containing the personal effects and various other items found with the skeletons. After twenty or more years in this climate, not much remained of these bodies except dirt-encrusted bones and teeth. At least that much was left; sometimes fragments were all they had to work with.

Nate was reading aloud from the accompanying reports. In that grim setting, his resonant voice sounded somehow obscene, echoing off the walls of the Quonset hut. "Number 784-A, found in jungle, twelve klicks west of Camp Hawthorne. Army dog tag nearby—name, Elmore Stukey, Pfc."

"The tag was lying nearby?" Guy asked. "Not around the neck?"

Nate glanced at the Vietnamese liaison officer, who was

standing off to the side. "Is that correct? It wasn't around the neck?"

The Vietnamese man nodded. "That is what the report said."

"Elmore Stukey," muttered Guy, opening the man's military medical record. "Six foot two, Caucasian, perfect teeth." He looked at the skeleton. Just a glance at the femur told him the man on the table couldn't have stood much taller than five-six. He shook his head. "Wrong guy."

"Cross off Stukey?"

"Cross off Stukey. But note that someone made off with his dog tag."

Nate let out a morbid laugh. "Not a good sign."

"What about these other three?"

"Oh, those." Nate flipped to another report. "Those three were found together eight klicks north of LZ Bird. Had that U.S. Army helmet lying close by. Not much else around."

Guy focused automatically on the relevant details: pelvic shape, configuration of incisors. "Those two are females, probably Asian," he noted. "But that one…" He took out a tape measure, ran it along the dirt-stained femur. "Male, five foot nine or thereabouts. Hmm. Silver fillings on numbers one and two." He nodded. "Possible."

Nate glanced at the Vietnamese liaison officer. "Number 786-A. I'll be flying him back for further examination."

"And the others?"

"What do you think, Guy?"

Guy shrugged. "We'll take 784-A, as well. Just to be safe. But the two females are yours."

The Vietnamese nodded. "We will make the arrangements," he said, and quietly withdrew.

There was a silence as Nate lit up another cigar, shook out the match. "Well, you sure made quick work of it. I wasn't expecting you here till tomorrow."

"Something came up."

"Yeah?" Nate's expression was thoughtful through the stinking cloud of smoke. "Anything I can help you with?"

"Maybe."

Nate nodded toward the door. "Come on. Let's get out of here. This place gives me the creeps."

They walked outside and stood in the dusty courtyard of the old military compound. Barbed wire curled on the wall above them. A rattling air conditioner dripped water from a window of the Quonset hut.

"So," said Nate, contentedly puffing on his cigar. "Is this business or personal?"

"Both. I need some information."

"Not classified, I hope."

"You tell me."

Nate laughed and squinted up at the barbed wire. "I may not tell you anything. But ask anyway."

"You were on the repatriation team back in '73, right?"

"Seventy-three through '75. But my job didn't amount to much. Just smiled a lot and passed out razors and toothbrushes. You know, a welcome-home handshake for returning POWs."

"Did you happen to shake hands with any POWs from Tuyen Quan?"

"Not many. Half a dozen. That was a pretty miserable camp. Had an outbreak of typhoid near the end. A lot of 'em died in captivity."

"But not all of them. One of the POWs was a guy named Luis Valdez. Remember him?"

"Just the name. And only because I heard he shot himself the day after he got home. I thought it was a crying shame.''

"Then you never met him?"

"No, he went through closed debriefing. Totally separate channel. No outside contact."

Guy frowned, wondering about that closed debriefing. Why had Intelligence shut Valdez off from the others?

"What about the other POWs from Tuyen Quan?" asked Guy. "Did anyone talk about Valdez? Mention why he was kept apart?"

"Not really. Hey, they were a pretty delirious bunch. All they could talk about was going home. Seeing their families. Anyway, I don't think any of them knew Valdez. The camp held its prisoners two to a cell, and Valdez's cellmate wasn't in the group.''

"Dead?"

"No. Refused to get on the plane. If you can believe it.''

"Didn't want to fly?"

"Didn't want to go home, period."

"You remember his name?"

"Hell, yes. I had to file a ten-page report on the guy. Lassiter. Sam Lassiter. Incident got me a reprimand.''

"What happened?"

"We tried to drag him aboard. He kept yelling that he wanted to stay in Nam. And he was this big blond Viking, you know? Six foot four, kicking and screaming like a two-year-old. Should've seen the Vietnamese, laughing at it all. Anyway, the guy got loose and tore off into the crowd. At that point, we figured, what the hell. Let the jerk stay if he wants to.''

"Then he never went home?"

Nate blew out a cloud of cigar smoke. "Never did. For a while, we tried to keep tabs on him. Last we heard, he was sighted over in Cantho, but that was a few years ago. Since then he could've moved on. Or died.'' Nate glanced around at the barren compound. ''Nuts—that's my diagnosis. Gotta be nuts to stay in this godforsaken country.''

Maybe not, thought Guy. *Maybe he didn't have a choice.*

''What happened to the other guys from Tuyen?'' Guy asked. ''After they got home?''

''They had the usual problems. Post-traumatic-stress reaction, you know. But they adjusted okay. Or as well as could be expected.''

''All except Valdez.''

''Yeah. All except Valdez.'' Nate flicked off a cigar ash. ''Couldn't do a thing for him, or for wackos like Lassiter. When they're gone, they're gone. All those kids—they were too young for that war. Didn't have their heads together to begin with. Whenever I think of Lassiter and Valdez, it makes me feel pretty damn useless.''

''You did what you could.''

Nate nodded. ''Well, I guess we're good for something.'' Nate sighed and looked over at the Quonset hut. ''At least 786-A's finally going home.''

THE RUSSIANS WERE SINGING again. Otherwise it was a pleasant enough evening. The beer was cold, the bartender discreetly attentive. From his perch at the rooftop bar, Guy watched the Russkies slosh another round of Stolichnaya into their glasses. They, at least, seemed to be having a good time; it was more than he could say for himself.

He had to come up with a plan, and fast. Everything he'd learned, from Alain Gerard that morning and from Nate Donnell that afternoon, had backed up what he'd already suspected: that Willy Maitland was in over her pretty head. He was convinced that the attack in Bangkok hadn't been a robbery attempt. Someone was out to stop her. Someone who didn't want her rooting around in Bill Maitland's past. The CIA? The Vietnamese? Wild Bill himself?

That last thought he discarded as impossible. No man, no matter how desperate, would send someone to attack his own daughter.

But what if it had been meant only as a warning? A scare tactic?

All the possibilities, all the permutations, were giving Guy a headache. Was Maitland alive? What was his connection to Friar Tuck? Were they one and the same man? Why was the Ariel Group involved?

That was the other part of the puzzle—the Ariel Group. Guy mentally replayed that visit they'd paid him two weeks ago. The two men who'd appeared in his office had been unremarkable: clean shaven, dark suits, nondescript ties, the sort of faces you'd forget the instant they walked out your door. Only when they'd presented the check for twenty thousand dollars did he sit up and take notice. Whoever they were, they had cash to burn. And there was more money waiting—a lot more—if only he'd do them one small favor: locate a certain pilot known as Friar Tuck. "Your patriotic duty," they'd called it. The man was a traitor, a red-blooded American who'd gone over to the other side. Still, Guy had hesitated. It wasn't his kind of job. He wasn't a bounty hunter.

That's when they'd played their trump card.

Ariel, Ariel. He kept mulling over the name. Something Biblical. Lionlike men. Odd name for a vets organization. If that's what they were.

Ariel wasn't the only group hunting the elusive Friar Tuck. The CIA had a bounty on the man. For all Guy knew, the Vietnamese, the French and the men from Mars were after the pilot, as well.

And at the very eye of the hurricane was naive, stubborn, impossible Willy Maitland.

That she was so damnably attractive only made things worse. She was a maddening combination of toughness and vulnerability, and he'd been torn between using her and protecting her. Did any of that make sense?

The rhythmic thud of disco music drifted up from a lower floor. He considered heading downstairs to find some willing dance partner and trample a few toes. As he took another swallow of beer, a familiar figure passed through his peripheral vision. Turning, he saw Willy head for a table near the railing. He wondered if she'd consider joining him for a drink.

Obviously not, he decided, seeing how determinedly she was ignoring him. She stared off at the night, her back rigid, her gaze fixed somewhere in the distance. A strand of tawny hair slid over her cheek, and she tucked it behind her ear, a tight little gesture that made him think of a schoolmarm.

He decided to ignore her, too. But the more fiercely he tried to shove all thought of her from his mind, the more her image seemed to burn into his brain. Even as he focused his gaze on the bartender's dwindling bottle of Stolichnaya, he felt her presence, like a crackling fire radiating somewhere behind him.

What the hell. He'd give it one more try.

He shoved to his feet and strode across the rooftop.

Willy sensed his approach but didn't bother to look up, even when he grabbed a chair, sat down and leaned across the table.

"I still think we can work together," he said.

She sniffed. "I doubt it."

"Can't we at least talk about it?"

"I don't have a thing to say to you, Mr. Barnard."

"So it's back to Mr. Barnard."

Her frigid gaze met his across the table. "I could call you something else. I could call you a—"

"Can we skip the sweet talk? Look, I've been to see a friend of mine—"

"You have friends? Amazing."

"Nate was part of the welcome-home team back in '75. Met a lot of returning POWs. Including the men from Tuyen Quan."

Suddenly she looked interested. "He knew Luis Valdez?"

"No. Valdez was routed through classified debriefing. No one got near him. But Valdez had a cellmate in Tuyen Quan, a man named Sam Lassiter. Nate says Lassiter didn't go home."

"He died?"

"He never left the country."

She leaned forward, her whole body suddenly rigid with excitement. "He's still here in Nam?"

"Was a few years ago anyway. In Cantho. It's a river town in the Delta, about a hundred and fifty kilometers southwest of here."

"Not very far," she said, her mind obviously racing. "I could leave tomorrow morning…get there by afternoon…"

"And just how are you going to get there?"

"What do you mean, how? By car, of course."

"You think Mr. Ainh's going to let you waltz off on your own?"

"That's what bribes are for. Some people will do anything for a buck. Won't they?"

He met her hard gaze with one equally unflinching. "Forget the damn money. Don't you see someone's trying to use *both* of us? I want to know why." He leaned forward, his voice soft, coaxing. "I've made arrangements for a driver to Cantho first thing in the morning. We can tell Ainh I've invited you along for the ride. You know, just another tourist visiting the—"

She laughed. "You must think I have the IQ of a turnip. Why should I trust you? Bounty hunter. Opportunist. *Jerk.*"

"Lovely evening, isn't it?" cut in a cheery voice.

Dodge Hamilton, drink in hand, beamed down at them. He was greeted with dead silence.

"Oh, dear. Am I intruding?"

"Not at all," Willy said with a sigh, pulling a chair out for the ubiquitous Englishman. No doubt he wanted company for his misery, and she would do fine. They could commiserate a little more about his lost story and her lost father.

"No, really, I wouldn't dream of—"

"I insist." Willy tossed a lethal glance at Guy. "Mr. Barnard was just leaving."

Hamilton's gaze shifted from Guy to the offered chair. "Well, if you insist." He settled uneasily into the chair, set his glass down on the table and looked at Willy. "What I wanted to ask you, Miss Maitland, is whether you'd consent to an interview."

"Me? Why on earth?"

"I decided on a new focus for my Saigon story—a daughter's search for her father. Such a touching angle. A sentimental journey into—"

"Bad idea," Guy said, cutting in.

"Why?" asked Hamilton.

"It…has no passion," he improvised. "No romance. No excitement."

"Of course, there's excitement. A missing father—"

"Hamilton." Guy leaned forward. "No."

"He's asking *me*," Willy said. "After all, it's about my father."

Guy's gaze swung around to her. "Willy," he said quietly, "think."

"I'm thinking a little publicity might open a few doors."

"More likely it'd close doors. The Vietnamese hate to hang out their dirty laundry. What if they know what happened to your father, and it wasn't a nice ending? They're not going to want the details all over the London papers. It'd be much easier to throw you out of the country."

"Believe me," said Hamilton, "I can be discreet."

"A discreet reporter. Right," Guy muttered.

"Not a word would be printed till she's left the country."

"The Vietnamese aren't dumb. They'd find out what you were working on."

"Then I'll give them a cover story. Something to throw them off the track."

"Excuse me..." Willy said politely.

"The matter's touchier than you realize, Hamilton," Guy said.

"I've covered delicate matters before. When I say something's off the record, I keep it off the record."

Willy rose to her feet. "I give up. I'm going to bed."

Guy looked up. "You can't go to bed. We haven't finished talking."

"You and I have definitely finished talking."

"What about tomorrow?"

"What about my story?"

"Hamilton," she said, "if it's dirty laundry you're looking for, why don't you interview *him?*" She pointed to Guy. Then she turned and walked away.

Hamilton looked at Guy. "What dirty laundry do you have?"

Guy merely smiled.

He was still smiling as he crumpled his beer can in his bare hands.

LORD, DELIVER ME FROM THE *jerks of the world,* Willy thought wearily as she stepped into the elevator. The doors slid closed. *Above all, deliver me from Guy Barnard.*

Leaning back, she closed her eyes and waited for the elevator to creep down to the fourth floor. It moved at a snail's pace, like everything else in this country. The stale air was rank with the smell of liquor and sweat. Through the creak of the cables she could hear a faint squeaking, high in the elevator shaft. Bats. She'd seen them the night before, flapping over the courtyard. Wonderful. Bats and Guy Barnard. Could a girl ask for anything more?

If only there was some way she could have the benefit of his insider's knowledge without having to put up with *him.* The man was clever and streetwise, and he had those shadowy but all-important connections. Too bad he couldn't be trusted. Still, she couldn't help wondering what it would be like to take him up on his offer. Just the thought of working cheek to cheek with the man made her stomach dance a little pirouette of excitement. An ominous sign. The man was getting to her.

Oh, she'd been in love before; she knew how unreasonable hormones could be, how much havoc they could wreak, cavorting in a deprived female body.

I just won't think about him. It's the wrong time, the wrong place, the wrong situation.

And definitely the wrong man.

The elevator groaned to a halt, and the doors slid open to the deserted outdoor walkway. The night trembled to the distant beat of disco music as she headed through the shadows to her room. The entire fourth floor seemed abandoned this evening, all the windows unlit, the curtains drawn. She whirled around in fright as a chorus of shrieks echoed off the building and spiraled up into the darkness. Beyond the walkway railing, the shadows of bats rose and fluttered like phantoms over the courtyard.

Her hands were still shaking when she reached her door, and it took a moment to find the key. As she rummaged in her purse, a figure glided into her peripheral vision. Some sixth sense—a premonition of danger—made her turn.

At the end of the walkway, a man emerged from the shadows. As he passed beneath the glow of an outdoor lamp, she saw slick black hair and a face so immobile it seemed cast in wax. Then something else drew her gaze. Something in his hand. He was holding a knife.

She dropped her purse and ran.

Just ahead, the walkway turned a corner, past a huge air-conditioning vent. If she kept moving, she would reach the safety of the stairwell.

The man was yards behind. Surely the purse was what he wanted. But as she tore around the corner, she heard his footsteps thudding in pursuit. Oh, God, he wasn't after her money.

He was after her.

The stairwell lay ahead at the far end of the walkway. Just one flight down was the dance hall. She'd find people there. Safety...

With a desperate burst of speed, she sprinted forward. Then, through a fog of panic, she saw that her escape route was cut off.

Another man had appeared. He stood in the shadows at

the far end of the walkway. She couldn't see his expression; all she saw was the faint gleam of his face.

She halted, spun around. As she did, something whistled past her cheek and clattered onto the walkway. A knife. Automatically, she snatched it up and wielded it in front of her.

Her gaze shifted first to one man, then the other. They were closing in.

She screamed. Her cry mingled with the dance music, echoed off the buildings and funneled up into the night. A wave of startled bats fluttered up through the darkness. *Can't anyone hear me?* she thought in desperation.

She cast another frantic look around, searching for a way out. In front of her, beyond the railing, lay a four-story drop to the courtyard. Just behind her, sunk into a square expanse of graveled roof, was the enormous air-conditioning vent. Through the rusted grating she saw its giant fan blades spinning like a plane's propeller. The blast of warm air was so powerful it made her skirt billow.

The men moved in for the kill.

CHAPTER SIX

SHE HAD NO CHOICE. She scrambled over the railing and dropped onto the grating. It sagged under her weight, lowering her heart-stoppingly close to the deadly blades. A rusted fragment crumbled off into the fan; the clatter of metal was deafening.

She inched her way over the grate, heading for a safe island of rooftop. It was only a few steps across, but it felt like miles of tightrope suspended over oblivion. Her legs were trembling as she finally stepped off the grate. It was a dead end; beyond lay a sheer drop. And a crumbling expanse of grating was all that separated her from the killers.

The two men glanced around in frustration, searching for a safe way to reach her. There was no other route; they would have to cross the vent. But the grating had barely supported her weight; these men were far heavier. She looked at the deadly whirl of the blades. They wouldn't risk it, she thought.

But to her disbelief, one of the men climbed over the railing and eased himself onto the vent. The mesh sagged but held. He stared at her over the spinning blades, and she saw in his eyes the impassive gaze of a man who'd simply come to do his job.

Trapped, she thought. *Dear God, I'm trapped!*

She screamed again, but her cry of terror was lost in the fan's roar.

He was halfway across, his knife poised. She clutched her knife and backed away to the very edge of the roof. She had two choices: a four-story drop to the pavement below, or hand-to-hand combat with an experienced assassin. Both prospects seemed equally hopeless.

She crouched, knife in trembling hand, to slash, to claw—anything to stay alive. The man took another step. The blade moved closer.

Then gunfire ripped the night.

Willy stared in bewilderment as the killer clutched his belly and looked down at his bloody hand, his face a mask of astonishment. Then, like a puppet whose strings have been cut, he crumpled. As dead weight hit the weakened grating, Willy closed her eyes and cringed.

She never saw his body fall through. But she heard the squeal of metal, felt the wild shuddering of the fan blades. She collapsed to her knees, retching into the darkness below.

When the heaving finally stopped, she forced her head up.

Her other attacker had vanished.

Across the courtyard, on the opposite walkway, something gleamed. The barrel of a gun being lowered. A small face peering at her over the railing. She struggled to make sense of why the boy was there, why he had just saved her life. Stumbling to her feet, she whispered, "Oliver?"

The boy merely put a finger to his lips. Then, like a ghost, he slipped away into the darkness.

Dazed, she heard shouts and the thud of approaching footsteps.

"Willy! Are you all right?"

She turned and saw Guy. And she heard the panic in his voice.

"Don't move! I'll come get you."

"No!" she cried. "The grate—it's broken—"

For a moment, he studied the spinning blades. Then, glancing around, he spotted a workman's ladder propped beneath a broken window. He dragged it to the railing, hoisted it over and slid it horizontally across the broken grate. Then he eased himself over the railing, carefully stepped onto a rung and extended his arm to Willy. "I'm right here," he said. "Put your left foot on the ladder and grab my hand. I won't let you fall, I swear it. Come on, sweetheart. Just reach for my hand."

She couldn't look down at the fan blades. She looked across them at Guy's face, tense and gleaming with sweat. At his hand, reaching for her. And in that instant she knew, without a shred of doubt, that he would catch her. That she could trust him with her life.

She took a breath for courage, then took the step forward, over the whirling blades.

Instantly his hand locked over hers. For a split second she teetered. Guy's rigid grasp steadied her. Slowly, jerkily, she lunged forward onto the rung where he balanced.

"I've got you!" he yelled as he swept her into his arms, away from the yawning vent. He swung her easily over the railing onto the walkway, then dropped down beside her. He pulled her into the safety of his arms.

"It's all right," he murmured over and over into her hair. "Everything's all right...."

Only then, as she felt his heart pounding against hers, did she realize how terrified he'd been for her.

She was shaking so hard she could barely stand on her own two legs. It didn't matter. She knew the arms now wrapped around her would never let her fall.

They both stiffened as a harsh command was issued in Vietnamese. The people gathered about them quickly stepped aside to let a policeman through. Willy squinted

as a blinding light shone in her eyes. The flashlight's beam
shifted and froze on the air-conditioning vent. From the
spectators came a collective gasp of horror.

"Dear God," she heard Dodge Hamilton whisper.
"What a bloody mess."

MR. AINH WAS SWEATING. He was also hungry and tired,
and he needed badly to use the toilet. But all these con-
cerns would have to wait. He had learned that much from
the war: patience. *Victory comes to those who endure.* This
was what he kept saying to himself as he sat in his hard
chair and stared down at the wooden table.

"We have been careless, Comrade." The minister's
voice was soft, no more than a whisper; but then, the voice
of power had no need to shout.

Slowly Ainh raised his head. The man sitting across
from him had eyes like smooth, sparkling river stones.
Though the face was wrinkled and the hair hung in silver
wisps as delicate as cobwebs, the eyes were those of a
young man—bold and black and brilliant. Ainh felt their
gaze slice through him.

"The death of an American tourist would be most embarrassing," said the minister.

Ainh could only nod in meek agreement.

"You are certain Miss Maitland is uninjured?"

Ainh cleared his throat. Nodded again.

The minister's voice, so soft just a moment before, took
on a razor's edge. "This Barnard fellow—he prevented an
international incident, something our own people seem incapable of."

"But we had no warning, no reason to think this would
happen."

"The attack in Bangkok—was that not a warning?"

"A robbery attempt! That's what the report—"

"And reports are never wrong, are they?" The minister's smile was disconcertingly bland. "First Bangkok. Then tonight. I wonder what our little American tourist has gotten herself into."

"The two attacks may not be connected."

"Everything, Comrade, is connected." The minister sat very still, thinking. "And what about Mr. Barnard? Are he and Miss Maitland—" the minister paused delicately "—involved?"

"I think not. She called him a…what is that American expression? A *jerk*."

The minister laughed. "Ah. Mr. Barnard has trouble with the ladies!"

There was a knock on the door. An official entered, handed a report to the minister and respectfully withdrew.

"There is progress in the case?" inquired Ainh.

The minister looked up. "Of a sort. They were able to piece together fragments of the dead man's identity card. It seems he was already well-known to the police."

"Then that explains it!" said Ainh. "Some of these thugs will do anything for a few thousand dong."

"This was no robbery." The minister handed the report to Ainh. "He has connections to the old regime."

Ainh scanned the page. "I see mention only of a woman cousin—a factory worker." He paused, then looked up in surprise. "A mixed blood."

The minister nodded. "She is being questioned now. Shall we look in on her?"

CHANTAL WAS SLOUCHED ON A wooden bench, aiming lethal glares at the policeman in charge of questioning.

"I have done nothing!" she spat out. "Why should I want anyone dead? An American bitch, you say? What, do you think I am crazy? I have been home all night! Talk to the old man who lives above me! Ask him who's been playing my radio all night! Ask him why he's been beating on my ceiling, the old crank! Oh, but I could tell you stories about *him*."

"You accuse an old man?" said the policeman. "*You* are the counterrevolutionary! You and your cousin!"

"I hardly know my cousin."

"You were working together."

Chantal snorted. "I work in a factory. I have nothing to do with him."

The policeman swung a bag onto the table. He took out the items, placed them in front of her. "Caviar. Champagne. Pâté. We found these in your cupboards. How does a factory worker afford these things?"

Chantal's lips tightened, but she said nothing.

The policeman smiled. He gestured to a guard and Chantal, rigidly silent, was led from the room.

The policeman then turned respectfully to the minister, who, along with Ainh, was watching the proceedings. "As you can see, Minister Tranh, she is uncooperative. But give us time. We will think of a way to—"

"Let her go," said the minister.

The policeman looked startled. "I assure you, she can be made to talk."

Minister Tranh smiled. "There are other ways to get information. Release her. Then wait for the fly to drift back to the honeypot."

The policeman left, shaking his head. But, of course, he would do as ordered. After all, Minister Tranh had far more experience in such matters. Hadn't the old fox honed his skills on years of wartime espionage?

For a long time, the minister sat thinking. Then he picked up the champagne bottle and squinted at the label. "Ah. Taittinger." He sighed. "A favorite from my days in Paris.'' Gently he set the bottle back down and looked at Ainh. ''I sense that Miss Maitland has blundered into something dangerous. Perhaps she is asking too many questions. Stirring up dragons from the past.''

''You mean her father?'' Ainh shook his head. ''That is a very old dragon.''

To which the minister said softly, ''But perhaps not a vanquished one.''

A LARGE BLACK COCKROACH crawled across the table. One of the guards slapped it with a newspaper, brushed the corpse onto the floor and calmly went on writing. Above him, a ceiling fan whirred in the heat, fluttering papers on the desk.

''Once again, Miss Maitland,'' said the officer in charge. ''Tell me what happened.''

''I've told you everything.''

''I think you have left something out.''

''Nothing. I've left nothing out.''

''Yes, you have. There was a gunman.''

''I saw no gunman.''

''We have witnesses. They heard a shot. Who fired the gun?''

''I told you, I didn't see anyone. The grating was weak—he fell through.''

''Why are you lying?''

Her chin shot up. ''Why do you insist I'm lying?''

''Because we both know you are.''

''Lay off her!'' Guy cut in. ''She's told you everything she knows.''

The officer turned, looked at Guy. ''You will kindly remain silent, Mr. Barnard.''

''And you'll cut out the Gestapo act! You've been questioning her for two hours now. Can't you see she's exhausted?''

''Perhaps it is time you left.''

Guy wasn't about to back down. ''She's an American. You can't hold her indefinitely!''

The officer looked at Willy, then at Guy. He gave a nonchalant shrug. ''She will be released.''

''When?''

''When she tells the truth.'' Turning, he walked out.

''Hang in,'' Guy muttered. ''We'll get you out of here yet.'' He followed the officer into the next room, slamming the door behind him.

The arguing went on for ten minutes. She could hear them shouting behind the door. At least Guy still had the strength to shout; she could barely hold her head up.

When Guy returned at last, she could see from his look of disgust that he'd gotten nowhere. He dropped wearily onto the bench beside her and rubbed his eyes.

''What do they want from me?'' she asked. ''Why can't they just leave me alone?''

''I get the feeling they're waiting for something. Some sort of approval....''

''Whose?''

''Hell if I know.''

A rolled up newspaper whacked the table. Willy looked over and saw the guard flick away another dead roach. She shuddered.

It was midnight.

At 1:00 a.m., Mr. Ainh appeared, looking as sallow as an old bed sheet. Willy was too numb to move from the bench. She simply sat there, propped against Guy's shoulder, and let the two men do the talking.

''We are very sorry for the inconvenience,'' said Ainh,

sounding genuinely contrite. "But you must understand—"

"Inconvenience?" Guy snapped. "Ms. Maitland was
nearly killed earlier tonight, and she's been kept here for
three hours now. What the hell's going on?"

"The situation is...unusual. A robbery attempt—on a
foreigner, no less—well..." He shrugged helplessly.

Guy was incredulous. "You're calling this an attempted
robbery?"

"What would you call it?"

"A cover-up."

Ainh shuffled uneasily. Turning, he exchanged a few
words in Vietnamese with the guard. Then he gave Willy
a polite bow. "The police say you are free to leave, Miss
Maitland. On behalf of the Vietnamese government, I apol-
ogize for your most unfortunate experience. What happened does not in any way reflect on our high regard and
warm feelings for the American people. We hope this will
not spoil the remainder of your visit."

Guy couldn't help a laugh. "Why should it? It was just
a little murder attempt."

"In the morning," Ainh went on quickly, "you are free
to continue your tour."

"Subject to what restrictions?" Guy asked.

"No restrictions." Ainh cleared his throat and made a
feeble attempt to smile. "Contrary to your government
propaganda, Mr. Barnard, we are a reasonable people. We
have nothing to hide."

To which Guy answered flatly, "Or so it seems."

"I DON'T GET IT. First they run you through the wringer.
Then they hand you the keys to the country. It doesn't
make sense."

Willy stared out the taxi window as the streets of Saigon

glided past. Here and there, a lantern flickered in the darkness. A noodle vendor huddled on the sidewalk beside his steaming cart. In an open doorway, a beaded curtain shuddered, and in the dim room beyond, sleeping children could be seen, curled up like kittens on their mats.

"Nothing makes sense," she whispered. "Not this country. Or the people. Or anything that's happened...."

She was trembling. The horror of everything that had happened that night suddenly burst through the numbing dam of exhaustion. Even Guy's arm, which had magically materialized around her shoulders, couldn't keep away the unnamed terrors of the night.

He pulled her against his chest, and only when she inhaled that comfortable smell of fatigue, felt the slow and steady beat of his heart, did her trembling finally stop. He kept whispering, "It's all right, Willy. I won't let anything happen to you." She felt his kiss, gentle as rain, on her forehead.

When the driver stopped in front of the hotel, Guy had to coax her out of the car. He led her through the nightmarish glare of the lobby. He was the pillar that supported her in the elevator. And it was his arm that guided her down the shadowed walkway and past the air-conditioning vent, now ominously silent. He didn't even ask her if she wanted his company for the night; he simply opened the door to his room, led her inside and sat her down on his bed. Then he locked the door and slid a chair in front of it.

In the bathroom, he soaked a washcloth with warm water. Then he came back out, sat down beside her on the bed and gently wiped her smudged face. Her cheeks were pale. He had the insane urge to kiss her, to breathe some semblance of life back into her body. He knew she wouldn't fight him; she didn't have the strength. But it wouldn't be right, and he wasn't the kind of man who'd take advantage of the situation, of her.

"There," he murmured, brushing back her hair. "All better."

She stirred and gazed up at him with wide, stunned eyes. "Thank you," she whispered.

"For what?"

"For…" She paused, searching for the right words. "For being here."

He touched her face. "I'll be here all night. I won't leave you alone. If that's what you want."

She nodded. It hurt him to see her look so tired, so defeated. *She's getting to me,* he thought. *This isn't supposed to happen. This isn't what I expected.*

He could see, from the brightness of her eyes, that she was trying not to cry. He slid his arm around her shoulders.

"You'll be safe, Willy," he whispered into the softness of her hair. "You'll be going home in the morning. Even if I have to strap you into that plane myself, you'll be going home."

She shook her head. "I can't."

"What do you mean, you can't?"

"My father…"

"Forget him. It isn't worth it."

"I made a promise…."

"All you promised your mother was an answer. Not a body. Not some official report, stamped and certified. Just a simple answer. So give her one. Tell her he's dead, tell her he died in the crash. It's probably the truth."

"I can't lie to her."

"You have to." He took her by the shoulders, forcing her to look at him. "Willy, someone's trying to kill you. They've flubbed it twice. But what happens the third time? The fourth?"

She shook her head. "I'm not worth killing. I don't know anything!"

"Maybe it's not what you know. It's what you might find out."

Sniffling, she looked up in bewilderment. "That my father's dead? Or alive? What *difference* does it make to anyone?"

He sighed, a sound of overwhelming weariness. "I don't know. If we could talk to Oliver, find out who he works for—"

"He's just a kid!"

"Obviously not. He could be sixteen, seventeen. Old enough to be an agent."

"For the Vietnamese?"

"No. If he was one of theirs, why'd he vanish? Why did the police keep hounding you about him?"

She huddled on the bed, her confusion deepening. "He saved my life. And I don't even know why."

There it was again, that raw edge of vulnerability, shimmering in her eyes. She might be Wild Bill Maitland's brat, but she was also a woman, and Guy was having a hard time concentrating on the problem at hand. Why was someone trying to kill her?

He was too tired to think. It was late, she was so near, and there was the bed, just waiting.

He reached up and gently stroked her face. She seemed to sense immediately what was about to happen. Even though her whole body remained stiff, she didn't fight him. The instant their lips met, he felt a shock leap through her, through him, as though they'd both been hit by some glorious bolt of lightning. *My God,* he thought in surprise. *You wanted this as much as I did....*

He heard her murmur, "No," against his mouth, but he knew she didn't mean it, so he went on kissing her until he knew that if he didn't stop right then and there, he'd do something he really didn't want to do.

Oh, yes I do, he thought with sudden abandon. *I want her more than I've wanted any other woman.*

She put her hand against his chest and murmured another "No," this one fainter. He would have ignored it, too, had it not been for the look in her eyes. They were wide and confused, the eyes of a woman pushed to the brink by fear and exhaustion. This wasn't the way he wanted her. Maddening as she could be, he wanted the living, breathing, *real* Willy Maitland in his arms.

He released her. They sat on the bed, not speaking for a while, just looking at each other with a shared sense of quiet astonishment.

"Why—why did you do that?" she asked weakly.

"You looked like you needed a kiss."

"Not from you."

"From someone, then. It's been a while since you've been kissed. Hasn't it?"

She didn't answer, and he knew he'd guessed the truth. *Hell, what a waste,* he thought, his gaze dropping briefly to that perfect little mouth. He managed a disinterested laugh. "That's what I thought."

Willy stared at his grinning face and wondered, *Is it so obvious?* Not only hadn't she been kissed in a long time, she hadn't *ever* been kissed like *that.* He knew exactly how to do it; he'd probably had years of practice with other women. For some insane reason, she found herself wondering how she compared, found herself hating every woman he'd ever kissed before her, hating even more every woman he'd kiss after her.

She flung herself down on the bed and turned her back on him. "Oh, leave me alone!" she cried. "I can't deal with this! I can't deal with you. I'm tired. I just want to sleep."

He didn't say anything. She felt him smooth her hair. It was nothing more than a brush of his fingers, but somehow, that one touch told her that he wouldn't leave, that he'd be there all night, watching over her. He rose from the bed and switched off the lamp. She lay very still in the darkness, listening to him move around the room. She heard him check the windows, then the door, testing how firmly the chair was wedged against it. Then, apparently satisfied, he went into the bathroom, and she heard water running in the sink.

She was still awake when he came back to bed and stretched out beside her. She lay there, worrying that he'd kiss her again and hoping desperately that he would.

"Guy?" she whispered.

"Yes?"

"I'm scared."

He reached for her through the darkness. Willingly, she let him pull her against his bare chest. He smelled of soap and safety. Yes, that's what it was. Safety.

"It's okay to be scared," he whispered. "Even if you are Wild Bill Maitland's kid."

As if she had a choice, she thought as she lay in his arms. The sad part was, she'd never wanted to be the daughter of a legend. What she'd wanted from Wild Bill wasn't valor or daring or the reflected glory of a hero.

What she'd wanted most of all was a father.

SIANG CROUCHED MOTIONLESS in a stinking mud puddle and stared up the road at Chantal's building. Two hours had passed and the man was still there by the curb. Siang could see his vague form huddled in the darkness. A police agent, no doubt, and not a very good one. Was that a snore rumbling in the night? Yes, Siang thought, definitely a snore. How fortunate that surveillance was always relegated to those least able to withstand its monotony.

Siang decided to make his move.

He withdrew his knife. Noiselessly he edged out of the alley and circled around, slipping from shadow to shadow along the row of hootches. Barely five yards from his goal, he froze as the man's snores shuddered and stopped. The shadow's head lifted, shaking off sleep.

Siang closed in, yanked the man's head up by the hair and slit the throat.

There was no cry, only a gurgle, and then the hiss of a last breath escaping the dead man's lungs. Siang dragged the body around to the back of the building and rolled it into a drainage ditch. Then he slipped through an open window into Chantal's flat.

He found her asleep. She awakened instantly as he clapped his hand over her mouth.

"You!" she ground out through his fingers. "Damn you, you got me in trouble!"

"What did you tell the police?"

"Get away from me!"

"What did you tell them?"

She batted away his hand. "I didn't tell them anything!"

"You're lying."

"You think I'm stupid? You think I'd tell them I have friends in the CIA?"

He released her. As she sat up, the silky heat of her breast brushed against his arm. So the old whore still slept naked, he thought with an automatic stirring of desire.

She rose from the bed and pulled on a robe.

"Don't turn on the lights," he said.

"There was a man outside—a police agent. What did you do with him?"

"I took care of him."

"And the body?"

"In the ditch out back."

"Oh, nice, Siang. Very nice. Now they'll blame me for that, too." She struck a match and lit a cigarette. By the flame's brief glow, he could see her face framed by a tangle of black hair. In the semidarkness she still looked tempting, young and soft and succulent.

The match went out. He asked, "What happened at the police station?"

She let out a slow breath. The smell of exhaled smoke filled the darkness. "They asked about my cousin. They say he's dead. Is that true?"

"What do they know about me?"

"Is Winn really dead?"

Siang paused. "It couldn't be helped."

Chantal laughed. Softly at first, then with wild abandon. "*She* did that, did she? The American bitch? You cannot finish off even a woman? Oh, Siang, you must be slipping!"

He felt like hitting her, but he controlled the urge. Chantal was right. He must be slipping.

She began to pace the room, her movements as sure as a cat's in the darkness. "The police are interested. Very interested. And I saw others there—Party members, I think—watching the interrogation. What have you gotten me into, Siang?"

He shrugged. "Give me a cigarette."

She whirled on him in rage. "Get your own cigarettes! You think I have money to waste on *you?*"

"You'll get the money. All you want."

"You don't know how much I want."

"I still need a gun. You promised me you'd get one. Plus twenty rounds, minimum."

She let out a harsh breath of smoke. "Ammunition is hard to come by."

"I can't wait any longer. This has to be—"

They both froze as the door creaked open. *The police,* thought Siang, automatically reaching for his knife.

"You're so right, Mr. Siang," said a voice in the darkness. Perfect English. "It has to be done. But not quite yet."

The intruder moved lazily into the room, struck a match and calmly lit a kerosene lamp on the table.

Chantal's eyes were wide with astonishment. And fear. "It's you," she whispered. "You've come back...."

The intruder smiled. He laid a pistol and a box of .38-caliber ammunition on the table. Then he looked at Siang. "There's been a slight change of plans."

CHAPTER SEVEN

SHE WAS FLYING. High, high above the clouds, where the sky was so cold and clear, it felt as if her plane were floating in a crystalline sea. She could hear the wings cut the air like knives through silk. Someone said, "Higher, baby. You have to climb higher if you want to reach the stars."

She turned. It was her father sitting in the copilot's seat, quicksilver smoke dancing around him. He looked the way she'd always remembered him, his cap tilted at a jaunty angle, his eyes twinkling. Just the way he used to look when she'd loved him. When he'd been the biggest, boldest Daddy in the world.

She said, "But I don't want to climb higher."

"Yes, you do. You want to reach the stars."

"I'm afraid, Daddy. Don't make me...."

But he took the joystick. He sent the plane upward, upward, into the blue bowl of sky. He kept saying, "This is what it's all about. Yessir, baby, this is what it's all about." Only his voice had changed. She saw that it was no longer her father sitting in the copilot's seat; it was Guy Barnard, pushing them into oblivion. "I'll take us to the stars!"

Then it was her father again, gleefully gripping the joystick. She tried to wrench the plane out of the climb, but the joystick broke off in her hand.

The sky turned upside down, righted. She looked at the

copilot's seat. Guy was sitting there, laughing. They went higher. Her father laughed.

"Who *are* you?" she screamed.

The phantom smiled. "Don't you know me?"

She woke up, still reaching desperately for that stump of a joystick.

"It's me," the voice said.

She stared up wildly. "Daddy!"

The man looking down at her smiled, a kind smile. "Not quite."

She blinked, focused on Guy's face, his rumpled hair, unshaven jaw. Sweat gleamed on his bare shoulders. Through the curtains behind him, daylight shimmered.

"Nightmare?" he asked.

Groaning, she sat up and shoved back a handful of tangled hair. "I don't usually have them. Nightmares."

"After last night, I'd be surprised if you didn't have one."

Last night. She looked down and saw she was still wearing the same blood-spattered dress, now damp and clinging to her back.

"Power's out," said Guy, giving the silent air conditioner a slap. He padded over to the window and nudged open the curtain. Sunlight blazed in, so piercing, it hurt Willy's eyes. "Gonna be a hell of a scorcher."

"Already is."

"Are you feeling okay?" He stood silhouetted against the window, his unbelted trousers slung low over his hips. Once again she saw the scar, noticed how it rippled its way down his abdomen before vanishing beneath the waistband.

"I'm hot," she said. "And filthy. And I probably don't smell so good."

"I hadn't noticed." He paused and added ruefully, "Probably because I smell even worse."

They laughed, a short, uneasy laugh that was instantly cut off when someone knocked on the door. Guy called out, "Who's there?"

"Mr. Barnard? It is eight o'clock. The car is ready."

"It's my driver," Guy said, and he unbolted the door.

A smiling Vietnamese man stood outside. "Good morning! Do you still wish to go to Cantho this morning?"

"I don't think so," said Guy, discreetly stepping outside to talk in private. Willy heard him murmur, "I want to get Ms. Maitland to the airport this afternoon. Maybe we can…"

Cantho. Willy sat on the bed, listening to the buzz of conversation, trying to remember why that name was so important. Oh, yes. There was a man there, someone she needed to talk to. A man who might have the answers. She closed her eyes against the window's glare, and the dream came back to her, the grinning face of her father, the sickening climb of a doomed plane. She thought of her mother, lying near death at home. Heard her mother ask, "Are you sure, Willy? Do you know for certain he's dead?" Heard herself tell another lie, all the time hating herself, hating her own cowardice, hating the fact that she could never live up to her father's name. Or his courage.

"So stick around the hotel," Guy said to the driver. "Her plane takes off at four, so we should leave around—"

"I'm going to Cantho," said Willy.

Guy glanced around at her. "What?"

"I said I'm going to Cantho. You said you'd take me."

He shook his head. "Things have changed."

"Nothing's changed."

"The stakes have."

"But not the questions. They haven't gone away. They'll never go away."

Guy turned to the driver. "Excuse me while I talk some sense into the lady...."

But Willy had already risen to her feet. "Don't bother. You can't talk sense into me." She went into the bathroom and shut the door. "I'm Wild Bill Maitland's kid, remember?" she yelled.

The driver looked sympathetically at Guy. "I will get the car."

THE ROAD OUT OF SAIGON was jammed with trucks, most of them ancient and spewing clouds of black exhaust. Through the open windows of their car came the smells of smoke and sun-baked pavement and rotting fruit. Laborers trudged along the roadside, a bobbing column of conical hats against the bright green of the rice paddies.

Five hours and two ferry crossings later, Guy and Willy stood on a Cantho pier and watched a multitude of boats glide across the muddy Mekong. River women dipped and swayed as they rowed, a strange and graceful dance at the oars. And on the riverbank swirled the noise and confusion of a thriving market town. Schoolgirls, braided hair gleaming in the sunshine, whisked past on bicycles. Stevedores heaved sacks of rice and crates of melons and pineapples onto sampans.

Overwhelmed by the chaos, Willy asked bleakly, "How are we ever going to find him?"

Guy's answer didn't inspire much confidence. He simply shrugged and said, "How hard can it be?"

Very hard, it turned out. All their inquiries brought the same response. "A tall man?" people would say. "And blond?" Invariably their answer would be a shake of the head.

It was Guy's inspired hunch that finally sent them into a series of tailor shops. "Maybe Lassiter's no longer blond," he said. "He could have dyed his hair or gone bald. But there's one feature a man can't disguise—his height. And in this country, a six-foot-four man is going to need specially tailored clothes."

The first three tailors they visited turned up nothing. It was with a growing sense of futility that they entered the fourth shop, wedged in an alley of tin-roofed hootches. In the cavelike gloom within, an elderly seamstress sat hunched over a mound of imitation silk. She didn't seem to understand Guy's questions. In frustration, Guy took out a pen and jotted a few words in Vietnamese on a scrap of newspaper. Then, to illustrate his point, he sketched in the figure of a tall man.

The woman squinted down at the drawing. For a long time, she sat there, her fingers knotted tightly around the shimmering fabric. Then she looked up at Guy. No words were exchanged, just that silent, mournful gaze.

Guy gave a nod that he understood. He reached into his pocket and lay a twenty-dollar bill on the table in front of her. She stared at it in wonder. American dollars. For her, it was a fortune.

At last she took up Guy's pen and, with painful precision, began to write. The instant she'd finished, Guy swept up the scrap of paper and jammed it into his pocket. "Let's go," he whispered to Willy.

"What does it say?" Willy whispered as they headed back along the row of hootches.

Guy didn't answer; he only quickened his pace. In the silence of the alley, Willy suddenly became aware of eyes, everywhere, watching them from the windows and doorways.

Willy tugged on Guy's arm. "Guy…"

"It's an address. Near the marketplace."

"Lassiter's?"

"Don't talk. Just keep moving. We're being followed."

"What?"

He grabbed her arm before she could turn to look. "Come on, keep your head. Pretend he's not there."

She fought to keep her eyes focused straight ahead, but the sense of being stalked made every muscle in her body strain to run. *How does he stay so calm?* she wondered, glancing at Guy. He was actually whistling now, a tuneless song that scraped her nerves raw. They reached the end of the alley, and a maze of streets lay before them. To her surprise, Guy stopped and struck up a cheerful conversation with a boy selling cigarettes at the corner. Their chatter seemed to go on forever.

"What are you doing?" Willy ground out. "Can't we get out of here?"

"Trust me." Guy bought a pack of Winstons, for which he paid two American dollars. The boy beamed and sketched a childish salute.

Guy took Willy's hand. "Get ready."

"Ready for what?"

The words were barely out of her mouth when Guy wrenched her around the corner and up another alley. They made a sharp left, then a right, past a row of tin-roofed shacks, and ducked into an open doorway.

Inside, it was too murky to make sense of their surroundings. For an eternity they huddled together, listening for footsteps. They could hear, in the distance, children laughing and a car horn honking incessantly. But just outside, in the alley, there was silence.

"Looks like the kid did his job," whispered Guy.

"You mean that cigarette boy?"

Guy sidled over to the doorway and peered out. "Looks clear. Come on, let's get out of here."

They slipped into the alley and doubled back. Even before they saw the marketplace, they could hear it: the shouts of merchants, the frantic squeals of pigs. Hurrying along the outskirts, they scanned the street names and finally turned into what was scarcely more than an alley jammed between crumbling apartment buildings. The address numbers were barely decipherable.

At last, at a faded green building, they stopped. Guy squinted at the number over the doorway and nodded. "This is it." He knocked.

The door opened. A single eye, iris so black, the pupil was invisible, peered at them through the crack. That was all they saw, that one glimpse of a woman's face, but it was enough to tell them she was afraid. Guy spoke to her in Vietnamese. The woman shook her head and tried to close the door. He put his hand out to stop it and spoke again, this time saying the man's name, "Sam Lassiter."

Panicking, the woman turned and screamed something in Vietnamese.

Somewhere in the house, footsteps thudded away, followed by the shattering of glass.

"Lassiter!" Guy yelled. Shoving past the woman, he raced through the apartment, Willy at his heels. In a back room, they found a broken window. Outside in the alley, a man was sprinting away. Guy scrambled out, dropped down among the glass shards and took off after the fugitive.

Willy was about to follow him out the window when the Vietnamese woman, frantic, grasped her arm.

"Please! No hurt him!" she cried. "Please!"

Willy, trying to pull free, found her fingers linked for

an instant with the other woman's. Their eyes met. "We won't hurt him," Willy said, gently disengaging her arm.

Then she pulled herself up onto the windowsill and dropped into the alley.

GUY WAS PULLING CLOSER. He could see his quarry loping toward the marketplace. It had to be Lassiter. Though his hair was a lank, dirty brown, there was no disguising his height; he towered above the crowd. He ducked beneath the marketplace canopy and vanished into shadow.

Damn, thought Guy, struggling to move through the crowd. *I'm going to lose him.*

He shoved into the central market tent. The sun's glare abruptly gave way to a close, hot gloom. He stumbled blindly, his eyes adjusting slowly to the change in light. He made out the cramped aisles, the counters overflowing with fruit and vegetables, the gay sparkle of pinwheels spinning on a toy vendor's cart. A tall silhouette suddenly bobbed off to the side. Guy spun around and saw Lassiter duck behind a gleaming stack of cookware.

Guy scrambled after him. The man leapt up and sprinted away. Pots and pans went flying, a dozen cymbals crashing together.

Guy's quarry darted into the produce section. Guy made a sharp left, leapt over a crate of mangoes and dashed up a parallel aisle. "Lassiter!" he yelled. "I want to talk! That's all, just talk!"

The man spun right, shoved over a fruit stand and stumbled away. Watermelons slammed to the ground, exploding in a brilliant rain of flesh. Guy almost slipped in the muck. "Lassiter!" he shouted.

They headed into the meat section. Lassiter, desperate, shoved a crate of ducks into Guy's path, sending up a cloud of feathers as the birds, freed from their prison, flapped loose. Guy dodged the crate, leapt over a fugitive duck and kept running. Ahead lay the butcher counters, stacked high with slabs of meat. A vendor was hosing down the concrete floor, sending a stream of bloody water into the gutter. Lassiter, moving full tilt, suddenly slid and fell to his knees in the offal. At once he tried to scramble back to his feet, but by then Guy had snagged his shirt collar.

"Just—just talk," Guy managed to gasp between breaths. "That's all—talk—"

Lassiter thrashed, struggling to pull free.

"Gimme a chance!" Guy yelled, dragging him back down.

Lassiter rammed his shoulders at Guy's knees, sending Guy sprawling. In an instant, Lassiter had leapt to his feet. But as he turned to flee, Guy grabbed his ankle, and Lassiter toppled forward and splashed, headfirst, into a vat of squirming eels.

The water seemed to boil with slippery bodies, writhing in panic. Guy dragged the man's head out of the vat. They both collapsed, gasping on the slick concrete.

"Don't!" Lassiter sobbed. "Please…"

"I told you, I just—just want to talk—"

"I won't say anything! I swear it. You tell 'em that for me. Tell 'em I forgot everything.…"

"Who?" Guy took the other man by the shoulders. "Who are *they?* Who are you afraid of?"

Lassiter took a shaky breath and looked at him, seemed to make a decision. "The Company."

"WHY DOES THE CIA WANT you dead?" Willy asked.

They were sitting at a wooden table on the deck of an old river barge. Neutral territory, Lassiter had said of this floating café. During the war, by some unspoken agree-

ment, V.C. and South Vietnamese soldiers would sit together on this very deck, enjoying a small patch of peace.
A few hundred yards away, the war might rage on, but
here no guns were drawn, no bullets fired.

Lassiter, gaunt and nervous, took a deep swallow of
beer. Behind him, beyond the railing, flowed the Mekong,
alive with the sounds of river men, the putter of boats. In
the last light of sunset, the water rippled with gold. Lassiter
said, "They want me out of the way for the same reason
they wanted Luis Valdez out of the way. I know too
much."

"About what?"

"Laos. The bombings, the gun drops. The war your av-
erage soldier didn't know about." He looked at Guy. "Did
you?"

Guy shook his head. "We were so busy staying alive,
we didn't care what was going on across the border."

"Valdez knew. Anyone who went down in Laos was in
for an education. If they survived. And that was a big *if*.
Say you did manage to eject. Say you lived through the
G force of shooting out of your cockpit. If the enemy
didn't find you, the animals would." He stared down at
his beer. "Valdez was lucky to be alive."

"You met him at Tuyen Quan?" asked Guy.

"Yeah. Summer camp." He laughed. "For three years
we were stuck in the same cell." His gaze turned to the
river. "I was with the 101st when I was captured. Got
separated during a firefight. You know how it is in those
valleys, the jungle's so thick you can't be sure which
way's up. I was going in circles, and all the time I could
hear those damn Hueys flying overhead, *right overhead*,
picking guys up. Everyone but me. I figured I'd been left
to die. Or maybe I was already dead, just some corpse
walking around in the trees...." He swallowed; the hand

clutching the beer bottle was unsteady. "When they finally boxed me in, I just threw my rifle down and put up my hands. I got force marched north, into NVA territory. That's how I ended up at Tuyen Quan."

"Where you met Valdez," said Willy.

"He was brought in a year later, transferred in from some camp in Laos. By then I was an old-timer. Knew the ropes, worked my own vegetable patch. I was hanging in okay. Valdez, though, was holding on by the skin of his teeth. Yellow from hepatitis, a broken arm that wouldn't heal right. It took him months to get strong enough even to work in the garden. Yeah, it was just him and me in that cell. Three years. We did a lot of talking. I heard all his stories. He said a lot of things I didn't want to believe, things about Laos, about what we were doing there...."

Willy leaned forward and asked softly, "Did he ever talk about my father?"

Lassiter turned to her, his eyes dark against the glow of sunset. "When Valdez last saw him, your father was still alive. Trying to fly the plane."

"And then what happened?"

"Luis bailed out right after she blew up. So he couldn't be sure—"

"Wait," cut in Guy. "What do you mean, 'blew up'?"

"That's what he said. Something went off in the hold."

"But the plane was shot down."

"It wasn't enemy fire that brought her down. Valdez was positive about that. They might have been going through flak at the time, but this was something else, something that blew the fuselage door clean off. He kept going over and over what they had in the cargo, but all he remembered listed on the manifest were aircraft parts."

"And a passenger," said Willy.

Lassiter nodded. "Valdez mentioned him. Said he was

a weird little guy, quiet, almost, well, *holy*. They could tell he was a VIP, just by what he was wearing around his neck."

"You mean gold? Chains?" asked Guy.

"Some sort of medallion. Maybe a religious symbol."

"Where was this passenger supposed to be dropped off?"

"Behind lines. VC territory. It was billed as an in-and-out job, strictly under wraps."

"Valdez told *you* about it," said Willy.

"And I wish to hell he never had." Lassiter took another gulp of beer. His hand was shaking again. Sunset flecked the river with bloodred ripples. "It's funny. At the time we felt almost, well, *protected* in that camp. Maybe it was just a lot of brainwashing, but the guards kept telling Valdez he was lucky to be a prisoner. That he knew things that'd get him into trouble. That the CIA would kill him."

"Sounds like propaganda."

"That's what I figured it was—Commie lies designed to break him down. But they got Valdez scared. He kept waking up at night, screaming about the plane going down...."

Lassiter stared out at the water. "Anyway, after the war, they released us. Valdez and the other guys headed home. He wrote me from Bangkok, sent the letter by way of a Red Cross nurse we'd met in Hanoi right after our release. An English gal, a little anti-American but real nice. When I read that letter, I thought, now the poor bastard's really gone over the edge. He was saying crazy things, said he wasn't allowed to go out, that all his phone calls were monitored. I figured he'd be all right once he got home. Then I got a call from Nora Walker, that Red Cross nurse. She said he was dead. That he'd shot himself in the head."

Willy asked, "Do you think it was suicide?"

"I think he was a liability. And the Company doesn't like liabilities." He turned his troubled gaze to the water. "When we were at Tuyen, all he could talk about was going home, you know? Seeing his old hangouts, his old buddies. Me, I had nothing to go home to, just a sister I never much cared for. Here, at least, I had my girl, someone I loved. That's why I stayed. I'm not the only one. There are other guys like me around, hiding in villages, jungles. Guys who've gone bamboo, gone native." He shook his head. "Too bad Valdez didn't. He'd still be alive."

"But isn't it hard living here?" asked Willy. "Always the outsider, the old enemy? Don't you ever feel threatened by the authorities?"

Lassiter responded with a laugh and cocked his head at a far table where four men were sitting. "Have you said hello to our local police? They've probably been tailing you since you hit town."

"So we noticed," said Guy.

"My guess is they're assigned to protect me, their resident lunatic American. Just the fact that I'm alive and well is proof this isn't the evil empire." He raised his bottle of beer in a toast to the four policemen. They stared back sheepishly.

"So here you are," said Guy, "cut off from the rest of the world. Why would the CIA bother to come after you?"

"It's something Nora told me."

"The nurse?"

Lassiter nodded. "After the war, she stayed on in Hanoi. Still works at the local hospital. About a year ago, some guy—an American—dropped in to see her. Asked if she knew how to get hold of me. He said he had an urgent message from my uncle. But Nora's a sharp gal, thinks fast on her feet. She told him I'd left the country, that I was living in Thailand. A good thing she did."

"Why?"

"Because I don't have an uncle."

There was a silence. Softly Guy said, "You think that was a Company man."

"I keep wondering if he was. Wondering if he'll find me. I don't want to end up like Luis Valdez. With a bullet in my head."

On the river, boats glided like ghosts through the shadows. A café worker silently circled the deck, lighting a string of paper lanterns.

"I've kept a low profile," said Lassiter. "Never make noise. Never draw attention. See, I changed my hair." He grinned faintly and tugged on his lank brown ponytail. "Got this shade from the local herbalist. Extract of cuttlefish and God knows what else. Smells like hell, but I'm not blond anymore." He let the ponytail flop loose, and his smile faded. "I kept hoping the Company would lose interest in me. Then you showed up at my door, and I—I guess I freaked out."

The bartender put a record on the turntable, and the needle scratched out a Vietnamese love song, a haunting melody that drifted like mist over the river. Wind swayed the paper lanterns, and shadows danced across the deck. Lassiter stared at the five beer bottles lined up in front of him on the table. He ordered a sixth.

"It takes time, but you get used to it here," he said. "The rhythm of life. The people, the way they think. There's not a lot of whining and flailing at misfortune. They accept life as it is. I like that. And after a while, I got to feeling this was the only place I've ever belonged, the only place I ever felt safe." He looked at Willy. "It could be the only place *you're* safe."

"But I'm not like you," said Willy. "I can't stay here the rest of my life."

"I want to put her on the next plane to Bangkok," said Guy.

"Bangkok?" Lassiter snorted. "Easiest place in the world to get yourself killed. And going home'd be no safer. Look what happened to Valdez."

"But *why?*" Willy said in frustration. "Why would they kill Valdez? Or me? I don't know anything!"

"You're Bill Maitland's daughter. You're a direct link—"

"To *what?* A dead man?"

The love song ended, fading to the *scritch-scritch* of the needle.

Lassiter set his beer down. "I don't know," he said. "I don't know why you're such a threat to them. All I know is, something went wrong on that flight. And the Company's still trying to cover it up...." He stared at the line of empty beer bottles gleaming in the lantern light. "If it takes a bullet to buy silence, then a bullet's what they'll use."

"DO YOU THINK HE'S RIGHT?" Willy whispered.

From the back seat of the car, they watched the rice paddies, silvered by moonlight, slip past their windows. For an hour they'd driven without speaking, lulled into silence by the rhythm of the road under their wheels. But now Willy couldn't help voicing the question she was afraid to ask. "Will I be any safer at home?"

Guy looked out at the night. "I wish I knew. I wish I could tell you what to do. Where to go..."

She thought of her mother's house in San Francisco, thought of how warm and safe it had always seemed, that blue Victorian on Third Avenue. Surely no one would touch her there.

Then she thought of Valdez, shot to death in his Houston rooming house. For him, even a POW camp had been safer.

The driver slid a tape into the car's cassette player. A Vietnamese song twanged out, sung by a woman with a sorrowful voice. Outside, the rice paddies swayed like waves on a silver ocean. Nothing about this moment seemed real, not the melody or the moonlit countryside or the danger. Only Guy was real—real enough to touch, to hold.

She let her head rest against his shoulder, and the darkness, the warmth, made sleep impossible to resist. Guy's arm came around her, cradled her against his chest. She felt his breath in her hair, the brush of his lips on her forehead. A kiss, she thought drowsily. It felt so nice to be kissed....

The hum of the wheels over the road seemed to take on a new rhythm, the whisper of the ocean, the soothing hiss of waves. Now he was kissing her all over, and they were no longer in the back seat of the car; they were on a ship, swaying on a black sea. The wind moaned in the rigging, a soulful song in Vietnamese. She was lying on her back, and somehow, all her clothes had vanished. He was on top of her, his hands trapping her arms against the deck, his lips exploring her throat, her breasts, with a conqueror's triumph. How she wanted him to make love to her, wanted it so badly that her body arched up to meet his, straining for some blessed release from this ache within her. But his lips melted away, and then she heard, ''Wake up. Willy, wake up....''

She opened her eyes. She was lying in the back seat of

the car, her head in Guy's lap. Through the window came
the faint glow of city lights.

"We're back in Saigon," he whispered, stroking her
face. The touch of his hand, so new yet so familiar, made
her tremble in the night heat. "You must have been tired."

Still shaken by the dream, she pulled away and sat up.
Outside, the streets were deserted. "What time is it?"

"After midnight. Guess we forgot about supper. Are
you hungry?"

"Not really."

"Neither am I. Maybe we should just call it a—" He
paused. She felt his arm stiffen against hers. "Now what?"
he muttered, staring straight ahead.

Willy followed his gaze to the hotel, which had just
swung into view. A surreal scene lay ahead: the midnight
glare of streetlights, the army of policemen blocking the
lobby doors, the gleam of AK-47s held at the ready.

Their driver muttered in Vietnamese. Willy could see
his face in the rearview mirror. He was sweating.

The instant they pulled to a stop at the curb, their car
was surrounded. A policeman yanked the passenger door
open.

"Stay inside," Guy said. "I'll take care of this."

But as he stepped out of the car, a uniformed arm
reached inside and dragged her out as well. Groggy with
sleep, bewildered by the confusion, she clung to Guy's arm
as voices shouted and men shoved against her.

"Barnard!" It was Dodge Hamilton, struggling down
the hotel steps toward them. "What the hell's going on?"

"Don't ask me! We just got back to town!"

"Blast, where's that man Ainh?" said Hamilton, glancing around. "He was here a minute ago...."

"I am here," came the answer in a shaky voice. Ainh,
glasses askew and blinking nervously, stood at the top of

the lobby steps. He was swiftly escorted by a policeman through the crowd. Gesturing to a limousine, he said to Guy, "Please. You and Miss Maitland will come with me."

"Why are we under arrest?" Guy demanded.

"You are not under arrest."

Guy pulled his arm free of a policeman's grasp. "Could've fooled me."

"They are here only as a precaution," said Ainh, ushering them into the car. "Please get in. Quickly."

It was the ripple of urgency in his voice that told Willy something terrible had happened. "What is it?" she asked Ainh. "What's wrong?"

Ainh nervously adjusted his glasses. "About two hours ago, we received a call from the police in Cantho."

"We were just there."

"So they told us. They also said they'd found a body. Floating in the river…"

Willy stared at him, afraid to ask, yet already knowing. Only when she felt Guy's hand tighten around her arm did she realize she'd sagged against him.

"Sam Lassiter?" Guy asked flatly.

Ainh nodded. "His throat was cut."

CHAPTER EIGHT

THE OLD MAN who sat in the carved rosewood chair appeared frail enough to be toppled by a stiff wind. His arms were like two twigs crossed on his lap. His white wisp of a beard trembled in the breath of the ceiling fan. But his eyes were as bright as quicksilver. Through the open windows came the whine of the cicadas in the walled garden. Overhead, the fan spun slowly in the midnight heat.

The old man's gaze focused on Willy. "Wherever you walk, Miss Maitland," he said, "it seems you leave a trail of blood."

"We had nothing to do with Lassiter's death," said Guy. "When we left Cantho, he was alive."

"I think you misunderstand, Mr. Barnard." The man turned to Guy. "I do not accuse you of anything."

"Who *are* you accusing?"

"That detail I leave to our people in Cantho."

"You mean those police agents you had following us?"

Minister Tranh smiled. "You made it a difficult assignment. That boy on the corner—an ingenious move. No, we're aware that Mr. Lassiter was alive when you left him."

"And after we left?"

"We know that he sat in the river café for another twenty minutes. That he drank a total of eight beers. And then he left. Unfortunately, he never arrived home."

"Weren't your people keeping tabs on him?"

"Tabs?"

"Surveillance."

"Mr. Lassiter was a friend. We don't keep…tabs—is that the word?—on our friends."

"But you followed *us*," said Willy.

Minister Tranh's placid gaze shifted to her. "Are you our friend, Miss Maitland?"

"What do you think?"

"I think it is not easy to tell. I think even you cannot tell your friends from your enemies. It is a dangerous state of affairs. Already it has led to three murders."

Willy shook her head, puzzled. "Three? Lassiter's the only one I've heard about."

"Who else has been killed?" Guy asked.

"A Saigon policeman," said the minister. "Murdered last night on routine surveillance duty."

"I don't see the connection."

"Also last night, another man dead. Again, the throat cut."

"You can't blame us for every murder in Saigon!" said Willy. "We don't even know those other victims—"

"But yesterday you paid one of them a visit. Or have you forgotten?"

Guy stared across the table. "Gerard."

In the darkness outside, the cicadas' shrill music rose to a scream. Then, in an instant, the night fell absolutely silent.

Minister Tranh gazed ahead at the far wall, as though divining some message from the mildewed wallpaper. "Are you familiar with the Vietnamese calendar, Miss Maitland?" he asked quietly.

"Your calendar?" She frowned, puzzled by the new twist of conversation. "It—it's the same as the Chinese, isn't it?"

"Last year was the year of the dragon. A lucky year, or so they say. A fine year for babies and marriages. But this year…" He shook his head.

"The snake," said Guy.

Minister Tranh nodded. "The snake. A dangerous symbol. An omen of disaster. Famine and death. A year of misfortune.…" He sighed and his head drooped, as though his fragile neck was suddenly too weak to support it. For a long time he sat in silence, his white hair fluttering in the fan's breath. Then, slowly, he raised his head. "Go home, Miss Maitland," he said. "This is not a year for you, a place for you. Go home."

Willy thought about how easy it would be to climb onto that plane to Bangkok, thought longingly of the simple luxuries that were only a flight away. Perfumed soap and clean water and soft pillows. But then another image blotted out everything else: Sam Lassiter's face, tired and haunted, against the sky of sunset. And his Vietnamese woman, pleading for his life. All these years Sam Lassiter had lived safe and hidden in a peaceful river town. Now he was dead. Like Valdez. Like Gerard.

It was true, she thought. Wherever she walked, she left a trail of blood. And she didn't even know why.

"I can't go home," she said.

The minister raised an eyebrow. "Cannot? Or will not?"

"They tried to kill me in Bangkok."

"You're no safer here. Miss Maitland, we have no wish to forcibly deport you. But you must understand that you put us in a difficult position. You are a guest in our country. We Vietnamese honor our guests. It is a custom we hold sacred. If you, a guest, were to be found murdered, it would seem…" He paused and added with a quietly whimsical lilt, "Inhospitable."

"My visa's still good. I want to stay. I *have* to stay. I was planning to go on to Hanoi."

"We cannot guarantee your safety."

"I don't expect you to." She added wearily, "No one can guarantee my safety. Anywhere."

The minister looked at Guy, saw his troubled look. "Mr. Barnard? Surely you will convince her?"

"But she's right," said Guy.

Willy looked up and saw in Guy's eyes the worry, the uncertainty. It frightened her to realize that even he didn't have the answers.

"If I thought she'd be safer at home, I'd put her on that plane myself," he said. "But I don't think she will be safe. Not until she knows what she's running from."

"Surely she has friends to turn to."

"But you yourself said it, Minister Tranh. She can't tell her friends from her enemies. It's a dangerous state to be in."

The minister looked at Willy. "What is it you seek in the North?"

"It's where my father's plane went down," she said. "He could still be alive, in some village. Maybe he's lost his memory or he's afraid to come out of the jungle or—"

"Or he is dead."

She swallowed. "Then that's where I'll find his body. In the North."

Minister Tranh shook his head. "The jungles are full of skeletons. Americans. Vietnamese. You forget, we have our MIAs too, Miss Maitland. Our widows, our orphans. Among all those bones, to find the remains of one particular man…" He let out a heavy breath.

"But I have to try. I have to go to Hanoi."

Minister Tranh gazed at her, his eyes glowing with a strange black fire. She stared straight back at him. Slowly, a benign smile formed on his lips and she knew that she had won.

"Does nothing frighten you, Miss Maitland?" he asked.

"Many things frighten me."

"And well they should." He was still smiling, but his eyes were unfathomable. "I only hope you have the good sense to be frightened now."

LONG AFTER THE TWO Americans had left, Minister Tranh and Mr. Ainh sat smoking cigarettes and listening to the screech of the cicadas in the night.

"You will inform our people in Hanoi," said the minister.

"But wouldn't it be easier to cancel her visa?" said Ainh. "Force her to leave the country?"

"Easier, perhaps, but not wiser." The minister lit another cigarette and inhaled a warm and satisfying breath of smoke. A good American brand. His one weakness. He knew it would only hasten his death, that the cancer now growing in his right lung would feed ravenously on each lethal molecule of smoke. How ironic that the very enemy that had worked so hard to kill him during the war would now claim victory, and all because of his fondness for their cigarettes.

"What if she comes to harm?" Ainh asked. "We would have an international incident."

"That is why she must be protected." The minister rose from his chair. The old body, once so spry, had grown stiff with the years. To think this dried-up carcass had fought two savage jungle wars. Now it could barely shuffle around the house.

"We could scare her into going home—arrange an incident to frighten her," suggested Ainh.

"Like your Die Yankee note?" Minister Tranh laughed

as he headed for the door. "No, I do not think she frightens easily, that one. Better to see where she leads us. Perhaps we, too, will learn a few secrets. Or have you lost your curiosity, Comrade?"

Ainh looked miserable. "I think curiosity is a dangerous thing."

"So we let her make the moves, take the risks." The minister glanced back, smiling, from the doorway. "After all," he said. "It is *her* destiny."

"YOU DON'T HAVE TO GO TO Hanoi," said Guy, watching Willy pack her suitcase. "You could stay in Saigon. Wait for me."

"While you do what?"

"While I do the legwork up north. See what I can find." He glanced out the window at the two police agents loitering in the walkway. "Ainh's got you covered from all directions. You'll be safe here."

"I'll also go nuts." She snapped the suitcase shut. "Thanks for offering to stick your neck out for me, but I don't need a hero."

"I'm not trying to be a hero."

"Then why're you playing the part?"

He shrugged, unable to produce an answer.

"It's the money, isn't it? The bounty for Friar Tuck."

"It's not the money."

"Then it's that skeleton dancing around in your closet." He didn't answer. "What are you trying to hide? What's the Ariel Group got on you, anyway?" He remained silent. She locked her suitcase. "Never mind. I don't really want to know."

He sat down on the bed. Looking utterly weary, he propped his head in his hands. "I killed a man," he said.

She stared at him. Head in his hands, he looked ragged,

spent, a man who'd used up his last reserves of strength. She had the unexpected impulse to sit beside him, to take him in her arms and hold him, but she couldn't seem to move her feet. She was too stunned by his revelation.

"It happened here. In Nam. In 1972." His laugh was muffled against his hands. "The Fourth of July."

"There was a war going on. Lots of people got killed."

"This was different. This wasn't an act of war, where you shoot a few men and get a medal for your trouble." He raised his head and looked at her. "The man I killed was American."

Slowly she went over and sank down beside him on the bed. "Was it…a mistake?"

He shook his head. "No, not a mistake. It was something I did without thinking. Call it reflexes. It just happened."

She said nothing, waiting for him to go on. She knew he *would* go on; there was no turning back now.

"I was in Da Nang for the day, to pick up supplies," he said. "Got a little turned around and wound up on some side street. Just an alley, really, a dirt lane, few old hootches. I got out of the jeep to ask for directions, and I heard this—this screaming.…"

He paused, looked down at his hands. "She was just a kid. Fifteen, maybe sixteen. A small girl, not more than ninety pounds. There was no way she could've fought him off. I—I just reacted. I didn't really think about what I was doing, what I was going to do. I dragged him off her, shoved him on the ground. He got up and swung at me. I didn't have a choice but to fight back. By the time I stopped hitting him, he wasn't moving. I turned and saw what he'd done to the girl. All the blood…"

Guy rubbed his forehead, as though trying to erase the image. "By then there were other people there. I looked around, saw all these eyes watching me. Vietnamese. One of the women came up, whispered that I should leave, that they'd get rid of the body for me. That's when I realized the man was dead.''

For a long time they sat side by side, not touching, not speaking. He'd just confessed to killing a man. Yet she couldn't condemn him; she felt only a sense of sadness about the girl, about all the silent, nameless casualties of war.

''What happened then?'' she asked gently.

He shrugged. ''I left. I never said a word to anyone. I guess I was scared to. A few days later I heard they'd found a soldier's body on the other side of town. His death was listed as an assault by unknown locals. And that was the end of it. I thought.''

''How did the Ariel Group find out?''

''I don't know.'' Restless, he rose and went to the window where he looked out at the dimly lit walkway. ''There were half a dozen witnesses, all of them Vietnamese. Word must've gotten around. And somehow the Ariel Group got wind of it. What I don't understand is why they waited this long.''

''Maybe they only just heard about it.''

''Or maybe they were waiting for the right chance to use it.'' He turned to look at her. ''Doesn't it bother you, how we got thrown together? That we *happened* to meet in Kistner's villa? That you *happened* to need a ride into town?''

''And that the man you've been asked to find just happens to be my father.''

He nodded.

''They're using us,'' she said. Then, with rising anger she added, ''They're using *me*.''

''Welcome to the club.''

She looked up. "What do we do about it?"

"In the morning I'll fly to Hanoi, start asking questions."

"What about me?"

"You stay where Ainh can watch you."

"Sounds like a lousy plan."

"Have you got a better one?"

"Yes. I come with you."

"You'll only complicate things. If your father's alive, I'll find him."

"And what happens when you do? Are you going to turn him in? Trade him for silence?"

"I've given up on silence," Guy said quietly. "I'll settle for answers now."

She hauled her packed suitcase off the bed and set it down by the door. "Why am I arguing with you? I don't need your permission. I don't need any man's permission. He's *my* father. I know his face. His voice. After twenty years, *I'm* the one who'll recognize him."

"You're also the one who could get killed. Or is that part of the fun, Junior, going for thrills? Hell." He laughed. "It's probably written in your genes. You're as loony as your old man. He loved getting shot at, didn't he? He was a thrill junkie, and you are, too. Admit it. You're having the time of your life!"

"Look who's talking."

"I'm not in this for thrills. I'm in it because I had to be. Because I didn't have a choice."

"Neither of us has a choice!" She turned away, but he grabbed her arm and pulled her around to face him. He was standing so close it made her neck ache to look up at him.

"Stay in Saigon," he said.

"You must really want me out of the way."

"I want you safe."

"Why?"

"Because I— You—" He stopped. They were staring at each other, both of them breathing so hard neither of them could speak. Without another word he hauled her into his arms.

It was just a kiss, but it hit her with such hurricane force that her legs seemed to wobble away into oblivion. He was all rough edges—stubbled jaw and callused hands and frayed shirt. Automatically, she reached up and her arms closed behind his neck, pulling him hard against her mouth. He needed no encouragement. As his body pressed into hers, those dream images reignited in her head: the swaying deck of a ship, the night sky, Guy's face hovering above hers. If she let it, it would happen here, now. Already he was nudging her toward the bed, and she knew that if they fell across that mattress, he'd take her and she'd let him, and that was that. Never mind what made sense, what was good for her. She wanted him.

Even if it's the worst mistake I'll ever make in my life?

The thump of her legs against the side of the bed jarred her back to reality. She twisted away, pushed him to arm's length.

"That wasn't supposed to happen!" she said.

"I think it was."

"We got our wires crossed and—"

"No," he said softly. "I'd say our wires connected just fine."

She crossed to the door and yanked it open. "I think you should get out."

"I'm not going."

"You're not staying."

But his stance, feet planted like tree roots, told her he

most certainly *was* staying. "Have you forgotten? Someone wants you dead."

"But *you're* the one who's threatening me."

"It was just a kiss. Has it been *that* long, Willy? Does it shake you up that much, just being kissed?"

Yes it does! she wanted to scream. *It shakes me up because I've never been kissed that way before!*

"I'm staying tonight," he said quietly. "You need me. And, I admit it, I need you. You're my link to Bill Maitland. I won't touch you, if that's what you want. But I won't leave, either."

She had to concede defeat. Nothing she could do or say would make him budge. She let the door swing shut. Then she went to the bed and sat down. "God, I'm tired," she said. "Too tired to fight you. I'm even too tired to be afraid."

"And that's when things get dangerous. When all the adrenaline's used up. When you're too exhausted to think straight."

"I give up." She collapsed onto the bed, feeling as if every bone in her body had suddenly dissolved. "I don't care what happens anymore. I just want to go to sleep."

He didn't have to say anything; they both knew the debate was over and she'd lost. The truth was, she was glad he was there. It felt so good to close her eyes, to have someone watching over her. She realized how muddled her thinking had become, that she now considered a man like Guy Barnard *safe.*

But safe was what she felt.

Standing by the bed, Guy watched her fall asleep. She looked so fragile, stretched out on the bedcovers like a paper doll.

She hadn't felt like paper in his arms. She'd been real flesh and blood, warm and soft, all the woman he could ever want. He wasn't sure just what he felt toward her. Some of it was good old-fashioned lust. But there was something more, a primitive male instinct that made him want to carry her off to a place where no one could hurt her.

He turned and looked out the window. The two police agents were still loitering near the stairwell; he could see their cigarettes glowing in the darkness. He only hoped they did their job tonight, because he had already crossed his threshold of exhaustion.

He sat down in a chair and tried to sleep.

Twenty minutes later, his whole body crying out for rest, he gave up and went to the bed. Willy didn't stir. What the hell, he thought, She'll never notice. He stretched out beside her. The shifting mattress seemed to rouse her; she moaned and turned toward him, curling up like a kitten against his chest. The sweet scent of her hair made him feel like a drunken man. Dangerous, dangerous.

He'd been better off in the chair.

But he couldn't pull away now. So he lay there holding her, thinking about what came next.

They now had a name, a tentative contact, up north: Nora Walker, the British Red Cross nurse. Lassiter had said she worked in the local hospital. Guy only hoped she'd talk to them, that she wouldn't think this was just another Company trick and clam up. Having Willy along might make all the difference. After all, Bill Maitland's daughter had a right to be asking questions. Nora Walker just might decide to provide the answers.

Willy sighed and nestled closer to his chest. That brought a smile to his face. *You crazy dame,* he thought, and kissed the top of her head. *You crazy, crazy dame.* He buried his face in her hair.

So it was decided. For better or worse, he was stuck with her.

CHAPTER NINE

THE FLIGHT ATTENDANT walked up the aisle of the twin-engine Ilyushin and waved halfheartedly at the flies swarming around her head. Puffs of cold mist rose from the air-conditioning vents and swirled in the cabin; the woman seemed to be floating in clouds. Through the fog, Willy could barely read the emergency sign posted over the exit: Escape Rope. Now *there* was a safety feature to write home about. She had visions of the plane soaring through blue sky, trailing passengers on a ten thousand-foot rope.

A bundle of taffy landed in her lap, courtesy of the jaded attendant. "You will fasten your seat belt," came the no-nonsense request.

"I'm already buckled in," said Willy. Then she realized the woman was speaking to Guy. Willy nudged him. "Guy, your seat belt."

"What? Oh, yeah." He buckled the belt and managed a tight smile.

That's when she noticed he was clenching the armrest. She touched his hand. "Are you all right?"

"I'm fine."

"You don't look fine."

"It's an old problem. Nothing, really…" He stared out the window and swallowed hard.

She couldn't help herself; she burst out laughing. "Guy Barnard, don't tell me you're afraid of *flying?*"

The plane lurched forward and began bumping along the tarmac. A stream of Vietnamese crackled over the speaker system, followed by Russian and then very fractured English.

"Look," he protested, "some guys have a thing about heights or closed spaces or snakes. I happen to have a phobia about planes. Ever since the war."

"Did something happen on your tour?"

"End of my tour." He stared at the ceiling and laughed. "There's the irony. I make it through Nam alive. Then I board that big beautiful freedom bird. That's how I met Toby Wolff. He was sitting right next to me. We were both high, cracking jokes as we taxied up the runway. Going home." He shook his head. "We were two of the lucky ones. Sitting in the last row of seats. The tail broke off on impact...."

She took his hand. "You don't have to talk about it, Guy."

He looked at her in obvious admiration. "You're not in the least bit nervous, are you?"

"No. I've been in planes all my life. I've always felt at home."

"Must be something you inherited from your old man. Pilot's genes."

"Not just genes. Statistics."

The Ilyushin's engines screamed to life. The cabin shuddered as they made their take-off roll down the runway. The ground suddenly fell away, and the plane wobbled into the sky.

"I happen to know flying is a perfectly safe way to travel," she added.

"Safe?" Guy yelled over the engines' roar. "Obviously, you've never flown Air Vietnam!"

In Hanoi, they were met by a Vietnamese escort known only as Miss Hu, beautiful, unsmiling and cadre to the core. Her greeting was all business, her handshake strictly government issue. Unlike Mr. Ainh, who'd been a fountain of good-humored chatter, Miss Hu obviously believed in silence. And the Revolution. Only once on the drive into the city did the woman offer a voluntary remark. Directing their attention to the twisted remains of a bridge, she said, "You see the damage? American bombs." That was it for small talk. Willy stared at the woman's rigid shoulders and realized that, for some people on both sides, the war would never be over.

She was so annoyed by Miss Hu's comment that she didn't notice Guy's preoccupied look. Only when she saw him glance for the third time out the back window did she realize what he was focusing on: a Mercedes with darkly tinted windows was trailing right behind them. She and Guy exchanged glances.

The Mercedes followed them all the way into town. Only when they pulled up in front of the hotel did the other car pass them. It headed around the corner, its occupants obscured behind dark glass.

Willy's door was pulled open. Heat poured in, a knockdown, drag-out heat that left her stunned.

Miss Hu stood waiting outside, her face already pearled with sweat. "The hotel is air-conditioned," she said and added, with a note of disdain, "for the comfort of *foreigners.*"

As it turned out, the so-called air-conditioning was scarcely functioning. In fact, the hotel itself seemed to be sputtering along on little more than its old French colonial glory. The entry rug was ratty and faded, the lobby furniture a sad mélange of battered rosewood and threadbare cushions. While Guy checked in at the reception desk,

Willy stationed herself near their suitcases and kept watch over the lobby entrance.

She wasn't surprised when, seconds later, two Vietnamese men, both wearing dark glasses, strolled through the door. They spotted her immediately and veered off toward an alcove, where they loitered behind a giant potted fern. She could see the smoke from their cigarettes curling toward the ceiling.

"We're all checked in," said Guy. "Room 308. View of the city."

Willy touched his arm. "Two men," she whispered. "Three o'clock..."

"I see them."

"What do we do now?"

"Ignore them."

"But—"

"Mr. Barnard?" called Miss Hu. They both turned. The woman was waving a slip of paper. "The desk clerk says there is a telegram for you."

Guy frowned. "I wasn't expecting any telegram."

"It arrived this morning in Saigon, but you had just left. The hotel called here with the message." She handed Guy the scribbled phone memo and watched with sharp eyes as he read it.

If the message was important, Guy didn't show it. He casually stuffed it into his pocket and, picking up the suitcases, nudged Willy into a waiting elevator.

"Not bad news?" called Miss Hu.

Guy smiled at her. "Just a note from a friend," he said, and punched the elevator button.

Willy caught a last glimpse of the two Vietnamese men peering at them from behind the fern, and then the door slid shut. Instantly, Guy gripped her hand. *Don't say a word,* she read in his eyes.

It was a silent ride to the third floor.

Up in their room, Willy watched in puzzlement as Guy circled around, discreetly running his fingers under lampshades and along drawers, opened the closet, searched the nightstands. Behind the headboard, he finally found what he was seeking: a wireless microphone, barely the size of a postage stamp. He left it where it was. Then he went to the window and stared down at the street.

"How flattering," he murmured. "We rate baby-sitting service."

She moved beside him and saw what he was looking at: the black Mercedes, parked on the street below. "What about that telegram?" she whispered.

In answer, he pulled out the slip of paper and handed it to her. She read it twice, but it made no sense.

Uncle Sy asking about you. Plans guided tour of Nam. Happy Trails. Bobbo.

Guy let the curtain flap shut and began to pace furiously around the room. By the look of him, he was thinking up a blizzard, planning some scheme.

He suddenly halted. "Do you want something for your stomach?" he asked.

She blinked. "Excuse me?"

"Pepto Bismol might help. And you'd better lie down for a while. That old intestinal bug can get pretty damn miserable."

"Intestinal bug?" She gave him a helpless look.

He stalked to the desk and rummaged in a drawer for a piece of hotel stationery, talking all the while. "I'll bet it's that seafood you ate last night. Are you still feeling really lousy?" He held up a sheet of paper on which he'd scribbled, "Yes!!!"

"Yes," she said. "Definitely lousy. I—I think I should lie down." She paused. "Shouldn't I?"

He was writing again. The sheet of paper now said, "You want to go to the hospital!"

She nodded and went into the bathroom, where she groaned loudly a few times and flushed the toilet. "You know, I feel really rotten. Maybe I should see a doctor...." It struck her then, as she stood by the sink and watched the water hiss out of the faucet, exactly what he was up to. *The man's a genius,* she thought with sudden admiration. Turning to look at him, she said, "Do you think we'll find anyone who speaks English?"

She was rewarded with a thumbs-up sign.

"We could try the hospital," he said. "Maybe it won't be a doctor, but they should have someone who'll understand you."

She went to the bed and sat down, bouncing a few times to make the springs squeak. "God, I feel awful."

He sat beside her and placed his hand on her forehead. His eyes were twinkling as he said, "Lady, you're really hot."

"I know," she said gravely.

They could barely hold back their laughter.

"SHE DID NOT SEEM ILL an hour ago," Miss Hu said as she ushered them into the limousine ten minutes later.

"The cramps came on suddenly," said Guy.

"I would say *very* suddenly," Miss Hu noted aridly.

"I think it was the seafood," Willy whimpered from the back seat.

"You Americans," Miss Hu sniffed. "Such delicate stomachs."

The hospital waiting room was hot as an oven and overflowing with patients. As Willy and Guy entered, a hush instantly fell over the crowd. The only sounds were the rhythmic clack of the ceiling fan and a baby crying in its mother's lap. Every eye was watching as the two Americans moved through the room toward the reception desk.

The Vietnamese nurse behind the desk stared in mute astonishment. Only when Miss Hu barked out a question did the nurse respond with a nervous shake of the head and a hurried answer.

"We have only Vietnamese doctors here," translated Miss Hu. "No Europeans."

"You have no one trained in the West?" Guy asked.

"Why, do you feel your Western medicine is superior?"

"Look, I'm not here to argue East versus West. Just find someone who speaks English. A nurse'll do. You have English-speaking nurses, don't you?"

Scowling, Miss Hu turned and muttered to the desk nurse, who made a few phone calls. At last Willy was led down a corridor to a private examination room. It was stocked with only the basics: an examining table, a sink, an instrument cart. Cotton balls and tongue depressors were displayed in dusty glass jars. A fly buzzed lazily around the one bare lightbulb. The nurse handed Willy a tattered gown and gestured for her to undress.

Willy had no intention of stripping while Miss Hu stood watch in the corner.

"I would appreciate some privacy," Willy said.

The other woman didn't move. "Mr. Barnard is staying," she pointed out.

"No." Willy looked at Guy. "Mr. Barnard is leaving."

"In fact, I was just on my way out," said Guy, turning toward the door. He added, for Miss Hu's benefit, "You know, Comrade, in America it's considered quite rude to watch while someone undresses."

"I was only trying to confirm what I've heard about

Western women's undergarments,'' Miss Hu insisted as she and the nurse followed Guy out the door.

"What, exactly, have you heard?'' asked Guy.

"That they are designed with the sole purpose of arousing prurient interest from the male sex.''

"Comrade,'' said Guy with a grin, "I would be delighted to share my knowledge on the topic of ladies' undergarments....''

The door closed, leaving Willy alone in the room. She changed into the gown and sat on the table to wait.

Moments later, a tall, fortyish woman wearing a white lab coat walked in. The name tag on her lapel confirmed that she was Nora Walker. She gave Willy a brisk nod of greeting and paused beside the table to glance through the notes on the hospital clipboard. Strands of gray streaked her mane of brown hair; her eyes were a deep green, as unfathomable as the sea.

"I'm told you're American,'' the woman said, her accent British. "We don't see many Americans here. What seems to be the problem?''

"My stomach's been hurting. And I've been nauseated.''

"How long now?''

"A day.''

"Any fever?''

"No fever. But lots of cramping.''

The woman nodded. "Not unusual for Western tourists.'' She looked back down at the clipboard. "It's the water. Different bacterial strains than you're used to. It'll take a few days to get over it. I'll have to examine you. If you'll just lie down, Miss—'' She focused on the name written on the clipboard. Instantly she fell silent.

"Maitland,'' said Willy softly. "My name is Willy Maitland.''

Nora cleared her throat. In a flat voice she said, "Please lie down."

Obediently, Willy settled back on the table and allowed the other woman to examine her abdomen. The hands probing her belly were cold as ice.

"Sam Lassiter said you might help us," Willy whispered.

"You've spoken to Sam?"

"In Cantho. I went to see him about my father."

Nora nodded and said, suddenly businesslike, "Does that hurt when I press?"

"No."

"How about here?"

"A little tender."

Now, once again in a whisper, Nora asked, "How is Sam doing these days?"

Willy paused. "He's dead," she murmured.

The hands resting on her belly froze. "Dear God. How—" Nora caught herself, swallowed. "I mean, how...much does it hurt?"

Willy traced her finger, knifelike, across her throat.

Nora took a breath. "I see." Her hands, still resting on Willy's abdomen, were trembling. For a moment she stood silent, her head bowed. Then she turned and went to a medicine cabinet. "I think you need some antibiotics." She took out a bottle of pills. "Are you allergic to sulfa?"

"I don't think so."

Nora took out a blank medication label and began to fill in the instructions. "May I see proof of identification, Miss Maitland?"

Willy produced a California driver's license and handed it to Nora. "Is that sufficient?"

"It will do." Nora pocketed the license. Then she taped the medication label on the pill bottle. "Take one four times a day. You should notice some results by tomorrow night.'' She handed the bottle to Willy. Inside were about two dozen white tablets. On the label was listed the drug name and a standard set of directions. No hidden messages, no secret instructions.

Willy looked up expectantly, but Nora had already turned to leave. Halfway to the door, she paused. ''There's a man with you, an American. Who is he? A relative?''

''A friend.''

''I see.'' Nora gave her a long and troubled look. ''I trust you're absolutely certain about your drug allergies, Miss Maitland. Because if you're wrong, that medication could be very, very dangerous.'' She opened the door to find Miss Hu standing right outside.

The Vietnamese woman instantly straightened. ''Miss Maitland is well?'' she inquired.

''She has a mild intestinal infection. I've given her some antibiotics. She should be feeling much better by tomorrow.''

''I feel a little better already,'' said Willy, climbing off the table. ''If I could just have some fresh air...''

''An excellent idea,'' said Nora. ''Fresh air. And only light meals. No milk.'' She headed out the door. ''Have a good stay in Hanoi, Miss Maitland.''

Miss Hu turned a smug smile on Willy. ''You see? Even here in Vietnam, one can find the best in medical care.''

Willy nodded and reached for her clothes. ''I quite agree.''

FIFTEEN MINUTES LATER, Nora Walker left the hospital, climbed onto her bicycle and pedaled to the cloth merchants' road. At a streetside noodle stand she bought a lemonade and a bowl of *pho*, for which she paid the vendor a thousand-dong note, carefully folded at opposite corners.

She ate her noodles while squatted on the sidewalk, beside all the other customers. Then, after draining the last of the peppery broth, she strolled into a tailor's shop. It appeared deserted. She slipped through a beaded curtain into a dimly lit back room. There, among the dusty bolts of silks and cottons and brocade, she waited.

The rattle of the curtain beads announced the entrance of her contact. Nora turned to face him.

"I've just seen Bill Maitland's daughter," she said in Vietnamese. She handed over Willy's driver's license.

The man studied the photograph and smiled. "I see there is a family resemblance."

"There's also a problem," said Nora. "She's traveling with a man—"

"You mean Mr. Barnard?" There was another smile. "We're well aware of him."

"Is he CIA?"

"We think not. He is, to all appearances, an independent."

"So you've been tracking them."

The man shrugged. "Hardly difficult. With so many children on the streets, they'd scarcely notice a stray boy here and there."

Nora swallowed, afraid to ask the next question. "She said Sam's dead. Is this true?"

The man's smile vanished. "We are sorry. Time, it seems, has not made things any safer."

Turning away, she tried to clear her throat, but the ache remained. She pressed her forehead against a bolt of comfortless silk. "You're right. Nothing's changed. Damn them. *Damn* them."

"What do you ask of us, Nora?"

"I don't know." She took a ragged breath and turned

to face him. "I suppose—I suppose we should send a message."

"I will contact Dr. Andersen."

"I need to have an answer by tomorrow."

The man shook his head. "That leaves us little time for arrangements."

"A whole day. Surely that's enough."

"But there are…" He paused. "Complications."

Nora studied the man's face, a perfect mask of impassivity. "What do you mean?"

"The Party is now interested. And the CIA. Perhaps there are others."

Others, thought Nora. Meaning those they knew nothing about. The most dangerous faction of all.

As Nora left the tailor shop and walked into the painful glare of afternoon, she sensed a dozen pairs of eyes watching her, marking her leisurely progress up Gia Ngu Street. The brightly embroidered blouse she'd just purchased in the shop made her feel painfully conspicuous. Not that she wasn't already conspicuous. In Hanoi, all foreigners were watched with suspicion. In every shop she visited, along every street she walked, there were always those eyes.

They would be watching Willy Maitland, as well.

"WE'VE MADE the first move," Guy said. "The next move is hers."

"And if we don't hear anything?"

"Then I'm afraid we've hit a dead end." Guy thrust his hands into his pockets and turned his gaze across the waters of Returned Sword Lake. Like a dozen other couples strolling the grassy banks, they'd sought this park for its solitude, for the chance to talk without being heard. Flame red blossoms drifted down from the trees. On the footpath ahead, children chattered over a game of ball and jacks.

"You never explained that telegram," she said. "Who's Bobbo?"

He laughed. "Oh, that's a nickname for Toby Wolff. After that plane crash, we wound up side by side in a military hospital. I guess we gave the nurses a lot of grief. You know, a few too many winks, too many sly comments. They got to calling us the evil Bobbsey twins. Pretty soon he was Bobbo One and I was Bobbo Two."

"Then Toby Wolff sent the telegram."

He nodded.

"And what does it mean? Who's Uncle Sy?"

Guy paused and gave their surroundings a thoughtful perusal. She knew it was more than just a casual look; he was searching. And sure enough, there they were: two Vietnamese men, stationed in the shadow of a poinciana tree. Police agents, most likely, assigned to protect them.

Or was it to isolate them?

"Uncle Sy," Guy said, "was our private name for the CIA."

She frowned, recalling the message. *Uncle Sy asking about you. Plans guided tour of Nam. Happy trails. Bobbo.*

"It was a warning," Guy said. "The Company knows about us. And they're in the country. Maybe watching us this very minute."

She glanced apprehensively around the lake. A bicycle glided past, pedaled by a serene girl in a conical hat. On the grass, two lovers huddled together, whispering secrets. It struck Willy as too perfect, this view of silver lake and flowering trees, an artist's fantasy for a picture postcard.

All except for the two police agents watching from the trees.

"If he's right," she said, "if the CIA's after us, how are we going to recognize them?"

"That's the problem." Guy turned to her, and the uneasiness she saw in his eyes frightened her. "We won't."

SO CLOSE. YET SO unreachable.

Siang squatted in the shadow of a pedicab and watched the two Americans stroll along the opposite bank of the lake. They took their time, stopping like tourists to admire the flowers, to laugh at a child toddling in the path, both of them oblivious to how easily they could be captured in a rifle's cross hairs, their lives instantly extinguished.

He turned his attention to the two men trailing a short distance behind. Police agents, he assumed, on protective surveillance. They made things more difficult, but Siang could work around them. Sooner or later, an opportunity would arise.

Assassination would be so easy, as simple as a curtain left open to a well-aimed bullet. What a pity that was no longer the plan.

The Americans returned to their car. Siang rose, stamped the blood back into his legs and climbed onto his bicycle. It was a beggarly form of transportation, but it was practical and inconspicuous. Who would notice, among the thousands crowding the streets of Hanoi, one more shabbily dressed cyclist?

Siang followed the car back to the hotel. One block farther, he dismounted and discreetly observed the two Americans enter the lobby. Seconds later, a black Mercedes pulled up. The two agents climbed out and followed the Americans into the hotel.

It was time to set up shop.

Siang took a cloth-wrapped bundle from his bicycle basket, chose a shady spot on the sidewalk and spread out a meager collection of wares: cigarettes, soap and greeting cards. Then, like all the other itinerant merchants lining the road, he squatted down on his straw mat and beckoned to passersby.

Over the next two hours he managed to sell only a single bar of soap, but it scarcely mattered. He was there simply to watch. And to wait.

Like any good hunter, Siang knew how to wait.

CHAPTER TEN

GUY AND WILLY slept in separate beds that night. At least, Guy slept. Willy lay awake, tossing on the sheets, thinking about her father, about the last time she had seen him alive.

He had been packing. She'd stood beside the bed, watching him toss clothes into a suitcase. She knew by the items he'd packed that he was returning to the lovely insanity of war. She saw the flak jacket, the Laotian-English dictionary, the heavy gold chains—a handy form of ransom with which a downed pilot could bargain for his life. There was also the Government-issue blood chit, printed on cloth and swiped from a U.S. Air Force pilot.

I am a citizen of the United States of America. I do not speak your language. Misfortune forces me to seek your assistance in obtaining food, shelter and protection. Please take me to someone who will provide for my safety and see that I am returned to my people.

It was written in thirteen languages.

The last item he packed was his .45, the trigger seat filed to a feather release. Willy had stood by the bed and stared at the gun, struck in that instant by its terrible significance.

"Why are you going back?" she'd asked.

"Because it's my job, baby," he'd said, slipping the

pistol in among his clothes. "Because I'm good at it, and because we need the paycheck."

"We don't need the paycheck. We need you."

He closed the suitcase. "Your mom's been talking to you again, has she?"

"No, this is me talking, Daddy. *Me.*"

"Sure, baby." He laughed and mussed her hair, his old way of making her feel like his little girl. He set the suitcase down on the floor and grinned at her, the same grin he always used on her mother, the same grin that always got him what he wanted. "Tell you what. How 'bout I bring back a little surprise? Something nice from Vientiane. Maybe a ruby? Or a sapphire? Bet you'd love a sapphire."

She shrugged. "Why bother?"

"What do you mean, 'why bother'? You're my baby, aren't you?"

"Your baby?" She looked at the ceiling and laughed. "When was I ever *your* baby?"

His grin vanished. "I don't care for your tone of voice, young lady."

"You don't care about anything, do you? Except flying your stupid planes in your stupid war." Before he could answer, she'd pushed past him and left the room.

As she fled down the hall she heard him yell, "You're just a kid. One of these days you'll understand! Grow up a little! Then you'll understand...."

One of these days. One of these days.

"I still don't understand," she whispered to the night.

From the street below came the whine of a passing car. She sat up in bed and, running a hand through her damp hair, gazed around the room. The curtains fluttered like gossamer in the moonlit window. In the next bed, Guy lay asleep, the covers kicked aside, his bare back gleaming in the darkness.

She rose and went to the window. On the corner below, three pedicab drivers, dressed in rags, squatted together in the dim glow of a street lamp. They didn't say a word; they simply huddled there in a midnight tableau of weariness. She wondered how many others, just as weary, just as silent, wandered in the night.

And to think they won the war.

A groan and the creak of bedsprings made her turn. Guy was lying on his back now, the covers kicked to the floor. By some strange fascination, she was drawn to his side. She stood in the shadows, studying his rumpled hair, the rise and fall of his chest. Even in his sleep he wore a half smile, as though some private joke were echoing in his dreams. She started to smooth back his hair, then thought better of it. Her hand lingered over him as she struggled against the longing to touch him, to be held by him. It had been so long since she'd felt this way about a man, and it frightened her; it was the first sign of surrender, of the offering up of her soul.

She couldn't let it happen. Not with this man.

She turned and went back to her own bed and threw herself onto the sheets. There she lay, thinking of all the ways he was wrong for her, all the ways they were wrong for each other.

The way her mother and father had been wrong for each other.

It was something Ann Maitland had never recognized, that basic incompatibility. It had been painfully obvious to her daughter. Bill Maitland was the wild card, the unpredictable joker in life's game of chance. Ann cheerfully accepted whatever surprises she was dealt because he was her husband, because she loved him.

But Willy didn't need that kind of love. She didn't need a younger version of Wild Bill Maitland.

Though, God knew, she wanted him. And he was right in the next bed.

She closed her eyes. Restless, sweating, she counted the hours until morning.

"A MOST CURIOUS TURN of events." Minister Tranh, recently off the plane from Saigon, settled into his hard-backed chair and gazed at the tea leaves drifting in his cup. "You say they are behaving like mere tourists?"

"Typical *capitalist* tourists," said Miss Hu in disgust. She opened her notebook, in which she'd dutifully recorded every detail, and began her report. "This morning at nine-forty-five, they visited the tomb of our beloved leader but offered no comment. At 12:17, they were served lunch at the hotel, a menu which included fried fish, stewed river turtle, steamed vegetables and custard. This afternoon, they were escorted to the Museum of War, then the Museum of Revolution—"

"This is hardly the itinerary of capitalist tourists."

"And then—" she flipped the page "—they went *shopping*." Triumphantly, she snapped the notebook closed.

"But Comrade Hu, even the most dedicated Party member must, on occasion, shop."

"For antiques?"

"Ah. They value tradition."

Miss Hu bent forward. "Here is the part that raises my suspicions, Minister Tranh. It is the leopard revealing its stripes."

"Spots," corrected the minister with a smile. The fervent Comrade Hu had been studying her American idioms again. What a shame she had absorbed so little of their humor. "What, exactly, did they do?"

"This afternoon, after the antique shop, they spent two hours at the Australian embassy—the cocktail lounge, to be precise—where they conversed in private with various suspect foreigners."

Minister Tranh found it of only passing interest that the Americans would retreat to a Western embassy. Like anyone in a strange country, they probably missed the company of their own type of people. Decades ago in Paris, Tranh had felt just such a longing. Even as he'd sipped coffee in the West Bank cafés, even as he'd reveled in the joys of Bohemian life, at times, he had ached for the sight of jet black hair, for the gentle twang of his own language. Still, how he had loved Paris....

"So you see, the Americans are well monitored," said Miss Hu. "Rest assured, Minister Tranh. Nothing will go wrong."

"Assuming they continue to cooperate with us."

"Cooperate?" Miss Hu's chin came up in a gesture of injured pride. "They are not aware we're following them."

What a shame the politically correct Miss Hu was so lacking in vision and insight. Minister Tranh hadn't the energy to contradict her. Long ago, he had learned that zealots were seldom swayed by reason.

He looked down at his tea leaves and sighed. "But, of course, you are right, Comrade," he said.

"IT'S BEEN A DAY NOW. Why hasn't anyone contacted us?" Willy whispered across the oilcloth-covered table.

"Maybe they can't get close enough," Guy said. "Or maybe they're still looking us over."

The way everyone else was looking them over, Willy thought as her gaze swept the noisy café. In one glance she took in the tables cluttered with coffee cups and soup bowls, the diners veiled in a vapor of cooking grease and cigarette smoke, the waiters ferrying trays of steaming food. *They're all watching us,* she thought. In a far corner, the two police agents sat flicking ashes into a saucer. And through the dirty street windows, small faces peered in, children straining for a rare glimpse of Americans.

Their waiter, gaunt and silent, set two bowls of noodle soup on their table and vanished through a pair of swinging doors. In the kitchen, pots clanged and voices chattered over a cleaver's staccato. The swinging doors kept slapping open and shut as waiters pushed through, bent under the weight of their trays.

The police agents were staring.

Willy, by now brittle with tension, reached for her chopsticks and automatically began to eat. It was modest fare, noodles and peppery broth and paper-thin slices of what looked like beef. Water buffalo, Guy told her. Tasty but tough. Head bent, ignoring the stares, she ate in silence. Only when she inadvertently bit into a chili pepper and had to make a lunge for her glass of lemonade did she finally put her chopsticks down.

"I don't know if I can take this idle-tourist act much longer." She sighed. "Just how long are we supposed to wait?"

"As long as it takes. That's one thing you learn in this country. Patience. Waiting for the right time. The right situation."

"Twenty years is a long time to wait."

"You know," he said, frowning, "that's the part that bothers me. That it's been twenty years. Why would the Company still be mucking around in what should be a dead issue?"

"Maybe they're not interested. Maybe Toby Wolff's wrong."

"Toby's never wrong." He looked around at the

crowded room, his gaze troubled. "And something else still bothers me. Has from the very beginning. Our so-called accidental meeting in Bangkok. Both of us looking for the same answers, the same man." He paused. "In addition to mild paranoia, however, I get also this sense of…"

"Coincidence?"

"Fate."

Willy shook her head. "I don't believe in fate."

"You will." He stared up at the haze of cigarette smoke swirling about the ceiling fan. "It's this country. It changes you, strips away your sense of reality, your sense of control. You begin to think that events are meant to happen, that they *will* happen, no matter how you fight it. As if our lives are all written out for us and it's impossible to revise the book."

Their gazes met across the table. "I don't believe in fate, Guy," she said softly. "I never have."

"I'm not asking you to."

"I don't believe you and I were *meant* to be together. It just happened."

"But something—luck, fate, conspiracy, whatever you want to call it—has thrown us together." He leaned forward, his gaze never leaving her face. "Of all the crazy places in the world, here we are, at the same table, in the same dirty Vietnamese café. And…" He paused, his brown eyes warm, his crooked smile a fleeting glimmer in his seriousness. "I'm beginning to think it's time we gave in and followed this crazy script. Time we followed our instincts."

They stared at each other through the veil of smoke. And she thought, *I'd like nothing better than to follow my instincts, which are to go back to our hotel and make love with you. I know I'll regret it. But that's what I want. Maybe that's what I've wanted since the day I met you.*

He reached across the table; their hands met. And as their fingers linked, it seemed as if some magical circuit had just been completed, as if this had always been meant to be, that this was where fate—good, bad or indifferent— had meant to lead them. Not apart, but together, to the same embrace, the same bed.

"Let's go back to the room," he whispered.

She nodded. A smile slid between them, one of knowing, full of promise. Already the images were drifting through her head: shirts slowly unbuttoned, belts unbuckled. Sweat glistening on backs and shoulders. Slowly she pushed her chair back from the table.

But as they rose to their feet, a voice, shockingly familiar, called to them from across the room.

Dodge Hamilton lumbered toward them through the maze of tables. Pale and sweating, he sank into a chair beside them.

"What the hell are *you* doing here?" Guy asked in astonishment.

"I'm bloody lucky to be here at all," said Hamilton, wiping a handkerchief across his brow. "One of our engines trailed smoke all the way from Da Nang. I tell you, I didn't fancy myself splattered all over some mountaintop."

"But I thought you were staying in Saigon," said Willy.

Hamilton stuffed the handkerchief back in his pocket. "Wish I had. But yesterday I got a telex from the finance minister's office. He's finally agreed to an interview— something I've been working at for months. So I squeezed onto the last flight out of Saigon." He shook his head. "Just about my last flight, period. Lord, I need a drink."

He pointed to Willy's glass. "What's that you've got there?"

"Lemonade."

Hamilton turned and called to the waiter. "Hello, there! Could I have one of these—these lemon things?"

Willy took a sip, watching Hamilton thoughtfully over the rim of her glass. "How did you find us?"

"What? Oh, that was no trick. The hotel clerk directed me here."

"How did *he* know?"

Guy sighed. "Obviously we can't take a step without everyone knowing about it."

Hamilton frowned dubiously as the waiter set a napkin and another glass of lemonade on the table. "Probably carries some fatal bacteria." He lifted the glass and sighed. "Might as well live dangerously. Well, here's to the trusty Ilyushins of the sky! May they never crash. Not with me aboard, anyway."

Guy raised his glass in a wholehearted toast. "Amen. From now on, I say we all stick to boats."

"Or pedicabs," said Hamilton. "Just think, Barnard, we could be pedaled across China!"

"I think you'd be safer in a plane," Willy said, and reached for her glass. As she lifted it, she noticed a dark stain bleeding from the wet napkin onto the tablecloth. It took her a few seconds to realize what it was, that tiny trickle of blue. Ink. There was something written on the other side of her napkin....

"It all depends on the plane," said Hamilton. "After today, no more Russian rigs for me. Pardon the pun, but I've been thoroughly dis-Ilyushined."

It was Guy's burst of laughter that pulled Willy out of her feverish speculation. She looked up and found Ham-

ilton frowning at her. Dodge Hamilton, she thought. He
was always around. Always watching.

She crumpled the napkin in her fist. "If you don't mind,
I think I'll go back to the hotel."

"Is something wrong?" Guy asked.

"I'm tired." She rose, still clutching the napkin. "And
a little queasy."

Hamilton at once shoved aside his glass of lemonade.
"I *knew* I should have stuck to whiskey. Can I fetch you
anything? Bananas, maybe? That's the cure, you know."

"She'll be fine," said Guy, helping Willy to her feet.
"I'll look after her."

Outside, the heat and chaos of the street were overwhelming. Willy clung to Guy's arm, afraid to talk, afraid
to voice her suspicions. But he'd already sensed her agi-
tation. He pulled her through the crowd toward the hotel.

Back in their room, Guy locked the door and drew the
curtains. Willy unfolded the napkin. By the light of a bedside lamp, they struggled to decipher the smudgy message.

"0200. Alley behind hotel. Watch your back."

Willy looked at him. "What do you think?"

He didn't answer. She watched him pace the room,
thinking, weighing the risks. Then he took the napkin, tore
it to shreds and vanished into the bathroom. She heard the
toilet flush and knew the evidence had been disposed of.
When he came out of the bathroom, his expression was
flat and unreadable.

"Why don't you lie down," he said. "There's nothing
like a good night's sleep to settle an upset stomach." He
turned off the lamp. By the glow of her watch, she saw it
was just after seven-thirty. It would be a long wait.

They scarcely slept that night.

In the darkness of their room, they waited for the hours
to pass. Outside, the noises of the street, the voices, the

tinkle of pedicab bells faded to silence. They didn't undress; they lay tensed in their beds, not daring to exchange a word.

It must have been after midnight when Willy at last slipped into a dreamless sleep. It seemed only moments had passed when she felt herself being nudged awake. Guy's lips brushed her forehead, then she heard him whisper, "Time to move."

She sat up, instantly alert, her heart off and racing. Carrying her shoes, she tiptoed after him to the door.

The hall was deserted. The scuffed wood floor gleamed dully beneath a bare light bulb. They slipped out into the corridor and headed for the stairs.

From the second-floor railing, they peered down into the lobby. The hotel desk was unattended. The sound of snoring echoed like a lion's roar up the stairwell. As they moved down the steps, the hotel lounge came into view, and they spotted the lobby attendant sprawled out on a couch, mouth gaping in blissful repose.

Guy flashed Willy a grin and a thumbs-up sign. Then he led the way down the steps and through a service door. Crates lined a dark and dingy hallway; at the far end was another door. They slipped out the exit.

Outside, the darkness was so thick, Willy found herself groping for some tangible clue to her surroundings. Then Guy took her hand and his touch was steadying; it was a hand she'd learned she could trust. Together they crept through the shadows, into the narrow alley behind the hotel. There they waited.

It was 2:01.

At 2:07, they sensed, more than heard, a stirring in the darkness. It was as if a breath of wind had congealed into something alive, solid. They didn't see the woman until she was right beside them.

"Come with me," she said. Willy recognized the voice: it was Nora Walker's.

They followed her up a series of streets and alleys, weaving farther and farther into the maze that was Hanoi. Nora said nothing. Every so often they caught a glimpse of her in the glow of a street lamp, her hair concealed beneath a conical hat, her dark blouse anonymously shabby.

At last, in an alley puddled with stagnant water, they came to a halt. Through the darkness, Willy could just make out three bicycles propped against a wall. A bundle was thrust into her hands. It contained a set of pajamalike pants and blouse, a conical hat smelling of fresh straw. Guy, too, was handed a change of clothes.

In silence they dressed.

On bicycles they followed Nora through miles of back streets. In that landscape of shadows, everything took on a life of its own. Tree branches reached out to snag them. The road twisted like a serpent. Willy lost all sense of direction; as far as she knew, they could be turning in circles. She pedaled automatically, following the faint outline of Nora's hat floating ahead in the darkness.

The paved streets gave way to dirt roads, the buildings to huts and vegetable plots. At last, at the outskirts of town, they dismounted. An old truck sat at the side of the road. Through the driver's window, a cigarette could be seen glowing in the darkness. The door squealed open, and a Vietnamese man hopped out of the cab. He and Nora whispered together for a moment. Then the man tossed aside the cigarette and gestured to the back of the truck.

"Get in," said Nora. "He'll take you from here."

"Where are we going?" asked Willy.

Nora flipped aside the truck's tarp and motioned for them to climb in. "No time for questions. Hurry."

"Aren't you coming with us?"

"I can't. They'll notice I'm gone."

"*Who'll* notice?"

Nora's voice, already urgent, took on a note of panic. "Please. Get in *now*."

Guy and Willy scrambled onto the rear bumper and dropped down lightly among a pile of rice sacks.

"Be patient," said Nora. "It's a long ride. There's food and water inside—enough to hold you."

"Who's the driver?" asked Guy.

"No names. It's safer."

"But can we trust him?"

Nora paused. "Can we trust anyone?" she said. Then she yanked on the tarp. The canvas fell, closing them off from the night.

IT WAS A LONG bicycle ride back to her apartment. Nora pedaled swiftly, her body slicing through the night, her hat shuddering in the wind. She knew the way well; even in the darkness she could sense where the hazards, the unexpected potholes, lay.

Tonight she could also sense something else. A presence, something evil, floating in the night. The feeling was so unshakable she felt compelled to stop and look back at the road. For a full minute she held her breath and waited. Nothing moved, only the shadows of clouds hurtling before the moon. *It's my imagination,* she thought. No one was following her. No one *could* have followed her. She'd been too cautious, taking the Americans up and down so many turns that no one could possibly have kept up unnoticed.

Breathing easier, she pedaled all the way home.

She parked her bicycle in the community shed and climbed the rickety steps to her apartment. The door was unlocked. The significance of that fact didn't strike her until she'd already taken one step over the threshold. By then it was too late.

The door closed behind her. She spun around just as a light sprang on, shining full in her face. Blinded, she took a panicked step backward. "Who—what—"

From behind, hands wrenched her into a brutal embrace. A knife blade slid lightly across her neck.

"Not a word," whispered a voice in her ear.

The person holding the light came forward. He was a large man, so large, his shadow blotted out the wall. "We've been waiting for you, Miss Walker," he said. "Where did you take them?"

She swallowed. "Who?"

"You went to the hotel to meet them. Where did you go from there?"

"I didn't—" She gasped as the blade suddenly stung her flesh; she felt a drop of blood trickle warmly down her neck.

"Easy, Mr. Siang," said the man. "We have all night."

Nora began to cry. "Please. Please, I don't know anything...."

"But, of course, you do. And you'll tell us, won't you?" The man pulled up a chair and sat down. She could see his teeth gleaming like ivory in the shadows. "It's only a question of when."

FROM BENEATH THE FLAPPING canvas, Willy caught glimpses of dawn: light filtering through the trees, dust swirling in the road, the green brilliance of rice paddies. They'd been traveling for hours now, and the sacks of rice were beginning to feel like bags of concrete against their backs. At least they'd been provided with food and drink. In an open crate they'd found a bottle of water, a loaf of

French bread and four hard-boiled eggs. It seemed sufficient—at first. But as the day wore on and the heat grew
suffocating, that single bottle of water became more and
more precious. They rationed it, one sip every half hour;
it was barely enough to keep their throats moist.

At noon the truck began to climb.

"Where are we going?" she asked.

"Heading west, I think. Into the mountains. Maybe the
road to Dien Bien Phu."

"Towards Laos?"

"Where your father's plane went down." In the shadows of the truck, Guy's face, dirty and unshaven, was a
tired mask of resolution. She wondered if she looked as
grim.

He shrugged off his sweat-soaked shirt and threw it
aside, oblivious to the mosquitoes buzzing around them.
The scar on his bare abdomen seemed to ripple in the
gloom. In silent fascination, Willy started to reach out to
him, then thought better of it.

"It's okay," he said softly, guiding her hand to the scar.
"It doesn't hurt."

"It must have hurt terribly when you got it."

"I don't remember." At her puzzled look, he added, "I
mean, not on any sort of conscious level. It's funny,
though, how well I remember what happened just before
the plane went down. Toby, sitting next to me, telling
jokes. Something about the pilot looking like an old buddy
of his from Alcoholics Anonymous. He'd heard in flight
school that the best military pilots were always the drunks;
a sober man wouldn't dream of flying the sort of junk heap
we were in. I remember laughing as we taxied down the
runway. Then—" He shook his head. "They say I pulled
him out of the wreckage. That I unbuckled him and
dragged him out just before the whole thing blew. They

even called me a hero.'' He uncapped the water bottle, took a sip. ''What a laugh.''

''Sounds like you earned the label,'' she said.

''Sounds more like I was knocked in the head and didn't know what the hell I was doing.''

''The best heroes in the world are the reluctant ones. Courage isn't fearlessness—it's acting in the face of fear.''

''Yeah?'' He laughed. ''Then that makes me the best of the best.'' He stiffened as the truck suddenly slowed, halted. A voice barked orders in the distance. They stared at each other in alarm.

''What is it?'' she whispered. ''What're they saying?''

''Something about a roadblock…soldiers are stopping everyone. Some sort of inspection.…''

''My God. What do we—''

He put a finger to his lips. ''Sounds like a lot of traffic in front. Could take a while before they get to us.''

''Can we back up? Turn around?''

He scrambled to the back of the truck and glanced through a slit in the canvas. ''No chance. We're socked in tight. Trucks on both sides.''

Willy frantically surveyed the gloom, searching for empty burlap bags, a crate, anything large enough in which to hide.

The soldiers' voices moved closer.

We have to make a run for it, thought Willy. Guy had already risen to a crouch. But a glance outside told them they were surrounded by shallow rice paddies. Without cover, their flight would be spotted immediately.

But they won't hurt us, she thought. *They wouldn't dare. We're Americans.*

As if, in this crazy world, an eagle on one's passport bought any sort of protection.

The soldiers were right outside—two men by the sound

of the voices. The truck driver was trying to cajole his way out of the inspection, laughing, offering cigarettes. The man had to have nerves of steel; not a single note of apprehension slipped into his voice.

His attempts at bribery failed. Footsteps continued along the graveled roadside, heading for the back of the truck.

Guy instinctively shoved Willy against the rice sacks, shielding her behind him. He'd be the one they'd see first, the one they'd confront. He turned to face the inevitable.

A hand poked through, gripping the canvas flap....

And paused. In the distance, a car horn was blaring. Tires screeched, followed by the thud of metal, the angry shouts of drivers.

The hand gripping the canvas pulled away. The flap slid shut. There were a few terse words exchanged between the soldiers, then footsteps moved away, crunching up the gravel road.

It took only seconds for their driver to scramble back into the front seat and hit the gas. The truck lurched forward, throwing Guy off his feet. He toppled, landing right next to Willy on the rice sacks. As their truck roared full speed around the traffic and down the road, they sprawled together, too stunned by their narrow escape to say a word. Suddenly they were both laughing, rolling around on the sacks, giddy with relief.

Guy hauled her into his arms and kissed her hard on the mouth.

"What was that for?" she demanded, pulling back in surprise.

"That," he whispered, "was pure instinct."

"Do you always follow your instincts?"

"Whenever I can get away with it."

"And you really think I'll let you get away with it?"

In answer, he gripped her hair, trapping her head against

the sacks, and kissed her again, longer, deeper. Pleasure leapt through her, a desire so sudden, so fierce, it left her voiceless.

"I think," he murmured, "you want it as much as I do."

With a gasp of outrage, she shoved him onto his back and climbed on top of him, pinning him beneath her. "Guy Barnard, you miserable jerk, I'm going to give you what you deserve."

He laughed. "Are you now?"

"Yes, I am."

"And what, exactly, do I deserve?"

For a moment she stared at him through the dust and gloom. Then, slowly, she lowered her face to his. "This," she said softly.

The kiss was different this time. Warmer. Hungrier. She was a full and willing partner; he knew it and he responded. She didn't need to be warned that she was playing a dangerous game, that they were both hurtling toward the point of no return. She could already feel him swelling beneath her, could feel her own body aching to accommodate that new hardness. And the whole time she was kissing him, the whole time their bodies were pressed together, she was thinking, *I'm going to regret this. As sure as I breathe, I'm going to pay for this. But it feels so right....*

She pulled away, fighting to catch her breath.

"Well!" said Guy, grinning up at her. "Miss Willy Maitland, I *am* surprised."

She sat up, nervously shoving her hair back into place. "I never meant to do that."

"Yes, you did."

"It was a stupid thing to do."

"Then why did you?"

"It was…" She looked him in the eye. "Pure instinct."

He laughed. In fact, he fell backward laughing, rolling around on the sacks of rice. The truck hit a pothole, bouncing her up and down so hard, she collapsed onto the floor beside him.

And still he was laughing.

"You're a crazy man," she said.

He threw an arm around her neck and pulled her warmly against him. "Only about you."

IN A BLACK LIMOUSINE WITH tinted windows, Siang sat gripping the steering wheel and cursing the wretched highway—or what this country called a highway. He had never understood why communism and decent roads had to be mutually exclusive. And then there was the traffic, added to the annoyance of that government vehicle inspection. It had given him a moment's apprehension, the sight of the armed soldiers standing at the roadside. But it took only a few smooth words from the man in the back seat, the wave of a Soviet diplomatic passport, and they were allowed to move on without incident.

They continued west; a road sign confirmed it was the highway to Dien Bien Phu. A strange omen, Siang thought, that they should be headed for the town where the French had met defeat, where East had triumphed over West. Centuries before, an Asian scribe had written a prophetic statement.

To the south lie the mountains,
The land of the Viets.
He who marches against them
Is surely doomed to failure.

Siang glanced in the rearview mirror, at the man in the

back seat. *He* wouldn't be thinking in terms of East versus West. *He* cared nothing about nations or motherlands or patriotism. Real power, he'd once told Siang, lay in the hands of individuals, special people who knew how to use it, to keep it, and *he* was going to keep it.

Siang had no doubt he would.

He remembered the day they'd first met in Happy Valley, at an American base the GIs had whimsically dubbed "the Golf Course." It was 1967. Siang had a different name then. He was a slender boy of thirteen, barefoot, scratching out a hungry existence among all the other orphans. When he'd first seen the American, his initial impression was of hugeness. An enormous fleshy face, alarmingly red in the heat; boots made for a giant; hands that looked strong enough to snap a child's arm in two. The day was hot, and Siang was selling soft drinks. The man bought a Coca Cola, drank it down in a few gulps and handed the empty bottle back. As Siang took it, he felt the man's gaze studying him, measuring him. Then the man walked away.

The next day, and every day for a week, the American emerged from the GI compound to buy a Coca Cola. Though a dozen other children clamored for his business, each waving soft drinks, the man bought only from Siang.

At the end of the week, the man presented Siang with a brand-new shirt, three tins of corned beef and an astonishing amount of cash. He said he was leaving the valley early the next morning, and he asked the boy to hire the prettiest girl he could find and bring her to him for the night.

It was only a test, as Siang found out later. He passed it. In fact, the American seemed surprised when Siang appeared at the compound gate that evening with an extraordinarily beautiful girl. Obviously, the man had expected Siang to take the money and vanish.

To Siang's astonishment, the man sent the girl away without even touching her. Instead, he asked the boy to stay—not as a lover, as Siang at first feared, but as an assistant. "I need someone I can trust," the man said. "Someone I can train...."

Even now, after all these years, Siang still felt that young boy's sense of awe whenever he looked at the American. He glanced at the rearview mirror, at the face that had changed so little since that day they'd met in Happy Valley. The cheeks might be thicker and ruddier, but the eyes were the same, sharp and all-knowing. Just like the mind. Those eyes almost frightened him.

Siang turned his attention back to the road. The man in the back seat was humming a tune: "Yankee Doodle." A whimsical choice, considering the Soviet passport he was carrying. Siang smiled at the irony of it all.

Nothing about the man was ever quite what it seemed.

CHAPTER ELEVEN

IT WAS LATE in the day when the truck at last pulled to a halt. Willy, half-asleep among the rice sacks, rolled drowsily onto her back and struggled to clear her head. The signals her body was sending gave new meaning to the word *misery*. Every muscle ached; every bone felt shattered. The truck engine cut off. In the new silence, mosquitoes buzzed in the gloom, a gloom so thick she could scarcely breathe.

"Are you awake?" came a whisper. Guy's face, gleaming with sweat, appeared above her.

"What time is it?"

"Late afternoon. Five or so. My watch stopped."

She sat up and her head swam in the heat. "Where are we?"

"Can't be sure. Near the border, I'd guess..." Guy stiffened as footsteps tramped toward them. Men's voices, speaking Vietnamese, moved closer.

The canvas flap was thrown open. Against the sudden glare of daylight, the faces of the two men staring in were black and featureless.

One of the men gestured for them to climb out. "You follow," he ordered. "Say nothing."

Willy at once scrambled out and dropped onto the spongy jungle floor. Guy followed her. They swayed for a moment, blinking dazedly, gulping in their first fresh air in hours. Chips of afternoon sunlight dappled the ground at their feet. In the branches above, an invisible bird screeched out a warning.

The Vietnamese man motioned to them to move. They had just started into the woods when an engine roared to life. Willy turned in alarm to see the truck rattle away without them. She glanced at Guy and saw in his eyes the same thought that had crossed her mind, *There's no turning back now.*

"No stop. Go, go!" said the Vietnamese.

They moved on into the forest.

The man obviously knew where he was going. Without a trail to guide him, he led them through a tangle of vines and trees to an isolated hut. A tattered U.S. Army blanket hung over the doorway. Inside, straw matting covered the earthen floor and a mosquito net, filmy as lace, draped a sleeping pallet. On a low table was set a modest meal of bananas, cracked coconuts and cold tea.

"You wait here," said the man. "Long time, maybe."

"Who are we waiting for?" asked Guy.

The man didn't answer; perhaps he didn't understand the question. He turned and, like a ghost, slipped into the forest.

For a long time, Willy and Guy lingered in the doorway, waiting, listening to the whispers of the jungle. They heard only the clattering of palms in the wind, the lonely cry of a bird.

How long would they wait? Willy wondered. Hours? Days? She stared up through the dense canopy at the last sunlight sparkling on the wet leaves. It would be dark soon. "I'm hungry," she said, and she turned back into the gloom of the hut.

Together they devoured every banana, gnawed every sliver of coconut from its husk, drank down every drop of tea. In all her life, Willy had never tasted any meal quite so splendid! At last, their stomachs full, their legs trembling with exhaustion, they crawled under the mosquito netting and, side by side, they fell asleep.

At dusk, it began to rain. It was a glorious downpour, monsoonlike in its ferocity, but it brought no relief from the heat. Willy, awake in the darkness, lay with her clothes steeped in sweat. In the shadows above, the mosquito net billowed and fell like a hovering ghost.

She clawed her way free of the netting. If she didn't get some air, she was going to smother.

She left Guy asleep on the pallet and went to the doorway, where she gulped in breaths of rain-drenched air. The swirl of cool mist was irresistible; she stepped out into the downpour.

All around her, the jungle clattered like a thousand cymbals. She shivered in the thunderous darkness as the water streamed down her face.

"What the hell are you doing?" called a sleepy voice. She turned and saw Guy in the doorway.

She laughed. "I'm taking a shower!"

"With your clothes on?"

"It's lovely out here! Come on, before it stops!"

He hesitated, then plunged outside after her.

"Doesn't it feel wonderful?" she cried, throwing her arms out to welcome the raindrops. "I couldn't take the heat any longer. God, I couldn't even stand the smell of my own clothes."

"You think that's bad? Just wait till the mildew sets in." Turning his face to the sky, he let out a satisfied growl. "Now *this* is the way we were meant to take a shower. The way the kids do it. When I was here during the war, I used to get a kick out of seeing 'em run around without their clothes on. Nothing cuter than all those little brown bodies dancing in the rain. No shame, no embarrassment.''

"The way it should be."

"That's right," he said. Softly he added, "The way it should be."

All at once, Willy felt him watching her. She turned and stared back. The palms clattered, and the rain beat its tattoo on the leaves. Without a word, he came toward her, stood so close to her, she could feel the heat rippling between them. Yet she didn't move, didn't speak. The rain streaming down her face was as warm as teardrops.

"So what are we doing with our clothes on?" he murmured.

She shook her head. "This isn't supposed to happen."

"Maybe it is."

"A one-night stand—that's all it'd be—"

"Better once than never."

"And then you'll be gone."

"You don't know that. I don't know that."

"I do know it. You'll be gone...."

She started to turn away, but he pulled her back, twisted her around to face him. At the first meeting of their lips, she knew it was over, the battle lost.

Better once than never, she thought as her last shred of resistance fell away. *Better to have you once and lose you than to always wonder how it might have been.* Reaching up, she threw her arms around his neck and met his kiss with her own, just as hungry, just as fierce. Their bodies pressed together so tightly, their fever heat mingled through the damp clothes.

He was already fumbling for the buttons of her blouse. She trembled as the fabric slid away and rain trickled down her bare shoulders. Then the warmth of his hand closed around her breast, and she was shivering not with cold but with desire.

Together they stumbled into the darkness of the hut. They were tugging desperately at each other's clothes now, flinging the wet garments into oblivion. When at last they faced each other with no barriers, no defenses, he pulled her face up and gently pressed his lips to hers. No kiss had ever pierced so true to her soul. The darkness swam around her; the earth gave way. She let him lower her to the pallet and felt the mosquito net whisper down around them.

Making love in the clouds, she thought as the whiteness billowed above. Then she closed her eyes and lost all sense of where she was. There was only the pounding of the rain and the magical touch of Guy's hands, his mouth. It had been so long since a man had made love to her, so long since she'd bared herself to the pleasure. The pain. And there *would* be pain after it was over, after he was gone from her life. With a man like Guy, the ending was inevitable.

She ignored those whispers of warning; she had drifted beyond all reach of salvation. She pulled him down against her, and whispered, "Now. Please."

He was already struggling against his own needs, his own urgencies. Her quiet plea slashed away his last thread of control.

"I give up," he groaned. Seizing her hands, he pinned her arms above her head, trapping her, his willing captive, beneath him.

His hardness filled her so completely, it made her catch her breath in astonishment. But her surprise quickly melted into pleasure. She was moving against him now, and he against her, both of them driving that blessed ache to new heights of agony.

The world fell away; the night seemed to swirl with mist

and magic. They brought each other to the very edge, and there they lingered, between pleasure and torment, unwilling to surrender to the inevitable. Then the jungle sounds of beating rain, of groaning trees were joined by their cries as they plummeted over the brink.

Even when she fell back to earth, she was still floating. In the darkness above, the netting billowed like parachute silk falling through the emptiness of space.

There was no need to speak; it was enough just to lie together, limbs entwined, and listen to the rhythms of the night.

Gently, Guy stroked a tangled lock of hair off her cheek. "Why did you say that?" he asked.

"Say what?"

"That I'd be gone. That I'd leave you."

She pulled away and rolled onto her back. "Because you will."

"Do you want me to?"

She didn't answer. What difference would it make, after all, to bare her soul? And did he really want to hear the truth: that after tonight, she would probably do anything to keep him, to make him love her?

"Willy?"

She turned away. "Why are we talking about this?"

"Because I want to talk about it."

"Well, I don't." She sat up and hugged her knees protectively against her chest. "It doesn't do anyone any good, all this babbling about what comes next, where do we go from here. I've been through it before."

"You really don't trust men, do you?"

She laughed. "Should I?"

"Is it all because your old man walked out on you? Or was it something else? A bad love affair? What?"

"You could say all of the above."

"I see." There was a long silence. She shivered at the touch of his hand stroking her naked back. "Who else has left you? Besides your father?"

"Just a man I loved. Someone who said he loved me."

"And he didn't."

"Oh, I suppose he did, in his way." She shrugged. "Not a very permanent way."

"If it's only temporary, it's not love."

"Now that sounds like the title of a song." She laughed. "A lousy song."

At once, she fell silent. She pressed her forehead to her knees. "You're right. A lousy song."

"Other people manage to get over rotten love affairs...."

"Oh, I got over it." She raised her head and stared up at the netting. "Took only a month to fall in love with him. And over a year to watch him walk away. One thing I've learned is that it doesn't fall apart in a day. Most lovers don't just get up and walk out the door. They do it by inches, step by step, and every single one hurts. First they start out with, 'Who needs to get married, it's just a piece of paper.' And then, at the end, they tell you, 'I need more space.' Then it's 'How can anyone promise forever?' Maybe it was better the way my dad did it. No excuses. He just walked out the door."

"There's no such thing as a good way to leave someone."

"You're right." She pushed aside the netting and swung her feet out. "That's why I don't let it happen to me anymore."

"How do you avoid it?"

"I don't give any man the chance to leave me."

"Meaning you walk away first?"

"Men do it all the time."

"Some men."

Including you, she thought with a distinct twinge of bitterness. "So how did you walk away from your girlfriend, Guy? Did you leave before or after you found out she was pregnant?"

"That was an unusual situation."

"It always is."

"We'd broken up months before. I didn't hear about the kid till after he was born. By then there was nothing I could do, nothing I could change. Ginny was already married to another man."

"Oh." She paused. "That made it simple."

"Simple?" For the first time she heard his anger, and she longed to take back her awful words, longed to cleanse the bitterness from his voice. "You've got some crazy notion that men are all the same," he said. "All of us trying to claw our way free of responsibility, never looking back at the people we've hurt. Let me tell you something, Willy. Having a Y chromosome doesn't make someone a lousy human being."

"I shouldn't have said that," she said, gently touching his hand. "I'm sorry."

He lay quietly in the shadows, staring up at the ceiling. "Sam's three years old now. I've seen him a grand total of twice, once on Ginny's front porch, once on the playground at his preschool. I went over there to get a look at him, to see what kind of kid he was, whether he looked happy. I guess the teachers must've reported it. Not long after, Ginny called me, screaming bloody murder. Said I was messing with her marriage. Even threatened to slap me with a restraining order. I haven't been near him since...." He paused to clear his throat. "I guess I realized I wouldn't be doing him any favors anyways, trying to shove my way into his life. Sam already has a father—a good one, from what I hear. And it would've hurt everyone if I'd tried to fight it out in court. Maybe later, when he's older, I'll find a way to tell him. To let him know how much I wanted to be part of his life.''

And my life? she thought with sudden sadness. *You won't be part of it, either, will you?*

She rose to her feet and groped around in the darkness for her scattered clothes. ''Here's a little advice, Guy,'' she said over her shoulder. ''Don't ever give up on your son. Take it from a kid who's been left behind. Daddies are a precious commodity.''

''I know.'' he said softly. He paused, then said, ''You'll never get over it, will you? Your father walking out.''

She shook out her wet blouse. ''There are some things a kid can't ever forget.''

''Or forgive.''

Outside, the rain had softened to a whisper. In the thatching above, insects rustled. ''Do you think I should forgive him?''

''Yes.''

''I suppose I could forgive him for hurting *me*. But not for hurting my mother. Not when I remember what she went through just to—'' Her voice died in midsentence.

They both heard it at the same time: the footsteps slapping through the mud outside.

Guy rolled off the pallet and sprang to his feet beside her. Shoes scraped over the threshold, and the shadow of a man filled the doorway.

The intruder held up a lantern. The flood of light caught them in freeze-frame: Willy, clutching the blouse to her naked breasts; Guy, poised in a fighter's crouch. The stranger, his face hidden in the shadow of a drab green poncho, slowly lowered the lantern and set it on the table. ''I am sorry for the delay,'' he said. ''The road is very bad tonight." He tossed a cloth-wrapped bundle down beside the lantern. "At ease, Mr. Barnard. If I'd wanted to kill you, you'd be dead now." He paused and added, "Both of you."

"Who the hell are you?" Guy asked.

Water droplets splattered onto the floor as the man shoved back the hood of his poncho. His hair was blond, almost white in the lantern light. He had pale eyes set in a moonlike face. "Dr. Gunnel Andersen," he said, nodding by way of introduction. "Nora sent word you were coming." Raindrops flew as he shook out the poncho and hung it up to dry. Then he sat down at the table. "Please, feel free to put on your clothes."

"How did Nora reach you?" Guy asked, pulling on his trousers.

"We keep a shortwave radio for medical emergencies. Not all frequencies are monitored by the government."

"Are you with the Swedish mission?"

"No, I work for the U.N." Andersen's impassive gaze wandered to Willy, who was self-consciously struggling into her damp clothes. "We provide medical care in the villages. Humanitarian aid. Malaria, typhoid, it's all here. Probably always will be." He began to unwrap the bundle he'd set on the table. "I assume you have not eaten. This isn't much but it's the best I could do. It's been a bad year for crops, and protein is scarce." Inside the bundle was a bamboo box filled with cold rice, pickled vegetables and microscopic flecks of pork congealed in gravy.

Guy at once sat down. "After bananas and coconuts, this looks like a feast to me."

Dr. Andersen glanced at Willy, who was still lingering in the corner, watching suspiciously. "Are you not hungry, Miss Maitland?"

"I'm starved."

"Then why don't you eat?"

"First I want to know who you are."

"I have told you my name."

"Your name doesn't mean a thing to me. What's your connection to Nora? To my father?"

Dr. Andersen's eyes were as transparent as water. "You've waited twenty years for an answer. You can surely wait a few minutes longer."

Guy said, "Willy, you need to eat. Come, sit down."

Hunger finally pulled her to the table. Dr. Andersen had brought no utensils. Willy and Guy used their fingers to scoop up the rice. All the time she was eating, she felt the Swede's eyes watching her.

"I see you do not trust me," he said.

"I don't trust anyone anymore."

He nodded and smiled. "Then you have learned, in a few shorts days, what took me months to learn."

"Mistrust?"

"Doubt. Fear." He looked around the hut, at the shadows dancing on the walls. "What I call the creeping uneasiness. A sense that things are not right in this place. That, just under the surface, lies some…secret, something…terrible."

The lantern light flickered, almost died. He glanced up as the rain pounded the roof. A puff of wind swept through the doorway, dank with the smells of the jungle.

"You sense it, too," he said.

"All I know is, there've been too many coincidences," said Guy. "Too many tidy little acts of fate. As though paths have been laid out for us and we're just following the trail."

Andersen nodded. "We all have roads laid out for us. We usually choose the path of least resistance. It's when we wander off that path that things become dangerous."

He smiled. "You know, at this very minute, I could be sitting in my house in Stockholm, sipping coffee, growing fat on cakes and cookies. But I chose to stay here."

"And has life become dangerous?" asked Willy.

"It's not my life I worry about now. It was a risk bringing you here. But Nora felt the time was right."

"Then it was her decision?"

He nodded. "She thought it might be your last chance for a reunion."

Willy froze, staring at him. "Did you—did you say *reunion?*"

Dr. Andersen met her gaze. Slowly, he nodded.

She tried to speak but found her voice was gone. The significance of that one word reduced her to numb silence.

Her father was alive.

It was Guy who finally spoke. "Where is he?"

"A village northwest of here."

"A prisoner?"

"No, no. A guest. A friend."

"He's not being held against his will?"

"Not since the war." Andersen looked at Willy, who had not yet found her voice. "It may be hard for you to accept, Miss Maitland, but there *are* Americans who find happiness in this country."

She looked at him in bewilderment. "I don't understand. All these years he's been alive…he could have come home.…"

"Many men didn't return."

"*He* had the choice!"

"He also had his reasons."

"Reasons? He had every reason to come home!"

Her anguished cry seemed to hang in the room. For a moment neither man spoke. Then Andersen rose to his feet. "Your father must speak for himself..." he said, and he started for the door.

"Then why isn't he here?"

"There are arrangements to be made. A time, a place—"

"When will I see him?"

The doctor hesitated. "That depends."

"On what?"

He looked back from the doorway. "On whether your father wants to see *you*."

LONG AFTER ANDERSEN HAD left, Willy stood in the doorway, staring out at the curtain of rain.

"Why *wouldn't* he want to see me?" she cried into the darkness.

Quietly Guy came to stand behind her. His arms came around her shoulders, pulled her into the tight circle of his embrace.

"Why wouldn't he?"

"Willy, stop."

She turned and pressed her face into his chest. "Do you think it was so terrible?" she sobbed. "Being my father?"

"Of course not."

"It must have been. I must have made him miserable."

"You were just a kid, Willy! You can't blame yourself! Sometimes men...change. Sometimes they need—"

"*Why?*" she cried.

"Hey, not all men walk out. Some of us, we hang around, for better or for worse."

Gently, he led her back to the sleeping pallet. Beneath the silvery mosquito net, she let him hold her, an embrace not of passion, but of comfort. The arms of a friend. It felt right, the way their making love earlier that evening had felt right. But she couldn't help wondering, even as she lay in his arms, when this, too, would change, when *he* would change.

It hurt beyond all measure, the thought that he, too, would someday leave her, that this was but a momentary mingling of limbs and warmth and souls. It was hurt she expected, but one she'd never, ever be ready for.

Outside, the leaves clattered in the downpour.

It rained all night.

AT DAWN THE JEEP APPEARED.

"I take only the woman," insisted the Vietnamese driver, planting himself in Guy's path. The man gestured toward the hut. "You stay, GI."

"She's not going without me," said Guy.

"They tell me only the woman."

"Then she's not going."

The two men faced each other, challenge mirrored in their eyes. The driver shrugged and turned for the jeep. "Then I don't take anybody."

"Guy, please," said Willy. "Just wait here for me. I'll be okay."

"I don't like it."

She glanced at the driver, who'd already climbed behind the wheel and started the engine. "I don't have a choice," she said, and she stepped into the jeep.

The driver released the brake and spun the jeep around. As they rolled away, Willy glanced back and saw Guy standing alone among the trees. She thought he called out something—her name, perhaps—but then the jungle swallowed him from view.

She turned her attention to the road—or what served as a road. In truth, it was scarcely more than a muddy track through the forest. Branches slashed the windshield; water flew from the leaves and splattered their faces.

"How far is it?" she asked. The driver didn't answer. "Where are we going?" she asked. Again, no answer. She sat back and waited to see what would happen next.

A few miles into the forest the mud track petered out, and they halted before a solid wall of jungle. The driver cut the engine. A few rays of sunlight shone dimly through the canopy of leaves. Only the cry of a single bird sliced through the silence.

The driver climbed out and walked around to the rear. Willy watched as he rooted around under a camouflage tarp covering the back seat. Then she saw the blade slide out from beneath the tarp. He was holding a machete.

He turned to face her. For a few heartbeats they stared at each other, gazes meeting over the gleam of razor-sharp steel. Then she saw amusement flash in his eyes.

"We walk now," he said.

A nod was the only reply she could manage. Wordlessly, she climbed out of the jeep and followed him into the jungle.

He moved silently through the trees, the only sound of his passage the whistle and slash of the machete. Vines hung like shrouds from the branches; clouds of mosquitoes swarmed up from stagnant puddles. He moved onward without a second's pause, melting like a phantom through the brush. Willy, stumbling in the tangle of trees, barely managed to keep the back of his tattered shirt in view.

It didn't take long for her to give up slapping mosquitoes. She decided it was a lost cause. Let them suck her dry; her blood was up for grabs. She could only concentrate on moving forward, on putting one foot in front of the other. She was sliding through some timeless vacuum where distance was measured by the gaps between trees, the span between footsteps.

By the time they finally halted, she was staggering from

exhaustion. Conquered, she sagged against the nearest tree and waited for his next command.

"Here," he said.

Bewildered, she looked up at him. "But what are you—"

To her astonishment, he turned and trotted off into the jungle.

"Wait!" she cried. "You're not going to leave me here!"

The man kept moving.

"Please, you have to tell me!" she screamed. He paused and glanced back. "Where am I? What is this place?"

"The same place we find *him*," was the reply. Then he slipped away, vanishing into the forest.

She whirled around, scanning the jungle, watching, waiting for some savior to appear. She saw no one. The man's last words echoed in her head.

What is this place?

The same place we find him.

"Who?" she cried.

In desperation, she stared up at the branches crisscrossing the sky. That's when she saw it, the monstrous silhouette rising like a shark's fin among the trees.

It was the tail of a plane.

CHAPTER TWELVE

SHE MOVED CLOSER. Gradually she discerned, amid the camouflage of trees and undergrowth, the remains of what was once an aircraft. Vines snaked over jagged metal. Fuselage struts reached skyward from the jungle floor, as bare and stark as the bleached ribs of a dead animal. Willy halted, her gaze drawn back to the tail above her in the branches. Years of rust and tropical decay had obscured the markings, but she could still make out the serial number: 5410.

This was Air America flight 5078. Point of origin: Vientiane, Laos. Destination: a shattered treetop in a North Vietnamese jungle.

In the silence of the forest, she bowed her head. A thin shaft of sunlight sliced through the branches and danced at her feet. And all around her the trees soared like the walls of a cathedral. How fitting that this rusted altar to war should come to rest in a place of such untarnished peace.

There were tears in her eyes when she finally forced herself to turn and study the fuselage—what was left of it. Most of the shell had burned or rotted away, leaving only a little flooring and a few crumbling struts. The wings were missing entirely—probably sheared off on impact. She moved forward to the remnants of the cockpit.

Sunlight sparkled through the shattered windshield. The navigational equipment was gutted; charred wires hung from holes in the instrument panel. Her gaze shifted to the bulkhead, riddled with bullet holes. She ran her fingers across the ravaged metal and then pulled away.

As she took a step back, she heard a voice say, ''There isn't much left of her. But I guess you could say the same of me.''

Willy spun around. And froze.

He came out of the forest, a man in rags, walking toward her. It was the gait she recognized, not the body, which had been worn down to its rawest elements. Nor the face.

Certainly not the face.

He had no ears, no eyebrows. What was left of his hair grew in tortured wisps. He came to within a few yards of her and stopped, as though afraid to move any closer.

They looked at each other, not speaking, perhaps not daring to speak.

''You're all grown up,'' he finally said.

''Yes.'' She cleared her throat. ''I guess I am.''

''You look good, Willy. Real good. Are you married yet?''

''No.''

''You should be.''

''I'm not.''

A pause. They both looked down, looked back up, strangers groping for common ground.

Softly he asked, ''How's your mother?''

Willy blinked away a new wave of tears. ''She's…dying.'' She felt a comfortless sense of retribution at her father's shocked silence. ''It's cancer,'' she continued. ''I wanted her to see a doctor months ago, but you know how she is. Never thinking about herself. Never taking the time to…'' Her voice cracked, faded.

''I had no idea,'' he whispered.

''How could you? You were dead.'' She looked up at

the sky and suddenly laughed, an ugly sound in that quiet circle of trees. "It never occurred to you to write to us? One letter from the grave?"

"It only would have made things harder."

"Harder than *what?* Than it's already been?"

"With me gone, dead, Ann was free to move on," he said, "to...find someone else. Someone better for her."

"But she didn't! She never even tried! All she could think about was *you.*"

"I thought she'd forget. I thought she'd get over me."

"You thought wrong."

He bowed his head. "I'm sorry, Wilone."

After a pause, she said, "I'm sorry, too."

A bird sang in the trees, its sweet notes piercing the silence between them.

She asked, "What happened to you?"

"You mean this?" He gestured vaguely at his face.

"I mean...everything."

"Everything," he repeated. Then, laughing, he looked up at the branches. "Where the hell do I start?" He began to walk in a circle, moving among the trees like a lost man. At last he stopped beside the fuselage. Gazing at the jagged remains, he said, "It's funny. I never lost consciousness. Even when I hit the trees, when everything around me was being ripped apart, I stayed awake all the way down. I remember thinking, 'So when do I get to see heaven?' Or hell, for that matter. Then it all went up in flames. And I thought, 'There's my answer. My eternity...'"

He stopped, let out a deep sigh. "They found me a short way from here, stumbling around under the trees. Most of my face was burned away. But I don't remember feeling much of anything." He looked down at his scarred hands. "The pain came later. When they tried to clean the burns.

When the nerves grew back. I'd scream at them to let me die, but they wouldn't. I guess I was too valuable.''

"Because you were American?"

"Because I was a pilot. Someone to pump for information, someone to trade. Maybe someone to spread the Party line back home...."

"Did they...hurt you?"

He shook his head. "I guess they figured I'd been hurt enough. It was a quieter sort of persuasion. Endless discussions. Relentless arguments as I recovered. I swore I wasn't going to let the enemy twist my head around. But I was weak. I was far from home. And they said things— so many things—I couldn't argue with. And after a while...after a while it made...well, sense. About this country being their house, about us being the burglars in the house. And wouldn't anyone with burglars in their house fight back?"

He let out a sigh. "I don't know anymore. It sounds so feeble now, but I just got tired. Tired of arguing. Tired of trying to explain what I was doing in their country. Tired of trying to defend God only knew what. It was easier just to agree with them. And after a while, I actually started to believe it. Believe what they were telling me." He looked down. "According to some people, that makes me a traitor."

"To some people. Not to me."

He was silent.

"Why didn't you come home?" she asked.

"Look at me, Willy. Who'd want me back?"

"*We* did."

"No, you didn't. Not the man I'd become." He laughed hollowly. "Everyone would be pointing at me, whispering behind my back, talking about my face. Is that the kind of father you wanted? The kind of husband your mother wanted? Back home, people expect you to have a nose and ears and eyebrows.'' He shook his head. ''Ann…Ann was so beautiful. I—I couldn't go back to that.''

''But what do you have here? Look at you, at what you're wearing, at how skinny you are. You're starving, wasting away.''

''I eat what the rest of the village eats. It's enough to live on.'' He picked at the rag that served as his shirt. ''Clothes, I never much cared about.''

''You gave up a family!''

''I—I found another family, Willy. Here.''

She stared at him, stunned.

''I have a wife. Her name's Lan. And we have children. A baby girl and two boys…eight and ten. They can speak English, and a little French….'' he said helplessly.

''*We* were at home!''

''But I was here. And Lan was here. She saved my life, Willy. She was the one who kept me alive through the infections, the fevers, the endless pain.''

''You said you begged to die.''

''Lan was the one who made me want to live again.''

Willy stared at that man with half a face, the man she'd once called her father. The lashless eyes looked back at her, unblinking. Awaiting judgment.

She still had a face, a normal life, she thought. What right did she have to condemn him?

She looked away. ''So. What do I tell Mom?''

''I don't know. Maybe nothing.''

''She has a right to know.''

''Maybe it would be kinder if she didn't.''

''Kinder to whom? You or her?''

He looked down at his feet in their dirty slippers. ''I suppose I deserve that. Whatever you have to say, I deserve it. But God knows, I wanted to make it up to her.

And to you. I sent money—twenty, maybe thirty thousand dollars. You got it, didn't you?''

"We never knew who sent it.''

"You weren't supposed to know. Nora Walker arranged it through a bank in Bangkok. It was everything I had. All that was left of the gold.''

She gave him a bewildered look and saw that his gaze had shifted toward the plane's fuselage. "You were carrying gold?''

"I didn't know it at the time. It was our little rule at Air America: Never ask about the cargo. Just fly the plane. But after she went down, after I crawled out of the wreckage, I saw it. Gold bars scattered all over the ground. It was crazy. There I was, half my damn face burned off, and I remember thinking, 'I'm rich. If I live through this, son of a bitch, I'm *rich*''' He laughed, then, at his own lunacy, at the absurdity of a dying man rejoicing among the ashes. "I buried some of the gold, threw some in the bushes. I thought—I guess I thought it would be my ticket out. That if I was captured, I could use it to bargain for my freedom.''

"What happened?''

He looked off at the trees. "They found me. NVA soldiers. And they found most of the gold.'' He shrugged. "They kept us both.''

"But not forever. You didn't have to stay—'' She stopped. "Didn't you *ever* think of us?''

"I never stopped thinking of you. After the war, after all that—that insanity was over, I came back here, dug up what gold they hadn't found. I asked Nora to get it out to you.'' He looked at Willy. "Don't you see? I never forgot you. I just…'' He stopped, and his voice dropped to a whisper. "I just couldn't go back.''

In the trees above, branches rattled in the wind. Leaves drifted down in a soft rain of green.

He turned away. "I suppose you'll want to go back to Hanoi. I'll see that someone drives you...."

"Dad?"

He halted, not daring to look at her.

"Your little boys. You—say they understand English?"

He nodded.

She paused. "Then we ought to understand each other, the boys and I." she said. "I mean, assuming they want to meet me...."

Her father quickly rubbed a hand across his eyes. But when he turned to look at her, she could still see the tears glistening there. He smiled...and held out his hand to her.

SHE'D BEEN GONE TOO LONG.

Three hours had passed, and Guy was more than worried. He was scared out of his head. Something wasn't right. It was that old instinct of his, that sense of doom closing in, and he was helpless to do anything about it. A dozen different images kept forming in his mind, each one progressively more terrible. Willy screaming. Dying. Or already dead in the jungle. When at last he heard the rumble of the jeep, he was hovering at the edge of panic.

Dr. Andersen was at the wheel. "Good morning, Mr. Barnard!" he called cheerily as Guy stalked over to him.

"Where is she?"

"She is safe."

"Prove it."

Andersen threw open the door and gestured for him to get in. "I will take you to her."

Guy climbed in and slammed the door. "Where are we going?"

"It is a long drive." Andersen threw the jeep into gear and spun them around onto a dirt track. "Be patient."

The night's rainfall had turned the path to muck, and on either side the jungle pressed in, close and strangling. They might have gone for miles or tens of miles; on a road locked in by jungle, distance was impossible to judge. When Andersen finally pulled off to the side, Guy could see no obvious reason for stopping. Only when he'd climbed out and stood among the trees did he notice the tiny footpath leading into the bush. He couldn't see what lay beyond; the forest hid everything from view.

"From here we walk," said Andersen, foraging around for a few loose branches.

"Why the camouflage?" asked Guy, watching Andersen drape the branches over the jeep.

"Protection for the village."

"What are they afraid of?"

Andersen reached under the tarp on the back seat and pulled out an AK-47. Casually, he slung it over his shoulder. "Everything," he said, and headed off into the jungle.

The footpath led into a shadowy world of hundred-foot trees and tangled vines. Watching Andersen's back, Guy was struck by the irony of a doctor lugging an automatic rifle. He wondered what enemy he planned to use it on.

The smells of rotting vegetation, of mud simmering in the heat were only too familiar. "The whole damn jungle smells of death," the GIs used to say. Guy felt his gait change to a silent glide, felt his reflexes kick into overdrive. His five senses were painfully acute; the snap of a branch under Andersen's boot was as shocking as gunfire.

He heard the sounds of the village before he saw it. Somewhere deep in the forest, children were laughing. And then he heard water rushing and the cry of a baby.

Andersen pushed ahead, and as the last curtain of

branches parted, Guy saw, beneath a towering stand of trees, the circle of huts. In the central courtyard, children batted a pebble back and forth with their feet. They froze as Guy and Andersen emerged from the forest. One of the girls called out; instantly, a dozen adults emerged from the huts. In silence they all watched Guy.

Then, in the doorway of one hut, a familiar figure appeared. As Willy came toward Guy, he had the sudden desire to take her in his arms and kiss her right then and there, in view of the whole village, the whole world. But he couldn't seem to move. He could only stare down at her smiling face.

"I found him," Willy said.

He shook his head. "What?"

"My father. He's here."

Guy turned and saw that someone else had emerged from the hut. A man without ears, without eyebrows. The horrifying apparition held out its hand; a fingertip was missing.

William Maitland smiled. "Welcome to Na Co, Mr. Barnard."

DR. ANDERSEN'S JEEP was easy to spot, even through the camouflage. How fortunate the rains had been so heavy the night before; without all that mud, Siang would never have been able to track the jeep to this trail head.

He threw aside the branches and quickly surveyed the jeep's interior. On the back seat, beneath a green canvas tarp, was a jug of drinking water, a few old tools and a weathered notebook, obviously a journal, filled with scribbling. The name "Dr. Gunnel Andersen" was written inside the front cover.

Siang left the jeep, tramped a few paces into the jungle and peered through the shadows. It took only a moment to spot the footprints. Two men. Dr. Andersen and who else? Barnard? He followed the tracks a short way and saw that, just beyond the first few trees, the footprints led to a distinct trail, no doubt an old and established path. The village of Na Co must lie farther ahead.

He returned to the limousine where the man was waiting. "They have gone into the forest," Siang said. "There's a village trail."

"Is it the right one?"

Siang shrugged. "There are many villages in these mountains. But the jeep belongs to Dr. Andersen."

"Then it's the right village." The man sat back, satisfied. "I want our people here tonight."

"So soon?"

"It's the way I work. In and out. The men are ready."

In fact the mercenary team had been waiting two days for the signal. They'd been assembled in Thailand, fifteen men equipped with the most sophisticated in small arms. As soon as the order went through, they would be on their way, no questions asked.

"Tell them we need the dogs as well," said the man. "For mopping up. The whole village goes."

Siang paused. "The children?"

"One mustn't leave orphans."

This troubled Siang a little, but he said nothing. He knew better than to argue with the voice of necessity. Or power.

"Is there a radio in the jeep?" asked the man.

"Yes," said Siang.

"Rip it out."

"Andersen will see—"

"Andersen will see nothing."

Siang nodded in instant understanding.

The man drove off in the limousine, headed for a rendezvous spot a mile ahead. Siang waited until the car had disappeared, then he trotted back to the jeep, ripped out the wires connecting the radio and smashed the panel for good measure. He found a cool spot beneath a tree and sat down. Closing his eyes, he summoned forth the strength needed for his task.

Soon he would have assistance. By tonight, the well paid team of mercenaries would stand assembled on this road. He wouldn't allow himself to think of the victims— the women, the children. It was a consequence of war. In every skirmish, there were the innocent casualties. He'd learned to accept it, to shrug it off as inevitable. The act of pulling a trigger required a clear head swept free of emotions. It was, after all, the way of battle.

It was the way of success.

"DOES SHE UNDERSTAND THE danger?" asked Maitland.

"I don't know." Guy stood in the doorway and gazed out at the leaf-strewn courtyard where the village kids were mobbing Willy, singing out questions. The wonderful bedlam of children, he thought wistfully. He turned and looked at the mass of scars that was Bill Maitland's face. "I'm not sure *I* understand the danger."

"She said things have been happening."

"Things? More like dead bodies falling left and right of us. We've been followed every—"

"Who's been following you?"

"The local police. Maybe others."

"The Company?"

"I don't know. They didn't come and introduce themselves."

Maitland, suddenly agitated, began to pace the hut. "If they've traced you here…"

"Who're you hiding from? The Company? The local police?"

"To name a few."

"Which is it?"

"Everyone."

"That narrows it down."

Maitland sat down on the sleeping pallet and rested his head in his hands. "I wanted to be left alone. That's all. Just left alone."

Guy gazed at that scarred scalp and wondered why he felt no pity. Surely the man deserved at least a little pity. But at that instant, all Guy felt was irritation that Maitland was thinking only of himself. Willy had a right to a better father, he thought.

"Your daughter's already found you," he said. "You can't change that. You can't shove her back into the past."

"I don't want to. I'm glad she found me!"

"Yet you never bothered to tell her you were alive."

"I couldn't." Maitland looked up, his eyes full of pain. "There were lives at stake, people I had to protect. Lan, the children—"

"Who's going to hurt them?" Guy moved in, confronted him. "It's been twenty years, and you're still scared. Why? What kind of business were you in?"

"I was just a pawn—I flew the planes, that's all. I never gave a damn about the cargo!"

"What *was* the cargo? Drugs? Arms?"

"Sometimes."

"Which?"

"Both."

Guy's voice hardened. "And which side took delivery?"

Maitland sat up sharply. "I never did business with the enemy! I only followed orders!"

"What *were* your orders on that last flight?"

"To deliver a passenger."

"Interesting cargo. Who was he?"

"His name didn't show up on the manifest. I figured he was some Lao VIP. As it turned out, he was marked for death." He swallowed. "It wasn't the enemy fire that brought us down. A bomb went off in our hold. Planted by *our* side. We were meant to die."

"Why?"

There was a long silence. At last, Maitland rose and went to the doorway. There he stared out at the circle of huts. "I think it's time we talked to the elders."

"What can they tell me?"

Maitland turned and looked at him. "Everything."

LAN'S BABY WAS CRYING in a corner of the hut. She put it to her breast and rocked back and forth, cooing, yet all the time listening intently to the voices whispering in the shadows.

They were all listening—the children, the families. Willy couldn't understand what was being said, but she could tell the discussion held a frightening significance.

In the center of the hut sat three village elders—two men and a woman—their ancient faces veiled in a swirl of smoke from the joss sticks. The woman puffed on a cigarette as she muttered in Vietnamese. She gestured toward the sky, then to Maitland.

Guy whispered to Willy. "She's saying it wasn't your father's time to die. But the other two men, the American and the Lao, they died because that was the death they were fated all their lives to meet...." He fell silent, mesmerized by the old woman's voice. The sound seemed to drift like incense smoke, curling in the shadows.

One of the old men spoke, his voice so soft, it was almost lost in the shifting and whispers of the audience.

"He disagrees," said Guy. "He says it wasn't fate that killed the Lao."

The old woman vehemently shook her head. Now there was a general debate about why the Lao had really died. The dissenting old man at last rose and shuffled to a far corner of the hut. There he pulled aside the matting that covered the earthen floor, brushed aside a layer of dirt and withdrew a cloth-wrapped bundle. With shaking hands he pulled apart the ragged edges. Reverently, he held out the object within.

Even in the gloom of the hut, the sheen of gold was unmistakable.

"It's the medallion," whispered Willy. "The one Lassiter told us about."

"The Lao was wearing it," said her father.

The old man handed the bundle to Guy. Gingerly, Guy lifted the medallion from its bed of worn cloth. Though the surface was marred by slag from the explosion, the design was still discernable: a three-headed dragon, fangs bared, claws poised for battle.

The old man whispered words of awe and wonder.

"He saw a medallion just like it once before," said Maitland. "Years ago, in Laos. It was hanging around the neck of Prince Souvanna."

Guy took in a sharp breath. "It's the royal crest. That passenger—"

"Was the king's half brother," said Maitland. "Prince Lo Van."

An uneasy murmur rippled through the gathering.

"I don't understand," said Willy. "Why would the Company want him dead?"

"It doesn't make sense," said Guy. "Lo Van was a

neutral, shifting to our side. And he was straight-arrow, a clean leader. With our backing, he could've carved us a foothold in Laos. That might have tipped the scales in our favor.''

"That's what he was *meant* to do," said Maitland. "That crate of gold was his. To be dropped in Laos."

"To buy an army?" asked Willy.

"Exactly."

"Then why assassinate him? He was on our side, so—"

"But the guys who blew up the plane weren't," said Guy.

"You mean the Communists planted that bomb?"

"No, someone more dangerous. One of ours."

The elders had fallen silent. They were watching their guests, studying them the way a teacher watches a pupil struggle for answers.

Once again the old woman began to speak. Maitland translated.

"'During the war, some of us lived with the Pathet Lao, the Communists in Laos. There were few places to hide, so we slept in caves. But we had gardens and chickens and pigs, everything we needed to survive. Once, when I was new to the cave, I heard a plane. I thought it was the enemy, the Americans, and I took my rifle and went out to shoot it down. But my cell commander stopped me. I could not understand why he let the plane land. It had enemy markings, the American flag. Our cell commander ordered us to unload the plane. We carried off crates of guns and ammunition. Then we loaded the plane with opium, bags and bags of it. An exchange of goods, I thought. This must be a stolen plane. But then the pilot stepped out, and I saw his face. He was neither Lao nor Vietnamese. He was like you. An American.'''

"Friar Tuck," said Guy softly.

The woman looked at them, her eyes dark and un-readable.

"I've seen him, too," said Maitland. "I was being held in a camp just west of here when he landed to make an exchange. I tell you, the whole damn country was an opium factory, money being made left and right on both sides. All under cover of war. I think that's why Lo Van was killed. To keep the place in turmoil. There's nothing like a dirty war to hide your profits."

"Who else has seen the pilot's face?" Guy asked in Viet-namese, looking around the room. "Who else remembers what he looked like?"

A man and a woman, huddled in a corner, slowly raised their hands. Perhaps there were others, too timid to reveal themselves.

"There were four other POWs in that camp with me," said Maitland. "They saw the pilot's face. As far as I know, not a single one made it home alive."

The joss sticks had burned down to ashes, but the smoke still hung in the gloom. No one made a sound, not even the children.

That's why you're afraid, thought Willy, gazing at the circle of faces. *Even now, after all these years, the war casts its shadow over your lives.*

And mine.

"COME BACK WITH US, Maitland," said Guy. "Tell your story. It's the only way to put it behind you. To be free."

Maitland stood in the doorway of his hut, staring out at the children playing in the courtyard.

"Guy's right," said Willy. "You can't spend your life in hiding. It's time to end it."

Her father turned and looked at her. "What about Lan?

The children? If I leave, how do I know the Vietnamese will ever let me back into the country?''

"It's a risk you have to take," said Guy.

"Be a hero—is that what you're telling me?" Maitland shook his head. "Let me tell *you* something, Barnard. The real heroes of this world aren't the guys who go out and take stupid risks. No, they're the ones who hang in where they're needed, where they belong. Maybe life gets a little dull. Maybe the wife and kids drive 'em crazy. But they hang in." He looked meaningfully at Willy, then back at Guy. "Believe me. I've made enough mistakes to know."

Maitland looked back at his daughter. "Tonight, you both go back to Hanoi. You've got to go home, get on with your own life, Willy."

"*If* she gets home," said Guy.

Maitland was silent.

"What do you think her chances are?" Guy pressed him mercilessly. "Think about it. You suppose they'll leave her alone knowing what she knows? You think they'll let her live?"

"So call me a coward!" Maitland blurted out. "Call me any damn name you please. It won't change things. I can't leave this time." He fled the hut.

Through the doorway, they saw him cross the courtyard to where Lan now sat beneath the trees. Lan smiled and handed their baby to her husband. For a long time he sat there, rocking his daughter, holding her tightly to his chest, as though he feared someone might wrench her from his grasp.

You have the world right there in your arms, Willy thought, watching him. *You'd be crazy to let it go.*

"We have to change his mind," said Guy. "We have to get him to come back with us."

At that instant Lan looked up, and her gaze met Willy's.

"He's not coming back, Guy," Willy said. "He belongs here."

"You're his family, too," Guy protested.

"But not the one who needs him now." She leaned her head in the doorway. A leaf fluttered down from the trees and tumbled across the courtyard. A bare-bottomed baby toddled after it. "For twenty years I've hated that man...." She sighed. And then she smiled. "I guess it's time I finally grew up."

"SOMETHING'S WRONG. Andersen should've been back by now."

Maitland stood at the edge of the jungle and peered up the dirt road. From where the doctor's jeep had been parked, tire tracks led northward. The branches he'd used for camouflage lay scattered at the roadside. But there was no sign of a vehicle.

Willy and Guy wandered onto the road, where they stood puzzling over Andersen's delay.

"He knows you're waiting for him," said Maitland. "He's already an hour late."

Guy kicked a pebble and watched it skitter into the bushes. "Looks like we're not going back to Hanoi tonight. Not without a ride." He glanced up at the darkening sky. "It's almost sunset. I think it's time to head back to the village."

Maitland didn't move. He was still staring up the road.

"He might have a flat tire," said Willy. "Or he ran out of gas. Either way, Dad, it looks like you're stuck with us tonight." She reached out and threaded her arm in his. "Guy's right. It's time to go back."

"Not yet."

Willy smiled. "Are you that anxious to get rid of us?"

"What?" He glanced at his daughter. "No, no, of

course not. It's just…'' He gazed up the road again. ''Something doesn't feel right.''

Willy watched him, suddenly sharing his uneasiness. ''You think there's trouble.''

''And we're not ready for it,'' he said grimly.

''What do you mean?'' said Guy, turning to look at him. ''The village must have some sort of defenses.''

''We have maybe one working pistol, a few old war relics that haven't been used in decades. Plus Andersen's rifle. He left it today.''

''How many rounds?''

''Not enough to—'' Maitland's chin suddenly snapped up. He spun around at the sound of an approaching car.

''Hit the deck!'' Guy commanded.

Willy was already leaping for the cover of the nearest bush. At the same instant, Guy and Maitland sprang in the other direction, into the foliage across the road from her.

She barely made it to cover in time. Just as she landed in the dirt, a jeep rounded the bend. Through the tangle of underbrush, she saw that it was filled with soldiers. As it roared closer, she tunneled frantically under the branches, mindless of the thorns clawing her face, and curled up among the leaves to wait for the jeep to pass. Something scurried across her hand. Instinctively she flinched and saw a fat black beetle drop off and scuttle into the shadows. Only then, as her gaze followed the insect, did she notice the strange chattering in the branches and she saw that the earth itself seemed to shudder with movement.

Dear God, she was lying in a whole nest of them!

Choking back a scream, she jerked sideways.

And found herself staring at a human hand. It lay not six inches from her nose, the fingers chalk white and frozen into a beckoning claw.

Even if she'd wanted to scream, she couldn't have uttered a sound; her throat had clamped down beyond all hope of any cry. Slowly her gaze traveled along the arm, followed it to the torso, and then, inexorably, to the face. Gunnel Andersen's lifeless eyes stared back at her.

CHAPTER THIRTEEN

THE SOLDIERS' jeep roared past.

Willy muffled her cry with her fist, desperately fighting the shriek of horror that threatened to explode inside her. She fought it so hard her teeth drew blood from her knuckles. The instant the jeep had passed, her control shattered. She stumbled to her feet and staggered backward.

"He's dead!" she cried.

Guy and her father appeared at her side. She felt Guy's arm slip around her waist, anchoring her against him. "What are you talking about?"

"Andersen!" She pointed wildly at the bushes.

Her father dropped to the ground and shoved aside the branches. "Dear God," he whispered, staring at the body.

The trees seemed to wobble around her. Willy slid to her knees. The whole jungle spun in a miserable kaleidoscope of green as she retched into the dirt.

She heard her father say, in a strangely flat voice, "His throat's been cut."

"Clean job. Very professional," Guy muttered. "Looks like he's been here for hours."

Willy managed to raise her head. "Why? Why did they kill him?"

Her father let the bushes slip back over the body. "To keep him from talking. To cut us off from—" He suddenly sprang to his feet. "The village! I've got to get back!"

"Dad! Wait—"

But her father had already dashed into the jungle.

Guy tugged her up by the arm. "We've gotta move. Come on."

She followed him, running and stumbling behind him on the footpath. The sun was already setting; through the branches, the sky glowed a frightening bloodred.

Just ahead, she heard her father shouting, "Lan! Lan!" As they emerged from the jungle, they saw a dozen villagers gathered, watching as Maitland pulled his wife into his arms and held her.

"These people have got to get out of here!" Guy yelled. "Maitland! Tell them, for God's sake! They've got to leave!"

Maitland released his wife and turned to Guy. "Where the hell are we supposed to go? The next village is twenty miles from here! We've got old people, babies." He pointed to a woman with a swollen belly. "Look at her! You think *she* can walk twenty miles?"

"She has to. We all have to."

Maitland turned away, but Guy pulled him around, forcing him to listen. "Think about it! They've killed Andersen. You're next. So's everyone here, everyone who knows you're alive. There's got to be somewhere we can hide!"

Maitland turned to one of the village elders and rattled out a question in Vietnamese.

The old man frowned. Then he pointed northeast, toward the mountains.

"What did he say?" asked Willy.

"He says there's a place about five kilometers from here. An old cave in the hills. They've used it before, other times, other wars...." He glanced up at the sky. "Almost sunset. We have to leave now while there's still enough light to cross the river."

Already, the villagers had scattered to gather their belongings. Centuries of war had taught them survival meant haste.

Five minutes was all the time Maitland's family took to pack. Lan presided over the dismantling of her household, the gathering of essentials—blankets, food, the precious family cooking pot. She spared no time for words or tears. Only outside, when she allowed herself a last backward glance at the hut, did her eyes brim. She swiftly, matter-of-factly, wiped away the tears.

The last light of day glimmered through the branches as the ragged gathering headed into the jungle. Twenty-four adults, eleven children and three infants, Willy counted. *And all of us scared out of our wits.*

They moved noiselessly, even the children; it was unearthly how silent they were, like ghosts flitting among the trees. At the edge of a fast-flowing river, they halted. A waterwheel spun in the current, an elegant sculpture of bamboo tubes shuttling water into irrigation sluices. The river was too deep for the little ones to ford, so the children were carried to the other bank. Soaked and muddy, they all slogged up the opposite bank and moved on toward the mountains.

Night fell. By the light of a full moon, they journeyed through a spectral land of wind and shadow where the very darkness seemed to tremble with companion spirits. By now the children were exhausted and stumbling. Still, no one had to coax them forward; the fear of pursuit was enough to keep them moving.

At last, at the base of the cliff, they halted. A giant wall of rock glowed silvery in the moonlight. The village elders conferred softly, debating which way to proceed next. It was the old woman who finally led the way. Moving unerringly through the darkness, she guided them to a set of stone steps carved into the mountain and led them up, along the cliff face to what appeared to be nothing more than a thicket of bushes.

There was a general murmur of dismay. Then one of the village men shoved aside the branches and held up a lit candle. Emptiness lay beyond. He thrust his arm into the void, into a darkness so vast, it seemed to swallow up the feeble light of the flame. They were at the mouth of a giant cavern.

The man crawled inside, only to scramble out as a flurry of wings whooshed past him. Nervous laughter rippled through the gathering.

Bats, Willy thought with a shudder.

The man took a deep breath and entered the cave. A moment later, he called for the others to follow.

Guy gave Willy a nudge. "Go on. Inside."

She swallowed, balking. "Do I have a choice?"

His answer was immediate. "None whatsoever."

THE VILLAGE WAS DESERTED.

Siang searched the huts one by one. He overturned pallets and flung aside mats, searching for the underground tunnels that were common to every village. In times of peace, those tunnels were used for storage; in times of war, they served as hiding places or escape routes. They were all empty.

In frustration, he grabbed an earthenware pot and smashed it on the ground. Then he stalked out to the courtyard where the men stood waiting in the moonlight, their faces blackened with camouflage paint.

There were fifteen of them, all crack professionals, rough-hewn Americans who towered above him. They had been flown in straight from Thailand at only an hour's notice. As expected, Laotian air defense had been a large-meshed sieve, unable to detect, much less shoot down, a lone plane flying in low through their airspace. It had taken a mere four hours to march here from their drop point just inside the Vietnamese border. The entire operation had been flawless.

Until now.

"It seems we've arrived too late," a voice said.

Siang turned to see his client emerge from the shadows, one more among this gathering of giants.

"They have had only a few hours head start," said Siang. "Their evening meals were left uneaten."

"Then they haven't gone far. Not with women and children." The man turned to one of the soldiers. "What about the prisoner? Has he talked?"

"Not a word." The soldiers shoved a village man to the ground. They had captured the man ten miles up the road, running toward Ban Dan. Or, rather, the dogs had caught him. Useful animals those hounds, and absolutely essential in an operation where a single surviving eyewitness could prove disastrous. Against such animals, the villager hadn't stood a chance of escape. Now he knelt on the ground, his black hair silvered with moonlight.

"Make him talk."

"A waste of time," grunted Siang. "These northerners are stubborn. He will tell you nothing."

One of the soldiers gave the villager a kick. Even as the man lay writhing on the ground, he managed to gasp out a string of epithets.

"What? What did he say?" demanded the soldier.

Siang shifted uneasily. "He says that we are cursed. That we are dead men."

The soldier laughed. "Superstitious crap!"

Siang looked around at the darkness. "I'm sure they sent other messengers for help. By morning—"

"By morning we'll have the job done. We'll be out of here," said his client.

"If we can find them," Siang said.

"Find a whole village? No problem." The man turned and snapped out an order to one of the soldiers. "That's what the dogs are for."

A DOZEN CANDLES FLICKERED in the cavern. Outside, the wind was blowing hard; puffs of it shuddered the blanket hanging over the cave mouth. Through the dancing shadows floated murmuring voices, the frantic whispers of a village under siege. Children gathered stones or twisted vines into rope. Women whittled stalks of bamboo, sharpening them into punji stakes. Only the babies slept. In the darkness outside, men dug the same lethal traps that had defended their homeland through the centuries. It was an axiom of jungle warfare that battles were won not by strength or weaponry but by speed and cunning and desperation.

Most of all, desperation.

"The cylinder's frozen," muttered Guy, sighting down the barrel of an ancient pistol. "You could squeeze off a single shot, that's all."

"Only two bullets left anyway," said Maitland.

"Which makes it next to worthless." Guy handed the gun back to Maitland. "Except for suicide."

For a moment Maitland weighed the pistol in his hand, thinking. He turned to his wife and spoke to her gently in Vietnamese.

Lan stared at the gun, as though afraid to touch it. Then, reluctantly, she took it and slipped away into the shadows of the cave.

Guy reached for Andersen's assault rifle and gave it a quick inspection. "At least this baby's in working order."

"Yeah. Nothing like a good old AK-47," said Maitland. "I've seen one fished out of the mud and still go right on firing."

Guy laughed. "The other side really knew how to make 'em, didn't they?" He glanced around as Willy approached. "How're you holding up?"

She sank down wearily beside him in the dirt. "We've carved enough stakes to skewer a whole army."

"We'll need more," said her father. He glanced toward the cave entrance. "My turn to do some digging...."

"I was just out there," said Guy. "Pits are all dug."

"Then they'll need help with the other traps—"

"They know what they're doing. We just get in the way."

"It's hard to belive," said Willy.

"What is?"

"That we can hold off an army with vines and bamboo."

"It's been done before," said Maitland. "Against bigger armies. And we're not out to win a war. We just have to hold out until our runners get through."

"How long will that take?"

"It's twenty miles to the next village. If they have a radio, we might get help by midmorning."

Willy gazed around at the sleeping children who, one by one, had collapsed in exhaustion. Guy touched her arm. "You need some rest, too."

"I can't sleep."

"Then just lie down. Go on."

"What about you two?"

Guy snapped an ammunition clip into place. "We'll keep watch."

She frowned at him. "You don't really think they'd find us tonight?"

"We left an easy trail all the way."

"But they'll need daylight—"

"Not if they have a local informant," said her father. "Someone who knows these caves. We found our way in the dark. So could they." He grabbed the rifle and slung it over his shoulder. "Minh and I'll take the first watch, Guy. Get some sleep."

Guy nodded. "I'll relieve you in a few hours."

After her father left, Willy's gaze shifted back to the sleeping children, to her little half brothers, now curled up in a tangle of blankets. *What will happen to them?* she wondered. *To all of us?* In a far corner, two old women whittled bamboo stalks; the scrape of their blades against the wood made Willy shiver.

"I'm scared," she whispered.

Guy nodded. The candlelight threw harsh shadows on his face. "We're all scared. Every last one of us."

"It's my fault. I can't stop thinking that if I'd just left well enough alone…"

He touched her face. "I'm the one who should feel responsible."

"Why?"

"Because I used you. For all my denials, I planned to use you. And if something were to happen to you now…"

"Or to you," she said, her hand closing over his. "Don't you ever make me weep over your body, Guy Barnard. Because I couldn't stand it. So promise me."

He pressed her hand to his mouth. "I promise. And I want you to know that, after we get out of here, I…" He smiled. "I plan to see a lot more of you. If you'll let me."

She returned the smile. "I'll insist on it."

What stupid lies we're telling each other, she thought. *Our way of pretending we have a future.* In the face of death, promises mean everything.

"What if they find us?" she whispered.

"We do what we can to stay alive."

"Sticks and stones against automatics? It should be a very quick fight."

"We have a defensible position. Traps waiting in the path. And we have some of the smartest fighters in the world on our side. Men who've held off armies with not much more than their wits." He gazed up at the darkness hovering above the feeble glow of candlelight. "This cave is said to be blessed. It's an ancient sanctuary, older than anyone can remember. Follow that tunnel back there, and you'll come out at the east base of the cliff. They're clever, these people. They never back themselves into a corner. They always leave an escape route." He looked at the families dozing in the shadows. "They've been fighting wars since the Stone Age. And they can do it in their bare feet, with only a handful of rice. When it comes to survival, *we're* the novices."

Outside, the wind howled; they could hear the trees groan, the bushes scrabbling against the cliff. One of the children cried out in his sleep, a sob of fear that was instantly stilled by his mother's embrace.

The little ones didn't understand, thought Willy. But they knew enough to be afraid.

Guy took her in his arms. Together, they sank to the ground, clinging to each other. There was no need for words; it was enough just to have him there, to feel their hearts beating together.

And in the shadows, the two old women went on whittling their stalks of bamboo.

WILLY WAS ASLEEP WHEN GUY rose to stand his watch. It wasn't easy leaving her. In the few short hours they'd clung together on the hard ground, their bodies had somehow melted together in a way that could never be reversed. Even if he never saw her again, even if she was suddenly swept out of his life, she would always be part of him.

He covered her with a blanket and slipped out into the night.

The sky was a dazzling sea of stars. He found Maitland huddled on a ledge a short way up the cliff face. Guy settled down beside him on the rock shelf.

"Dead quiet," said Maitland. "So far."

They sat together beneath the stars, listening to the wind, to the bushes thrashing against the cliff. A rock clattered down the mountain. Guy glanced up and saw, on a higher ledge, one of the village men silhouetted against the night sky.

"Did you get some sleep?" asked Maitland.

Guy shook his head. "You know, I used to be able to sleep through anything. Chopper landings. Sniper fire. But not now. Not here. I tell you, this isn't my kind of fight."

Maitland handed the rifle to Guy. "Yeah. It's a whole different war when people you love are at stake, isn't it?" He rose to his feet and walked off into the darkness.

People you love? It filled Guy with a sense of wonder, the thought that he *was* in love. Though it shouldn't surprise him. On some level, he'd known it all along: he had fallen hard for Bill Maitland's daughter.

It was something he'd never planned on, something he'd certainly never wanted. He wasn't even sure *love* was the right word for what he felt. They'd just spent a week together in hell. *And in heaven,* he thought, remembering that night in the hut, under the mosquito net. He knew he couldn't stand the thought of her being hurt, that he'd do anything to keep her safe. Was *love* the name for that feeling?

Somewhere in the night, an animal screamed.

He tightened his grip on the rifle.

Four more hours until dawn.

AT FIRST LIGHT the attack came.

Guy had already handed the rifle to the next man on watch and was starting down the cliff face when a shot rang out. Sheer reflexes sent him diving for cover. As he scrambled behind a clump of bushes, he heard more automatic gunfire and a scream from the ledge above, and he knew his relief man had been hit. He peered up to see how badly the man was hurt. Through fingers of morning mist, he could make out the man's bloodied arm dangling lifelessly over the ledge. More gunfire erupted, spattering the cliff face. There was no return fire; the village's only rifle now lay in the hands of a dead man.

Guy glanced down and saw the other villagers scrambling for cover among the rocks. Unarmed, how long could they defend the cave? It was the booby traps they were counting on now, the trip wires and the pits and the stakes that would hold off the attackers.

Guy looked up at the ledge where the rifle lay. That precious AK-47 could make all the difference in the world between survival and slaughter.

He spotted a boulder a few yards up, with a few scraggly bushes as cover along the way. There was no other route, no other choice. He crouched, tensing for the dash to first base.

WILLY WAS STIRRING a simmering pot of rice and broth when she heard the gunshots. Her first thought as she leapt to her feet was, *Guy. Dear God, has he been hurt?*

But before she could take two steps, her father grabbed her arm. "No, Willy!"

"He may need help—"

"You can't go out there!" He called for his wife. Somehow, Lan heard him through the bedlam and, taking her arm, pulled Willy toward the back of the cave. Already the other women were herding the children into the escape tunnel. Willy could only watch helplessly as the men grabbed what primitive weapons they had and scrambled outside.

More gunfire thundered in the distance, and rocks clattered down the mountainside.

Where's our return fire? she thought. *Why isn't anyone firing back?*

Outside, something skittered across the ground and popped. A finger of smoke wafted into the cave, its vapor so sickening it made Willy reel backward, gasping for air.

"Get back, get back!" her father yelled. "Into the tunnel, all of you!"

"What about Guy?"

"He can take care of himself! Go and get the kids out of here!" He gave her a brutal shove into the tunnel. *"Move!"*

There was no other choice. But as she turned to flee and heard the rattle of new gunfire, she felt she was abandoning a part of herself on the embattled cliff.

The children had already slipped into the tunnel. Just ahead, Willy could hear a baby crying. Following the sound, she plunged into pitch blackness.

A light suddenly flickered in the passage. It was a candle. By the flame's glow, she saw the leathery face of the old woman who'd guided them to the cave. She was now leading the frightened procession of women and children.

Willy, bringing up the rear, could barely keep track of the candle's glow. The old woman moved swiftly; obviously, she knew where she was going. Perhaps she'd fled this way before, in another battle, another war. It offered some small comfort to know they were following in the footsteps of a survivor.

The first step down was a surprise. For an instant, Willy's heel met nothingness, then it landed on slippery stone. How much farther? she wondered as she reached out to steady herself against the tunnel wall. Her fingers met clumps of dried wax, the drippings of ancient candles. How many others before her had felt their way down these steps, had stumbled in terror through these passages? The fear of all those countless other refugees seemed to permeate the darkness.

The tunnel took a sharp left and moved ever downward. She wondered how far they'd come; it began to seem like miles. The sound of gunfire had faded to a distant *tap-tap-tap*. She wouldn't let herself think about what was happening outside; she could only concentrate on that tiny pinpoint of light flickering far ahead.

Suddenly the light seemed to flare brighter, exploding into a dazzling luminescence. No, she realized with sudden wonder as she rounded the curve. It wasn't the candle. It was daylight!

Murmurs of joy echoed through the passageway. All at once, they were all scrambling forward, dashing toward the exit and into the blinding sunshine.

Outside, Willy stood blinking painfully at trees and sky and mountainside. They were on the other side of the cliff. Safe. For now.

Gunfire rattled in the distance.

The old woman ordered them forward, into the jungle. At first Willy didn't understand the urgency. Was there some new danger she hadn't recognized? Then she heard what was frightening the old woman: dogs.

Now the others heard the barking, too. Panic sent them all dashing into the forest. Lan alone didn't move. Willy spotted her standing perfectly still. Lan appeared to be listening to the dogs, gauging their direction, their distance. Her two boys, alarmed by their mother's refusal to run, stood watching her in confusion.

Lan shoved her sons forward, commanding them to flee. The boys shook their heads; they wouldn't leave without their mother. Lan gave the baby to her eldest son, then gave both boys another push. The younger boy was crying now, shaking his head, clinging to her sleeve. But his mother's command could not be disobeyed. Sobbing, he was led away by his older brother to join the other children in flight.

"What are you doing?" Willy cried. Had the woman gone mad?

Calmly, Lan turned to face the sound of the dogs.

Willy glanced ahead at the forest, saw the children fleeing through the trees. They were so small, so helpless. How far would they get?

She looked back at Lan, who was now purposefully shuffling through the dirt, circling back toward the dogs. Suddenly Willy understood what Lan was doing. She was leaving her scent for the dogs. Trying to make them follow her, to draw them away from the children. By this action, this choice, the woman was offering herself as a sacrifice.

The barking grew louder. Every instinct Willy possessed told her to run. But she thought of Guy and her father, of how willingly, how automatically they had assumed the role of protectors, had offered themselves to the enemy. She saw the last of the children vanish into the jungle. They needed time, time no one else could give them.

She, too, began to stamp around in the dirt.

Lan glanced back in surprise and saw what Willy was doing. They didn't exchange a word; just that look, that sad and knowing smile between women, was enough.

Willy ripped a sleeve off her blouse and trampled the torn cloth into the dirt. The dogs would surely pick up the scent. Then she turned and headed south, back along the cliff base. Away from the children. Lan, too, headed away from the villagers' escape route.

Willy didn't hurry. After all, she was no longer running for *her* life. She wondered how long it would take for the dogs to catch up. And when they did, how long she could hold them off. A weapon was what she needed. A club, a stick. She snatched up a fallen branch, tore off the twigs and swung it a few times. It was good and heavy; it would make the dogs think twice. Prey she might be, but she'd damn well fight back.

The barking grew steadily closer, a demon sound, relentless and terrifying. But now it mingled with something else, a rhythmic, monotonous thumping that, as it grew louder, seemed to make the ground itself shudder. Not gunfire…

A helicopter!

Wild with hope, she glanced up at the sky and saw, in the distance, a pair of black specks against the vista of morning blue. Was it the rescue party they'd been waiting for?

She scrambled up on a mound of rocks and began waving her arms. It was their only chance—Guy's only chance—for survival.

All her attention focused on those two black pinpricks hovering in the morning sky, she didn't see the dogs moving in until it was too late.

A flash of brown shot across her peripheral vision. She jerked around as a pair of jaws lunged straight for her throat. Her response was purely reflex. She twisted away and a hundred pounds of fur and teeth slammed into her shoulder. Thrown to the ground, she could only cry out as powerful jaws clamped onto her arm.

Footsteps thudded close. A voice shouted, "Back off! I said back *off!*"

The dog released her and stood back, growling.

Slowly Willy raised her head and saw two men in camouflage garb towering above her. *Americans,* she thought in confusion. What were they doing here?

Rough hands hauled her to her feet. "Where are the others?" one of the men demanded.

"You're hurting me—"

"Where are the others?"

"There are no others!" she screamed.

His savage blow knocked her back to the ground. Too dazed to move, she sprawled helplessly at their feet and fought to clear her head.

"Finish her off."

No, she thought. *Please, no...*

But she knew that no amount of begging would change their minds. She lay there, hugging herself, waiting for the end.

Then the other soldier said, "Not yet. She might come in handy."

She was dragged back to her feet to stand, sick and swaying, before them.

An expressionless face, blackened with camouflage grease, stared down at her. "Let's see what the good Friar thinks."

CHAPTER FOURTEEN

MADE IT TO THIRD BASE. Time to go for that home run.

Guy, sprawled behind a boulder, scouted out the next twenty yards to the gun. His only cover would be a few bushes and, midway, a pathetic excuse for a tree. He could see the AK-47's barrel extending over the rock ledge, so close, he could practically spit at it, but still beyond reach.

Slowly, he rose to a crouch and got ready for the final dash.

Gunfire splattered the cliff. Instantly, he flopped back to the dirt. *This is a crazy-ass idea, Barnard. The dumbest idea you've ever had.*

He glanced below and saw Maitland trying to signal him. What the hell was he trying to say? Guy couldn't be sure, but Maitland seemed to be telling him to wait, to hold on. But there was so little time left. Already, Guy spotted men in camouflage fatigues moving through the brush toward the cliff base. Toward the first booby trap. *God, slow 'em down. Give us time.*

He heard, rather than saw, the first victim drop into the trap. A shriek echoed off the cliff face, the cry of a man who had just slid into a bed of stakes. Now there were other shouts, curses, the sounds of confusion as soldiers dragged their injured comrade to safety.

Just a taste, fellas, Guy thought with a grim sense of satisfaction. *Wait till you see what comes next.*

The attackers didn't delay long. A shouted order sent a

half-dozen soldiers scrambling up the cliff path, closer and closer to the second trap: a trip wire poised to unleash a falling tree trunk. But now the attackers were warned; they knew that every step was a gamble, and they were searching for hazards, considering every rock, every bush with the practiced eyes of men well versed in jungle combat.

We're almost down to our last resort, thought Guy. *Prayer.*

Then he heard it. They all heard it. A familiar rumble that made them turn their gazes to the sky. Choppers.

That was the instant Guy ran, when everyone's eyes were focused on the heavens. His sudden dash took the soldiers by surprise, left them only a split second to respond. Then the maelstrom broke loose as bullets chewed the ground, throwing up a storm cloud of dust. By then he was halfway to his goal, scrambling through the last thicket. Time seemed to slow down. Each step took an eternity. He saw puffs of dirt explode near his feet, heard a far-off shriek and the thud of the poised tree trunk, the second trap, slamming onto the soldiers in the path.

He launched himself through the air and tumbled onto the ledge. Time leapt to fast forward. He yanked the AK-47 out of the dead man's grasp, took aim and began firing.

One soldier, standing exposed below, went down at once. The others beat a fast retreat into the jungle. Two lay dead on the path, victims of the latest booby trap.

Welcome to the Stone Age, Rambo.

Guy held his fire as the attackers slipped out of view and into the cover of trees. He watched, waiting for any flash of movement, any sign of a renewed attack. A standoff?

He turned his gaze to the sky and searched for the choppers. To his dismay, they were moving away; already they had faded to mere specks. In despair he watched them slip away into a field of relentless blue.

Then, from below, he heard shouts in Vietnamese and saw smoke spiral up the cliff face, the blackest, most glorious smoke he'd seen in his whole damn life. The villagers had set the mountainside on fire!

Quickly he scanned the heavens again, hoping, praying. Within seconds he spotted them, like two flies hovering just above the horizon. Was it only wishful thinking, or were they actually moving closer?

A new hint of movement at the bottom of the cliff drew his attention. He looked down to see two figures emerge from the forest and approach the cliff base. Automatically, he swung his gun barrel to the target and was about to squeeze off a round when he saw who it was standing below. His finger froze on the trigger.

A man stood clutching a human shield in front of him. Even from that distance, Guy recognized the prisoner's face, could see her blanched and helpless expression.

"Drop it, Barnard!" The command of an unseen man, hidden among the trees, echoed off the mountainside. The voice was disturbingly familiar.

Guy remained frozen in the pose of a marksman, his finger on the trigger, his cheek pressed against the rifle. Frantically he wracked his brain for a plan, for some way to pull Willy out of this alive. A trade? It was the only possibility: her life for his. Would they go for it?

"I said *drop it!*" the disembodied voice shouted.

Willy's captor raised a pistol barrel to her head.

"Or would you like to see what a bullet will do to that pretty face?"

"Wait!" Guy screamed. "We can trade—"

"No deals."

The barrel was pressed to Willy's temple.

"No!" Guy's voice, harsh with panic, reverberated off the cliff.

"Then drop the gun. *Now*."

Guy let the AK-47 fall to the ground.

"Kick it away. Go on!"

Guy gave the gun a kick. It tumbled off the ledge and clattered to the rocks below.

"Out where I can see you. Come on, come on!"

Slowly, Guy rose to his full height, expecting an instantaneous hail of bullets.

"Now come down. Off the cliff. You, too, Maitland! I haven't got all day, so *move*."

Guy made his way down the cliff path. By the time he reached bottom, Maitland was already waiting there, his arms hooked behind his head in surrender. Guy's first concern was Willy. He could see she'd been hurt; her shirt was torn and bloodied, her face alarmingly white. But the look she gave him was one of heartwrenching courage, a look that said, *Don't worry about me. I'm okay. And I love you.*

Her captor smiled and let the pistol barrel drop from her head. Guy instantly recognized his face: it was the same man he'd tackled on the terrace of the hotel in Bangkok. The Thai assassin—or was he Vietnamese?

"Hello, Guy," said a shockingly familiar voice.

A man strolled into the sunshine, a man whose powerful shoulders seemed to strain against the fabric of his camouflage fatigues.

Maitland took in a startled breath. "It's him," he murmured. "Friar Tuck."

"Toby?" said Guy.

"Both," said Tobias Wolff, smiling. He stood before them, his expression hovering somewhere between tri-

umph and regret. "I didn't want to kill you, Guy. In fact,
I've done everything I could to avoid it."

Guy let out a bitter laugh. "Why?"

"I owed you. Remember?"

Guy frowned at Toby's legs, noticing there were no
braces, no crutches. "You can walk."

Toby shrugged. "You know how it is in army hospitals.
The surgeons gave me the bad news, said there was nothing they could do and then they walked away. Shoved me
into a corner and forgot about me. But I wasn't a lost
cause, after all. First I got the feeling back in my toes.
Then I could move them. Oh, I never bothered to tell Uncle
Sam. It gave me the freedom to carry on with my business.
That's the nice thing about being a paraplegic. No one
suspects you of a damn thing." He grinned. "Plus, I get
that monthly disability check."

"A real fortune."

"It's the principle of things. Uncle Sam owes me for
all those years of loyal service." He glanced at Maitland.
"He was the only detail that worried me. The last witness
from Flight 5078. I'd heard he was alive. I just didn't know
how to find him."

He squinted up at the sky as the rumble of the choppers
drew closer. They were moving in, attracted by the smoke
from the cliff fire. "Time's up," said Toby. Turning, he
yelled to his men, "Move out!"

At once, the soldiers started into the woods in a calm
but hasty retreat. Toby looked at the hit man and nodded.
"Mr. Siang, you know what to do."

Siang shoved Willy forward. Guy caught her in his
arms; together, they dropped to their knees. There was no
time left for last words, for farewells. Guy wrapped himself around her in a futile attempt to shield her from the
bullets.

"Finish it," said Toby.

Guy looked up at him. "I'll see you in hell."

Siang raised the pistol. The barrel was aimed squarely at Guy's head. Still cradling Willy, Guy waited for the explosion. The darkness.

The blast of the pistol made them both flinch.

In wonderment, Guy realized he was still kneeling, still breathing. *What the hell? Am I still alive? Are we both still alive?*

He looked up in time to see Siang, shirt bloodied, crumple to the ground.

"There! She's there!" Toby shouted, pointing at the trees.

In the shadow of the forest they saw her, clutching the ancient pistol in both hands. Lan stood very still, as though shocked by what she'd just done.

One of the soldiers took aim at her.

"No!" screamed Maitland, flinging himself at the gunman.

The shot went wild; Maitland and the soldier thudded to the ground, locked in combat.

From the cliff above came shouts; Guy and Willy hit the dirt as arrows rained down. Toby cried out and fell. What remained of his army scattered in confusion.

In the melee, Guy and Willy managed to crawl to cover. But as they rolled behind a boulder, Willy suddenly realized her father hadn't followed them.

"Dad!" she screamed.

A dozen yards away, Maitland lay bloodied. Willy turned to go to him, but Guy dragged her back down.

"Are you nuts?" he yelled.

"I can't leave him there!"

"Wait till we're clear!"

"He's hurt!"

"There's nothing you can do!"

She was sobbing now, trying to wrench free, but her protests were drowned out by the *whomp-whomp* of the helicopters moving in. An army chopper hovered just above them. The pilot lowered the craft through a slot in the trees. Gently, the skids settled to the ground.

The instant it touched down, a half-dozen Vietnamese soldiers jumped out, followed by their commanding officer. He pointed at Maitland and barked out orders. Two soldiers hurried to the wounded man.

"Let me go," Willy said and she broke free of Guy's grasp.

He watched her run to her father's side. The soldiers had already opened their medical field kit, and a stretcher was on the way. Guy's gaze shifted back to the chopper as one last passenger stepped slowly to the ground. Head bowed beneath the spinning blades, the old man made his way toward Guy.

For a long time, they stood together, both of them silent as they regarded the rising cloud of smoke. The flames seemed to engulf the mountain itself as the last of the village men scrambled down the cliff path to safety.

"A most impressive signal fire," said Minister Tranh. He looked at Guy. "You are unhurt?"

Guy nodded. "We lost some people…up on the mountain. And the children—I don't know if they're all right. But I guess…I think…"

He turned and watched as Willy followed her father's stretcher toward the chopper. At the doorway, she stopped and looked back at Guy.

He started toward her, his arms aching to embrace her. He wanted to tell her all the things he'd been afraid to say, the things he'd never said to any woman. He had to tell her now, while he still had the chance, while she was still there for him to touch, to hold.

A soldier suddenly blocked Guy's way and commanded, "Stay back!"

Dust stung Guy's eyes as the chopper's rotor began to spin. Through the tornadolike wash of whirling leaves and branches, Guy saw a soldier in the chopper shout at Willy to climb aboard. With one last backward glance, she obeyed. Time had run out.

Through the open doorway, Guy could still see her face gazing out at him. With a sense of desolation, he watched the helicopter rise into the sky, taking with it the woman he loved. Long after the roar of the blades had faded to silence, he was staring up at that cloudless field of blue.

Sighing, he turned back to Minister Tranh. That's when he noticed that someone else, just as desolate, had watched the chopper's departure. At the forest edge stood Lan, her gaze turned to the sky. At least she, too, had survived.

"We are glad to find you alive," Minister Tranh said.

"How *did* you find us?" Guy asked.

"One of the men from the village reached Na Khoang early this morning. We'd been concerned about you. And when you vanished…" Minister Tranh shook his head. "You have a talent for making things difficult, Mr. Barnard. For us, at least."

"I had to. I didn't know who to trust." Guy looked at the other man. "I still don't know who to trust."

Minister Tranh considered this statement for a moment. Then he said quietly, "Do we ever really know?"

"A TOAST," SAID Dodge Hamilton, leaning against the hotel bar. "To the good fight!"

Guy stared down moodily at his whiskey glass and said,

"There's no such thing as a good fight, Hamilton. There are only fights you can't avoid."

"Well—" grinning, Hamilton raised his drink "—then let's drink to the unavoidable."

That made Guy laugh, though it was the last thing he felt like doing. He supposed he *ought* to be celebrating. The ordeal was over, and for the first time in days, he felt human again. After a good night's sleep, a shower and a shave, he could once again stand the sight of his own face in the mirror. *For all the difference it makes,* he thought bleakly. *She's not here to notice.*

He was having a hell of a time adjusting to Willy's absence. Over and over he replayed that last image of her sad backward glance as she'd climbed into the chopper. No last words, no goodbyes, just that look. He wished he could erase the image from his memory.

No, no, that wasn't what he wanted.

What he wanted was another chance.

He set the whiskey glass down and forced a smile to his lips. "Anyway, Hamilton," he said, "looks like you got your story, after all."

"Not quite the one I expected."

"Think it's front-page material?"

"Indeed! It has everything. Old war ghosts come to life. Ex-enemies joining sides. *And* a happy ending! A story that ought to be heard. But…" He sighed. "It'll probably get shoved to the back page to make room for some juicy royal scandal. As if the fate of the world depends on who does what to whom in Buckingham."

Guy shook his head and chuckled. Some things, it seemed, never changed.

"He'll be all right, won't he? Maitland?"

Guy looked up. "I think so. Willy called me from Bang-

kok a few hours ago. Maitland's stable enough to be transferred.''

"They're flying him to the States?''

"Tonight.''

Hamilton cocked his head. "Aren't you joining them?''

"I don't know. I've got a job to wrap up, a few last
minute details. And she'll be busy with other things.…''

He looked down at his whiskey and thought of that last
phone conversation. They'd had a lousy connection, lots
of static on the line, and they'd both been forced to shout.
She'd been standing at a hospital telephone; he'd been on
his way out to meet Vietnamese officials. It had hardly
been the time for romantic conversation. Yet he'd been
ready to say anything, if only she'd given him some hint
that she wanted to hear it. But there'd been only awkward
how-are-yous and is-your-arm-all-right and yes-it's-fine-
I'm-all-patched-up-now and then, in the end, a hasty goodbye.

When he'd hung up the receiver, he'd known she was
gone. *Maybe it's for the best,* he thought. Every idiot knew
wartime romances never lasted. When you were huddled
together in the trenches and the bullets were whizzing
overhead, it was easy to fall in love.

But now they were back in the real world. She didn't
need him any longer, and he liked to think he didn't need
her either. After all, he'd never needed anyone before.

He drained his whiskey glass. "Anyway, Hamilton,'' he
said, "I guess I'll have a hell of a story to tell the guys
back home. How I fought in Nam all over again—this time
with the other side.''

"No one'll believe you.''

"Probably not.'' Guy looked off at a painting on the
wall—Ho Chi Minh smiling like someone's merry uncle.
"You know, I have a confession to make.'' He looked

back at his drinking partner. "At one point, I was so paranoid that I thought *you* were the CIA."

Hamilton burst out laughing.

"Can you believe it?" Guy said, laughing as well. "You of all people!"

Hamilton, still grinning, set his glass down on the counter. "Actually," he said after a pause, "I am."

There was a long silence. "What?" said Guy.

Hamilton gazed back, his expression blandly pleasant and utterly unrevealing. "General Kistner sends his regards. He's happy to hear you're alive and well."

"Kistner sent you?"

"No, he sent *you.*"

Guy stiffened. "You got it wrong. I don't work for those people. I was on my own the whole—"

"Were you, now?" Hamilton's smile was maddening. "Quite a stroke of luck, wouldn't you say, that meeting between you and Miss Maitland at Kistner's villa? Damned odd about her driver vanishing like that, just as you were heading back to town."

Guy looked down at his glass, swirled the whiskey. "I *was* set up," he muttered. "That mysterious appointment with Kistner—"

"Was to get you and Miss Maitland together. She was in dangerous waters, already floundering. We knew she'd need help. But it had to be someone completely unconnected with the Company, someone the Vietnamese wouldn't suspect. As it turned out, *you* were it."

Guy's fists tightened on the countertop. "I did your dirty work—"

"You did Uncle Sam a favor. We knew you were slated to go to Saigon. That you knew the country. A bit of the language. We also knew you had a…shall we say, *vulnerable* aspect to your past." He gave Guy a significant look.

They know, Guy thought. *They've probably always known.* Slowly, he said, "That visit from the Ariel Group…"

"Ah, yes. Ariel. Lovely ring to it, don't you think? It happens to be the name of General Kistner's youngest granddaughter." Hamilton smiled. "You needn't worry, Guy. We can be discreet. Especially when we feel we've been well served."

"What if you'd been wrong about me? What if I was working for Toby Wolff? I could have killed her."

"You wouldn't."

"I had a 'vulnerable' aspect to my past, remember?"

"You're clean, Guy. Even with your past, you're cleaner than any flag-waving patriot in Washington."

"How would you know?"

Hamilton shrugged. "You'd be amazed at the things we know about you. About everyone."

"But you couldn't predict what I'd do! What Willy would do. What if she'd told me to go to hell?"

"It was a gamble. But she's an attractive woman. And you're a resourceful man. We took a chance on chemistry."

And it worked, thought Guy. *Damn you, Hamilton, the chemistry worked just fine.*

"At any rate," said Hamilton, sliding a few bills onto the bar, "you'll be rewarded with the silence you crave. I'm afraid the bounty's out of the question, though— budget deficit and all. But you'll have the distinct pleasure of knowing you served your country well."

That's when Guy burst into unstoppable laughter. He laughed so hard, tears came to his eyes; so loud, a dozen heads turned to look at him.

"Have I missed the joke?" Hamilton inquired politely.

"The joke," said Guy, "is on me."

He laughed all the way out the door.

CHAPTER FIFTEEN

HER FATHER, once again, was leaving.

Early on a rainy morning, Willy stood in the bedroom doorway and watched him pack his suitcase, the way she'd watched him pack it long ago. She'd had him home such a short time, only a few days since his release from the hospital. And he'd spent every moment pining for his family—his other family. Oh, he hadn't complained or been unkind, but she'd seen the sadness in his gaze, heard his sighs as he'd wandered about the house. She'd known it was inevitable: that he'd be walking out of her life again.

He took one last look in the closet, then turned to the dresser.

She glanced down at a pair of brand-new loafers that he'd set aside in the closet. "Dad, aren't you taking your shoes?" she asked.

"At home, I don't wear shoes."

"Oh." *This used to be your home,* she thought.

She wandered into the living room, sat down by the window and stared out at the rain. It seemed as if a lifetime of sorrow had been crammed into these past two weeks she'd been home. While her father had recuperated in a military hospital, in a civilian hospital a few miles away, her mother had lain dying. It had been wrenching to drive back and forth between them, to shift from seeing her father regain his strength to seeing her mother fade. Ann's death had come more quickly than the doctors had predicted; it was almost as if she'd held on just long enough to see her husband one last time, then had allowed herself to quietly slip away.

She'd forgiven him, of course.

Just as Willy had forgiven him.

Why was it always women who had to do the forgiving? she'd wondered.

"I'm all packed," her father said, carrying his suitcase into the living room. "I've called a cab."

"Are you sure you've got everything? The kids' toys? The books?"

"It's all in here. What a delivery! They're going to think I'm Santa Claus." He set the suitcase down and sat on the couch. They didn't speak for a moment.

"You won't be coming back, will you?" she said at last.

"It may not be easy."

"May I come see you?"

"Willy, you know you can! Both you and Guy. And next time, we'll make it a decent visit." He laughed. "Nice and quiet and dull. Guy'll appreciate that."

There was a long silence. Her father asked, "Have you spoken to him lately?"

She looked away. "It's been two weeks."

"That long?"

"He hasn't called."

"Why haven't you called him?"

"I've been busy. A lot of things to take care of. But you know that."

"He doesn't."

"Well, he *ought* to know." Suddenly agitated, she rose and paced the room, finally returning to the window. "I'm not really surprised he hasn't called. After all, we had our little adventure, and now it's back to life as usual." She glanced at her father. "Men hate that, don't they? Life as usual."

"Some men do. On the other hand, some of us change."

"Oh, Dad, I've been around the block. I can tell when things are over."

"Did Guy say that?"

She turned and gazed back out the window. "He didn't have to."

Her father didn't comment. After a while, she heard him go back into the bedroom, but she didn't move. She just kept staring out at the rain, thinking about Guy. Wondering for the first time if maybe *she* had done the running away.

No, it wasn't running. It was facing reality. Together they'd had the time of their lives, a crazy week of emotions gone wild, of terror and exhilaration, when every breath, every heartbeat had seemed like a gift from God.

Of course, it hadn't lasted.

But whose fault was that?

She felt herself drawn almost against her will to the telephone. Even as she dialed his number, she wondered what she'd say to him. *Hello, Guy. I know you don't want to hear this, but I love you.* Then she'd hang up and spare him the ordeal of admitting the feeling wasn't mutual. She let it ring twelve times, knowing it was 4:00 a.m. in Honolulu, knowing he *should* be home.

There were tears in her eyes when she finally hung up. She stood staring down at the phone, wondering how that inanimate collection of wires and plastic could leave her feeling so betrayed. *Damn you,* she thought. *You never even gave me the chance to make a fool of myself.*

The sound of tires splashing across wet streets made her look out the window. Through pouring rain she saw a cab pull up at the curb.

"Dad?" she called. She went to her father's bedroom. "Your taxi's here."

"Already?" He glanced around to see if he'd forgotten anything. "Okay. I guess this is it, then."

The doorbell rang. He threw on his raincoat and strode across the living room. Willy wasn't watching as he opened the door, but she heard him say, "I don't believe it." She turned.

"Hello, Maitland," said Guy.

The two men, both wearing raincoats, both holding suitcases, grinned at each other across the threshold.

Guy shook the raindrops from his hair. "Mind if I come in?"

"Gee, I don't know. I'd better ask the boss." Maitland turned to his daughter. "What do you think? Can the man come in?"

Willy was too stunned to say a word.

"I guess that's a yes," her father said, and he motioned for Guy to enter.

Guy stepped over the threshold and set his suitcase down. Then he just stood there, looking at her. Rain had plastered his hair to his forehead, lines of exhaustion mapped his face, but no man had ever looked so wonderful. She tried to remind herself of all the reasons she didn't want to see him, all the reasons she should throw him out into the rain. But she couldn't seem to find her voice. She could only stare at him in wonder and remember how it had felt to be in his arms.

Maitland shuffled uneasily. "I...uh...I think I forgot to pack something," he muttered, and he discreetly vanished into the bedroom.

For a moment, the only sound was the water dripping from Guy's raincoat onto the wood floor.

"How's your mother?" Guy asked.

"She died, five days ago."

He shook his head. "Willy, I'm sorry."

"I'm sorry, too."

"How are you? Are you okay?"

"I'm...fine." She looked away. *I love you,* she thought.

And yet here we are, two strangers engaging in small talk. "Yeah, I'm fine," she repeated, as though to convince him—to convince herself—that the anguish of these past two weeks had been a minor ache not worth mentioning.

"You look pretty good, considering."

She shrugged. "You look terrible."

"Not too surprising. Didn't get any sleep on the plane. And there was this baby screaming in the next seat, all the way from Bangkok."

"Bangkok?" She frowned. "You were in Bangkok?"

He nodded and laughed. "It's this crazy business I'm in. Got home from Nam, and a week later, they asked me to fly back...for Sam Lassiter." He paused. "I admit I wasn't thrilled about getting on another plane, but I figured it was something I had to do." He paused and added quietly, "No soldier should have to come home alone."

She thought about Lassiter, about that evening in the river café, the love song scratching from the record player, the paper lanterns fluttering in the wind. She thought about his body drifting in the waters of the Mekong. And she thought about the dark-eyed woman who'd loved him. "You're right," she said. "No soldier should have to come home alone."

There was another pause. She felt him watching her, waiting.

"You could have called me," she said.

"I wanted to."

"But you never got the chance, right?"

"I had plenty of chances."

"But you didn't bother?" She looked up. All the hurt, all the rage suddenly rose to the surface. "Two weeks with no word from you! And here you have the gall to show up unannounced, walk in my door and drop your damn suitcase in my living—"

The last word never made it to her lips. But he did. She

was dragged into a rain-drenched embrace, and everything she'd planned to say, all the hurt and angry words, were swept away by that one kiss. The only sound she could manage was a small murmur of astonishment, and then she was whirled up in a wild maelstrom of desire. She lost all sense of where she ended and he began. She only knew, in that instant, that he had never really left her, that as long as she lived, he'd be part of her. Even as he pulled back to look at her, she was still drunk with the taste of him.

"I *did* want to call you. But I didn't know what to say…"

"I kept waiting for you to call. All these days…"

"Maybe I was…I don't know. Scared."

"Of what?"

"Of hearing it was over. That you'd come to your senses and decided I wasn't worth the risk. But then, when I got to Bangkok, I stopped at the Oriental Hotel. Had a drink on the terrace for old time's sake. Saw the same sunset, the same boats on the river. But it just didn't feel the same without you." He sighed. "Hell, nothing feels the same without you."

"You never told me. You just dropped out of my life."

"It never seemed like…the right time."

"The right time for what?"

"You know."

"No, I don't."

He shook his head in irritation. "You never make it easy, do you?"

She stepped back and gave him a long, critical look. Then she smiled. "I never intended to."

"Oh, Willy." He threw his arms around her and pulled her tightly against his chest. "I can see you and I are going to have a lot of things to settle."

"Such as?"

"Such as…" He lowered his mouth to hers and whispered, "Such as who gets to sleep on the right side of the bed...."

"Oh," she murmured as their lips brushed. "You will."

"And who gets to name our firstborn...."

She settled warmly into his arms and sighed. "I will."

"And who'll be first to say 'I love you.'"

There was a pause. "That one," she said with a smile, "is open to negotiation."

"No, it's not," he said, tugging her face up to his.

They stared at each other, both longing to hear the words but stubbornly waiting for the other to give in first.

It was a simultaneous surrender.

"I love you," Willy heard him say, just as the same three words tumbled from her lips.

Their laughter was simultaneous, too, bright and joyous and ringing with hope.

The kiss that followed was warm, seeking, but all too brief; it left her aching for more.

"It gets even better with practice," he whispered.

"Saying 'I love you?'"

"No. Kissing."

"Oh," she murmured. She added in a small voice, "Then can we try it again?"

Outside, a horn honked, dragging them both back to reality. Through the window they saw another taxi waiting at the curb.

Reluctantly Willy pulled out of Guy's arms. "Dad?" she called.

"I'm coming, I'm coming." Her father emerged from the bedroom, pulling on his raincoat again. He paused and looked at her.

"Uh, why don't you two say goodbye," said Guy, diplomatically turning for the front door. "I'll take your suitcase out to the car."

Willy and her father were left standing alone in the

room. They looked at each other, both knowing that this, like every goodbye, could be the last.

"Are things okay between you and Guy?" Maitland asked.

Willy nodded.

There was another silence. Then her father asked softly, "And between you and me?"

She smiled. "Things are okay there, too." She went to him then, and they held each other. "Yes," she murmured against his chest, "between you and me, things are definitely okay."

A little reluctantly, he turned to leave. In the doorway, he and Guy shook hands.

"Have a good trip back, Maitland."

"I will. Take care of things, will you? And, Guy—thanks a lot."

"For what?"

Maitland glanced back at Willy. It was a look of regret. And redemption. "For giving me back my daughter," he said.

As Wild Bill Maitland walked out the door, Guy walked in. He didn't say a thing. He just took Willy in his arms and hugged her.

As the taxi drove away, she thought, *My father has left me. Again.*

She looked up at Guy. *And what about you?*

He answered her unspoken question by taking her face in his hands and kissing her. Then he gave the door a little kick; with a thud of finality, it swung shut.

And she knew that this time, the man would be staying.

NO WAY BACK
Debra Webb

First, I would like to thank Harlequin Books
and my editor, Denise O'Sullivan, for affording me the
opportunity to bring my stories to life. I would also like
to convey a very special thanks to you the reader.
Thank you for reading my stories…for taking this
journey with me. Finally, this book is dedicated to the
one and only Fran Woodard, a lovely lady, a
compassionate human being, a true champion of the
written word and one heck of a secret agent—the
latter, of course, is only in my very vivid imagination.

PROLOGUE

PARIS...it never changed.

He watched from the third-story window of the shop he had seized in the middle of the day along boulevard Saint-Michel. Outside, pigeons fluttered and squawked. Nearby, a waiter moved between the tables of a crowded open-air café. Natives and tourists alike chatted over drinks, never suspecting or caring what nasty business was taking place only a few meters away. He studied each face before moving on. To this day he could not stop himself from looking for *her*.

He shook his head. It had been two long years. She was gone. And even if she were here, her fate would be like that of the traitors bound and gagged downstairs. He turned his attention back to the sidewalk below and the pedestrians strolling along completely oblivious to anything other than the beauty of the day...of the place.

But here, where he was, there was no beauty...no good. Only the evil that men could do.

He closed his eyes and blocked the images that haunted him day and night. When would this nightmare end?

"Pardon," came from the door behind him. *"Nous sommes prêts."*

He opened his eyes. His men were ready, but he needed another moment. *"Dans un moment."* A vague smile tugged at his lips. He had trained them well. Without thought, they spoke the language of those around them. In

Paris they were Parisians, speaking the language as well as the natives.

As the messenger returned downstairs to those waiting patiently, their leader braced himself for the inevitable. It was time. He could not wait any longer. There would be no last-minute salvation. His orders stood.

Mentally preparing himself for the next step, he left the room. His footfalls echoed in the expectant silence as he descended the three flights of stairs. Supplications for forgiveness would be pointless. So he didn't bother. Whatever awaited him at the end of this existence would not be pleasant. His crimes were far too great. But, unfortunately, necessary.

"What do we do with them?" One of his men, Carlos, gestured to the four bound men lying on the floor in the middle of the *boulangerie*. The scent of freshly baked bread did little to mask the smell of fear, of death looming.

As he, their respected leader, the one who must show no weakness, moved down the final step, he glanced at the frightened faces of those anxiously awaiting his decree. He turned his attention back to Carlos. There was no room for hesitation or remorse. "Kill them."

CHAPTER ONE

"BLOOD PRESSURE?" Dr. Roland yelled above the organized chaos of the trauma room.

"One hundred over sixty-five," Ami Donovan, R.N., reported. "Pulse is seventy and thready."

"Where the hell is Mason?" Roland demanded.

"Dr. Mason's on his way," Jane, another R.N. on duty, told him as she shoved the X rays onto the viewing box.

Frowning, Roland took a moment to scan the views. "Let's get this guy typed and crossed," he barked, his attention refocusing on the patient and the two leaking wounds where the bullets had entered the upper left area of his chest.

"Doing that as we speak," Lonnie, the lab tech, advised as warm, red blood filled the tube in his hand.

"Seventy over fifty," Ami cut in, her own blood pressure rising with a new surge of anxiety. Internal bleeding was taking its toll on their patient.

"Get that second IV in now! Sixteen-gauge," Roland ordered. "Let's get this guy's pressure back up."

Ami dabbed Betadine on the inside of the patient's arm and positioned the needle for insertion. The patient, Natan Olment, was a foreign VIP of some sort. Whoever he was, they'd had a hell of a time clearing his security detail from the trauma room. Only one of the bodyguards had spoken some English. From what she'd discerned of the broken conversation as they'd wheeled Mr. Olment into the ER, he'd apparently been a victim of an assassination attempt.

The patient jerked at the needle prick. Ami quickly taped the second intravenous catheter into place, then adjusted the flow of the tube. Mr. Olment stared up at her now, his eyes wide above the hissing oxygen mask, his breath coming in short, desperate puffs.

"It's all right, sir," she felt compelled to assure him. "We're going to take very good care of you."

The doors suddenly burst open behind her and Dr. Mason, the thoracic surgeon on call, breezed into the room. "Bring me up to speed!" he snapped.

"Two gunshot wounds to the chest. The X rays indicate—"

Roland's assessment was abruptly halted by the patient's sudden scramble to get up and off the gurney. He grabbed at Ami, his left hand waving frantically for purchase.

Startled into action, she restrained his flailing arm, preventing him from reaching his target. He screamed something at her, his words muffled behind the oxygen mask. He elbowed Ami away with his right arm, almost tearing loose the IV tubes. Jane, Lonnie and Dr. Roland forced the man back down onto the gurney.

Olment tugged free of Lonnie's hold, his desperate, muffled shouts clearly directed at Ami, his horrified gaze fixated on her. The whole team looked at her then, confusion claiming their faces. Rattled, she pulled back a step, her presence obviously somehow threatening to the man.

When Olment was fully restrained in a four-point hold, they all took a breath, including Ami.

"Get that blood to the lab," Roland ordered, his tone weary. "This guy must be on something," he added under his breath.

Ami carefully moved back into position and checked the

IV connections, then the man's blood pressure. One-ten over eighty. Well, at least, his numbers were up. His dark gaze, wild with unreadable emotion, never left her, trekked her every move. She resisted the urge to look directly into those accusing depths. Whatever this guy's problem, it had nothing to do with her. And right now she had a job to do…helping to save his life.

"Let's get him to the OR," Dr. Mason announced, sending the team into another practiced routine of organized chaos.

AMI PULLED her navy sweater and purse from her locker and slammed the door. God, she was glad her shift was over. The ER had stayed unusually busy this afternoon, forcing a hectic pace for every staff member on duty. There must be something in the air today, she mused. Then again, tonight there would be a full moon. All the weirdos were likely warming up. Some sort of subconscious urging prompting them to drive recklessly, take nosedives out of buildings, and shoot at people they would at any other time consider friends.

She pulled the scrunchie from her hair, allowing the forever-unruly locks to fall around her shoulders. Just one more day of duty and she'd have a full four days off. Ami smiled. Four days with her little boy. And maybe some quality time with Robert. She felt as if she had drifted further from him the past few months. It was time she did something about it. He was too good to her and her son for her to continue to neglect him this way. It was time she got her act together and put the past behind her once and for all.

"That was some wild shit in the ER today, huh, Ami?" She glanced up at Lonnie, the lab tech who'd been on duty with her. "Yeah," she agreed. "A little too wild for my liking."

He pulled his gym bag from his locker and dropped it onto the bench that flanked the row of gray metal storage units. Lonnie worked out every single day and it showed in his lean, athletic physique. She should start working out again. She'd really let herself go since becoming a member of the mommy brigade. But there was just never enough time.

"Tonight's a full moon, you know," he said almost as an afterthought. "The crazies must've decided to come out early."

Ami nodded. "I'm glad I'm not on duty tonight."

"That makes two of us." Lonnie suddenly stalled, one hand on his locker door, the other on the handle of his gym bag. "That sheikh guy was a trip, wasn't he?"

Despite her exhaustion, she had to laugh. "He's not a sheikh. According to Jane, he's some sort of aide to the Israeli prime minister."

Lonnie closed his locker door and shrugged. "Whatever. He damn sure freaked out." A grin slid across the tech's freckled face.

When he smiled like that, he reminded Ami of Opie from the old *Andy Griffith Show*. Though she couldn't imagine Opie spouting the kind of language Lonnie was known to use.

"What'd you do to him, anyway?" he teased.

Ami rolled her eyes and heaved an impatient sigh. She'd been asked that question at least a dozen times today. "I didn't do anything to him. He probably forgot his lithium this morning." She pulled on her sweater. "Or maybe he had too much of something else."

"Actually," Lonnie began, his face suddenly serious. "He was clean." He shook his head from side to side as if he couldn't believe it himself. "No scripts, no street candy. Nothing."

A chill sank clear to her bones. "Oh." It was all she could think to say. The patient had been drug-free…no reason why he hadn't been lucid. No reasonable explanation for him to go postal. No reason for him to look at Ami the way he had. The uneasiness she'd barely kept at bay all day reared its ugly head. She told herself it was the combination of pain and fear, but why turn it all against her in particular? There had been several others present. Why her?

"See ya tomorrow." Lonnie hefted his gym bag and gave her a little salute. "We've got the same shift again."

Doing her level best to ignore the uneasiness, she waved him off. She liked Lonnie. He was good at his job and he could always be counted on for a laugh. She was glad he would be here tomorrow. If it turned out anything like today, they would need some comic relief.

Ami left the locker room and headed back to the ER. That was the most direct route to the parking garage. She was too tired to take the long way around. "Have fun," she offered to Jane as she passed her in the corridor.

"I will when I get my paycheck," her friend returned smugly.

Jane was working half a shift over since another nurse had called in sick. Ami was enormously thankful Dr. Roland hadn't asked her to stay. She just wanted to go home. But Jane had her reasons for putting her mind and body through twelve hours of ER abuse. As a single parent, extra money was always handy.

Ami's footsteps echoed in the deserted stairwell as she descended to the basement level. She trudged across the quiet parking garage, trying without success to not think about Mr. Olment and his strange reaction to her. Her busy shift had kept the disturbing thoughts away, but now, as silence closed in around her, the incident nagged at her again. It didn't mean anything, she reminded herself. She would talk to Robert tonight. He was a psychiatrist, a damn good one at that. He would be able to explain away the episode. He always had an explanation for everything.

Ami climbed into her Volvo wagon and drove across town more or less on autopilot. She turned right onto Piedmont Street and slowed at the gate to allow the security guard to identify her. He motioned for her to continue and she entered the quiet neighborhood she'd called home for the past year. A sense of relief and contentment instantly started to melt away the day's tension.

The first time Robert had brought her here and showed her the new, exclusive, high-security housing development she'd fallen in love. The homes and their small yards were stunningly picturesque. The well-planned, gated community had all the amenities one would expect in a ritzy neighborhood that catered to Chicago's young professionals. But it was the security she'd loved most. With a new baby, safety was number one on her priority list, as well as Robert's.

She parked in her drive, next to Mrs. Perry's Taurus, powered the window down and just sat for a while, absorbing the feeling of home. Leaves, tinged with the first hues of fall, danced across the well-manicured lawn. It was only September, but most yards, including her own, were decorated for Halloween. Pumpkins, scarecrows and the usual cornstalks and hay bales embellished the small plots of dormant grass. A few painted wood ghosts, witches and black cats were scattered around, some bordered by freshly planted mums and pansies.

Warmth welled inside her, chasing away the lingering coldness of an ER shift. This was a wonderful neighborhood. They were so lucky to live here. Nicholas would have lots of friends to play with when he was older. Next door, the Petreys' little boy, who'd had his first birthday last month, would go to preschool with Nicholas. Ami was glad for that. The Petreys were nice people; the father, a doctor like Robert, the mother, a schoolteacher. The perfect family. Ami surveyed the houses on her right, then her left for as far as she could see. They were all perfect families, living in a perfect neighborhood.

That reality sent a new chill racing up her spine, where it camped at the base of her skull, a precursor to the dread now filling her. Everything was perfect…except her. No matter how hard she tried, she would never be. Her past was a big black hole that left her permanently flawed. The image of Natan Olment imposed itself amid her depressing thoughts.

"Stop obsessing, Ami," she scolded as she got out of the car and started up the walk. "This day is over, you're home, put it behind you."

She slipped her key into the door, unlocked it and stepped inside. "Hello," she called. "I'm home." *At last,* she thought with a sigh.

Ami could hear Nicholas squealing with delight even before Mrs. Perry rounded the corner into the entry hall, sixteen-month-old Nicholas toddling along beside her, his arms outstretched for his mommy. Ami didn't feel whole until he was in her arms. She hugged him as tightly as she dared and inhaled the sweet baby scents of lotion and powder.

"He's had his dinner and his bath," Mrs. Perry reported as she did every day she cared for Nicholas. "I hope you had a nice day, Miss Donovan."

Ami kept her pleasant smile in place in spite of a jab of irritation. She preferred to give Nicholas his bath. She'd told Mrs. Perry that time and again, to no avail. "It was fine, Mrs. Perry. And how were things here?"

"Oh, we had a marvelous day."

The woman literally beamed, the sincerity of it banishing Ami's irritation. How could she be angry with a woman who took such joy in caring for Nicholas? She and Robert were very fortunate to have found her. Most of the children on this street went to day-care centers—good ones, but centers nonetheless. Nicholas received one-on-one care from the grandmotherly type. A friend of Robert's whose child had just entered elementary school had highly recommended her. Her other references had been impeccable, as well. She was *perfect*.

"We took a stroll in the park," Mrs. Perry continued. "We watched *Sesame Street*, then read Dr. Seuss until nap time."

Ami adopted a wowed expression for her son. "My, my, young man." She kissed his chubby cheek. "It sounds like you've had a full day. Do you have any fun left in you for Mommy?" His answering gurgle and chorus of *da-da* warmed her heart.

"I'll see you tomorrow then." Mrs. Perry gathered her purse and all-weather jacket from the hall closet. "Have a pleasant evening, Miss Donovan."

"You, too. Thank you, Mrs. Perry."

Ami waited until the older woman had settled into her car before she closed the door. She smiled at Nicholas who was engrossed with the ID badge pinned to her nurse's smock. "How about another bath?"

Nicholas's dark eyes brightened at the prospect. He grinned, a wide, gap-toothed gesture, then babbled *da-da* again.

"Want to play in the water?" His eager bounce in her arms was all the encouragement she needed. "We just won't tell, Mrs. Perry,'' Ami whispered. ''It'll be our secret. And while we're at it, let's practice *ma-ma*.''

LATER, Ami stood next to Nicholas's crib and watched him sleep. She glanced at the Winnie the Pooh clock. Seven already and Robert still wasn't home. He'd probably had a last-minute consultation that ran longer than he expected, or maybe an emergency at the hospital. Psychiatric patients were even more prone to full moon dementia, she supposed.

Her attention refocused on her sleeping child. She trailed a finger over one silky, rose-colored cheek. Her heart squeezed. She loved him so much. He was the only part of the real her. The one she couldn't remember. Ami studied his features for a time. The thick, dark hair. The long, almost feminine lashes splayed against his olive skin. Those equally dark eyes, which were almost black.

''Where did you get those?'' she murmured softly. Her own hair was a light brown with so many gold streaks that it looked more blond than brown. And her eyes were blue. Ami closed her eyes and tried to imagine a man with Nicholas's features, but she could only call to mind the shadowy image that haunted her dreams far too often.

She sighed and peered down at her baby. ''Doesn't matter,'' she answered herself. ''You're my son. No matter who your father was, you're all mine now.''

By ten-thirty Ami had grown seriously worried. Robert always called when he was going to be this late.

She clicked off the television. The newscaster had reported this morning's shooting as an assassination attempt on American Economic Advisor Frank Lowden. Mr. Olment had inadvertently stepped into the path of the bullet intended for Mr. Lowden. The images the cameras had captured made Ami shiver. Why did they have to show such graphic scenes on television? She frowned. Where was Robert?

Feeling more alone than she had in a very long time, she reached for the telephone to call his cellular number, but a sound downstairs stopped her. She held her breath and listened, her fingers still clutching the cordless receiver, an uncharacteristic hint of fear trickling through her. This was a secure neighborhood. She never worried about intruders.

The front door opened, then closed. She tensed, ready to dial 9-1-1. The sound of the dead bolt being set into place and the clink of keys hitting the hall table announced that Robert was home.

Ami exhaled the breath she'd been holding and dropped the receiver back into its cradle. The familiar rhythm of Robert's footfalls on the stairs chased away any lingering anxiety. She shook her head at how foolishly she was behaving. What was wrong with her tonight?

The episode with Mr. Olment in the ER, she admitted. It had shaken her far too deeply. She turned on her bedside lamp and sat up. Discussing her feelings with Robert never failed to help. He would be able to explain everything. He always did. He was her knight in tailored Armani.

"You're still up," he commented, surprise as well as concern marring his handsome brow as he strode through the door. He draped his suit jacket over the nearest chair and tugged at his tie, his expectant gaze searching hers.

"I was worried." She clasped her arms around her bent legs, propped her chin on her knees and waited for him to realize he hadn't called.

A frown pulled his lips downward. "Why would—?" He swore, something he rarely did. "I didn't call," he realized out loud. He sat on the edge of the bed, next to her, and pressed his forehead to hers. "I am so sorry, baby.

It was an emergency meeting of the board. They're stressing over that lawsuit against Jacobs. I didn't have time to think of anything else. I swear I'll make it up to you.''

She kissed his nose. "Forgiven." Then she fixed him with a firm look. "But don't ever do it again.''

A deep chuckle rumbled from his chest. "Shall I make it up to you tonight?" He brushed a kiss across her lips. "It might be late, but I'm not that tired.''

She studied his teasing gray eyes, worry twisting unreasonably in her stomach. She did care so for this man. She just wasn't quite sure that what she felt was love, which was why she still hadn't agreed to become Mrs. Robert Allen. But she did care deeply for him. "Maybe," she offered in an attempt to hang on to the playful moment a little bit longer. "But first we have to talk.''

He arched a skeptical brow. "Talk?" He stood and pulled his shirt from his slacks, then began to unbutton it. "This sounds serious. Did Josh Cowden leave his bicycle in the driveway again?''

Ami patted the spot he'd vacated. "Sit. This *is* serious.''

His fingers stilled in their work, his expression instantly turning as solemn as her own. "Has something happened?" He eased back down onto the mattress. "Is Nicholas all right?''

"He's fine. It's not that kind of serious.''

His sigh of relief was audible.

Ami moistened her lips and tried to decide how to tell him what had happened and how she felt without sounding hormonal or totally paranoid. "There's some kind of international financial summit in town, did you know that?''

He lifted one shoulder and dropped it in a halfhearted shrug. "I may have heard something about it. But I didn't have time to more than glance at the news this morning.'' His gaze searched hers, his frown deepening. "Why?''

"There was an assassination attempt." She splayed her palms, as uncertain of the exact details as the newscaster who'd reported them. "The man who was shot came in on my ER shift."

Robert dragged the undone tie from around his neck. "Who was he?"

"Natan Olment. He's an aide to the Israeli prime minister. According to the news, he stepped in front of the intended target just as the shot was fired."

"Bad timing for him." Robert's tie dropped silently to the carpeted floor. "Did he survive?"

She nodded. "He's in ICU in stable condition. But something strange happened in the ER."

"Don't keep me in suspense. Tell me," he urged. His shirt hit the floor next.

Ami took a moment of reprieve to appreciate his well-defined torso. He was a wonderful man, and very nice to look at, blond hair, kind gray eyes. Why hadn't she said yes months ago? What was it that made her hesitate when he had done so very much for her? He'd been there for her every step of the way, even when she'd longed for a career after Nicholas's birth. Robert had been the one to notice her unusual grasp of medical terminology. A battery of tests had quickly revealed an undeniable education from her previous life in the medical field. He helped her get licensed as well as to obtain the position she now held.

"Ami," he prompted firmly. "Tell me what happened."

"Just before we sent him up to the OR, I was adding another IV line and he..." Her mind quickly replayed every frantic moment like a video on fast forward. "He looked straight at me and just went ballistic." She shook her head, still finding the whole episode unbelievable. She knew how it sounded, but she was there, she also knew what she saw. "He was screaming something at me. Something none of us could understand, of course." She took a breath and forced herself to calm. "Even with two bullets in his chest, he tried to get away." She looked straight into Robert's eyes. "He tried to get away from *me*. He seemed scared to death."

"Drugs?" Robert suggested.

"That's the really weird part, his tox screen was clean."

Robert took her hands in his. "Look," he said gently. "Just because the guy freaked, doesn't mean it had anything to do with you. He was probably suffering from trauma-induced hallucinations. You've seen it happen before."

This was true, but today was different somehow. She just couldn't seem to make him understand that. Ami squeezed his hands, holding on with all her might. "You don't think it could've had anything to do with...before?"

He smiled patiently, the expression full of the assurance she needed so desperately. "Of course not. It was just a coincidence that his attention focused on you when the episode started."

Still not fully convinced, she went on. "It was like he knew me. And whatever he knew wasn't good."

"Ami." Robert slipped into his therapist mode. The tone of his voice not quite so patient as before, his posture a little stiffer, his expression closed, free of emotion. She remembered it all well from when they'd first met. Before he'd turned her case over to someone else so that the two of them could pursue a personal relationship.

"You have focal retrograde amnesia. You're always going to wonder whenever anyone looks at you just the right way if they somehow know you. There's nothing wrong with that."

She let go a heavy breath. "Then why does it feel so...wrong?"

"Because you keep hoping someone will simply walk up to you and fill in all the blanks." He shook his head slowly, sympathy filling those gray eyes now despite the irritation she knew he must feel. They'd had this discussion a hundred times. "It's not going to happen. You have to accept that."

She looked away. "I know. It's like I sprang forth fully grown just two years ago." She thought of her sweet baby. "And four weeks' pregnant."

"But you know that's not the case." He took her face in his hands, his hold tender, certain. "You came from somewhere, we just may never know where. And that doesn't matter to me, but it matters to you. That's why you're reading too much into an injured man's hallucinations."

"Maybe I am," she relented. "It just felt so real. The whole trauma team noticed it."

Robert pressed a kiss to her forehead, then looked deeply into her eyes. "Your past is gone, Ami. None of the therapy we tried worked, and we tried it all. That past isn't coming back."

She wound her arms around his neck and relished the security of having him near. "You're right. I know."

"You're Ami Donovan," he murmured close to her ear, the words, his voice, soothing. "Whoever you were before is gone for good."

CHAPTER TWO

SHE WAS DREAMING of *him* again. Only this time he pulled her into the shadows with him. Not a threatening gesture, but one of fierce need. He whispered to her, his voice deep and alluring, the words soothing, sensual, and in some foreign language she somehow understood.

He kissed her and fire rushed through Ami's body. Her fingers splayed over his chest. Warm skin, stretched taut over powerful muscle, sent her every nerve ending on alert. She knew instinctively that he could kill her in an instant, but instead he was making her come. Her loins ached from his masterful touch. Pleasure cascaded over her as his lips tasted, teased, and his hands skimmed her body. His long, dark hair brushed against her skin like a medieval warrior's. And his eyes were even darker…almost bottomless, but deeply sensual and alluring. She wanted nothing but to be with him…forever.

Ami jerked awake. For a moment time and place escaped her. Her skin was hot and damp with sweat, her heart pounding in sync with her ragged breaths. The lavender sheets were tangled around and beneath her. Her feminine muscles throbbed with the receding waves of orgasm. She reached out to find the other side of the bed cold and empty. She turned her head and stared at the pillow next to hers, confirming the lack of a warm body beside her. Robert had left for the office without waking her. She frowned. That was odd, he always—

A cry pierced the morning silence.

Nicholas.

Ami sat straight up and peered at the digital clock on the bedside table—6:15 a.m. Damn. She was late. Nicholas cried out again.

She bounded out of bed and rushed down the hall to her baby's room. He stood at the foot of his crib, his face flushed from crying, huge tears flowing down his cheeks. Ami lifted him into her arms. He was wet and hungry and she'd overslept. *Damn.*

"Oh, baby, Mommy's sorry," she cooed. "Let's get this diaper changed and we'll get you some breakfast. Okay?" She tapped his nose and a smile finally peeked past the tears. "That's better," she murmured, happiness blooming in her chest. Late or not, holding her son always put her in a good mood.

"Good morning!"

Ami's good mood drooped like a summer flower after an early frost at the sound of Mrs. Perry's greeting. She didn't want the epitome of punctuality to know she'd overslept and would still be sleeping if Nicholas hadn't cried out or the dream hadn't been so...

She shook off the lingering sensations of the too vivid dream. She'd analyze that later. Right now she had to get her baby fed, both of them dressed, and herself off to work.

"Oh, my, you aren't dressed."

Ami looked up to find Mrs. Perry in the doorway. "I overslept," she said lamely. God, why did she have to sound so guilty? It wasn't her fault she'd dreamed of making love with some raven-haired stranger. Nicholas's dark features nagged at her as if she should remember something. Was she dreaming of his father? Could the man be an actual memory slipping through the wall her mind had erected between her and her past? Or was it just that, a dream?

"Here, I'll take him. You'd better get dressed."

Before Ami could protest, Mrs. Perry had taken Nicholas and headed to the changing table. Ami started to snatch him back and to tell the woman that she was capable of caring for her own child, but common sense prevailed. She was late. She should get dressed and get going. Mrs. Perry had done the right thing. As always.

But Ami didn't have to like it.

UNBELIEVABLY Ami arrived at work ten minutes before her scheduled shift began. She grabbed a cup of coffee from the nurse's lounge and headed for the bank of elevators. According to Jane, Mr. Olment had been moved from ICU to a room on the fourth floor late last night since he was stable and they needed his bed. Apparently the full moon had caused two major pileups, both with serious injuries. Jane had ended up working the entire second shift last night. The dark smudges under her eyes this morning told the tale of how little sleep she'd gotten after going home. Pulling a double shift in the ER was just plain dumb, not to mention against hospital policy. But sometimes it just couldn't be avoided. And the extra money would buy school clothes for Jane's kids.

Ami stabbed the elevator call button. She knew it was foolish, but she had to know. She had to see if the man would react the same way now that his condition had stabilized.

Robert would tell her that she was feeding her own paranoia by going to the man's room or even allowing herself to continue thinking about him. But she simply had to know. She would never stop playing that awful scene over and over in her head until she reconciled herself to the fact that it was, as Robert had said, trauma-induced hallucinations and nothing more.

On the fourth floor the three nurses at the station were busily preparing for their shift to end. Ami was relieved to see Kathi Stevens on duty. She knew Kathi from a CPR recertification course they'd taken together a few months ago. Kathi had a daughter about the same age as Nicholas.

"Good morning, ladies. Did you have a good shift last night?" Ami propped on the counter and sipped her coffee.

Kathi smiled and winked. "Oh, we had a glorious night. We always do when there's a full moon."

A heavyset lady Ami knew only as Ginny, glowered at Kathi and then at Ami. "It was the shift from hell."

Ami took another sip of coffee to prevent a giggle. "That bad, huh?"

The youngest of the three, a new girl Ami had never met, piped up next. "The man in four-twelve ranted the entire first half of the shift." She shook her head ruefully. "It must be really frightening to be in a foreign country and in the hospital."

Mr. Olment, Ami presumed.

Kathi lifted a brow at the girl's naiveté. "I would think the frightening part was when someone was shooting at him."

The girl blushed. "Well, you know what I mean."

"The Feds coming in and out didn't help," Ginny added irritably. "I don't know what they expected the man to tell them. He was too out of it to know his own name, much less what happened."

"Speaking of Mr. Olment..." Ami ventured. "How's he doing this morning?"

"I was just about to go check his vitals," Kathi told her, selecting his medical chart from the rack.

"I'm glad it's you and not me," the younger woman said, relieved. "Those guards give me the willies."

"Would you like to join me?" Kathi asked Ami, ignoring her co-worker's remark.

"Sure." Ami tossed her empty foam cup into a trash bin and followed Kathi. She was older than Ami, thirty maybe. But her blond hair, perpetual tan and petite figure made her look far younger than her years.

"So Olment had a rough night?" Ami inquired nonchalantly.

Kathi nodded. "We had to up his meds for him to get any real rest at all. He kept mumbling in something besides English and every once in a while he'd try to climb out of his bed. We finally had to put him in restraints."

"Did evening shift have the same trouble?"

Kathi paused, taking a moment to glance at his chart. "They're the ones who got the order for a sedative to be added to his meds not long after he left ICU. The dosage was too low, though. It wore off in no time."

Ami didn't have to ask which room was Olment's. The guards posted on either side of his door left no doubt. The two dark, grim-faced men gave Ami the willies, too. When the stiff-looking soldiers let them pass, Ami took a deep breath before going into the room. She had to do this for her own peace of mind. Her pulse skittered into overdrive and her palms began to sweat. This was the right thing to do. She needed to see if Olment would react to her presence this morning. She…had to know.

Once again luck was not going to be on her side. He was asleep. Disappointment flooded Ami. Dammit, why did he have to be asleep right now? Kathi moved to his bedside, leaving Ami at the foot, and began the routine of checking vitals, which was second nature to a nurse. Oh, well, it wasn't as though Ami could kick his bed or any-

294

thing and hope he'd wake up. She'd just have to come by again on her break. If her friend Miranda was on duty today, she wouldn't mind Ami tagging after her to the man's room.

"How is he this morning?"

The male voice that sounded from the doorway behind Ami was heavily accented, just like Mr. Olment's. Kathi looked up at the same time Ami turned to face the man.

"Everything looks fine," Kathi said as she removed the BP cuff from Mr. Olment's arm.

In spite of the fact that Kathi had spoken to him, the man hadn't taken his eyes off Ami. A strange feeling stirred in the pit of her stomach. She watched in morbid fascination as recognition flared in the newcomer's eyes. She didn't have time to react or to even think before a pallor slid over his face and a barely banked fury devoured all other emotion in his eyes.

"You!" he snarled.

Whatever he said next was in his native tongue and completely lost on Ami. He shouted something to the guards and they came running.

Kathi moved next to Ami at the end of the bed. "What the hell is going on?" she whispered.

Ami shook her head, her voice suddenly paralyzed by a terror she couldn't quite name. The guards seized her, one on either side of her, forcing Kathi away. Only then did Ami's brain register the imminent threat and issue an appropriate response.

"What are you doing?" she demanded.

"Let her go!" Kathi shouted.

Ami struggled, but it was as if iron manacles had been clamped around her arms. She could hardly move, much less hope to break free. The man who'd issued the order was snarling at her in that foreign language again. What was he saying? Why were they doing this?

"I'm calling Security!" Kathi warned.

During the seemingly endless minutes it took Security to reach the room, everything lapsed into slow motion for Ami. All sound grew distorted, including the man's voice as he continued to rail at her. She shook her head in denial of whatever he was charging. She tried again to break free, but the men holding her were too strong. She blinked, the effort taking what felt like forever. Some instinct deep inside her urged her to flee, but she could neither understand it nor act upon it. She could only stand there, stunned.

Hospital Security charged into the room, shattering the strange slow-motion scene. "What the hell is going on here?"

Ami thought she recognized that deep commanding voice and craned her neck to see if the security guard speaking was Jason Stanford. It was. Thank God. She'd been on shift when Jason had worked a few incidents in the ER. He would know how to handle this.

"They've lost their minds!" Kathi shouted. "That man started barking orders and they—" she pointed to the two guards "—grabbed Ami. They won't turn her loose."

Jason moved in toe-to-toe with the guard closest to him. "Step aside," he said in a tone that brooked no argument. The Israeli man didn't move. Hell, he probably didn't even understand a word Jason said. Ami's anxiety rocketed to a new level.

Jason turned back to the man in the richly tailored suit, the one who seemed to be in charge. "Sir, you will ask your men to release this woman. Her name is Ami Donovan. She's a nurse at this hospital. I don't know what you think is going on here, but whatever it is, you're wrong."

The man merely looked at Jason for several seconds,

then shifted his attention back to Ami. "*You* are a nurse in this facility?"

Ami struggled to keep from trembling. Who did he think she was? She had the white uniform and the damned ID. Couldn't he see that she was a member of the hospital staff? "Yes," she said shakily. "Kathi and I came in to check Mr. Olment's vitals."

The man said something in that foreign language again and the two guards released her and returned to their posts outside the door. She exhaled the breath she hadn't even been aware she'd been holding. This was beyond crazy. She rubbed her bruised arms and her knees almost buckled.

Jason bracketed a protective arm around her as if sensing her waning ability to stay vertical. "Would you like to explain what happened?" he asked the man who continued to stare suspiciously at Ami.

"I have obviously made a mistake," the man said stiffly, his attention now focused on Jason. "You must excuse me." He turned that unapologetic gaze back to Ami. "I won't make the same mistake again."

Fear sliced straight through her. Every instinct warned her that his words were more threat than apology. But how could that be? She didn't know this man. Why would he threaten her?

Jason extended his free hand. "My name is Jason Stanford. I'm chief of hospital security."

After a hesitation that lasted far too long for comfort, the man accepted Jason's hand. "I am Amos Amin. I am head of Mr. Olment's security," he returned in a tone that sounded forced, clipped.

"If you have any problems, Mr. Amin, you should let me know first." There was no question what Jason meant by his statement. He would not tolerate Amin or any member of his security crossing the line he'd just drawn. Jason squeezed Ami's shoulders. "You ladies through in here?"

"Yes," Kathi said, her voice sounding almost as shaky as Ami felt.

Ami nodded, dredging up a smile for Jason. As she left the room, she felt Amin's gaze on her back like a dagger poised to thrust deep. Who the hell was this man? Who was Olment? And why in God's name did they think they knew her?

Kathi and Ami exchanged unsteady goodbyes at the nurses' station. She didn't miss the strange looks the other two nurses stole in her direction. Ami forced herself to go on, immensely grateful that Jason walked with her to the elevator. Her mind reeled with conflicting emotions. She felt scared, angry, and extremely...anxious. Her entire being wanted to deny the episode that had just taken place.

"Do you have a clue what that was all about?" Jason asked as he depressed the call button.

She shook her head, her body literally humming with emotion and a kind of dread she couldn't quite comprehend. It was as if she should know something that she didn't. She folded her arms over her middle and tried to warm herself. She was cold. Cold and scared.

"I must remind them of someone they know," she said finally, then choked out a humorless sound. "On a Wanted poster, obviously."

Jason laughed at that. "It sure looks that way. Maybe you should avoid this floor until these guys are out of here. I'll see what I can find out about them. I don't know why I wasn't informed of their presence in the first place. I swear, by the time the official word gets to me the guy will probably have been released." The elevator doors slid open and Jason ushered her into the waiting car.

"I think you're right," Ami agreed without reservation.

"I'll just stay in the ER until they go back to their homeland."

As the elevator bumped into downward motion, Ami closed her eyes and tried to gather her composure. Going to that room had been a huge error in judgment. What were the odds that two men from the same foreign country would think they knew her? She had a very bad feeling that she wouldn't like the answer.

Ami and Jason parted ways on the first floor. She hurried to the ER, ten minutes late rather than ten minutes early. Had it only been twenty minutes? It felt like a lifetime since she'd gotten on that elevator headed for Olment's room. And worst of all, she had more questions now than she'd had when she got out of bed this morning. Her little adventure hadn't proven anything at all.

Well, maybe it had proven something...that she didn't ever need to take a trip to the Middle East.

CHAPTER THREE

AN HOUR BEFORE her ER shift ended, Ami finally took a break. She hadn't had a moment to worry about the past or the Israelis on the fourth floor, though, apparently word of the incident had spread like a plague through the hospital. Lunch had come and gone in a flash of sutures and EKGs. The day after the full moon was proving to be worse than the day before.

The one moment of quiet she'd had, she'd used to call home, only to get the machine. She told herself not to worry, that Mrs. Perry had probably taken Nicholas for a stroll. But it was raining outside. Ami then rationalized that just because it was raining downtown didn't mean it was in her 'burb outside of town. Still feeling uneasy, she'd called Robert and was told that he would be out of the office all day. He never went to work without saying goodbye...and now he was unavailable. This was just too weird. The whole day had been the pits, starting with the incident on the fourth floor and going downhill from there.

A cup of coffee in her hand, Ami sat on the well-worn couch in the nurses' lounge, closed her eyes and leaned her head back. It felt so good just to sit. And the quiet. Oh, that was heavenly. Jane and Lonnie had made a cafeteria run. The doctor on call was poring over reports in the tiny room designated as the on-call physician's private sanctuary. The triage nurse was holding the fort at the front desk.

All Ami needed was five minutes of quiet and this cup of coffee. She took a deep swallow and moaned her satisfaction. No one made coffee like Jane did.

The squeak of the door echoed in the quiet and Ami reluctantly opened her eyes expecting to find the triage nurse with word that another onslaught of patients had arrived. To her surprise, a stranger—a man wearing a travel-wrinkled suit—entered the lounge and closed the door behind him. He was tall, she noted. Black hair...nice tan. Ami was pretty sure he wasn't on staff here, which meant he was probably lost.

Annoyed at the intrusion, she sat up a little straighter. Maybe he was here with a patient. A father or brother or son. She supposed in his distress he could think this was a public lounge.

"May I help you?" she asked.

He just looked at her.

Ami stood, trepidation belatedly setting in. "If you're looking for the cafeteria, it's on the opposite end of the building. This is the nurses' lounge." When he continued to stand there staring a hole through her, she added a bit more firmly, "I'll have to ask you to leave."

"Jesus H. Christ," he murmured, disbelief evident in his voice as well as his expression as he sagged against the door behind him.

Ami had the sudden almost overwhelming urge for fight or flight. Another of those feelings she couldn't quite place or name welled inside her.

He pushed off from the door and moved toward her. She backed up a step, only to be halted by the couch she'd vacated seconds ago.

"My name is Jack Tanner." Ami's breath caught as he reached into his inside jacket pocket. He smiled as if he understood. "Don't worry, it's just my ID." He flipped

open a black leather credentials case. "Miss Donovan, I'm
from the Central Intelligence Agency."

Ami blinked. The CIA? Yeah, right. She understood
now. This was a joke. She was going to kill Lonnie. It
wasn't bad enough that he'd ragged her all day about the
Israeli guys. "Look, I don't know who you are, but I've
had—"

"Like I told you," he cut in smoothly, moving a few
steps closer, "I'm Jack Tanner from the CIA. I just need
a few minutes of your time."

He was serious and still holding his ID in plain sight.
Ami stared at the credentials now. *Tanner, Jack. Central
Intelligence Agency.* This guy was for real. She shook her
head in confusion. Why would anyone from the CIA want
to talk to her? The answer that reverberated through her
made her go cold. Her hands shaking, she placed her coffee cup on the table before she dropped it.

"I don't understand," she offered, then blinked, her vision all at once cloudy. The floor seemed to shift beneath
her feet, making her feel unsteady. She took a deep breath
to counter the wave of dizziness. Her blood sugar level
must have bottomed out, she reasoned. Lunch. She
shouldn't have skipped lunch, but there hadn't been time.
"Why would you want to speak with me?" she eventually
managed to ask.

"May I?" He gestured to the chair directly across the
coffee table from her.

She moistened her lips and tried to think of a reason to
say no but found none. "Sure," she relented.

He sat, his gaze steady on her. "I'd like you to join me,
if you will."

Ami eased back down onto the couch, still feeling a bit
unsteady. She wasn't sure why she did as he asked. Maybe,
deep down, she was afraid not to. He was CIA, after all.

"Miss Donovan, you were in the ER when Natan Olment was brought in?"

"Yes." He was here about the Israeli guys. Relief, so profound she could barely hold herself upright, rushed through her. He was investigating the assassination attempt. Why hadn't she thought of that?

"I understand that Mr. Olment reacted as if he knew you somehow?" Tanner went on.

Uneasiness stirred again. "Well, yes. It was kind of odd. But the…doctor said that his reaction was probably trauma-induced hallucinations." Well, Robert had said it and he was a doctor.

Tanner nodded. "And then this morning another gentleman, Mr. Amos Amin, also reacted *oddly* to your presence?"

Ami swallowed. Her throat felt viciously dry. Where was he going with this? What did it have to do with the assassination attempt? And how the hell did he know about it? "Yes, he did. We had to call Security."

"Have you considered why these two incidents occurred?"

"No," she lied. "I don't have any idea."

Tanner lowered his gaze, staring at the floor for a time. Ami found that move far more unnerving than if he'd continued that relentless stare directly into her eyes.

When he at last met her gaze again, he asked, "You really don't know me, do you?"

She did not know him. She didn't know either of the men on the fourth floor. This had to be some sort of bizarre mistake. She shook her head. At least she thought she did. She wasn't sure the movement was much more than a pathetic twitch.

Tanner reached into his pocket once more. This time he pulled out a couple of photographs. He laid them on the table in front of her. "Do you know the woman in these pictures?"

Don't look! Don't look! a little voice deep inside her cried. A part of her was certain that if she looked, something very bad would happen. She sucked in a ragged breath and tried to calm herself. Why was she so afraid? They were only pictures. The knot of fear twisted in her stomach. She had to look, didn't she? She forced away the questions whirling in her head and stared down at the pictures. The inner trembling she'd been restraining for hours erupted inside her. Her hands shook with the force of it.

In the photographs was a woman, a couple of years younger maybe, but she looked exactly like Ami. Exactly. Down to the unruly ponytail in which she wore her hair.

"It's not me," she breathed, her voice scarcely more than a whisper. She felt the color leech out of her face. This had to be some sort of joke. It couldn't be real. "It's someone else. Someone who looks like me. A mistake," she insisted.

"Miss Donovan," Tanner said quietly, "I'm afraid there is no mistake. For two years we've thought you were dead."

Two years. She'd been found wandering in the park two years ago. For all intents and purposes, her life began two years ago. "No." She shook her head again, harder this time. She had to make him see that he was wrong. His last statement abruptly reverberated in her ears. "'We'?"

"The CIA," he explained.

"It's not me," she repeated. She'd never even met anyone in the CIA—at least not until today.

"Your real name is Jamie Dalton. You were born in Baltimore, Maryland."

She didn't want to hear this but she couldn't seem to

think of the right words to make him go away. This couldn't be real. Maybe she was hallucinating.

"I don't know a Jamie Dalton," she told him flatly, and yet she rolled the name around in her mind to see if it stirred a response. *Jamie.* It didn't feel wrong, but it couldn't be right. No, she denied. She wasn't the Jamie he was talking about. She couldn't be. She was Ami Donovan now. Her past was gone.

"You were a second-year medical student when we met." He averted his gaze briefly as if it pained him to remember. "Your father was Jamison Dalton, a politically connected man who knew his way around the wealthy and the powerful in this country. His ability to pull together financing made him a strategic player in the success of a new, top-secret antiterrorism force. The private sector had been secretly helping certain elements of the government, of which I'm not at liberty to discuss, put together this joint force. Your father was assassinated by someone who wanted that effort to fail."

Tanner was silent for a moment, allowing her to absorb what he'd said so far. She understood his words, yet every fiber of her being rejected it as truth. This simply could not be.

"You were devastated by his death. It was when I was investigating his murder that I first saw you. I couldn't believe my eyes. You were the exact double of Amira Peres."

When Ami frowned, he hastened to explain, "Yael Peres was the man responsible for your father's death. We—the CIA—approached you about helping us bring him down. You agreed. We would never have been able to get close to him without your help. He was too good at hiding his wrongdoing…too well thought of in his home country, which he rarely left."

Whoa! She couldn't listen to any more of this. It was too, too much. Ami held up a hand for him to stop right there. "Mr. Tanner—"

"Jack," he interrupted. "You called me Jack…before."

She tried to read what exactly he meant by that statement but this was all far too confusing. It couldn't be real. "Jack, I don't know this Jamie Dalton. And I don't know you. There has to be some kind of mix-up."

"You have a birthmark on your left hip. It's shaped like a star. And you absolutely hate strawberries."

Ice slid slowly through her veins. How could he know those things? He…he couldn't know her. She didn't know him. None of this felt right. She didn't want to be Jamie Dalton.

"It took me six weeks to get you ready," he continued. "We worked together day and night." He pressed her with that deep brown gaze, urging her to remember.

She shook her head. "I don't remember you." He flinched. Had they…? No. No. That couldn't be. This was crazy.

"You went undercover as Peres's estranged daughter. You were under for three months. I lost contact with you that last month. And then we lost you. We…" His voice trailed off and silence hung between them for three endless beats. "We thought the Israelis had executed you."

Enough! "Why would they want to execute me?" she demanded, ready to march out of this room and call Security to take this nutcase away. This was the craziest story she'd ever heard. It sounded like a movie, not someone's life. Certainly not hers. She lived on Piedmont Street in a nice little home with perfect neighbors with the perfect man who loved her and whom she'd foolishly refused to marry.

"You set up Peres. He was a highly respected man and a personal friend of the Israeli prime minister's."

"Set him up?" Ami shook her head. "I don't know what you're talking about."

"You made sure he was in the right place at the right time and your lover killed him."

Ami lunged to her feet, her sluggish self-protective instincts charging into high gear. "You, Mr. Tanner, are either mistaken or totally insane. I am not a killer or an undercover agent. I'm just an ER nurse whose break time is over." She smoothed her sweating palms over her smock. "Now, if you'll excuse me."

Tanner stood, blocking her path when she would have walked away. He reached into his pocket yet again and brought out another photograph. "This man is Michal Arad. He's the single most vicious freelance terrorist in the world today. You were his lover for those three months. You talked him into taking down Peres."

Ami stared at the dark man in the picture. His long black hair was fastened at his nape. Sunglasses shielded his eyes, but nothing could hide the power that emanated from him even in a slightly out-of-focus, worn photograph. Something moved in a distant corner of her heart…something she couldn't name and didn't want to feel.

"This is the only photograph we have of him. He's elusive as well as vicious. But during the Peres mission he took the bait just like a lovesick puppy."

Ami's gaze shifted upward to Tanner. She had been the bait, if all he said was true. But it couldn't be true. She wouldn't let it be true. "I don't know this man and I don't know you." She stepped around him and headed for the door.

"Miss Donovan…Jamie—"

She turned to find him two steps behind her. "I'm going

to summon Security," she warned. "If I were you, I'd find my way to the nearest exit."

"I can understand how all this must sound to you. But you have to believe me. Your life depends upon it."

"And how is that?" she snapped, her nerves jangling and raw. This was beyond insane. None of this could be true. He surely didn't expect her to believe this ridiculous nonsense.

"I told you that we've thought you were dead for the past two years," he urged. "Well, so have the Israelis. Now they know different. If word got to me within a few hours, how long do you think it will take them to order an assassin team to finish the job they started two years ago?"

She lifted her chin and glared at him. "You need help, Mr. Tanner. Get this straight, I am not who you think I am."

He exhaled a heavy breath. "Think what you will, but if you don't listen to me, I doubt you'll live through the night."

His last statement unleashed a fresh wave of fear inside her. "I have to go." She had to get home. To ensure Nicholas was safe. Surely this insanity hadn't found its way to her home. She'd have to call the police. Maybe even before she left the hospital. This had gone entirely too far.

"The Israelis aren't the only ones who will want you dead," he added, jerking her attention back to him. "Michal Arad knows you set him up. He'll likely want his own revenge, as well."

A new kind of anxiety surged through her at the mention of the man in the photograph. "Stay away from me." Ami reached for the doorknob behind her without taking her eyes off him. "Just stay away." She didn't want to hear any more of this. She wanted out of here.

"If you won't do it for yourself," Tanner said, stalling

her by bracing one hand against the door. "Do it for your son. They'll kill him just to get back at you. I have to warn you that if Arad or the Israelis get their hands on you first, there's no way back. There will be nothing we can do to help you at that point. You have to let me help you *now*...before it's too late."

Hot tears streamed down her cheeks. She wanted to rant at him, but words failed her. Instead she jerked the door open and ran from the room.

"Ami! What's wrong?" Jane asked as they almost collided in front of the nurses' station.

Ami ignored her. She had to get out of here. She rushed down the corridor, dodging patients and personnel until she burst into the stairwell. She didn't stop until she was in the parking garage next to her car. She had to get to her son. Had to find Robert. He would know what to do. Her head ached and spun wildly. She braced her hands against the cold metal surface of her car until the spinning stopped. Her heart hammered beneath her sternum, making a deep breath impossible. She couldn't think straight, but she knew what she had to do. She had to get out of here.

Her keys.

"Shit!" she hissed. She'd left her purse in the locker room. Now she'd have to go back for it. She prayed Tanner would be gone by now.

She started to turn but a strong arm snaked around her waist at the same time a hand closed over her mouth. She kicked...tried to scream, but the attempt died in her throat. The sound of metal sliding on metal echoed behind her. Her captor dragged her into a van. Voices, too low to understand. The door slamming shut. Tires squealing.

Oh, God, oh, God! she cried silently. *Help me!*

She had to get to her baby. A needle pierced her skin.

She struggled to break away, but her strength vanished before she could take her next breath.

She had to…

Darkness dragged her down, down, down…until there was nothing else.

CHAPTER FOUR

PRESTON FOWLER, CIA Deputy Director of Closed Ops, Antiterrorism Division, sat behind his government-issue desk like the heartless son of a bitch he was and denied Jack Tanner's request.

"You know he'll kill her," Jack said from between clenched teeth. "There's not even a frigging question."

Fowler shrugged one massive shoulder. "Maybe. But I'm not sending in a retrieval team for one skinny broad whose head is already screwed up. No way. You offered her a chance, she didn't accept. She has no one to blame but herself."

Jack rocketed to his feet and paced the narrow space between Fowler's desk and the two upholstered chairs in front of it. How did he get this through that thick skull? "So we're just supposed to let her die."

"It won't be the first time we've sacrificed someone for the greater good. We all know this going in. Get a grip here, Tanner. You didn't just fall off the turnip truck." Fowler straightened his hundred-dollar tie. "Try to act like a professional."

Fury flashed anew inside Jack. He didn't want to hear this crap. He halted his pacing abruptly, flattened his palms on the too neat desk and leaned in his boss's direction in a blatant attempt at intimidation that was doomed to failure. "I trained her myself. She's mine. I'm not going to write her off as a calculated loss."

A nasty grin inched across Fowler's heavily lined features. "You always did have a thing for her, didn't you?"

Jack shook with the rage building beneath his barely controlled exterior. But he couldn't lose it. That would only make matters worse. He'd already given away far too much about just how personal this was to him. "We've already taken enough from her. She deserves to be cut some goddamn slack."

"Sit down, Tanner," his boss growled, all signs of amusement gone.

"I want some damn backup here," Jack demanded.

"Sit down."

His fists clenched for battle, but his brain recognizing his proximity to maxing Fowler's tolerance level for grief, Tanner dropped back into his chair. This was the part he hated about this damn job. The lack of compassion in those who sat behind a desk and had long ago forgotten what it was like to be out there risking his life for his flag.

"We're pretty sure it's Arad who has her, right?" Fowler suggested, feigning actual interest in the case.

Tanner forced himself to take a breath and think reasonably. "According to our intel the Israelis haven't made a move yet. It has to be Arad. He's the only one besides the Israelis who has an interest and the know-how and ability to move this quickly."

Fowler nodded. "I agree. But I disagree with your assumption that he'll kill her."

Jack rolled his eyes. "He will kill her. She set him up. He has to know that."

"But we also know that he liked having her in his bed."

A new blast of fury had to be repressed before Jack could respond in a normal tone. "She wouldn't be the first old lover he's killed."

Fowler flared his palms. "But the other one was a spy

for the French D.S.T. France had no business trying to get one of their intelligence operatives in bed with him. Arad is convinced our girl is the neglected and vengeful daughter of the late Yael Peres. That makes her like him…as far as he knows.''

''The man is smart,'' Jack argued impatiently. ''If he hasn't figured out her connection to us already, it won't take him long.''

''We'll just have to wait and see, won't we?''

Jack knew by the look in Fowler's eyes that there was no changing his mind, but that didn't stop him. ''We owe her. She's one of ours,'' he urged in a last-ditch effort to sway the unmovable. ''She gave up a lot for us.'' He sighed. ''More than even she knows.''

''You're right,'' Fowler agreed, to Jack's complete surprise. ''She is one of ours. And if she lives, I intend to use her to our benefit.''

Uneasiness nudged Jack. This was not a good thing. ''What do you mean, *use her?*''

''Arad has gotten too powerful. The decision has already been made. It's time to take him out of the picture. He makes too many people nervous, including some of our Israeli friends. She can help us do that.''

Jack laughed out loud, but the sound held no humor. ''She'll be dead long before we can put whatever the hell plan you've got up your sleeve into motion. Don't you get it?'' he demanded. ''She's probably dead already!''

''Then what's the big deal?'' Fowler demanded in that too reasonable tone of his. ''If she survives, we'll use her. If she doesn't, then we'll be saving the taxpayers a few dollars not having to keep her up.''

Jack pushed to his feet again. He wanted to climb across that perfectly organized desk and beat the hell out the thick-skulled bastard. But that would accomplish nothing.

The last thing he needed was to get any further on Fowler's bad side. Right now Jack was the only hope Ami had…and that wasn't saying much.

"What do you want me to do?" he asked, resignation heavy in his voice.

"See if you can get a line on where Arad's taken her. Take some time and see what her status is with her old lover. If this plays out like I believe it will, once we've established that she's back in tight with him, we'll move ahead."

"He's probably in France. Finding his approximate location won't be that difficult, but getting close will be impossible. You know how he works." This was a waste of time. "Nobody gets close to him. He knew that other woman was D.S.T. before he ever welcomed her into his tight little group. He had his reasons. He used her before she even knew what was happening. It's a miracle Ami fooled him."

Fowler grinned, another of those sick surface conventions that made Jack want to reach across his desk and throttle him. "Love is blind. Besides, I have every faith in your ability, Tanner. You'll get close enough to find out what's going on. You've got a personal stake in this. Just like Arad."

"Yeah, right." *Fuck you, too,* Jack didn't add.

He left Fowler's office with a bad feeling in his gut. He waffled between wanting to kill someone with his bare hands and wanting to get rip-roaring drunk. But neither of those things would help Ami. He wasn't sure anything outside a miracle straight from God would make a difference. At this point, it probably didn't matter in which direction the pendulum swung for her, she was likely dead either way.

AWARENESS CAME in slow, gradual degrees. Though she couldn't move, Ami could feel a bed beneath her and a cool sheet over her skin. It was too soft to be her bed at home. Robert preferred a firm mattress. There was a distinctly bad taste in her mouth. She tried to swallow, but the effort proved too monumental a task so she drifted back to sleep.

Sometime later, though she still couldn't open her eyes, she did hear voices. The whispered words were too hushed to distinguish. Was she in a hospital? County General, maybe? She remembered rushing to her car.

But what had happened after that?

More voices and images filled her head. The sound of a door slamming…the squeal of tires. Fear welled inside her. She'd been kidnapped. Tanner…the CIA guy. Terrorists. She tried to shake her head. To deny the memories slowly seeping back into her skull. This couldn't be real. She didn't know anyone in the CIA, and she sure didn't know any terrorists. Maybe she was having a breakdown of some sort. That would explain everything.

There was only one way to prove it was all just a bad dream. She had to open her eyes and look. Ami focused intently on the task, but her body wouldn't cooperate. Finally her lids drifted open. Unaccustomed to the light, she snapped them shut again. But she had to see. Slowly she opened her eyes once more, blinking to adjust. Large windows or doors of some sort lined the wall she was facing.

She could hear the voices again. A little louder now. Her head felt as if it was stuffed with cotton, but at the same time as heavy as a bowling ball. She couldn't move. All she wanted to do was to go back to sleep. But if she went back to sleep she would never know where she was or why she was here.

With a groan she managed to roll onto her back. A large

fan slowly circled above her. Richly stained wooden beams appeared dark against the white ceiling. Where was she?

If Arad or the Israelis get their hands on you first, there's no way back.

She'd been kidnapped, her mind told her again, more firmly this time.

Ami bolted upright. She groaned and held her head in her hands until it stopped spinning. Finally she lifted her gaze and blinked until her eyes had regained focus. Oversized furniture lined this new wall she faced. An armoire and a couple of chairs with a table between them. At first it felt as if she were seeing everything in black and white since there appeared to be no color in the room other than varying shades of gray. She looked to her right again, at the wall of windows she'd seen before. The blue sky that reached down to touch the green and brown earth beyond the glass allayed that concern.

But where was she?

Ami pushed the sheet away and gingerly dropped her feet to the bare wood floor. Take it slow, she told herself. She grabbed hold of the bedpost and was distracted a moment by the intricately carved detailing of the stout wooden post. She pulled herself up and stood absolutely still for a time to relieve the vertigo. She took in a deep, steadying breath. There was something vaguely familiar about the way the room smelled, but she couldn't grasp the fleeting memory. Finally, when the dizziness had passed, she took one tiny step at a time until she reached the wall of windows.

French doors stood between two massive windows. A balcony sprawled in front of her. Beyond that was the autumn-colored forest she'd seen reaching up to the blue sky. The sun was low, almost hidden behind the treetops. Nothing she saw looked even vaguely familiar. She reached for the lever to open the door but a voice stopped her.

"That would be a mistake."

The deep, erotic sound of the accented voice stroked across her senses, shimmered through her soul, stirring something hidden and long forgotten. But with the dangerous lure of the sound came fear, stark and deep, making her flesh pebble with goose bumps. Slowly, she turned to face the man who'd spoken.

He stood in the shadows on the far side of the room, watching her. Hair as black as midnight fell around his broad shoulders. Without the white shirt he would have disappeared completely into those deepening shadows.

"If you step out onto that balcony, the guards have orders to shoot." He said this with cold, calculating calm.

Ami reached way down deep for any courage she could find and asked, "Where am I?" Her voice sounded small and as shaky as she felt. She trembled before she could stop herself. She was cold, she rationalized, and hugged her arms around her middle. Only then did she think to look down to see what she was wearing. A man's shirt. The worn soft fabric whispered against her bare skin. The masculine scent that clung to it elicited an alien yet somehow familiar yearning deep inside her.

He moved toward her. Her head came up, not because she'd heard him, for he made no sound, but because she felt him. Felt him move closer to her as if his presence was somehow connected to her own. She flattened against the door as the thick tension radiating from him slowly closed in around her.

When he stood only three or four feet away, he stopped, the reality of his size slamming into her full-force then. He was tall. Broad shoulders tapered into a lean waist and narrow hips. Long, muscular legs filled out the jeans he wore. Her gaze traveled back up to his face. There was no denying that this was an extraordinarily good-looking man, all angles and shadow, but it was his eyes that were the most compelling of his assets. Deep, dark, pools of heat that could see right through her. That familiar yearning…a recognition of sorts flared, making her shiver.

"Do you know who I am?" he asked, his silky voice now rough with impatience.

She shook her head. "Please, I just want to go home." Tears welled in her eyes and she blinked rapidly to hold them at bay. She didn't want to cry. She wanted to be strong. Strong enough to somehow convince this man that he'd make a mistake. A terrible mistake.

"I am Michal Arad." That intent gaze bored more deeply into hers, watching, analyzing. "This name means nothing to you?"

Her lips trembled and a sob escaped before she could stop it. "I'm sorry. I don't know who you are or why I'm here, but there must be a mistake. I have to go home." *I need to hold my baby,* her heart cried. "Please," she whispered, emotion choking her. "Please, just let me go home."

"So Gil was right. You remember nothing." He crossed his arms over his chest and stroked his chin. The sound of a day's beard growth rasped beneath his fingers. She shivered, her gaze settling on his full lips. They moved slowly, sensually, as he spoke. "Even with the sodium pentathol. Interesting."

Sodium pentathol? That's why she felt so groggy. They'd drugged her. She suddenly remembered the prick of a needle when she'd first been dragged into the van in the hospital parking garage. How long ago had that been? Where was she now? She pivoted and stared out the window, desperation surging through her with every beat of her heart. She didn't recognize anything at all about the landscape. How could she hope to get away when she had no idea where she was?

"Where am I?" she heard herself ask again, her voice weary now. The fierce emotions were draining out of her, leaving a kind of resigned numbness. She was going to die. The CIA guy named Tanner had warned her and she hadn't listened. And now it was too late. ...*no way back*.

"You are in my home. That is all I will tell you until I have made a decision."

Ami shivered again with something more than fear, then almost laughed out loud. She was pathetic. Despite her dire circumstances the man's deep, compelling voice still had the power to make her tremble with a mixture of emotions that frightened her even more than the thought of death.

She faced him again, knowing that nothing she said or did at this point would make a difference. She was dead. It was only a matter of time. She would never see her baby again. And who would raise him? Would Robert still care for Nicholas now that she was out of the picture? She prayed with all her heart that he would. Why hadn't she married him a year ago? Then there would be no question. She'd been such a fool.

"What decision?" she asked...no, it wasn't a question, it was a demand, she realized as the harshly uttered words echoed in the room. Feeling suddenly brave, or maybe too incredibly stupid to care, she lifted her gaze and stared directly into his. "What decision do you have to make?"

He touched her then. Her breath caught, but to her credit she didn't pull away. Those long fingers lingered on her cheek, then trailed along the column of her throat, making her tremble yet again.

"The decision," he said, his accented voice soft yet

undeniably lethal, "as to what I will do with you now that I've found you."

She looked away, unable to tolerate that penetrating gaze a second longer. "Whatever you believe I've done to you, you're wrong." She stared fully into those dark eyes. "I'm not who you think I am."

He flattened his hands on the door on either side of her and leaned in closer, so close she could feel the whisper of his warm breath on her face.

"It is not a matter of what I believe," he told her, his voice just as soft, just as deadly as before. "It is a matter of what I know. I know what you've done. And I know exactly who you are."

CHAPTER FIVE

MICHAL LEFT THE ROOM, his senses humming with a mélange of emotions. Need had somehow surged to the fore-
front and overtaken all others, however, and that infuriated
him beyond reason. He did not *need* this woman.

He would not fall prey to her seemingly innocent temptation again. For he knew firsthand that she was not innocent. His jaw tightened with the fury building inside him
at his own stupidity. She had plotted the assassination of
her own father and had used him to accomplish that end.
She had made him drunk with her wicked, feminine
wiles…had given up her body entirely to him. Whatever
he had wanted she had given until he had grown blind
with lust, driven only by need, and finally becoming completely obsessed.

She had been his one obsession, his one mistake.

Then he had lost her.

He closed his eyes and fought the emotion that accompanied that last thought. For two endless years he had believed her dead. He had grieved the loss, prayed for his
own death, apathetic of his destiny without her. In their
short time together she had become everything to him.

And now he'd found her again…alive and well.

His eyes opened wide with renewed determination. He
would not fall under her spell this time. She was evil…a
harlot. A bitch who cared for no one other than herself.

Wherever she had been hiding, whatever she had been

doing all this time, mattered little to him. She was here now and *now* she would pay for her betrayal.

The word had traveled swiftly to him. Some imbecile had failed in his attempt to assassinate Natan Olment. The press had insisted that the American was the target, but Michal knew better. Olment was high on the list of those wanted dead by the supporters of the fallen Taliban. Though forced underground to carry out its machinations, money was no obstacle for the crippled organization. The payment for making such a kill would be substantial, the task a simple one. Olment and his security advisor were fools. Michal could have taken him out on numerous occasions, had played the scenario over in his mind and laughed at the ease with which he could accomplish the hit if he so chose.

Now that ridiculously lax security would be tightened. The security advisor replaced, as should have been done months ago. Those with less skill than Michal would bemoan the loss of potential opportunity. To him it made no difference. The reputation he had earned spoke for itself. Lucky for him, Olment had no part in his plans for the immediate future.

Of course that could change, but Michal didn't see that happening as things stood. Olment dabbled in nothing that interested him.

The woman on the other side of the door he braced against dragged his attention back to the present. He had a more pressing quandary at the moment than what his next crusade would be. He had to decide what to do with her. His jaw tightened again. She had to die. There was no real question there. But he would be the one to decide when her fate was to be carried out.

If his heart proved too weak to exact the necessary ven-

geance, he would cut it out. It was worthless to him, anyway. The organ merely continued to beat, nothing more.

He moved away from the door as if her very essence
could somehow penetrate the heavy wood and reach him,
ultimately making him weak. He would not consider the
issue further now, he decided as he moved toward where
the others waited. When he was stronger, when the shock
of seeing her again had passed, would be the proper time
for such a course of action. He would need all of his
strength, all of his powers of concentration, to do what had
to be done.

She had to pay.

Just not today.

"Why is she still alive?"

The irate tone of his comrade heightened Michal's already mounting frustration. He stared at Carlos, his right
arm—the man who had proven his worth over and over
again. But, to Michal's way of thinking, in the last twenty-
four hours that worth had lessened considerably. A comrade's value could only be accurately measured by his will-
ingness to follow his leader and/or his orders to the death.

Michal was not accustomed to being questioned where
his decisions were concerned.

"She is alive," he said to his friend, his tone lethal, his
words leaving no room for discussion, "because I allow
it. Do you have a problem with that?"

His defiance never wavering, Carlos openly questioned
Michal's authority for the first time. He sauntered a step
closer, his posture growing even more belligerent. "I
watched the effect this woman had on you two years ago."
One dark eyebrow slanted high above the other. "She dis-
tracts you," he suggested in the thick accent that gave
away his Israeli roots. "We—" he motioned magnani-
mously to the others lounging in the room "—were almost

captured because of her.'' He banged a fist against his chest. ''Our own brothers despise us now, attempt to bring us down at every opportunity because of her. *That* is my problem!''

Tamping down his fury to a more tolerable level, Michal closed the remaining distance between them. ''You have stated your objections. *This*—'' he looked straight into his old friend's eyes ''—will be the end of it. The decision as to what will become of her is mine and mine alone.''

Absolute silence reigned in the room. No one dared to even move. The others waited for the outcome, not one had the courage to side with Carlos, yet not one would dispute him since he wanted to live to see another day. The tension built so swiftly, so thickly, that the very air evacuated the room.

''Mark my words,'' Carlos said, ''she will be the death of us all.''

Michal laughed softly, but didn't relax his battle-ready stance. Staying in control was crucial. ''So now you are a prophet, is that the way of it?''

Carlos grunted a halfhearted laugh. ''Clearly you are not. But, as you say, the decision is yours.''

Michal turned to the others, taking his time, studying each familiar face in turn. These were the men with whom he had worked for the past three years. He had earned their respect under the tutelage of their former leader, a man known only as the Wolf. After his assassination, Michal had risen to the challenge as his successor. No one had questioned the move, not even Carlos who had worked with the Wolf for a longer period of time. Carlos claimed that he preferred the chain of command just as it was. He had no desire to lead, only to follow.

Michal had an uneasy feeling about that now. He'd noted Carlos's need to have more of a say during recent strategy meetings. He imagined his days were numbered to Carlos's way of thinking. Michal did not fear the confrontation. He had long ago decided that death might be a relief.

Until now.

Now everything had changed.

"Is there anyone else who would question my authority?"

Heads wagged from side to side, negative responses were grunted all the way around the room. All eyes remained fixed on Michal; no one had the nerve to meet Carlos's unrelenting gaze as they, however belatedly, openly professed their loyalty.

"Then we are in agreement, no?" Michal turned back to the man at his side, watching and waiting for some indication of just how far he intended to take this vie for power.

The corners of Carlos's mouth curled into a sly smile. "We are in agreement."

Michal nodded. "A wise decision." He surveyed the group once more. "We must take advantage of this time to rest and hone our skills. We have some time yet before our next mission. This one will be tricky. Keen focus will be the key. No one—" He shot a sidelong glance at Carlos. "No one can be distracted. This is assuredly not the time for division."

Carlos merely stared back at him, his previous display of aggression reined in for the most part. *"No one,"* he agreed pointedly.

Michal left it at that and sought refuge outside in the coming gloom. The air was cool and he filled his lungs with the pleasant scents of the changing season. He closed his eyes and tried to remember how his homeland smelled. But it had been far too long since he had set foot upon that soil and, in an effort to keep his sanity, he had worked far too diligently to banish it from his mind to recall it now. A high price had been leveled on his head there; he was considered a murderer and worse. In reality, he had no homeland. But he no longer cared. He had stopped caring about anything at all two years ago.

Forcing his thoughts away from the woman inside, he surveyed the grounds for as far as he could see in the encroaching dusk. The perimeter guards moved around soundlessly, all of whom would have taken note of his presence the instant he exited the house. Michal had many dedicated men at his disposal, any of which would willingly die for him. Except, perhaps, for Carlos. Until a few days ago he would have said the same for him. But he had changed of late, particularly since Amira's return. That, too, seemed suspect to Michal. Though Carlos's rationale for being disturbed by her presence was sound, there was something more going on.

Only time would reveal this unknown factor. Michal turned and stared up at the room—his room—where he held Amira prisoner. Just as time would also determine her fate.

HE WASN'T COMING back.

Ami sucked in another shaky breath, mentally commanding herself to pull it together. She had to think. She couldn't just stand here and wait for him to return. She had to run. To hide. Something.

She pushed off from the door where she'd remained glued even after he'd walked out of the room. She simply hadn't had the strength or courage to move away from the support it gave or the hope it offered since it led to the balcony outside. But the guards were out there, as well. He'd said they had orders to shoot. She shuddered.

Clothes. First, she needed clothes.

She looked down at herself again and fought another wave of terror as she considered that he, or someone who worked for him, had undressed her. That was done. Nothing she could do about it. She looked around the room and decided to start with the armoire. All she had to do was make it across the room.

Putting one foot in front of the other, she slowly made the journey, praying with each step that the floor wouldn't creak, giving her movements away. She felt certain there would be a guard right outside her door.

Slowly she opened the armoire doors, her heart thudding so hard she could scarcely hear herself think. She scanned the folded items on the shelves, then opened each drawer in turn, sorting through the contents as carefully as possible so as not to leave anything out of place.

Nothing she had been wearing when she rushed out of the hospital.

Jeans, shirts…all, she presumed, belonging to her captor.

She turned to survey the room once more. Where were her clothes? Surely they wouldn't have thrown them away.

Moving more quickly now, she got down on her hands and knees and looked under the bed. Nothing.

She pushed to her feet and rushed to the en suite bathroom and came up empty-handed again. Towels and facecloths, toiletries.

Her pulse fluttering wildly, she moved back into the large bedroom. Everything she'd been wearing was gone. She remembered that she hadn't had her purse with her so she had no ID other than her hospital badge, and no money.

A phone.

She glanced around frantically. She needed a phone.

An old-fashioned, rotary-base telephone sat on the table between the two chairs next to the armoire. She ran toward it, almost stumbling in her haste, and snatched up the receiver.

The line was dead.

She had to bite down on her lower lip to hold back a cry of panic and to regulate the breathing that was coming in ragged spurts. Why wasn't there a dial tone?

She got down on her hands and knees and traced the line leading from the telephone to the wall.

Two inches from the wall jack the line lay on the floor, severed completely. She jammed the ends together and tried to think of some way to tape it. That would work, wouldn't it?

She scrambled up and back to the bathroom in search of any kind of tape. Bandages, gauze tape, anything. She flung the contents of the various drawers to the floor, no longer concerned with caution.

Nothing.

No kind of tape and not a single item she could use for a weapon.

She sank to the floor and hugged her arms around her knees. It was hopeless.

Long minutes later, maybe thirty, maybe more, she heard the telltale creak of the bedroom door opening. She didn't bother gathering the scattered items on the floor. She was dead. What difference would a mess make?

He was going to kill her and there was nothing she could do about it. She would never see her baby again.

When he stopped in the doorway, she peered up at him. She could feel the scald of tears on her cheeks, but she no longer cared about that, either. She was numb inside.

She was going to die.

Michal watched her for a moment, uncertain what she

might do next. Judging by the disarray of the room, panic had clearly gotten the better of her. He brutally squashed the first sensations of sympathy that tried to bore into his hardened heart. He would feel nothing for her except the desire he could not conquer.

"I brought you a change of clothes." He angled his head toward the bed behind him. "When you've bathed, you may dress for dinner."

She continued to stare at him as if he hadn't spoken at all. A jolt of fury screwed his gut into knots when the pangs of sympathy would not abate. He took her by the arm, ensuring that his fingers bit deeply into her flesh, and jerked her to her feet.

"Do it now," he growled near her face.

She flinched but didn't bother trying to pull free of his hold. He shoved her away, his hand tingling from even that brief encounter with her smooth skin.

He turned his back on her and strode to the bed. He grabbed the package he'd sent one of his men to collect from a boutique in Marseilles and carried it back to the bathroom. He tossed it onto the floor and glowered at her since she still stood exactly where he'd left her.

"I said, prepare for dinner."

She moved slowly, keeping him in the edge of her vision as she opened the shower door and adjusted the spray of water.

"It'll take me a few minutes," she said shakily, her gaze still not meeting his.

"Fine," he snapped. "I have all night." He crossed his arms over his chest and leaned against the door frame.

Her eyes widened when she realized he had no intention of giving her any privacy.

He knew his actions would prove a mistake, but he simply could not help himself. He wanted to watch. No. He needed to watch.

She reached for the first button on the shirt, her hands trembling, tears welling in her pale blue eyes. He gritted his teeth against the softer emotions that threatened his control.

One button after the other, she released until there were no more. She looked up at him then and something changed in her eyes. She turned around, giving him her back, and allowed the shirt to drift down to the cold tile floor.

His breath caught in spite of his efforts not to allow it, in spite of the fact that he'd already seen her nude while she was unconscious. But this was different. She was awake, her creamy-smooth skin flushed with humiliation. The gentle curves of her feminine body all the more alluring.

With all that made him male, he wanted to touch her…to take her. He wanted to bury himself inside her until she pleaded for his forgiveness…until she screamed his name and begged for mercy. He wanted to fuck her long and hard, until he spilled out two long years of frustration and pain.

He wanted her. His loins hardened to the point of readiness in a mere instant of simply looking at her…thinking of plunging into her sweet, hot depths.

She stepped into the shower and he turned away, disgusted with himself.

Whatever good had ever existed inside him was gone. He was nothing. He had nothing but his work.

And he was very, very good at his work.

No one had ever reached this point before.

No one.

He was hated by all, feared by most, and revered by a chosen few.

He was the only link.

HER HANDS SHAKING, Ami toweled her hair dry as best she could. She paused in her efforts and stared at the woman in the mirror. Her skin was pink and fresh from the scrubbing she'd given it. The idea that he had touched her...

She closed her eyes and told herself again that even the thought repulsed her. But, in truth, it was the heat that swelled inside her even when he looked at her that bothered her the most. He had kidnapped her. Had told her in no uncertain terms that she was going to die and still she could not completely disregard her body's reaction to him.

She shook off the awareness that plagued her when she so much as called to mind his image. She squeezed her eyes shut and cursed herself. What was wrong with her? None of this could be true. She couldn't have worked for the CIA or had an affair with this man. She certainly wouldn't have had anything to do with anyone's murder. There had to be a mistake.

She'd read about cases like this, had even seen a movie or two with this very plotline. The problem was, she must look strikingly similar to the real Amira Peres. Tanner had said as much. That coincidental resemblance had her in deep trouble. Hurt twisted inside her again when she thought of her baby. How long had it been since she'd seen him? Twenty-four hours? Longer?

It was dark now. She had to have been gone more than twenty-four hours. It had been almost dark when she'd been grabbed in the basement garage at the hospital. She'd been drugged and interrogated and when she'd awakened it had been daylight. Yes, she was sure of it. Just over twenty-four hours had passed.

She ran her fingers through her still-damp hair and exhaled a heavy breath. She had to find a way to escape. But before she could do that she needed to get the lay of the land, so to speak. If she could keep her cool, she would eventually learn where she was being held and how many of his men were here.

She squared her shoulders and made a promise to her reflection. She would find a way out of this. She had to. Nicholas was counting on her.

Another thought crashed into her musings. That Tanner guy. Jack. The CIA guy. He'd said she was in danger, that she was one of them. Surely the CIA would be looking for her since Robert had most likely reported her missing. A glimmer of relief warmed her chest. If what Tanner said was true, which she couldn't see how it was, but still, if he thought it was, she was not only an American citizen, she was CIA. They would have to look for her. And Tanner knew where to look. He'd mentioned Michal Arad by name.

Her hopes shored up with that last thought, she smoothed her hands over the new jeans and checked her blouse to see that it covered all that it should. It was a little tight and a little revealing, but it was better than wearing that shirt of his. She shivered at the remembered scent that was uniquely his. That was definitely something she didn't need cluttering her senses.

She moved to the bedroom door but hesitated before opening it. What if she opened the door and the guard took the move as one of aggression and shot her? She forced the idea away. She was expected for dinner. Besides, it was probably locked.

To her surprise the door opened when she turned the

knob. Holding her breath she peeked into the hallway. The sight of the man holding a large, ugly weapon pointed directly at her registered instantly and she squealed before she could clamp her hand over her mouth.

"Come with me."

Her gaze swung to the man who'd spoken. Arad waited, a few steps away. The guard immediately lowered his weapon, but his hate-filled glare stayed firmly in place.

Thankful to be free of the room, she followed Arad along a dimly lit corridor. She passed other closed doors and she couldn't help wandering if anyone else was being held prisoner behind one of those doors. Or if one of them led to the outside. Nothing she encountered gave her any indication of where she was or how she'd gotten here.

The corridor finally gave way into a large room, like a great room. A couple of sofas and several chairs were scattered around. There was a huge stacked-stone fireplace and a television. The walls were wood, the decor rustic. And not a telephone in sight. She missed a step when her gaze fell on the enormous double-entry doors. Though the doors were barred like the entry to a fortress, the desire to run toward them was nearly irresistible.

Ami bumped into Arad's broad chest as she moved forward once more and before she realized he had stopped and turned around.

"You are not to speak to any of my men. You will eat and then you will return to your room." His next words told her he hadn't missed her preoccupation with the doors. "There is a state-of-the-art security system. If you open an exterior door, an alarm will sound and, as I told you before, the guards have orders to shoot you on sight if, at any time, you are found outside the house without being accompanied by me."

She nodded, too overwhelmed to speak. How could she

feel anything but utter hatred for this savage? She hated him. Her fingers balled into fists as the need to do him bodily injury rushed through her veins.

He smiled, obviously reading her mind yet again. "You should have killed me two years ago."

With a wave of his arm he ordered her to precede him into the kitchen. Helpless to do otherwise, she did as instructed. Several men pushed away from the table and filed out of the huge dining room, each glaring down at her as he passed. She counted six and there were more outside. One man, a barbaric-looking brute with long brown hair tied back into a ponytail, remained at the other end of the table. Tears burned at the backs of Ami's eyes. How could she ever hope to escape with odds like this? She couldn't.

She dropped into the chair Arad pulled from the table and admitted defeat. She was going to die and there was nothing she could do about it.

He placed a stoneware plate, laden with a generous portion of roast beef and mixed vegetables, in front of her. Even the smell made her stomach roil. She didn't know when she'd eaten last, but the idea was more than she could deal with at the moment. She was going to die, why did it matter if she ate?

Her heart lurched. Was Robert seeing to Nicholas at this very moment? Feeding him? Bathing him and readying him for bed? She blinked back the moisture gathering. Would he remind her baby that she loved him? Would he tell Nicholas as he grew older that she hadn't wanted to leave him? That some terrible man had kidnapped her?

"Eat."

Her gaze connected with Arad's and she couldn't hold back the tears. She tried. She really did. But they would be contained no longer.

Fury tightened the features of his face, sending a new

wave of fear through her. He scooped up a spoonful of potatoes and held it close to her mouth. "Eat."

She moistened her lips and tried to open her mouth, told herself that she had to do as he said, but she just couldn't. She shook her head. "I'm sorry…I—"

He grabbed her chin and held it firmly, forcing her mouth to open as he shoved the spoon inside. Her throat and stomach rebelled against the intrusion. She clamped her hand over her mouth to keep from spitting out the food. She instinctively knew that if she did she would regret it. After a few moments of fighting the gag reflex, she finally chewed and allowed the potatoes, little by little, to slide down her throat.

When she wiped her mouth with the back of her hand, he shoved another spoonful toward her.

She couldn't do this. Her stomach contracted once more at the very sight of the food. "I can't…"

He grabbed her by the chin once more and forced her to look directly into his eyes. "You can and you will."

Something in his eyes… The fury or maybe the other emotion she saw there. A hurt that didn't quite mesh with the evil persona.

A sob burst from her before she could stop it. "Why?" she cried. "Why do you care if I eat? You're going to kill me anyway."

"The date and means of your death," he snarled, "will not be your decision. It will be mine." He released her as if touching her had somehow burned him. He barked something in a language she did not understand to the man at the other end of the table. The man pushed to his feet and stamped down to where she sat. He grabbed her by the arm and dragged her from the table, overturning her chair in the process.

Hysteria setting in now, Ami looked from the brute to

Arad and back; he only stared after her as she was dragged away. She stumbled as she tried to keep up with the man's long strides. Her heart thundered so hard in her chest she couldn't draw in a breath. When he shoved her into the bedroom where she'd awakened, relief washed over her. Thank God. At least they weren't going to kill her yet.

As long as she was alive there was still hope.

The man looked her up and down and smirked. "Sleep well, whore, for tomorrow you die."

CHAPTER SIX

THE DREAM came again. No matter that she tried to banish it. She couldn't escape the exquisite pull…like the ocean's tide beneath the influence of the full moon, it was destiny. He lay next to her. She didn't have to open her eyes…she could feel him there. Long, dark hair against the linens. Skin that was bronzed as much by the sun as by genetics and stretched taut over muscle sculpted by danger.

His deep voice whispered against her skin. *You will always belong to me.* Her fingers tightened in the sheet as images evolved, moving the dream from one moment in time to the next. Moments she had spent with him…in his arms. Then she saw a new face. An older man. He stared up at her in startled amazement. Blood bloomed from the place where a dagger protruded from his chest. With one bloody hand he reached for her…

"W-why?"

Ami bolted upright in bed, shattering the final image of her nightmare, her breath coming in uneven spurts.

Her hands shook as she pushed the hair back from her face. Sweat dampened her skin. Dreaming. She'd only been dreaming, she told herself as she struggled to gain her bearings.

She squeezed her eyes shut against the vivid picture of the bloody hand reaching out to her…the broken voice asking why. Though she didn't recognize that face, she did know the other one that had haunted her yet again.

Forcing her respiration to quiet, she clenched her fists in preparation and turned her head in infinitesimal increments until she ensured that the other side of the bed was empty. She dragged in a lungful of blessed relief. Thank God. This time the dream had felt so real. It was as if he'd actually been right there next to her…touching her… whispering intimate words to her. She shivered and pulled her knees up so that she could press her forehead there.

Reality crashed in on her all over again. It was the same every morning. She would wake up from the powerful dreams, her skin still warm from the touch of his hand, whether real or imagined. But it damn sure felt real. Then she would gather her wits and she would know.

She was a prisoner.

Somewhere in France. She had gleaned that much from a glimpse of a television news program some of the men had been watching.

Three days he had kept her here. Forcing her to eat…to bathe…to wait. To obey his every order. The way he looked at her—she shivered again—terrified her on several levels. He despised her, wanted to hurt her somehow. The disgust was almost always there in those dark, dark eyes. But other times she saw something else. Pain. Need. Something along those lines. She could only assume that what he said was true and that this Amira Peres brutally betrayed him.

But she was not Amira Peres. She was Ami Donovan. The tears rose instantly, burning her eyes and reminding her of the defeat sucking at her very existence.

Dear God, she only wanted to get back to her son. To hold her sweet baby in her arms.

She tried to be strong. Looked for any avenue of escape, but they watched her every moment of every day.

The sobs started deep inside her, like the threatening rumbles of a volcano before it built to overflowing. When she could contain the misery no longer, she wept openly, loudly. Not for herself, but for her child.

She prayed again that Robert would be a good father to Nicholas. She wished for the hundredth time that she had married him as he'd asked on so very many occasions. Then she begged God to send Jack Tanner to rescue her. Surely the CIA wouldn't just forget about her.

Scrubbing her face with the heels of her hands, she dredged up a smidgen of courage and fumbled for her composure as she climbed from the bed. Lying there crying would accomplish nothing. She had to find a way to escape.

The mere idea sent hope soaring inside her. She had to escape. It was the only way. She was the only woman here, as far as she had seen. That could be an advantage.

Renewed determination steadied her trembling limbs and firmed her resolve. Why hadn't she thought of this already? All she had to do was befriend one of the guards and use him to unknowingly facilitate her escape.

She shuddered at the possibility of what that kind of maneuver might cost her, but whatever it cost it would be worth the price if she could get free. If she made it to a nearby house she could use the phone and call for help. There would be an American embassy in Paris, though she didn't know how far she was from Paris. She would find a way to get there or, at the very least, get a call through to the police. She didn't speak French, but she felt certain the word "help" was universal.

The image of her son was fixed steadfastly in her mind. She would do anything to get back to him. *Anything.*

Ami showered and dressed in another of the outfits Michal had purchased for her. He had apparently decided he would keep her alive for quite some time since he'd outfitted her with a fairly complete wardrobe. This time she would not rue the tight-fitting, revealing clothing. This time she would flaunt the assets her captor insisted on displaying.

She chewed her lip as she stared at her reflection in the steam-fogged mirror. If he really thought she was this Amira Peres who had betrayed him so cruelly, then why hadn't he killed her already? Why did he dress her like a trashy Barbie doll and toy with her emotionally and physically? She tossed the brush aside and braced her hands on the basin to think about that for a bit. Maybe he was still in love with Amira Peres.

Turning that concept over in her mind, Ami straightened and paced the length of the small room. If he was still in love with the woman he thought her to be, that made him vulnerable on some level. She hesitated midturn. She could use that…pretend to be whatever he wanted her to be until just the right moment presented itself. She swung around and stared at her reflection once more. She could do that. The images from the dreams that haunted her each time she closed her eyes sent a quiver through her.

For her son she could do most anything.

The face of the older man, the one with the knife stuck into his chest, intruded on her musings. A frown marred her brow and something deep inside her shifted painfully. Who was the man? Had she conjured up the image from the horrible tales Michal Arad had told her? Or maybe Tanner had told her that she'd helped assassinate Amira Peres's father? Was her subconscious somehow confusing fact with fiction?

She shook herself and pushed the concept aside. She had to focus here. Finally she had a plan. One that might just work. She pulled in a deep, steadying breath. One that could just as easily get her killed. But then, she was dead anyway, right?

She had to make this work. However she had to approach this new avenue cautiously. Too abrupt a change in her behavior would give her away. She had to proceed very, very carefully. If he suspected for one second that she was up to anything…

He would kill her. He wanted to already, but something held him back. A number of his men, especially the one named Carlos, didn't like her being there. She'd have to see what she could do about that, as well. Win them over, in a manner of speaking.

You were undercover for three months…

Jack Tanner's words echoed inside her. According to his side of all this she'd agreed to work for the CIA as some sort of undercover agent. She still couldn't believe she'd done all that and had no memory of it. The last thing Robert had said to her reverberated through her with the force of a physical blow.

Whoever you were before is gone for good.

The realization hit with such intensity…such clarity that she stumbled from the weight of it.

Everything Tanner said could be true. She had no idea who she was before she was found wandering in that park two years ago. She blinked and peered more intently at her image in the mirror. Was she capable of being a spy? Setting up a man, no matter how ruthless, to die?

Tanner had said that she'd done it because this man, this Yael Peres, had her father assassinated. She supposed that revenge could motivate a person to do most anything. Somehow it just didn't feel right…but that didn't make it wrong.

Whoever she was and whatever she'd done in the past had gotten her into this predicament. It was no longer reasonable to assume that it was all a matter of mistaken identity. Too many people recognized her…too many verifying memories flickered through her mind for it to be mere coincidence or subliminal suggestion. This whole scenario held more merit than she wanted to admit. So she wouldn't. She would simply use the situation to her advantage. She would assume that *if* she'd worked as a spy before, she could again. That *if* she'd been her captor's lover before, she could now. That *if* she could fool them all, including her lover then, she could now.

She had to try.

She remembered now that Tanner had warned her there would be no way back if Michal Arad or the Israelis got their hands on her first. Bottom line: she couldn't count on the CIA to come and rescue her.

She had to do this herself.

For Nicholas.

AT THE END of a narrow brick-and-stone street between the tightly packed old houses and refurbished ancient buildings in the Panier district of Marseilles, Ron Doamiass stood in the shadows. But not so much so that Michal could not discern the expression on his face. Ron did not like where this conversation was going. The brooding medieval village on the north side of the Quai du port, which Michal had chosen for the rendezvous, did not help his mood.

Too bad. Michal had had enough.

"I want out." He looked straight into his old friend's eyes and made the statement that had been a very long time in coming. "Three years is too long."

Ron sighed and shook his head. He had worked for the Israeli Mossad twice as long as Michal's seven years. Ron had moved up the ranks quickly. His knowledge of on-

going operations and level of clearance marked him as a
member of the chosen few in the hierarchy of the covert
organization. His influence could very well sway the decision by those in power as to Michal's fate.

"I can no longer do this." Michal turned away, unwilling to allow his friend to see the depth of the pain he
suffered. He had become one of "them." His entire existence sickened him. He'd lost count of the number of
men he had killed. All in the name of the greater good. At
first he had anticipated this assignment with the kind of
excitement borne of naiveté. Wished for the occasion to
rid this earth of the scum that he now lived among. His
burning need to right at least a few of the world's wrongs
and to serve his country to the fullest extent possible had
driven him to excel beyond all expectations. The high of
success had carried him the first year under deep cover.
He'd utilized his American education in international law
and his privileged Israeli upbringing among the politically
elite to make himself indispensable to those who obeyed
no man's law.

Michal Arad had not only infiltrated the international
terrorist group led by the Wolf, he had become the ruthless
leader's right arm. He had worked his way to the top of
the food chain, devouring anyone who got in his way.
Then, utilizing the intelligence he'd gathered, the Wolf had
been assassinated during a particularly ingenious operation
masterminded by top Israeli strategists like Ron himself.
A feat neither the Americans nor the Europeans had been
able to accomplish.

Michal was a hero.

But no one could ever know. He had been ordered to
retain his cover…to live with those he despised and to
continue to provide the intelligence no one before him had
ever been in a position to know. The very people he risked

his life to protect, feared and despised him the most. The fewer people who knew the truth, the less risk to his cover. Less than half a dozen men were privy to Michal's actual status.

"No one has ever been inside this deep," Ron, his only friend as well as superior, said, echoing Michal's thoughts. "You know how important the intel you provide is to the security of not only our country, but also numerous others. Look at the number of catastrophes we've been able to avoid in the past two years. All because you are trusted by those who wish to do harm and ravage our American friends as well as our own people."

Michal whipped around and glared at his old friend. His posture went instantly to that of the ruthless savage he portrayed each day. It was second nature now. He had to consciously restrain the fury as well as the urge to grab his friend and shake him. "Do you think I don't know that? I have risked my life dozens of times to provide those warnings. Even now Carlos grows more suspicious of me each day. When is it enough?" He looked away, battling the rage that he so liberally unleashed on a regular basis amid his cutthroat associates.

"Michal." Ron gripped his arm reassuringly; Michal flinched and pulled away. "No one understands more than I what you have sacrificed. But your role is far too vital to our continued stability to allow the mission to come to an end. You must not waver."

Michal unclenched his hands and scrubbed them over his face then through his hair. Could he do this another day? Another hour? His thoughts went immediately to Amira and he forced the resulting images away. With every fiber of his being he wanted to believe that she was one of those he hated, but his heart would not allow him the luxury. His men were already suspicious of his allow-

NO WAY BACK

ing her to live this long. Carlos, in particular, had pushed the issue. This continued unrest among the ranks of his followers would undermine his absolute control, ultimately getting him killed. To a degree, death would be a relief. It was the other that kept him from simply shirking off all cares. The vow he had made to serve his country.

The damage control he could assert from the position he held as Michal the Executioner was priceless. Even he could see no way anyone else could match the level of power he had attained.

He almost laughed out loud when he considered how the Americans likened their CIA to the Mossad. If they only knew. The Mossad was more aggressive and more ruthless than the CIA could even imagine. Even those CIA officers who worked closely with their Mossad counterparts had no idea just how far the Mossad would go to accomplish their intended mission.

"It's the woman, isn't it?"

Ron's question brought Michal up short.

He didn't hide the surprise in his expression quickly enough. "I knew it was you," Ron went on. He pushed off from the stone wall, allowing a slash of sunlight to fall over his profile. "When the woman was discovered alive and well and then came up missing, I knew." He turned to Michal. "You know that her existence jeopardizes this mission. She could ruin everything."

A muscle ticked in Michal's tightly clenched jaw.

Ron glanced first right then left, noting the children racing after the goat that had escaped their watch. "My CIA contact says she has no memory of any of the events from two years ago." His gaze locked with Michal's once more. "The risk that she might remember is far too great. You must take the proper steps."

Michal inclined his head, his barely banked fury no

doubt blazing in his eyes. "And if I choose otherwise, what will you do? Kill me?" He smirked. "I think not."

Enough talk. Michal turned away. There was nothing more to say...not even to the man who was his only friend, the only soul on earth he could trust. He walked away.

"Michal."

Though he hesitated, he did not turn around to face the other man.

"What happened two years ago was a necessary risk. *This* is not. You know what has to be done."

The warning fell on deaf ears.

Whether Amira lived or died was Michal's decision.

His alone.

"I'D LIKE TO TAKE a walk."

Ami stared into the cold, beady eyes of the man named Carlos and prayed he would not deny her request. Michal had allowed her to go outside for short periods each day for the past three. Since he'd been gone all morning she could see no reason one of the other men couldn't do the same. She just hadn't expected to find Carlos outside the door of the bedroom turned prison. Why did it have to be his turn to watch her?

His glare turned more venomous but, to her credit, she held her ground. She knew he, more so than any of the others, despised her. As with all else related to her current situation, she had no idea why. She only knew that she had to find a way to escape. Nothing else mattered.

"Go back into the room. I have no time or desire to bother with a whore such as you."

Fear raced up her spine, but she held herself rigid against it. "I am allowed to take a walk. Michal said so," she argued, working hard to keep her voice from quavering. "I want to do it now."

Carlos made a dismissive sound and turned away from her. He folded his arms over his chest and propped against the wall next to her door as if that were the end of the subject.

She had to do this. Michal was gone. This might be her only chance to get outside without him watching her every move. "Fine." She swallowed back the terror rising in her throat. "I'll just ask one of the other men to accompany me."

When he didn't respond, she focused her gaze on the end of the hall where it opened into the massive great room and started in that direction. Her heart thudded so hard against her rib cage she could scarcely take a breath. One foot in front of the other, she reminded her sluggish brain. She was almost there and Carlos hadn't demanded that she stop. As she came to the entryway leading into the great room she could see three men lounged around the room. One had been nicer to her than the others. Kolin, she was pretty sure. Kolin from Ireland. It seemed that Michal Arad's band of terrorists were multinational.

Not merely a ragtag group of multinational terrorists. These men are highly trained, the cream of the crop. Their ruthlessness is rivaled only by their superior intelligence and innate instincts. No one has been able to stop them.

Ami jerked to a halt as the words crashed into her thoughts, shattering all else. She blinked. Where had she heard those words before? The voice sounded vaguely familiar. She frowned, concentrating with all her might.

Tanner.

His voice. Had he said those words to her in the nurses' lounge when he'd tried to warn her about all this craziness? Why hadn't she listened? Uncertainty turned the hardwood floor beneath her feet to mire. How could she hope to escape?

Suddenly aware that all eyes in the room were on her, Ami jerked her attention back to the matter at hand. She sucked in a bolstering breath and manufactured a shaky smile. "Kolin." She looked directly at the only man who had shown a glimmer of kindness toward her. "I'd like to take a walk now. Would you mind—"

The rest of the words trapped in her throat when someone grabbed a handful of her hair, snapping her head back. Carlos, she realized, terror claiming her all over again. He jerked her against him and pressed his face close to hers. "You disobeyed me," he snarled. "No one disobeys me."

"I—I just wanted—"

"Shut up!" He tightened his fist in her hair. "When I'm finished with your punishment you won't forget to obey me again."

She cried out as he jerked her backward, toward the bedroom that was her prison. Begging for help would be pointless. None of the other men would dare defy Carlos. He was the second in command.

"Carlos, please…I…"

He shoved her into the room. For one second she prayed he would slam the door and leave her be. The next second she knew that was not going to happen. He slammed the door behind him and moved toward her like the evil predator he was.

Fear sent her stumbling backward. Her heart stuttered to a halt in her chest as the fury in his eyes turned to a sinister gleam. Her throat closed in fear. He was…

He slapped her hard, knocking her off her feet.

"You may have Michal fooled," he bellowed, "but I know what you're up to." Her jerked her to her feet when she tried to scramble away from him. "You've come back to finish the job you started two years ago." He pounded his chest with his free hand. "I know this. I am not blinded by your whorish temptation."

She tried to claw his fingers away as they closed around her throat. The coppery tang of blood leeched from her lip into her mouth. "Stop," she whimpered, his punishing grip very nearly overpowering her ability to speak. She tried to knee him in the groin, but he twisted away from her feeble effort. He slammed her against the nearest wall and jabbed the barrel of his weapon into her temple.

"Who sent you here?" he demanded, his face only inches from hers, the stale smell of whiskey on his breath.

She tried to shake her head. To deny his accusations. But his brute strength pinned her helplessly to the wall.

The barrel of the weapon bore more deeply into her skull. "You will tell me or you will die."

"Laissez-la partir."

Though she didn't understand the words, the stone-cold voice belonged to Michal.

"I said, let her go," Michal repeated.

Relief flooded Ami, making her legs so weak beneath her that she collapsed to the floor the instant Carlos released her. Her chest ached with the harsh banging of her heart.

Carlos turned on Michal. "She makes you weak," he accused, the pitch of his voice rising to match his fury.

Ami cradled her bruised throat with her hands, gasping to fill her lungs more fully with life-giving air, but her gaze was locked on the two men squaring off only a few feet away. Carlos still held his gun in his hand. Michal stared him down, his own hands empty but clenched into hard fists at his sides.

"Your orders are only to see that she does not escape," he said firmly.

Carlos waved his gun at her. Ami gasped and curled

into herself protectively. "She makes a fool of you, my friend. She was sent here to destroy us...just like before."

Michal's dark gaze remained steady on Carlos, his composure never faltered. "That is for me to decide. You—" he moved a step closer to Carlos "—will never touch her again. Is that understood?"

For three long beats Ami wasn't sure if Carlos was going to back down. His fingers tightened around his weapon as the face-off continued for another seemingly endless second, then he said, "You will regret this day, my friend."

Carlos walked out of the room, not waiting for Michal to say more.

Thank God. A sob burst loose from her chest. She closed her eyes and tried hard to hold back the tears, but it was impossible. If Michal had not arrived when he had...

Strong arms suddenly scooped her up. She tried to escape, but he held her firmly against his chest. What was he going to do with her? Fear pumped through her veins once more. She stared up at Michal and tried to make her lips form the words to ask that very question, but she didn't have the strength.

He carried her into the bathroom and settled her on her feet. She seized the opportunity to put some distance between them, moving around to the far side of the sink. She pressed against the wall, trying to make herself small and unnoticeable. Some of the panic had receded, but the fear lingered still. He planned to kill her...he'd made no bones about that. She couldn't fathom why he'd bothered to save her from Carlos.

Unless...he wanted the honor for himself.

She shivered uncontrollably. That was it. He'd said as

much. It would be *his* decision. He would no doubt do the deed personally.

Emotion brimmed behind her lashes as she thought again of her sweet baby and the idea that she would never see him again. Another sob wrenched from her heart.

Michal moved toward her, trapping her between the wall and his powerful body. Her fingers fisted against her sides, the urge to run or to fight so fierce she could scarcely resist the impulse to do one or the other. He growled savagely beneath his breath in that language she thought to be French. She didn't understand the words, but he looked furious.

Her breath caught as he reached toward her.

That dark, dark gaze collided with hers. "Don't move," he ordered softy but, even tempered, the tone echoed with the danger that emanated from every square inch of him.

As gently as if she were an injured child, he cleaned her bleeding lip with a damp cloth, dabbing tenderly. Stunned by the act of mercy, she could only stare at him and watch the startling metamorphosis of emotions on his face. This close she could see the tiny lines that marred the smooth complexion of his skin. Lines that spoke of years of close calls with death and wielding that same power over others. The hard set to his chiseled jaw told her more about the unyielding determination he possessed than any words could have. His entire body was honed to lethal perfection. And yet the tenderness exposed in the beard-shadowed, granite-like features of that same face shifted something deep inside her.

He could kill her in an instant, but instead he was making her come.

The breath hissed past her lips. It was him that she'd been dreaming of…even before the episode in the ER with the injured Israeli man…before the startling conversation with Jack Tanner.

Michal Arad was the man she'd dreamed of making love with so often that she'd been unable to commit to Robert. The dark image that had haunted her dreams had rendered the possibility of a future with the real, flesh-and-blood man in her life impossible. Robert hadn't had a chance, she realized ironically. He'd been competing with a ghost…

A ghost from her past.

"They all want you dead," Michal murmured as he studiously worked to soothe the bruised skin of her throat with the cool, damp cloth. That dark, dark gaze lifted to meet hers. "What am I to do?"

Later, when she could think back on that moment, Ami couldn't say what made her do it—some long-buried instinct or self-protective urge—but she thrust her arms around his neck and buried her face in his chest and sobbed.

She didn't want to die.

Somehow she knew that though he appeared to have the most reason to want her dead, he was the only one who could save her.

CHAPTER SEVEN

AMI KEPT HER EYES CLOSED, feigning sleep until he left
the room. At last she opened them and blinked to adjust
to the pale dawn hues sifting through the wall of windows.
Her gaze went immediately to the chair where he sat each
night and watched her. She shoved the thin coverlet aside
and sat up in the bed, the cool air easily penetrating the
gossamer-thin gown she wore, making her shiver. She
stared down at the silky pale pink garment, wondering
what had made him give it to her last night.

He'd stayed closer than usual since the incident with
Carlos two days ago. That memory sent a shudder quaking
through her. She consciously set aside the other memories
related to that exchange, especially the one where she'd
thrown her arms around Michal and held on tightly as if
he were her only anchor in violent waters. He had allowed
the unexpected display for a few moments before pushing
her away, his expression going instantly from tender to
threatening.

No matter what she thought she saw as he'd tended the
hurt Carlos had inflicted, he was still determined to have
his vengeance. To make her pay for her betrayal two years
ago. Ami trudged to the bathroom and took care of necessary business, including a change of clothes.

As she brushed her forever unruly hair she considered
the face in the mirror. Could she really have played the
part of Amira Peres as Jack Tanner had said? Was she

really capable of those kinds of exploits? The dreams she'd experienced night after night the past two years seemed to indicate a past with Michal. But she couldn't be certain. The dreams could be nothing but dreams. Just because his features were dark didn't make him the father of her child. She trembled with something totally unrelated to fear for her life at that thought. If that were true and he ever found out about Nicholas…

She shook off the concept. For that matter Tanner could be the father. He'd insinuated that something had gone on between them while he'd trained her for the mission. His coloring was dark, as well.

Ami shook her head. Maybe Carlos was right. Maybe she had been nothing but a bought-and-paid-for whore who'd done the CIA's bidding or anyone else's, ultimately betraying Michal.

But he was a terrorist. Another shiver danced up her spine. The single most ruthless terrorist on the planet, Tanner had said. Somehow it didn't fit. She had yet to see him harm another human being. Not even when Carlos overstepped his bounds did Michal use violence to control the situation. It was true that he'd manhandled her to a degree, but he hadn't actually hurt her. She studied the fading bruises left over from her encounter with Carlos. Now there was a man she was certain was capable of horrible violence.

Ami sighed and rubbed her hands over her face. This was all insane. She was a nurse, for Pete's sake. A mother. She didn't know anything about terrorists except what she saw in the news. She barely kept up with politics. How could she be this Jamie Dalton, undercover agent for the CIA, that Tanner told her about? How could she have played the part of Amira Peres and then orchestrated the murder of Yael Peres?

She shook her head. It just wasn't possible. Of course, the coincidence that the name Ami could be derived from both Amira and Jamie wasn't lost on her. When she'd been found wandering in that park two years ago the name Ami Donovan was all she'd known. She'd stuck by the name, insisting that, despite her inability to remember anything about her past, she was indeed Ami Donovan. The police and even the FBI had searched every data base available and found nothing on an Ami Donovan. For all intents and purposes, she simply did not exist.

"But here you are," she argued with the weary-looking reflection. "Caught in the middle of a nightmare."

The dreams hadn't relented, either. Each night the images played across the private theater of her mind. Nothing was ever clear enough for her to actually identify a face or place. But there was always, always the irresistible lure of the dark man who knew her so intimately.

Ami sagged against the sink and closed her eyes, summoning the face of her sweet baby. At least seven days had passed since she'd held him in her arms. She replayed every moment of that last night they'd spent together. She'd bathed him and they'd played until he'd scarcely stayed awake long enough to be tucked into bed. What she would give to hold him now. An overwhelming pain arced through her, tightening her chest.

She straightened and forced her eyes open. She hadn't given up on her plan. Since Michal had warned Carlos about pushing her around, the other men had treated her a bit more kindly. Perhaps kind was an overstatement, but their unsympathetic, hateful attitudes toward her had relaxed just a fraction. One man, Kolin, had actually smiled at her. She was certain she could befriend him if given the opportunity.

With this new relaxed attitude had come a little more

freedom. She could now leave the room as long as the guard assigned to watch her accompanied her wherever she went. Her outside time was still quite limited. Michal didn't want her outdoors unless he was with her.

But that could change if she played her cards right.

And if she stayed alive.

Determined more each day to make her escape plan a reality, Ami took a deep breath and exited her room. She smiled for the man who immediately stood at attention when she stepped through the open doorway.

"Good morning," she said at a loss for his name.

"Señorita," was his only acknowledgment.

She remembered then that they called him the Spaniard. So far she had discerned that there were a dozen men in Michal's group. Two members whose native tongue was unquestionably Spanish, as the one guarding her, Kolin, from Ireland, Carlos, whose origin she couldn't even guess, at least three Frenchmen, and four of Middle Eastern decent. The whole group appeared to be multilingual. She didn't even want to hazard a guess as to the other talents they possessed. Tanner's words kept echoing in her head each time she considered what these men were capable of. That she was a prisoner among them felt surreal, like a bad movie she'd been forced to watch over and over.

But it was real. And somehow she had to escape.

Had to get back to her son.

"I'd like breakfast," she said to the Spaniard and smiled again, injecting as much sensuality as she could muster into it. The slight flare of his nostrils told her she'd been successful. Nausea roiled in her stomach, but she ignored it. Whatever the price, she reminded herself.

As Ami made her way through the house to the enormous gourmet kitchen she noted a curious tension in the air. The men were hovered in groups in the great room conversing quietly, all were, as usual, armed to the hilt. Their furtive glances as she'd passed through the room nudged at her, made her stomach tighten. Something was up. She had grown accustomed to the Uzi machine guns and various handguns, but this was different.

With as much nonchalance as she could manage, once in the kitchen she sliced a piece of bread from the thick loaf and slathered it with butter. A cup of coffee and she was set.

Pretending to ignore the murmurings of the men, she strolled back into the great room and peered out the floor to ceiling windows facing the front of the property as she negligently nibbled on her bread. The house sat high on a ridge above the valley below. If she squinted she could see the profile of a city in the distance and the sea beyond that. Miles away, she estimated. But even risking the journey through the unknown terrain that lay between here and there was not beyond her scope of comprehension. Better to die in the wilderness than at the hands of one of these terrorists. She suppressed a shudder. She needed to pay attention. Something was definitely going on. Whatever it was it could be important to her.

Ami nibbled and sipped and watched the birds fly past outside the windows, but not for a second did her full attention stray from the quiet voices behind her. Some of the conversation was carried on in a language she didn't understand, but most of it was in English. Kolin and another of the men had gone into town early that morning to deliver a package. God only knew what the package contained. Ami felt certain she didn't want to know. Kolin had spotted someone. She frowned, rolling the phrase he'd used over in her mind. *Traitre*. He said it again, with fervor. Another of the men shouted, "*Adversaire*."

Then she knew.

Traitor. Adversary.

Her throat went suddenly dry.

She gulped the cooled coffee. Kolin and the other man had run into an adversary, a traitor. They'd brought him here. Her blood went cold. At least these terrorists she knew, a stranger put a whole new bend in the situation. She trembled with a new kind of fear, but forced herself to pay attention. She needed to know more.

In English, one of the men mentioned that Michal was interrogating the traitor in the cellar at that very moment. Laughter rumbled through the group. Carlos had gone back into town with three other men to sweep the city just to be sure none of the traitor's friends were hanging around. Another thought that sent her tension to new heights.

Slowly, so as not to attract their attention, Ami turned around. The Spaniard, her guard for the day, had joined his buddies in the discussion about the traitor.

Carefully dividing her attention between the men and her destination, she eased from the room. Once beyond the doorway, she moved faster, heading for the kitchen. She placed her cup and uneaten bread on the table and braced her hands against the smooth wooden surface until she'd fully summoned enough courage to go through with the next step. From the corner of her eye she looked at the door that led to the cellar. Carlos had taunted her with the possibility of being locked down there a couple of times. She shivered again as dread punctuated the thought.

Sparing one last glance toward the expansive hall that connected the kitchen to the great room, Ami wove her way through the kitchen to the door.

Her fingers wrapped around the cold brass door handle. She held her breath as she pressed downward, releasing the latch with a click that rent the air like a shotgun blast in her overcharged imagination. One minuscule increment at a time she opened the door, praying the hinges wouldn't whine. The wooden stairs that lay on the other side of the door dove downward, a bald low-wattage bulb casting their depths in gloom.

Ami swallowed at the lump of fear clogging the back of her throat. She had to know…had to see if Michal Arad was the ruthless killer Tanner had said he was. Was he the kind of man who would end her life only to assuage his need for vengeance when she clearly had no memory of betraying him?

Ami closed her eyes and hesitated before stepping down onto the first tread. What she really wanted to know was if the man who'd touched her so tenderly two days ago as he'd seen to her split lip and bruises was really capable of cold-blooded murder.

Holding her breath all over again, she took the first step. It didn't creak. Relief made her knees weak. One more step. Then another. And another until she was midway down the steep incline. At this point, if she crouched she could see the dank, musty cellar almost in its entirety. A floor-to-ceiling rack filled with dusty, unopened bottles of wine lined one wall. Storage shelves covered the wall opposite the staircase.

"You will tell me!"

Ami almost jumped at the shouted words. She cautiously leaned forward a bit more. In the corner, very nearly behind the staircase, was Michal. He stood over a man who looked to be tied to a wooden, straight-backed chair. Michal moved slightly to the side and her assumption was confirmed. The man, who looked about thirty with blond hair and a light complexion, was definitely tied to the chair. His face was bloody and he wore an expression of infinite pain underscored by blatant insolence. She wondered if Kolin and the others had worked him over or if this was Michal's doing.

Just then Michal raised his hand and hit the man across the face; his head snapped back. The sound of the blow made Ami jump as if she'd felt it herself. Blood gushed anew from his nose. Even in the low light and from the span of twenty or so feet Ami could see that it was broken. Her heart lurched when Michal raised his hand once more.

"You will tell me *now!*" he shouted.

"Go to hell!" his prisoner barked then winced.

To her astonishment Michal lowered his hand. He stepped away from the man and she froze. If he turned around right then he'd see her.

He moved in the other direction; she released the breath she'd been holding. Taking his time, he unbuttoned the crisp white shirt he wore. Ami blinked, confused. But his movements soon mesmerized her, made her forget all about the prisoner tied up a few feet away. The white shirts Michal wore reminded her of those pirates must have worn as they'd ravaged the ships of old. The sleeves were billowy, the front double-breasted. When he shouldered out of the flattering fabric, her breath trapped in her lungs all over again at the sight of his broad, broad shoulders and back. He laid the shirt aside on a crate and turned back to his prisoner.

Ami shook off the ridiculous curiosity with his male features and focused on the poor man in the chair. If she made her presence known, could she somehow prevent further harm to him? Or would she only call Michal's rage down on her. Her gaze went back to the man. Before she could decide if he was worth the risk, Michal had his gun in his hand and had pressed the tip of the barrel against the man's forehead. Her eyes went wide with disbelief.

"It is my favorite shirt," Michal explained. "I can see that this is going to get very messy."

The man blinked rapidly. The sudden slump of his shoulders told Ami he'd admitted defeat on some level.

"You think you are invincible," he said to Michal, sneering in spite of his obvious no-win situation.

"Enough games," Michal said wearily. "Give me the information I need and I will make this as swift and painless as possible. Who was behind the Bellatti hit?"

The man laughed for a moment, then his expression turned somber. "Your old friend Lofgren, for the good that information will do you. He will bring you down yet. My only regret is that I will not be there to see it."

The weapon abruptly fired. Fine droplets of crimson spewed from the neat round hole that appeared in the man's forehead. But the spray of blood and matter across the wall behind him was what startled Ami from the shock that had paralyzed her with the first echo of the blast. She braced to run. She couldn't let him catch her spying on him like this.

MICHAL LOWERED his weapon.

It was done.

One more name to scratch off the endless list. One more piece of the intelligence puzzle.

Would it never be enough?

The empty abyss that was his soul felt suddenly even more hollow than before. There was nothing left that set him apart from those he executed for the good of the world. He was no better than the dead man now taking up space in his cellar. *He* was a killer.

He stared at the gun in his hand and then at the spray of blood staining his skin before unconsciously tucking the weapon back into the waistband of his trousers. He had done what he'd had to...what he'd been ordered to do.

A creak on the stairs jerked his attention in that direction. His gaze locked with Amira's wide blue one. The fear in her eyes told him that she'd witnessed everything. She looked ready to bolt.

His last thought evolved into action at the same time that she scrambled to her feet. Michal was charging up the steps before she could reach the door. He grabbed her by the waist and quickly twisted as they went down on the treads, allowing his body to take the brunt of the impact.

"Let me go!" She flailed her arms, banging her fists against him anywhere she could.

He jerked his head first left then right to avoid her panicked attack. Before she could get in a proper blow he'd manacled her wrists.

"What are you doing here?" he demanded, his fury mounting at the idea that she'd not only given her guard the slip, but that no one had come looking for her.

She swallowed convulsively, the movement of delicate muscles along the slender length of her throat distracting him for one long moment. "You killed that man."

The disgust in her voice stabbed deep into his gut. He looked away from her accusing eyes and got to his feet, dragging her upward with him. "This is none of your concern." He tugged her after him as he headed toward the door.

She stalled, tried to jerk away from his hold. When he glared a warning at her she muttered thinly, "You *are* a murderer."

In that instant several emotions coalesced at once. The realization that she truly had no memory of their former time together absorbed fully; the depth of her absolute fear of him slammed into his gut with all the force of a physical blow; the undeniable hurt he suffered as a result.

He yanked her up hard against him. "Unless you want to be the next to die, I would suggest that you obey me." He snarled the words like a wounded animal. The rage at his own vulnerability—a vulnerability only she had the power to effect—mushroomed inside him with each passing second. The heart of stone that beat in his chest felt strangely fragile.

"Your wish is my command," she muttered disdainfully, yet her eyes gave her away. She blinked rapidly, but not quickly enough to hide the brightness that glimmered there. However fearless she wanted to appear at the moment, he knew she was terrified.

Terrified of him.

Of what he was.

He burst into the kitchen with her in tow. She tried to wrench away from him, which only fueled his anger. He didn't stop, though he knew she could hardly keep up with him, as he passed through the main room where his obviously inept men loitered like the fools they were.

With his savage glare, a hush fell over the room. He said nothing. No words were necessary. All six of those present understood their error.

Once in his room he slammed and locked his door. She fought his hold, a new kind of fear apparently taking root. As it should. He clenched his jaw against the rage building, but it did no good.

He glowered down at her, stilling her struggles in an instant. But his own inner battle would not so easily be subdued. He longed to shake her until she admitted the rightness of his ways. He wanted to make her see the truth. But to what end? What did it matter? "You would call me a murderer," he roared, arguing the point in spite of the stupidity and uselessness of the effort. He slapped his chest with his palm, as angry with himself as he was with her. "The man in the cellar is a victim of my murderous ways, is that it?"

She trembled visibly, but did not turn away as he'd expected. Instead she lifted her chin and countered, "I've heard your men talking. You're not just a murderer," she threw back at him. "You're a monster."

White-hot fury blindsided him, obliterating all other emotion, all other thought. He pulled back his hand but caught himself, shaking with the effort of suppressing the reaction that was far too automatic in this tainted world in which he lived.

She cowered in anticipation of the blow, but she did not run from him.

He blinked and dragged in a ragged breath. It took a full ten seconds to master the beast inside him and lower the hand with which he'd intended to punish her. Never once had he laid a hand on her in that manner. Even though she had betrayed him, sentencing herself to death from more sources than one, he could not bring himself to do *this*.

He leaned closer to her, using his size and physical strength to intimidate her instead. "You call me a monster," he growled back at her. "That rotting bastard in the cellar was instrumental in the deaths of dozens of women and children. He cared not who got in his way." He pressed her with the fiercest glare he could summon. "He will harm no more innocents. His reign of terror is over."

Still she didn't back down. "What about yours?" she snapped right back at him. "When will your reign end?"

Something shattered inside him…some protective mental barrier that allowed him to ignore what the world thought of him. That made him oblivious to it all. He snagged her wrist and jerked her close…close enough to feel the heat of his breath on those luscious lips parted by her abrupt, fear-inspired gasp.

"I am fighting a war," he murmured harshly. "You will treat me with the respect of a warrior or suffer the consequences."

She tugged at his hold, his threatening words only making her more visibly determined, infuriating him beyond all reason. "What're you going to do, *Michal?*" she demanded consciously, or perhaps not, putting emphasis on his name the way she had before. In a single heartbeat his fury morphed into need, pooling in his loins like a sea of fire.

"Are you going to kill me, too?" she taunted. "You've been tiptoeing around it all week. Why don't you just get it over with?" She moved in on him, eliminating the few centimeters between them. "Just go ahead and kill me and give your men a new subject to speculate about." She glanced at his chest and then his hands. "You already have blood on your hands, what's a little more?"

Her insolence maddened him so completely he could not form a coherent thought. He looked at his hands and then at her and said from between clenched teeth, "You will honor my victory over my enemy by cleansing this tainted blood from my body."

Her lips thinned into a grim line, but she said nothing as he hauled her into the bathroom. He waited, impatience pounding inside him, as she turned reluctantly to the sink. Her movements stiff and jerky, she dampened a cloth and waited for him to move nearer. He saw her breath catch as he did so. Was true fear for her life only now sinking in?

A definite tremble in her touch, she smoothed the cloth over his flesh, slowly but surely cleansing away the blood and, at the same time, somehow converting his fury to something hot and wild, sending it pulsing through his veins, only to reignite the heat still smoldering in his loins.

Over and over she rinsed the delicate white cloth and moved it across his skin, her fingers kneading, gliding, until he was rigid with need. The pulse at the base of her throat fluttered frantically, whether from fear or her own desire, he could not say. Michal only knew that he could not bear her touch a moment longer.

"Enough." He flung her hand away when she reached for him once more. If she touched him again...

Glaring at him as if she wished the blood had come from his body, she threw the soiled cloth into the sink but said nothing.

Michal closed his eyes and took in a long, deep breath. He brutally squashed the softer emotions that tried to surface. Those feelings had no place in his life now. He set his jaw hard against them. This was his life now. Even if this mission ended today, he wasn't sure he could ever go back to being the man he once was. That man was gone. Lost to the unfeeling monster he had become.

She had been right when she'd called him a monster.

He was that and worse.

"Are you finished with me now?"

Rage renewed inside him ending his moment of self-deprecating reverie. She stood right in front of him, arms folded over her breasts, staring directly at him with utter disgust.

"There is nothing else I will ever need from you." He hurled the words at her, making her flinch, but to his surprise, she quickly recovered.

"Then why don't you let me go?" she challenged.

He could almost believe the bravado and arrogance she flaunted, but then he saw a flicker of the truth. She was playing him…trying to trip him up. The momentary glint of fear in those blue eyes gave away her true self.

She was still afraid of him. Didn't trust him. Didn't remember him…

"Answer me, dammit," she demanded sharply, a definite quiver in her voice now. She knew he'd seen the truth and her frustration made her weak. "Why don't you let me go?"

"Because I cannot bring myself to let you go."

Her heart slamming mercilessly against her rib cage, Ami saw the truth of his statement in his eyes a fraction of a second before he moved. Those strong arms snaked out and hauled her up against him, pressing her breasts against the solid wall of his chest, rendering any thoughts of escape futile.

"Is that what you wanted to hear?" he growled savagely. "That I cannot bear to exact the revenge you deserve?" The troubling emotions straining his voice swirled and darkened in his deep brown eyes. "That killing you would be like cutting out my own heart—the heart that I had thought dead these two long years?"

Her brain told her to push him away…not to believe the need-filled words he spoke, but her heart wouldn't let her. "Yes," she whispered instinctively. Some part of her that she either didn't understand or didn't remember wanted to hear exactly that.

His mouth claimed hers before she could take back the solitary word that revealed far too much of the confusion and fear twisting inside her. His kiss was hard and punishing and at the same time incredibly needy. She flattened her palms against his chest to push him away, at that same instant she felt him tremble. Just once. And her internal battle was lost.

She surrendered to the desperate words he'd said…to

the heat of his skin...the feel of his muscular body as he held her closer, tighter in those powerful arms. The last gauzy-thin resistance faded as he deepened the kiss. His tongue invaded her mouth, seeking, teasing, needing. Unable to restrain her own need, her arms went around his neck, pulling him nearer, allowing her the added pleasure of aligning intimately against him. His savage groan sent heat searing through her veins.

He lifted her against him and carried her to the bed. It was too late to resist...too late for her and too late for him. No matter what he'd done or who he was, she needed him right now. Needed him in ways she couldn't explain...needed him to help her forget for just one moment...

His fingers fumbled with the buttons to her blouse, his knuckles scraping her pearled nipples through the thin fabric. Impatient to feel more of his touch, she pushed his hands away and ripped the blouse from her body, bearing her upper torso to him. For a long while he only stood there, staring at her breasts, as if making up for lost time. Then he dropped to his knees and patiently tugged off her jeans, her panties, his eyes devouring every inch he bared.

He kissed her slowly, fully, moving over her thighs, across her abdomen and up her rib cage. He lowered her onto the bed and continued his erotic journey until his mouth covered one aching breast. Her body arched like a bow and she cried out before she could stop herself. She writhed in pleasured agony as he sucked deeply from first one breast and then the other. When she was certain she would simply die of it, he moved on, feathering kisses along her throat, over her chin, until he possessed her mouth once more.

His kiss was slow and deep, tender with a barely restrained ferocity. He dragged out the kiss, laving her with his full attention and a seemingly endless patience when she wanted nothing more than for him to finish this. To fill her with the hard length she felt pressing against her. He moved between her thighs, cradling himself there so intimately she would have screamed with the unparalleled ecstasy of it had his mouth not been fully sealed over hers. He pumped his hips slowly, erotically, sliding his pulsing length along her throbbing feminine channel. She locked her legs around his, urging him to fill her…to bring her the completion her body sought.

"I can't lose you again," he murmured against her lips, his gaze seeking and finding hers.

His tender words wound around her heart and tightened like a vise while the insistent nudge of his sex as he positioned for entry sent the tension in her body soaring. She lifted her hips instinctively and whimpered with need when he held back.

His fingers threaded into her hair and twisted to the point of pain at the same instant fury flashed in the dark depths of his eyes. Her body humming with desire, on the very brink of climax, the intensity of the rage suddenly glaring down at her caused her thundering heart to shudder to a near stop.

"But if you betray me again, I will kill you."

He plunged fully inside her, bringing her to an instantaneous orgasm and obliterating all other thought.

CHAPTER EIGHT

MICHAL SAT QUIETLY as the sun rose, spilling light through the windows behind him. He watched Amira sleep as he had done every night since bringing her to his secret estate just over one week ago. He would sleep a few minutes here and there as necessary, however the slightest shift in her position or change in the pattern of her breathing and he awoke instantly.

But this morning it was different…it was like when they had been together two years ago. They would make love over and over during the night and he would awaken early to watch her sleep. To dream of a life together that, even then, he'd known was impossible. She had come to mean everything to him—kept him from losing his sanity completely as he carried out mission after mission… assassination after assassination. Then she had betrayed him, disappearing afterward like a fleeting phantom of his imagination. He'd awakened in the middle of the night crying out her name for weeks that turned into months until his heart hardened so completely he no longer cared if he lived or died. He continued to follow his orders, hoping that each mission would be the last…that he would be finally released from the misery of existing.

But it never happened. Each time he survived, more victorious than the last. The world feared him. Even his own men, except possibly for Carlos, were in awe of his ruthless and creative methods. He was the Executioner. A freelance mercenary, terrorist—whatever the latest buzz-word for cold-blooded killer—with no cause or country. As far as the world knew, his talent for slaying, whether by up-close-and-personal means or methods of mass destruction, was for sale to the highest bidder. It was always about the money.

Michal closed his eyes and leaned his head back in the chair that had served as his resting place since Amira's return. In a few days, if not sooner, he would receive new orders and someone else would die. For the most part those slain were the scum of the earth, the true terrorists who cared for nothing but their cause. Those who had made the mistake of plotting boldly against the free world. The Americans and Europeans had long attempted to set into play a plan such as this, but they had failed. The failures had not risen from their lack of accurate strategizing or highly trained operatives. They had failed because their operatives were too closely monitored, never entirely abandoned to do what must be done. Nor did they possess the genetic predisposition to fit in where it counted most.

Michal, on the other hand, had been born in Israel. His Middle Eastern heritage, to the way of thinking of most, fit the proper profile. He had no remaining family ties, another advantage in this line of work, and he had spent months building this cover before going active. He had alienated himself among his peers in the political circles of his homeland, working hard to disentangle himself from any emotional bonds to country or patriotism of any sort. He had chosen new friends who associated with known terrorists. And then he had become one. His cover was so authentic that it fooled even him at times.

His eyes opened and he clenched his jaw against the bitterness that welled in his chest. He'd gone too far. Even he recognized that now. How could the Mossad ever re-

claim him? His infamous exploits, though carried out under strict orders, at times caused the deaths of those who
had not deserved such a cruel and final punishment. In
truth, his reputation had been bolstered somewhat by connecting his name to events that had not actually been carried out by him. No one would ever believe he was, in
actuality, a silent warrior for his country…for the world.
He blinked and considered that reality. How long had he
been hiding from that truth? Too long. When the powers
that be were finished with him he would be terminated just
as numerous others had been once their respective purposes were served.

There was no way back to his old life. His fate was
sealed, as was Amira's.

His gaze roved over the slender curves of her sheet-
draped body and he hardened instantly. Though his superior, Ron, would not push the issue, but if Michal allowed
her to live much longer, the order would be issued from
above and then he would have no choice. She would die
without ever understanding why or even remembering
what had brought her to this lethal precipice.

Emotion twisted into a granite-like knot in his gut. How
could he hurt her when the only thing he wanted was for
her to remember their time before…for her to want him
as she'd seemed to then. But she had used him, had she
not? A frown creased his brow. Could he have been so
wrong about what he thought he felt? It would seem so.
But he knew better than anyone that things were not always as they appeared.

Until the order was formally issued he had no intention
of harming her, unless, of course, she betrayed him again.
When the order came…well, he would deal with that when
the time arrived. A wave of dread washed over him at the
mere thought of losing her again. He decided then and

there that he had to know if she had truly betrayed him two years ago or if she had been somehow set up. He had suspected something was very wrong the moment the hit had gone down. It was as if she had realized the wrongness of what she had orchestrated as her father took his dying breath. The shock and regret on her face had been real. Before he'd had time to question her sudden about-face all hell had broken loose and she'd been captured by Peres's private security. He would have been captured, as well, had it not been for his men. They had dragged him from the scene. Injured and fighting to maintain consciousness, he had not been able to argue otherwise.

The word had spread like wildfire that Yael Peres had been assassinated and that his daughter had been executed for the deed. The people of Israel had mourned the loss of a beloved political fixture who had influenced their world for nearly half a century. Michal knew differently, of course, but no one else ever would. The world was a safer place without him, but no one wanted to tarnish the memory since it would serve no real purpose.

Michal pushed to his feet. Enough. He had business to attend to. Including making sure his men did not question his decision to allow Amira to live another day. And later, for lunch perhaps, he intended to take her into town for an afternoon of pleasantness. Something else his men would not like…but he was the one who had the final say. He hesitated at the door and looked back at her. It would have made things so much simpler if only he could have stayed angry with her, if he could have believed fully that her betrayal was complete, but he could not.

All he could do now was protect her from the many others who would like nothing more than to take credit for killing the daughter who had choreographed the slaying of her own father—at least he could until he was ordered to take that very step himself.

AMI STUDIED THE PROFILE of the man beside her as the Hummer bumped along the cliff road that descended toward where the sky met the sea and the city that hugged its coastline. Michal had said little to her today. She fixed her gaze straight ahead and mentally railed at herself for growing warm inside just looking at him. How could she have allowed this to happen? Was she suffering from some sort of hostage syndrome?

No, that wasn't it. It was far more than some bizarre emotional connection between hostage and kidnapper. She'd dreamed of him again last night. This time the images were more vivid than usual. She could see herself with him. Endless days and nights of touching, making love, never being able to get enough of each other. The danger had only heightened the sexually explosive bond between them. She remembered it clearly. Ami was nearly certain she had, two years ago, been in love with Michal Arad.

How could that be possible? He was a savage! A murderer. She'd seen him kill a man scarcely twenty-four hours ago. And still she'd been drawn to him while the blood of his victim cooled on his flesh. She squeezed her eyes shut and gave her head a little shake. There had to be something wrong with her. Some intrinsic genetic defect or heretofore undiagnosed mental illness. How else could she love a killer?

Her gaze shifted back to him. He'd pulled his long dark hair back into a loose queue. He wore his trademark white shirt and black trousers and leather boots, which only added to his mystique. She considered the lean, chiseled features of his handsome face, the perfectly formed blade of his nose, and then those generous lips. Every instinct told her that he was not what he seemed.

But she was pretty sure she'd lost a grip on her instincts at the same time that she'd lost her memory. After all, how good could instincts honed only over a two-year period be?

Just then he looked straight at her, catching her staring at him. She turned away abruptly, her cheeks heating with humiliation. How could she have made love with this man? He'd abducted her from her workplace, keeping her away from her child, and had emotionally abused her beyond reason. Even in the throes of passion he had warned her that he would kill her if she betrayed him again.

How could she be such a fool?

Forcing her attention back to her surroundings she told herself to make the most of this outing. Try to judge how far the city was from the house. Look for an embassy. Find a way to let someone know she was being held against her will.

A tall order when four other men accompanied them. She almost laughed out loud. A tall order period when in the presence of Michal Arad who missed nothing.

She'd decided that Jack Tanner and the CIA had written her off. Decided they considered it too much trouble to bother rescuing her. *She* was her only hope.

No matter how risky, she had to find a way to escape for Nicholas's sake.

Marseilles was larger than she'd expected. Cosmopolitan and exuberant, the city had a magnificent ambience about it. As they drove through the medieval-village-style neighborhoods, the city's age became instantly apparent. Ancient would describe it best. Ancient but lovely. Museums, small walking alleys, terrace cafés, boutiques and shops dominated the charming city. Yet nothing was as beautiful as the Old Port, lined by its seaside walks, filled with fishing boats and yachts, surrounded by small streets teeming with seafood restaurants and shops. Pedestrians strolled leisurely on the wide seaside walks, enjoying the September sun.

Carlos parked in an alley near a terrace café reminiscent of ones she'd seen in movies. If she'd ever been to a place like this she had no recall whatsoever of it. Big surprise, she mused dryly.

Michal kept his left hand at the small of her back as they emerged from the vehicle and walked the short distance to the café. She could feel the tension in him as he constantly scanned the area. Nothing escaped his notice. He was like a stealthy panther moving through the crowd, constantly alert to threat, postured for battle.

Once they were seated with his back to the wall of the café, her next to him and the others spread out around them as a security barrier, Michal ordered his as well as her lunch. He insisted that she had always loved the *bouillabaisse du pêcher* and the Cassis white wine, which was produced locally.

Ami dredged up a smile and managed a thank-you. She'd have to take his word for that. The main thing was, she was out of the house. She had to make the most of it. If she responded to his generosity, maybe he'd bring her out more often, providing more opportunities for escape.

She blinked and looked away from him. The lurch in her stomach at the thought of never seeing him again made her want to scream. She'd made love with the man. Hadn't been able to help herself. It was done. Dammit, she couldn't fall for him, no matter how she'd felt about him two years ago. Whatever and whoever she had been two years ago, she wasn't that person anymore. She was a mother. She had a son to get back to. He needed her and his safety was all that mattered. This life—she glanced at Michal—was certainly no life for a child. She knew without question that Michal would want his son with him if he knew of his existence. But Nicholas might not be Michal's child, she reasoned.

Yet she was nearly certain he was.

She sighed and pushed the thoughts away. This was the first time she'd been away from the house, paying attention to the details was her top priority right now. She tucked the tender memories and thoughts of her baby into a faraway corner of her mind—far away from this horrible nightmare.

As she took in the street and the splendid view of the boats moored nearby, she wondered if she could escape and hide on one of them where she would end up. Did it even matter as long as she was out of here? She inhaled deeply of the salt air and decided that idea was worth more thought. Before their entrées were served the waitress brought fresh-baked bread with olive oil, cold meats and cheese. Ami nibbled as the men conversed about some militant group who'd made a move to corner their market in Libya.

"If their aggression continues," Michal was saying, "we will act. They have been warned."

Carlos nodded. "At least two of our old customers have used them recently. They work cheaper."

Michal smiled, it was not pleasant. "They will die cheaply, as well," he mused. The men laughed, apparently amused by the prospect.

Ami shivered, her mind again having trouble reconciling the man who'd made love to her—who'd tended her wounds from her run-in with Carlos—with this ruthless leader who plotted death so easily.

She gulped a long drink from her wineglass, needing to

numb her raw nerves. Michal refilled it immediately, as if sensing her need.

"Thank you," she murmured.

"Ah." He nodded to the waitress approaching with a tray. "You will enjoy this, I am certain."

The bouillabaisse the waitress set in front of her looked huge, though Michal had commented that it was smaller and lighter than the others and contained only three varieties of fish rather than the usual six. If Ami had ever eaten this dish—her stomach roiled in protest—she was certain she couldn't now. She didn't even like fish.

As the waitress placed the final order on the table, she bumped Ami's glass, knocking it over, the contents splashing over her blouse. She jumped up from her chair, but not quickly enough to avoid a lapful.

Michal swore hotly. Though Ami didn't know the language he used, she instinctively understood the meaning. "What are you doing, you clumsy woman?" he demanded as he moved next to Ami and offered his linen napkin. He repeated the words in French, the harshness no less evident in the sensual language.

"*Pardon, Monsieur,*" the waitress cried, her expression mortified. "*Je le regrette beaucoup, Mademoiselle!*"

The waitress sputtered the next few phrases far too quickly for Ami to even guess what she was saying. She gestured repeatedly for Ami to follow her. She indicated the wet spots on Ami's clothes and repeated her request.

"Go with her," Michal said to Carlos.

Ami looked from Michal to Carlos and then to the frantic waitress and finally realized what she wanted. She followed the exasperated woman through the restaurant. A few people looked up and raised an eyebrow, but most simply continued to eat. When they reached the narrow hall that led to the rest rooms the waitress glared at Carlos

and said something cross to him. He only rolled his eyes
and propped against the wall to wait.

Startled that the waitress could get away with such high-
handedness with a man like Carlos, Ami allowed her to
usher her toward the ladies' room. She decided it was the
older woman's gray hair and attractive matriarchal features. She reminded Ami of a schoolteacher she'd once
had. Or maybe a librarian.

The moment the door to the ladies' room had closed
behind them, the kindly waitress shoved Ami against the
wall, face first, and patted her down like a vice cop in an
episode of *N.Y.P.D. Blue*. Before she could regain her
voice and demand to know what the hell the woman was
doing, the waitress straightened and looked Ami dead in
the eye.

"Don't say a word," she said quietly and in perfect
English. "You have five minutes, use them wisely." Then
she ushered Ami through the inner door that led from the
powder room to the stalls.

Still reeling from the encounter, Ami stumbled drunkenly into the room. Six stalls lined one wall, three sinks
and a long mirror made up the other. There was no window, no avenue of escape and, as far as she could see, no
one else around. When she would have turned to question
what she was supposed to be looking for, a stall door
opened and Jack Tanner stepped out.

"You!"

He pressed a finger against his lips in reminder that her
guard was not so far away. By now, maybe even right
outside the door marked Femmes.

She walked straight up to him, fury exploding inside
her. "What the hell took you so long? Couldn't you get
here before now? You had to know where I was." Pain

wrenched through her. "How's my baby? Where is he? Is he okay?"

"Keep your voice down," Tanner warned again.

Her rage burst through the softer emotion. "Listen, you bastard," she snapped, "I want to know what the hell is going on here. I'm an American citizen. I was kidnapped. Get me the hell out of here. I've been waiting every single day for you to rescue me."

Those brown eyes fixed fully onto hers and dread settled like a rock on her chest. "I'm not here to rescue you."

"What?" Ami bit down on her bottom lip to hold back the scream that burgeoned in her throat. When she had regained some measure of control, she demanded, "What does that mean?" This couldn't be happening. How could he do this? How could the CIA do this? It was crazy. All of it! Slashes of memory from the week's events whipped through her mind, shaking her to the core of her being.

"We have another mission for you."

"Are you insane?" She flung her arms helplessly. "Those men are terrorists. It's a miracle they haven't killed me already. They killed a man just yesterday right in front of my eyes."

"We know."

She shook her head. "That's all you can say? You know!"

His patient expression remained unchanged. "Your orders are to stay put. If Arad hasn't killed you already, he probably won't."

How reassuring! "Orders? Don't you get it? I know you think I'm this Jamie Dalton person," she allowed sharply, "and that I once worked for your company." She shook her head, confusion only fueling her hysteria. "Even if that's all true, I don't remember how to be a spy! Whoever

I was is gone. I'm just a nurse. A mother," she added emphatically. "I can't do this."

"Three minutes," the waitress announced in a stage whisper as she stuck her head through the door.

"Who the hell is she?" Ami demanded, infuriated all the more by the woman's intrusion.

"She's Fran Woodard." Tanner nodded to the woman and she disappeared again, presumably to keep watch. "One of our top European operatives. You're lucky she was in the area and knows the guy who owns this café. I've been watching Arad's estate for days. This was the first time I've had a chance to get close to you, but I couldn't have done it without Fran—"

"Look," Ami cut him off. "I can't do this. Do you understand? I'm not a spy."

Tanner reached into his inside jacket pocket and pulled out a photograph. He handed it to Ami. It was Nicholas. Her heart lurched. "Oh, God," she cried, tears welling before she could stop them. "He's okay." She looked up at Tanner. "He is, isn't he?" Whether it was the dullness of indifference in his eyes or pure intuition, realization dawned. He hadn't shown her the picture to make her feel better…

"If you ever want to see your son again, you have to do exactly as I tell you." Regret flashed briefly in his eyes, but it did nothing to lessen the new dread mounting in Ami's stomach. He retrieved the photo from her limp fingers. "This is the way it has to be. I'll give you more specific orders as soon as I can. For now, stay put, keep Arad happy."

"Just tell me he's okay," she said from between clenched teeth. For days she'd prayed Tanner would show up and rescue her. Now all she wanted was to hurt him. Her fingers curled into fists. She wanted to scream the indignity of it all to the world. But she had no choice in any of this.

"He's fine. Your friend Robert and the nanny he hired are taking very good care of him."

Another kind of emotion slammed into her belly at the mention of Robert's name. She'd cheated on him. God, how could she have done such a thing? He'd stood by her all this time, treated her son as his own, and this was how she repaid him. Every ounce of emotion she possessed bled from her, left her completely numb.

"Clean yourself up," Tanner prompted. "It's time to go."

Moving on autopilot, Ami grabbed a handful of paper towels and quickly dampened them so that she could dab listlessly at the wine spots on her blouse and slacks.

"It's time," Fran announced from the doorway. "We drag this out any longer and they'll be coming in looking for her."

Ami tossed the wad of towels in the trash receptacle, resurrected a calm she did not feel, and turned to go.

"Try to keep yourself alive," Tanner urged softly. "We don't want to lose you again."

A new thought struck Ami, adding yet another complexity to the already insane mixture. She stopped and faced him. "Just tell me one thing."

To his credit, his calm, casual expression never wavered. She supposed that poker face was part of his training. "What's that?" he asked.

"Who am I *really?*"

For two long beats she was certain he wasn't going to answer, then he said, "You're Jamie Dalton, field operative for the Central Intelligence Agency."

She blinked once, twice, absorbing that information. "And where is the real Amira Peres?"

His guard went up this time. The change was so abrupt, she blinked and looked again just to make sure she'd read it right. "That's classified," he said tightly, "but, rest assured, she's alive and well."

"We gotta go," Fran said as she tugged Ami toward the door.

Ami's gaze locked with Tanner's one last time before the door closed between them and she knew for absolute certainty where she stood then.

She was on her own.

JACK KICKED THE WALL in frustration.

How the hell could he let this happen again?

He braced his hands against the wall and closed his eyes as he struggled to regain his composure. He had to keep it together here.

There was nothing he could do to stop any of this. He'd tried to keep her safe. If that damned assassination attempt hadn't gone down and Nathan Olment hadn't ended up in the ER where Ami worked, none of this would have happened.

She'd still be dead as far as the world knew.

That had been her only protection.

Now the only hope of survival she had was Arad.

Jack laughed a self-deprecating sound. It was just too damned ironic. Arad was the only hope she had of staying alive and *she* was the best shot the CIA had at seeing that Arad didn't.

CHAPTER NINE

NO MORE...

Ami pushed back from the table and stood. She couldn't bear another day of this.

The intense discussion of those around her, the clatter of silver against stoneware and the slosh of wine as it spilled into stemmed goblets abruptly ceased. The eyes of all those seated around the table instantly turned in her direction.

Michal's gaze collided with hers.

Before he could put voice to the question reflected there, Ami rushed from the dining room. Blood pounded in her temples. She couldn't think...couldn't tolerate the perpetually building tension a second longer. She slammed the door shut behind her as she fled into the bedroom that was both hell and heaven on earth.

Night after night he lured her into his arms and made love to her so infinitely tenderly and yet with such intensity that she was certain each time that she would not survive the next. And each night she dreamed of the past they had shared, more and more pieces of the puzzle that was her former life falling into place. Then Jack Tanner's voice would haunt her, sending ice through her veins.

They had another mission for her.

Ami pressed her fingertips to her forehead to stem the insistent pressure there and dropped onto the foot of the bed. She couldn't do this. She'd told Tanner as much four days ago when he'd appeared in the ladies' room of that restaurant like some kind of ghost who could materialize and vanish at will. But that wasn't the case at all. He'd gotten to France—to her—by the usual means and he'd left that way, as well, without once offering to take her with him.

She was a hostage, dammit! Fury whipped through her, momentarily blotting out the skull-shattering tension. She was an American citizen who needed rescuing. But he'd left her here, insisting that she had to follow his orders exactly.

Or else.

No matter how hard she'd tried, she couldn't remember being a spy. Didn't they understand that? No. No, they didn't. Or maybe they simply didn't care. The only thing she knew for certain was that she had to give it her best shot. A moan of agony wrenched through her. She hugged herself and rocked forward with the fierceness of it. Her baby. Dear God, they were using her baby for leverage to blackmail her into doing their bidding.

Where were her rights? She was the victim here! How could they qualify her freedom? Her safety?

Ami looked around the room, at her prison, and a stillness fell over her. She had to be stronger than this. Survival…getting back to her child depended on her and her alone. She had to do whatever it took. She squeezed her eyes shut and tamped down another wave of agony. But the waiting… It was pure hell. She could feel herself drawing closer to Michal—couldn't stop it. He was like an obsession. She exhaled a weary sigh. How could she feel this way about a man who committed murder for money? There was no explanation for it. Her emotions were a total wreck. Her physical reactions to the man confused her so

completely that she could scarcely think straight most of
the time.

The CIA was counting on that. Ami stilled again. That
was it. *For now, stay put, and keep Arad happy.* Tanner's
words sifted through her head. Michal was some sort of
weakness for her. She toyed with that concept for a moment. As she was to him. Like kryptonite to Superman.
That's why he hadn't killed her already. Dread swelled in
her stomach. He couldn't…

Whatever her mission was to be, it undoubtedly involved keeping Michal distracted. *Happy.* But why? What
purpose did that serve?

Ami wiped her eyes and clenched her jaw. What did it
matter? She had to follow orders or risk losing her son
forever. That was a risk she wouldn't take.

Who was to say she was as much a victim as she
thought, anyway. The image of the older man, a knife
plunged deeply into his chest, kept clawing its way into
her dreams…into her every waking thought. Was she really responsible for his death? Had he truly been convinced
that she was his daughter? She shook her head. She did
not know the man. There had to be a mistake. She blinked
and forced the disturbing image away. She wasn't a murderer. Nothing anyone told her would ever make her believe that.

But she could be a spy or practically anything else required if it meant getting back home to her child.

She would do anything to make that happen.

MICHAL HESITATED outside the bedroom door. He did not
look forward to this confrontation. Instead of lessening, her
troubles had continued to build the past few days. He had
thought that taking her into the city would ease her mind,
help her remember. But it had not. She appeared more ill

at ease than before. Even their lovemaking had not allayed her unrest. He had hoped that with their restored physical union that she would recall their past together and that things would be as they once were. But that had not happened by any stretch of the imagination.

Though she responded to him physically in a manner that encouraged him greatly, there were still reservations. Reservations she refused to discuss at length. Though she adamantly denied his suspicions, he could feel her holding back.

Michal no longer doubted her amnesia. But there was more. Something else stood between them—kept her from submitting to him completely.

The answer hit him with all the force of a physical blow. There had been someone else. Muscle after muscle went rigid until he felt forged of stone.

What did he expect?

Two years was a very long time. He could not claim celibacy on his part, either. Yet, the sexual gratification he had allowed himself from time to time had meant nothing…had changed nothing. Could she say the same? The mere idea of Amira with another man sent fire roaring through his veins, melting the granite-like weight that had pinned him to the spot. His movements spawned by fury, he burst through the bedroom door and glared straight into her startled gaze when she looked up.

"I will know the secret you are hiding from me." He closed the distance between them with three long strides. "I will know it now, Amira." The initial trepidation in her eyes morphed instantly into a fury that matched his own, the heat of it blazed from those deep blue depths as she rocketed to her feet. He leaned intimidatingly nearer and added, "If you lie to me, you will regret it."

"Don't call me that name," she said with all the ferocity of a tigress. "My name is Ami Donovan."

"Deny it until the end of time," he shouted, "but Amira is your name. And Yael Peres was your father."

She trembled but did not back away. "How is that possible?" She pushed up the sleeve of her blouse. "Look at my skin...and my hair." She splayed her fingers through perpetually tousled golden tresses for emphasis. "I'm not Israeli." She glanced at his hair and his skin to validate her point. "I'm Ami Donovan, an American-born citizen."

The challenge remained in her stance, but the certainty in her eyes wavered when her gaze once more leveled on his.

"You are an American-born citizen, that is true enough," he allowed more calmly as he touched her hair. She stiffened, which made him want to wrap his fingers in those long tresses and kiss her long and deep until she whimpered in submission. He tamped down his emotions, refusing to be baited by her show of will. "Your mother was fair with the same eyes the color of the sea."

She searched his eyes, as if looking for the truth and hoping she would not find it.

"You hated your father," he went on, unable to help himself despite knowing how his words would make her feel. "Hadn't seen him since you were a small girl. You'd lived all those years in the United States with your mother."

His fingertips trailed down the smooth expanse of creamy flesh along the length of her slender neck. She shivered. "After your mother died you decided to seek out your father." Her gaze locked with his, a new kind of heat glimmering there now. He smiled at the knowledge of how his touch affected her. "Apparently you didn't like what you found."

She jerked away from him. "Stop it!" She trembled visibly. He resisted the need to reach out to her…to undo the hurt he'd just wielded to assuage his own ego. Why did he force the issue? He knew she did not want to speak of it…wanted to pretend it never happened. But when she denied herself, she denied what they had once shared.

"It's true, Amira. The sooner you come to terms with the truth the better."

She shook her head and backed away from him, stopping only when the bed blocked her path. "I can't take any more of this." She wrapped her arms around herself, as if needing the additional support he so wanted to give her but which she refused to accept.

He closed the distance between them once more, his need to know the full truth pounding in his brain. "There is someone else, is that the problem?" Rage blinded him for two beats. He wanted to kill the man who had touched her.

Ami tried to control her reaction to the question, but she was too late. She couldn't. Recognition flared instantly in Michal's eyes.

"This other man," he demanded savagely, "did he touch you the way I touch you?"

Ami wanted to lie. She didn't want to give him the satisfaction of hearing the truth. The corded muscles of his neck, the rigid set of his broad shoulders and the hard, chiseled features of his darkly handsome face demolished any hope she had of holding her own. The temptation of those sensuous lips and the fire in those deep, dark eyes would not permit her to conceal the truth he wanted.

"No one has ever touched me the way you do," she murmured, at once hating her vulnerability to him and loving the instantaneous physical response her words wrought. His nostrils flared and his gaze went straight to her mouth as if he longed to taste her.

The memory of the secret visit from Tanner poked through the swirling emotions reminding her of what she'd had to promise him. She would help with whatever mission they were orchestrating in exchange for being reunited with her son. Anxiety charged to the front of all else. As easily as Michal read her...

"I have to get out of here." She spun away from him, praying she could keep the guilt out of her eyes. How could she do this? This breaking point had been building for four days. She'd held it together pretty well until today and something had finally just snapped inside her. Now she was falling apart. She prayed for the strength to hang on.

She kept thinking about how long it had been since she'd seen her baby and how very far away he was. What if he got sick while she was away? She had to get back home. Had to find a way. There was only one way.

She closed her eyes and swallowed back the wail of agony that rose in her throat.

"Tell me what frightens you so, *Ami.*"

She fought back the sobs and hugged herself more tightly at his gesture. This was the first time he'd called her Ami. She knew it was only to mollify her. That he, a man who killed as easily as he took a breath, would go that far to appease her simply didn't make sense.

"I just need to get out of here." Her breath hitched as his arms came around her and anchored her against his powerful body. She felt the steady beat of his heart and the fullness of his loins.

"I do not believe it is my company you wish to escape," he whispered close to her ear.

Ami shivered and bit her lower lip to stave off a moan

of need. How could he do this to her? Convert her anxiety and anger into something else altogether.

"Tell me what I can do," he urged softly.

Another thought surfaced abruptly. Maybe she could use this to her advantage. Renewed guilt assaulted her with equal abruptness. She pushed it away, focused her mind on her son. She had to get back to him…whatever it took. "It's the men," she said carefully, testing the waters. She felt the tension in him increase. "They watch me constantly, make me feel like an outsider."

He turned her slightly in his arms to look directly into her eyes and asked, "Has one of my men done something to make you feel this way?"

She had to really be cautious here. One wrong word could get someone killed. And though each and every one of his men were sadistic killers, she didn't want to be responsible for a death. She shrugged, avoiding his eyes. "I feel like I'm in prison. Why can't we go somewhere together *alone?* I'm sick to death of guards and guns."

She held her breath and waited for his reaction.

He turned her around to fully face him and studied her more closely. For one endless second she was certain he'd seen through her ruse, then he said, "If it will make you happy we will take some time together." He leveled that dark-as-midnight gaze on hers. *"Alone."*

"THIS IS NOT THE WAY we do things!" Carlos argued bitterly as he paced the room.

Michal relaxed fully in his chair and sipped the whiskey the Spaniard had poured in celebration of their next quest. The order had come this morning. The hit was to be quick; one man and his four bodyguards. Simple. But before he died, the target would be held hostage for twenty-four hours until all his assets were drained. Therein lay the less than desirable part of the assignment.

Michal suffered not the slightest twinge of guilt for the target since he had made his vast fortune with drugs and the marketing of children he stole from the streets of various cities. His reputation for depravity was known far and wide. He did not deserve to live. But that was not the reason for his selection by the powers that be for execution. This target used his endless funds to support even more notorious terrorist activities. For this, he would die.

The man was immensely fortunate he had lasted this long in the cutthroat world of kill or be killed in which he appeared to prefer of late. That he had lasted so long was testament to his not having crossed the wrong path or pissed off the wrong organization. At least until now.

Michal inclined his head and studied the man who could so easily become his most challenging enemy as he continued to pace like a caged animal. This new need to display his self-importance became more blatant with each passing day. He arrogantly tested the limits of Michal's patience. It was time to bring to an end to what could only result in a bad outcome, perhaps for both of them.

"You are right, my friend," Michal confessed with a dash of proper humility.

Carlos did an about-face and stared at him, surprise clear on every hard contour of his face.

"However," Michal continued, "this is the way we shall proceed this time. You and the others will go ahead of me. I will meet you at the rendezvous point in twenty-four hours." Michal infused all the lethal finality he possessed into his gaze then. "Do you still have questions?"

The fury flared anew in Carlos's eyes. "None. I already know the only answer I need." He pointed in the direction of the bedroom where Amira rested. "This is because of her. I warn you, Michal, she will cost you everything. She betrayed you once before. How long before she betrays you yet again? You might not be so lucky this time."

Michal set his whiskey glass aside and stood, facing the challenge Carlos had tossed out. Luck had played no part in his survival the last time. His men, including Carlos, had saved his life. "And if she does," Michal suggested, his tone as calm as the sea on a summer's morn, "you will succeed me, will you not?"

Carlos looked stunned that Michal would say such a thing out loud. "That...that is not the issue. The issue—"

"Is," Michal cut in, "whether or not you intend to follow my orders or face my wrath."

AMI BREATHED DEEPLY of the hot, salty air and surveyed the quiet Mediterranean city Michal had brought her to late last evening. At first when he'd told her they were coming to Libya, she balked. She didn't know a lot about the country but what she did was not good. She remembered flashes of news about how Libya's ruler openly supported terrorism and, vaguely, something about U.S. sanctions levied. The headdress Michal had insisted she wear reminded her of how they treated their women, as well.

It seemed odd now to think of this place as a hotbed of evil terrorist activities as she walked the wide avenues. They had arrived too late yesterday to do any sight-seeing. Dinner at the best local restaurant and a night in the finest hotel, which was a far cry from five stars but had a charm of its own, had proved the agenda for the evening. Michal had even abstained from wooing her into sex. He had, however, held her close all night, burrowing deeper still into her heart. If she could not escape him soon he would surely own her heart completely. She closed her eyes for a moment and let the past memories of their time together flicker by like a video on fast forward. Maybe he already owned her, heart and soul.

But the fate of her son hung in the balance.

She snapped her eyes open and forced her mind to take note of the details of the city of Tripoli. She'd decided that today would be the day. She would make a run for it today. She wasn't waiting for Tanner to rescue her. She'd likely be dead before that happened. She was going home one way or another. Whatever they expected her to help them do that somehow involved Michal Arad, they could simply forget it. She was not a spy or an undercover operative. She was just Ami Donovan. The sooner they all realized that, the better off everyone would be.

She wouldn't be able to see Robert again. A pang of hurt speared her. He had been good to her and her child. But she and Nicholas would have to disappear completely. It was the only way they would ever be safe. Ami flinched, startled, when Michal slid his arm around her waist. He glanced at her and somehow she managed to produce a convincing smile as they continued to stroll down the avenue.

Pay attention, she ordered. Details. She had to remember the details. Tripoli wasn't that large even if it was the capital city. There was a quaint, palm-tree-lined port with boats, that was one option. And the airport they'd arrived at wasn't that far away. She'd noticed the black-and-white taxis. She had a couple of options. All she needed was the right moment and a clear memory of the city's myriad lanes that formed a mazelike pattern. It wouldn't do her any good to escape only to get lost.

Tiny cafés and open-air workshops lined the wide avenue they traveled, which she presumed to be the main street. Skilled craftsmen worked at their trade. Ami slowed as they passed one who busily fashioned elaborate jewelry.

The beat of his hammer kept a steady rhythm amid the voices and sounds of negotiating and conversation she couldn't understand that carried on the air. The smell of welding mingled with the other more natural scents of the city.

The architecture fascinated her. Michal had told her that it had been influenced by various worlds over the centuries, Roman, Greek, Italian. Heavy wooden doors topped with rusty ironworks provided the only means of entry into the ancient-looking buildings painted varying shades of blue, yellow and brown. The merciless sun caressed the crumbling structures, highlighting the cracks and patches of time. Drying laundry served as makeshift shutters to the windows high above the street. Electrical wires wove a tangled web from house to house, a not so subtle reminder of the present. Barefoot children played in the streets. A dusty, beat-up car could be found here and there.

It took scarcely half an hour to travel the length of the city. They encountered numerous workshops and cafés, a disused Jewish school and well-kept mosques along the way. Turning to smile back at her as if he knew some secret, Michal led her into a mosque.

She felt a little breathless as she took in the expansive, dimly lit interior. Ancient pillars supported the vaulted ceiling of the deserted prayer room. It was so old. Ami was certain she'd never seen architecture this antiquated except for the day Michal had taken her into Marseilles. How could she have been exposed to the likes of this and not remember it?

Michal stroked a hand over one of the stone pillars, his own awe evident. "If only they could speak," he said, amusement as well as something resembling wonder in his tone. "Roman mysteries, Byzantine feasts and Muslim prayers.'' He sighed deeply. ''The deep, dark history we could learn.''

Why would such a ruthless man care about history? Each day she learned something new from him...some part she hadn't expected, didn't want to know. Such as the tender way he'd held her last night with no demands of his own despite the readiness of his male body. She'd felt how much he wanted her...but he had deprived himself for her comfort.

A paradox, she decided.

Michal Arad was a paradox she was certain she could spend a lifetime exploring and never know all there was to be learned.

Just watching him move around the large room, touching the ancient walls and speaking so reverently, made her want to weep. It was as if they'd stepped back into time. Michal fit the part perfectly. The way his dark hair fell over his shoulders, the contrast of his dark skin against the white shirt. He looked as if he'd just stepped off a proud ship, exploring this seemingly desolate land for the first time and finding its hidden treasure. The walls built by human hands. Walls that bore the marks and the whispered echo of centuries of both good and evil.

As if seeing him for the first time, Ami knew at once that Michal Arad was very much like that. Despite the evil he had seen, had wielded even, something good still existed there. She could almost touch it.

''Does this place trouble you?''

His deep, sensual voice tugged her back to the present. He was standing close enough to touch her, smiling down at her as if he'd read her thoughts and was pleased by her conclusion.

She shook her head, suddenly too breathless to speak.

''Perhaps you only need nourishment.'' He slid his arm

around her waist and ushered her toward the exit. "Food would be good about now. I must leave in a few hours. You'll stay at the hotel with Raoul. I would trust your safety to few others."

"Why are you leaving me here?" On the deserted street, she stopped and peered up at him. Her heart picked up its pace for two reasons. She feared what this meant for him. But then, this could be her chance. Only one man would be guarding her. She knew Raoul. He seemed to like her. The hopeful part of her rejoiced...but that other part of her—a part Michal had touched far too deeply—worried that this was not a good thing. Where was he going? A mission? Something dangerous?

It was then and there that Ami realized just how much he cared for her. He stared deeply into her eyes and, for the first time, allowed her to see the depth of his emotions. He raised his hand and gently tucked an errant strand of hair behind her head covering. Another epiphany struck on the heels of the first one. This man was more dangerous than she first suspected. He held the power to tear her life apart, starting with her most vital organ...her heart.

"You are not to concern yourself. I will return for you in twenty-four hours. You have my word."

Her anxiety crossed a whole new threshold. Before she could demand more answers, his mouth swooped down and captured hers. The heat and insistent pressure of his lips soon banished all other thought. It didn't matter that they were standing in an empty street in a place where death lurked, especially for a woman, around every corner. There was only him and the way he kissed her, as savagely as a starving barbarian and yet with all the infinite finesse of a masterful lover.

It had to be the last time.

Ami knew at that instant that if she didn't go now—today—she would never be able to leave him without telling him the truth.

The whole truth.

CHAPTER TEN

IN THE HOTEL, Ami relaxed on the bed, feigning interest in a French magazine. Michal had ordered issues of every fashion and beauty magazine available from the little tourist shop across the street, for the good it did since she didn't know any of the languages. In their former life together she must have been multilingual, though she couldn't imagine it now. Somehow, there had to be a mistake. Yes, she dreamed of him…or someone like him. Before Michal had yanked her into his world, she'd only sensed what the man in her dreams looked like. It wasn't beyond the scope of reason that she might have subconsciously superimposed his image into her dreams after the abduction. In fact, if Robert were here, he would insist that was precisely the answer to her current dilemma.

She couldn't possibly be this Amira Peres that Michal believed she was, or Jamie Dalton as the CIA insisted. Everything inside her stilled. The Israelis were wrong, as well. They were all wrong. She wasn't even a shrink and that sounded foolish to her. How could everyone else be wrong?

She shuddered and pushed the unpleasant thoughts away. It was almost time. She glanced around the room, noting the serving cart that room service had delivered. Michal had ordered the fruit, cheese and wine for her, as well, before he'd left. He wanted her to lack for nothing during his absence. Raoul had consumed most of it at Ami's urging.

She stole a sidelong look at him now. It had taken all of her persuasive powers to talk him into partaking of the wine. He was on duty, he'd told her over and over. But her persistence had won out. No one knew they were here, she'd argued. Michal would never have left her here were it not completely safe. Raoul had nothing to worry about. He should eat, drink and enjoy his day off.

He had done just that. Now he lit another cigarette causing her nose to wrinkle, drained the bottle into the delicate stemmed glass and then gulped it down just as quickly. She stifled a smile. Why hadn't he simply turned up the bottle and saved the wear and tear on his wrist pouring the stuff?

She'd plotted her strategy all day. Michal had departed the city shortly before noon to join his men. She didn't know the rendezvous point or what the mission was, but she had garnered that it would take approximately twenty-four hours. It was almost dark now. Raoul had to have a slight buzz. If she could get out of the room she could hide out on one of the boats. The hotel wasn't that far from the port. While they had enjoyed that leisurely stroll this morning, Michal had told her that boats arrived and departed from the port at all hours of the day and night. She repressed another shudder when she considered what their cargo might be. She'd have to be extremely careful in her selection or she'd end up in more trouble than she was now.

Her plan didn't include leaving the country aboard one of the vessels, she only wanted to hide out there until Michal and his men stopped searching for her. She'd noticed one large fishing boat that was under repair, that one surely wouldn't be going anywhere.

Michal would expect her to flee the city. With that in mind, he and his men would do a quick sweep of the city and then start searching for her beyond that perimeter. She, meanwhile, would leave the boat and take a taxi to the closest embassy. Though she didn't have any money of her own, Michal had left what appeared to be a sizable tip for the room service waiter. Ami swallowed tightly. She had taken it before the cart arrived. Raoul hadn't noticed or didn't care.

Ami had never stolen anything in her life—at least in the part of her life that she remembered. But extreme situations called for desperate measures. This, she concluded gravely, was as extreme as it got.

"I think I'll take a bath." She sprang up from the bed and gave Raoul a big smile. "Let me know if anything exciting happens."

Raoul tamped out his cigarette. "*Señora,* I fear the only excitement will be in my imagination." His slow perusal of her body and accompanying wolfish grin told her he was thinking about her naked in that enormous tub.

She kept her smile tacked into place as she headed toward the en suite bath. On second thought, she hesitated at the armoire long enough to take out one of the silky gowns Michal had purchased for her. When she closed the drawer, she made sure a pair of black lacy panties dangled from it. She crossed the room, the gown tossed over her shoulder, and turned on the stereo so that sensuous music drifted from its decades' old speakers. She had no idea what the words to the song meant, but they sounded sexy enough.

"You don't mind, do you?" she asked of the man staring openmouthed at her. When she started to unbutton her blouse, his eyes bulged.

Raoul's harsh intake of breath was indication enough

that he would be preoccupied while she pretended to bathe. Belatedly, he shook his head in answer to her question.

"Good." She crossed the room, taking care to sway her hips provocatively. When she reached the door, she paused. "I'll be a while," she purred, gifting him with another wide, teasing smile before she closed and locked the door behind her.

She threw the gown to the floor and quickly turned on the water in the lavish tub. Who would have thought that such elegant amenities would exist in a hotel that hadn't been renovated in several decades? She remembered then that Michal had mentioned that in the 1960s the place had been a hotel casino. Maybe that was why it was decorated so extravagantly. What had most likely been quite elegant more than forty years ago put a new slant on the phrase "shabby chic."

It would serve her purpose nicely.

She pushed up her sleeves and, using the cheap stopper, since the original drain mechanism apparently no longer worked, she adjusted the drain to suit her. This would allow the water to escape to an extent but would simultaneously permit the tub to fill enough to create the volume of splashing noise she wanted. The idea was to make sure it was noisy, but didn't overflow anytime soon.

With that out of the way, she quickly dried her arms and moved to the window. The casing and sashes were old, the latch slightly rusty. But, with effort, she managed to open it. The window wasn't large, but she could fit through. Since the sashes opened inward she was able to lean fully out through the opening. The room was on the third floor, but she'd already decided on an escape route. An old rusty pipe about six inches in diameter, probably a drainpipe of some sort, was attached to the building's facade about eighteen to twenty inches from the window.

Every few feet there was a raised collar-like section that appeared to connect the lengths of pipe. That would, hopefully, keep her from sliding straight down too fast and injuring herself.

Taking one last look over her shoulder at the closed door, she said a final prayer and climbed out the window. Holding her breath, she swung one arm then one leg over to the pipe. Once she'd locked on tightly with both arms and both legs, she eased up just a little on her grip so that she would slide downward fireman-pole style. The rust bit into her palms like sandpaper, but she ignored it. She had to hold on tightly, ease down just a little at a time.

The blood roared in her ears so loudly she wasn't sure she would have heard anyone if they had screamed her name. When she reached the dusty ground, she took a moment to regain her footing before she moved. Her entire body felt weak with a numbing mixture of fear and adrenaline. But she was down. She'd almost made it to freedom!

Looking carefully left to right, she started forward through the shadows. It was nearly dark now. Too late, she wished she'd remembered the head covering. The lightness of her hair would work against her in the dark. Not to mention it was illegal for a woman to leave the house without it.

She swore softly. She just couldn't get caught, that's all. This might be her only chance.

Moving soundlessly, she edged around the corner of the building. This would be the tough part. She had to cross the street. Then she could stay in alleyways until she reached the port…but crossing this one street was necessary. Though there weren't any streetlights to speak of, there was light from windows. The businesses had closed their doors before dusk and most of the cafés were a few blocks in the other direction. The area around the hotel was pretty deserted at this hour other than the occasional patron going and coming from its entrance. But those who lived above the shops had turned on lights.

Her gaze shifted up the block to a car parked at the side of the street. That would help. She stay pressed against the walls of the closed shops as she made her way to the car. Holding her breath again, she worked up her courage and moved swiftly across the street.

Once in the adjacent alleyway, she let go the breath that ached in her lungs. Thank God. No one shouted for her to stop. No one called out her name. She glanced up at the third floor of the hotel across the street and wondered if Raoul had noticed she was gone yet. Probably not or she'd hear him ranting all the way over here.

Peering into the darkness further down the alleyway until she was convinced no one hovered in the shadows, she began to make her way to the rear of the block that would open out onto the port side.

The unmistakable sound of a footfall a few feet behind her skimmed her auditory senses. Then nothing. She froze. The hair on the back of her neck stood on end.

Slowly, careful not to make even the slightest sound, she turned around. From behind her a hand snaked out and covered her mouth. Strong arms slammed her against a hard body.

She fought valiantly, kicking and scratching at the hand holding her. It couldn't be over this quickly. She was so close!

Her heel connected with a shin and a string of French profanities hissed past the lips mere inches from her head. Instinctively she bent her head forward then threw it back, hitting her assailant in the nose or mouth or both.

The arms suddenly loosened.

She was free.

She lunged forward.

Something hit her hard in the back of the head.

The ground flew up to meet her.

Bitch! was the last thing she heard as the darkness swallowed her.

PAIN SPLIT her skull.

Ami moaned.

Her lids were so heavy she couldn't make her eyes open. What had happened to her...she...?

The man grabbing her in the darkness...trying to run...the pain shattering through her skull.

She'd gotten away from Michal's guard.

But someone else had grabbed her.

Fear ripped through her chest.

Or maybe it was another of Michal's men. Someone who'd been watching from a distance to make sure she didn't run.

Carlos...or one of the others.

Now he would know.

Summoning all of her willpower, she opened her eyes.

She blinked against the dim lighting, but her eyes slowly adjusted. A rickety old fan stirred overhead. The ceiling was dingy and stained by long-term water leaks.

Not the hotel. It had been shabby, but not like this. Whoever had taken her, she wasn't back at the hotel.

She turned her head to see more. Pain sliced through her. She squeezed her eyes shut and clenched her teeth until it passed. When she opened her eyes once more she saw that a woman was sitting in a chair only a few feet away, her attention focused on the paperback book she was reading.

Confusion joined the pain swirling inside her brain as Ami studied the woman's features. Gray hair, the soft, glistening kind, was swept up and back. She was dressed in dark slacks, maybe navy or black, and a pale blouse, white or soft blue. She definitely did not look like the type Ami had expected to find guarding her. She looked like that actress…what was her name? Katharine Hepburn. Or maybe a schoolteacher.

Recognition suddenly crashed into her like a train bursting from a dark tunnel.

The waitress.

CIA operative.

Fran Woodard.

"Welcome back," Fran said, her gaze now focused on Ami instead of the book.

Somehow, in spite of the skull-cracking pain and drunken feeling that accompanied it, Ami sat up. Her clothes were dirty, rust was smeared down the front of her blouse from where she'd shimmied down that pipe. She looked up at the woman and the room spun wildly for about five seconds.

"You don't have a concussion, but it's a pretty nasty contusion. Hurts like hell, huh?"

From out of nowhere fury ignited inside Ami. What the hell was this woman doing here? Did that mean Tanner was here, as well?

Fran stood and smoothed her free hand over her slacks to straighten the wrinkles from sitting so long watching her charge. "I'll get the boss." She left, closing the door behind her.

Fear, stark and vivid, surged through Ami once more. What if Fran was a double agent? What if she had plans of her own for Ami? What would the Israelis pay to get their hands on her? Was there a price on her head already?

Her heart pumped so hard her chest ached, momentarily distracting her from the insistent throbbing in her brain.

She had to protect herself. Ami moved as quickly as she could, searching the meager furnishings of the room for some sort of weapon.

There was nothing.

The door suddenly opened once more.

Ami's head came up from her futile search.

Jack Tanner stood in the doorway, glowering at her.

"What the hell did you think you were doing?"

"You did this?" she accused, her breath catching as another stab of pain speared through her.

He shook his head, regret rearranged the features of his face, softening the signs of anger that had been there only a second or so ago.

"One of my men." His temper flared again. "But he claims he had no choice."

Ami vaguely remembered kicking and clawing, and then the coup de grace, the head butt. "Why didn't he identify himself?" she snapped, then winced. "I thought I was about to be raped—" her gaze met Tanner's "—or worse."

He crossed the room and visually examined her, as if looking for other signs of mishandling. "Worse was what you were headed for." He glared at her then. "If you'd been caught by any of the locals, do you have any idea what they would have done to you? You weren't properly attired and—"

"I don't want to hear it," she cut him off. "They didn't catch me, you did. I want to know why you've been following me and haven't tried to contact me." Pain seared through her again. What she really wanted to know was why he hadn't gotten her out of here.

"Following you is my job," he said tightly. "And keeping you alive, *if* I can."

Yeah, right. Her own temper rushed toward the boiling

point. "For how long? Until I accomplish whatever task it is the CIA needs me to do?" He wasn't going to rescue her...not until she'd done whatever the hell it was he wanted.

He didn't have to respond. She saw the answer in his eyes. "That's it, isn't it? I'm expendable. Once I've done your bidding, it doesn't matter whether I survive or not."

"That's not true," he countered savagely. "I will keep my word. I'll get you back to your son. I won't go back on that promise."

As if she could trust him. She didn't even know the man.

"Forgive me if I don't put a lot of stock in that guarantee," she tossed back at him. The whole world had gone mad as far as she could see. The only thing she wanted to do was to go home. But no one would let her.

"Why didn't you just let me go?" she asked, the anger pulsing out of her like the blood from a severed artery. There was no need to ask him how her son was, he'd never gone back. He'd been tailing her...her and Michal.

He looked away then. "I can't do that. Not until this is finished."

She threw up her hands in surrender. "To hell with it. I give up. I'm never going to see my child again and we both know it." She rounded on him then. "Why not just admit that and be done with it? I'm dead, right?"

Ten long seconds ticked by before he answered. "As far as anyone else is concerned, your survival is not essential to the mission," he admitted wearily.

She started to shake her head, but then remembered the hot ball of pain pulsing at the base of her skull. She laughed instead, a dry, brittle sound. "I knew it."

"But that's not the way I see it," he pressed. "I'll keep my word, Ami. You have to trust me."

She glared up at him from beneath her lashes. "Like hell. I can't trust anyone."

"I have everything set," he said more quietly as if fearing someone would overhear him. "I have a backup plan that no one else knows about. Your son is safe. I'll see that you're reunited with him. But you've got to do exactly what I tell you. I can't help you if you get me killed or one of my operatives spotted by Arad or his people. I can't help you if I'm out of the picture," he reiterated.

She took the final step that stood between them. "Swear to me that you won't let anything happen to my child and that if I survive this you'll get me to him."

"I swear." He started to say more but didn't or couldn't. Slowly, without taking his eyes from hers, he lifted his hand and stroked her cheek. "I won't let you down."

For that brief moment a memory surfaced—him holding her...kissing her. She blinked the image away. She remembered something he'd said that first day they'd met...something about their relationship before.

"Did we...?" Her gaze locked with his and she pleaded for the whole truth. She didn't want any more lies. She was so sick and tired of deception.

"Yes." He lowered his hand and backed off emotionally. She felt his withdrawal. "But that was before. Our...personal relationship ended when you went undercover."

That meant only one thing. "He's Nicholas's father." The words were scarcely a whisper, a mere breath, but the realization was so profound she staggered beneath the weight of it. On some level she'd known.

"Yes," Tanner admitted. "He's the father. Do you understand what that means?"

She looked up at him once more.

"If he finds out about the child, he'll do whatever necessary to get his hands on him. Is this the kind of life you want for your child?''

She shook her head slowly from side to side, the pain now relegated to some rarely used area of gray matter. As the rest of her hurts, it no longer mattered. "I don't want that.''

"Then this mission is your only hope. As long as Arad is alive, you and your son won't be safe from his reach. He's too powerful…too ruthless.''

They were going to kill him, Ami realized. The thought seemed to come from some faraway place. She felt somehow outside her body as she watched her mind absorb the implication of his statement. She'd suspected that, as well.

"You want me to help you kill him.''

Again his eyes answered before he did. "Yes.''

How could she do that? He was her son's father…he was her…lover. Emotion twisted inside her. She wasn't a murderer. No matter what anyone said, she would not believe that.

"Look at it this way,'' Tanner said, calling her attention to him once more, ''one more sick terrorist will be dead and you and your son will be free of him once and for all.''

She backed up a step, putting her hands up in a stop fashion. "If he's so bad, why hasn't the CIA done this already? Why wait for me to come along? Surely I can't be that important to the success of the mission.''

Tanner plowed his fingers through his hair, apparently annoyed that she didn't just go along with his plan. But none of this made sense.

"It's complicated,'' he hedged.

Her fury kindled again. "Don't let my simple mind stop you from giving an explanation your best shot.''

He held up a hand in protest. "I didn't mean it that way. There's just some things that I can't tell you."

She gritted her teeth to the count of five in hopes of slowing her anger's ascent. It didn't work. "Well, tell me what you can."

"Arad has served a purpose in the past."

Disbelief shook her. "So the CIA deals in terrorists? Let them live as long as they serve a purpose. Please, no wonder you guys got your hands slapped after—"

"I told you," he interrupted pointedly, "that there were certain parts I had to leave out. A perfectly logical explanation regarding his status is one of those things you don't have clearance for."

She rolled her eyes. "Whatever."

"He's gotten too powerful, too arrogant. We need him out of the picture."

"So you people can't do this?" Ami deadpanned. "You need me—a civilian—to do it for you?" She looked heavenward in exasperation.

"Again," he said, his patience clearly thinning, "it's not that simple. And you're not merely a civilian."

Apprehension welled inside her. She didn't want to talk about this anymore. Things between her and Michal were—as Tanner so eloquently put it—complicated.

"When this goes down, no one can know we're responsible. The setup with you is perfect." Tanner splayed his hands as if the answer were clear. "Think about it. Everyone knows you betrayed him two years ago, now you're back. It won't come as any surprise if he comes up dead with you hanging around again."

Ami felt certain he had no idea how his words affected her. Her whole body rejected the idea...but some brain cell connected to long-term memory that had lain dormant for two long years suddenly went active and she knew Tanner was right. "So it's true, I did betray him?"

Tanner's guard came up. "We've been over this before. You went undercover to set up Yael Peres. You used Arad to accomplish that and left him to face the Israelis' wrath. That he escaped was pure luck."

She searched his eyes, looking for any indication that he was lying to her. "Why did I do that? Set up Peres, I mean?"

Tanner shifted, his impatience palpable now, his gaze averted. "We've been over that part, too," he said crisply.

"No." Ami waited until he looked at her again. "Not that part. I need to know why the CIA wanted Peres out of the way."

His anger resurfacing, Tanner's jaw hardened. "Because he was secretly using his influence in the Israeli government to undermine Israeli-U.S. relations." He had to pause a moment to contain his emotions. She saw the muscle jerking rhythmically in his jaw, saw the vein throb on his forehead. He took a deep breath and continued, "If you watch the news you know how vital that relationship is. We can't let anything jeopardize it."

She nodded. Even she could see the necessity in that. But Michal… An ache banded around her chest at even the thought of having anything to do with hurting him. She knew she shouldn't feel that way. He was a terrorist. A kidnapper. A murderer.

Her son's father…her lover… But if she didn't do this she would never see her son again. Michal had chosen his own path. As helpless as she was at the moment, she had, as well. But her son was the true innocent in all this.

She closed her eyes and forced all emotion aside. "What do you want me to do?"

Jack swallowed back the regret that stuck in his craw.

He hated this shit. He should just take her right now and get her the hell out of here. He set his jaw hard and forced himself to do what had to be done.

"Arad will take on another job in a few days. I'll need specifics in order to catch him off guard. Times, rendezvous points, anything you can get. Then I'll take care of the rest. It's going to look as if someone trying to get at you took him down."

A frown furrowed its way across her brow. "But how can I do that now? Raoul has probably already sent word to him that I—"

"You have to go back," Jack interjected. "It's the only way."

She retreated a step as if preparing to flee. "How can I do that? Raoul—"

"Is dead," he cut in again.

Jack allowed the impact of those two words to sink in before he continued. "As soon as my team recognized what you were up to, we sent someone in and terminated him. We've since pretty much wrecked the room so that it'll look like someone broke in, killed Raoul and nabbed you."

Her complexion turned ashen. "Because I tried to escape, you had him killed?"

Jack considered whether he should tell her the truth or not, but opted to keep things on the level. "We had no choice. We need your cover intact."

She blinked, looking far too close to fainting for his liking, but he couldn't let her see anything less than complete detachment on his part.

"What do we do now?" Her voice sounded small, like a lost child's.

He brutally squashed the urge to tell her everything...to take her and run as far and fast as he could. "Most likely someone in the hotel, an associate of Arad's, has already informed him of the incident and he's probably on his way back here right now or may even be here as we speak. We'll release you on the street and you'll say that you escaped.'' He gestured to the room at large. ''Tell him you were kept here. We've planted evidence to indicate a local group of extremists were responsible for the incident.''

''What am I supposed to tell him they did to me?''

She trembled and he had to restrain the need to reach out to her. Every instinct told him this wasn't right. But, like her, he had no choice.

''You tell him that they tried to beat information about his whereabouts out of you, but that you didn't know anything. Tell him that you managed to escape when one of the men tried to...to rape you.''

She blinked but didn't clear the confusion totally from her gaze. ''What if he doesn't believe me?''

This part was almost more than Jack could live with and yet it was the most crucial element...her survival depended upon it. ''We have to make him believe it.''

''How?''

Jack stepped to the door and gestured to the man waiting outside. When he entered the room, Ami gasped, obviously recognizing him from the claw marks on his forearms and cheeks as well as the swollen nose. She'd worked the guy over pretty good in her efforts to escape.

When her frightened gaze swung to his, regret pierced Jack like a dagger straight through the heart. ''I wish there was another way.''

He turned away from the shock and confusion in her eyes before the first blow landed, unable to watch the brutality necessary to make her cover story real.

The story that would ultimately save her life.

CHAPTER ELEVEN

AMI LAY PRONE in the dusty street, her face turned to one side, her eyes unblinking. She stared, seeing nothing. Her mind as well as her body was numb.

She felt nothing.

People gathered around her. She sensed more than heard or saw them.

She wondered briefly if she was dead.

Something ached through the numbness.

Her son. She would never see her baby again.

Arms lifted her and she did not resist.

They turned her over with a great deal of care.

She didn't recognize the voices or the faces around her.

She no longer cared where she was.

Darkness tugged at her.

A bolt of pain erupted, screamed through her, awakening the other senses her mind had shut down hours ago. She groaned, unable to do more. Her tongue slid forward, to dampen her dry, cracked lips and fire rushed through her once more.

Finally she did the only thing she could, she closed her eyes and surrendered to the blessed oblivion.

MICHAL PACED the outer room of the tiny clinic, rage churning inside him. Someone would pay for this. His jaw hardened. Someone would pay dearly.

Anguish squeezed his heart each time he thought of how

badly she'd been beaten…of what could have happened had she not escaped the imbeciles who had taken her hostage. To get at him, he knew for a certainty. He'd grown complacent when it came to this city. Felt untouchable. He was respected and feared here. Obviously not feared enough.

That would change.

Carlos and four of his men were scouring Tripoli at that very moment to determine how this had happened. A physician Michal trusted was doing all he could to make Amira comfortable as he tended her injuries. He'd insisted Michal leave the room since his presence appeared to upset the patient. The few patients in the clinic when he and his men arrived had chosen to come back later.

Michal kicked the closest object. The chair skidded across the floor and crashed into the wall. The Spaniard and Thomas moved yet again to avoid his path as he began to pace once more. He kept seeing her lying on that shop floor, crumpled and broken-looking. The owner and his wife had seen her stagger into the street and fall facedown. They had thought her dead the way she'd lain so still and with her eyes wide open, unblinking. Michal could not banish the images their words evoked. The shop owner had called the authorities who had reported her whereabouts directly to Michal.

She was bruised badly, her arms, upper torso, and even her legs. Her left cheek was swollen and discolored, as well. One cracked rib.

His mind went black for several seconds before he could again regain control of the consuming rage.

Thank God she had not been raped.

This was bad enough.

She had told him that she'd barely escaped the man.

There had been three, but only one had been with her when she'd managed to break free.

Michal's fingers curled into fists. This man would die. As would the others.

This wasn't supposed to happen. She should have been safe, here of all places.

Word had come swiftly to him. The mission had been accomplished, but this necessity had required that he leave earlier than planned. And still it had taken what felt like a lifetime to reach her.

Michal's gaze moved back to the door that stood between them. He would see that this never happened again. He closed his eyes and fought the urge to roar like a lion with the emotions twisting inside him.

He should have protected her. He had failed.

The fear she must have suffered at the hands of those brutes haunted him. Made him sick with disgust.

This was no life for her. He inhaled sharply, his chest heavy with too many regrets. She was different now. Before she had seemed to enjoy the thrill of living on the edge, the dangerous lure of how he lived. He remembered well when she'd first sought him out. Michal had been certain he had never met a woman more like himself—utterly fearless.

In no time she had worked her way into his heart, and then she had demanded to know his price for killing her father. Shocked at first, Michal had played off her suggestion. But Amira had been insistent. Then the word had come down that Peres was to be added to his list. Michal had not questioned the coincidence at the time, his only concern had been keeping Amira pleased with him. He wanted to make her father suffer for the hurt and neglect she had suffered because of him.

He frowned and stared at the door as if he could see

through it, see what the physician was doing now, by sheer force of will. Her continued assertion since her return that she was not Amira Peres nagged at him. Could she have fooled him, as well as Yael Peres? Michal could only assume that her amnesia was so complete that even the most remote aspect of her past was now gone forever. The only other conclusion would be that she was not Amira Peres. He shook his head in protest of that reasoning. That was not possible.

Still, she was quite different now. Whatever bitterness that lurked in her soul two years ago had disappeared along with her memory. She was not the same. But on every other level she felt the same.

This Amira—Ami—was more vulnerable, softer, with no idea how to function in his world. And he had failed to protect her. Leaving her helpless to defend herself and a perfect target for those who would seek to bring him down.

The door opened and the physician waved him inside. His feet moving him forward, Michal's heart shuddered to a near stop as his gaze fell upon her once more.

She sat on the examination table, her ribs wrapped tightly beneath her torn blouse. Another blast of fury thundered through him. The blood had been cleansed from her skin and her hair had been combed. His gaze flitted to the nurse standing next to her. The nurse's doing, he imagined. The entire staff of the small clinic had been terrified by his volatile emotions. He was certain they wanted to appease him in any way possible in hopes of surviving this encounter.

"She will be fine," the physician told him in stilted English. "She must take care for a time until the rib is healed properly. There is no concussion despite the lump on her head. There is nothing more I can do."

Michal nodded. "Good." He knew he should at least glance at the doctor and thank him, but he couldn't take his eyes off Ami. She sat so very still, her eyes glazed and empty.

"We can go now?" he asked, finally sparing the physician a glance.

"Yes."

Michal stepped closer to her, but she made no move to reach out to him or to even stand. She simply sat there, staring at nothing. The nurse scurried to the other side of the room as far away from Michal as possible.

He reached an arm around Ami's shoulders and she flinched. A blade of hurt skewered him as if he'd been run through with a sword. "We can go now," he murmured as reassuringly as the emotion clogging his throat would allow. She made no response. Worry thudded in his temples. "You are sure she will be fine?" he asked, suddenly certain the physician had missed some aspect of her injury.

"The shock," he offered. "It will take time to recover from the shock."

Satisfied with that diagnosis, Michal gently urged Ami toward the edge of the table until she scooted off the rest of the way on her own. Once on her feet, she wobbled for a moment, but he steadied her against him. He didn't bother saying anything else as he led Ami from the room. His man, Thomas, would generously reward the physician and his nurse. No other discussion was necessary.

Outside, he helped Ami into the back of the car and slid in next to her. She leaned back in the seat and closed her eyes as if too weary to do otherwise. Thomas and the Spaniard climbed into the front, Thomas behind the wheel.

"I'm taking you home," Michal told her softly, again hoping she would respond to his words. "You'll be safe there."

A cellular telephone buzzed and Thomas quickly silenced it by answering the call. He pulled out onto the street as he listened. Michal only half listened until Thomas demanded to know the address, then his instincts soared to a higher state of alert. Carlos had found something. He was sure of it.

Thomas ended the call and glanced at him in the rearview mirror. "Carlos found him. He's holding him at the house where they took her. The other two men have not been found."

"Take me there," Michal ordered, his fury burning bloodred, clouding his vision.

Ami tensed in his arms. "Don't worry," he soothed, his voice still gruff despite his best efforts. "You will be safe. I swear it."

The ride took only five minutes. Ami prayed every second of those few minutes that she could keep up the pretense. Tears burned behind her eyes, but it was the fear that pounded in her chest that made her weak…made her want to run. If Michal found out what really happened.

She would be dead. *If you betray me again I will kill you.* His words as he'd made love to her that first time echoed inside her skull.

The car bumped over a rut in the road and she had to close her eyes against the pain that seared through her sides. Her whole body ached, her lower lip felt raw from the split there.

She tried to block the memory of that jerk coming at her, slapping her repeatedly with the back of his hand, shoving her against the wall and then to the floor where he'd kicked her. Had Tanner not interceded, things could have gotten a lot worse. The jerk had been extremely pissed at her. She'd sobbed harder with each blow, hadn't wanted to, but the pain had been overwhelming. She'd been certain that the extent of the beating wasn't necessary—that the guy had been out for revenge rather than simply following orders. She tried to think now if Tanner could have stopped him sooner. Maybe not. Maybe he'd done the right thing.

She was definitely thankful for the indisputable evidence of her innocence the brutal beating provided. If Tanner wasn't going to get her out of this, and he likely wasn't, she definitely didn't want Michal suspicious of her.

She pushed away the thought of what Tanner expected her to do. She couldn't think about that right now. She only wanted out of this godforsaken country. Her thoughts were too fragmented, too scattered to analyze the situation.

She would do what she had to.

A single tear rolled down her cheek at the reality of exactly what that entailed. She pushed it away again, determined not to let it into her thoughts until she could think more clearly.

Her heart lurched when the car stopped in front of the crumbling building where Tanner's people had held her last night. Where she'd been beaten to within an inch of her life or what felt like it. What if they'd forgotten something? Something that could link her to the CIA?

"I don't want to go in there," she said, pulling away from Michal's hold. Wanting desperately to crawl out the passenger-side door and run like hell. She wasn't cut out for this cloak-and-dagger stuff. "Please." Her gaze shot to Michal's. "I can't."

His eyes turned even darker with some raw, savage emotion that went way beyond rage. He took her by the arm, less gently than before. "You must. It is necessary."

Terror clawing at her, she slid across the seat and allowed him to help her from the car. Every move she made sent pain radiating across her nerve endings. Outside the

contusion and the fractured rib, most of her injuries were
superficial. Why did she have to come back here? Why
was vengeance necessary? Why did it matter who did it?
She just wanted to leave.

She shivered as she recalled Tanner saying that he
would plant evidence. She didn't know what kind or about
whom; she didn't want to know. She didn't want to be
here. She stalled at the entryway, but Michal prodded her
into forward motion. He wasn't going to leave it alone.
She might as well face facts. She doubted he would even
consider leaving the country until he'd exhausted all his
resources.

Inside the gloomy structure that smelled of urine and
disuse, it was evident the place had been ransacked. She
remembered distinctly that the front room, the one she now
stood in, had been vacant. The room where she'd awakened had been furnished with only a cot, a chair and a
rickety old armoire.

She surveyed the room once more as they moved
through it. The overturned furniture and shattered crockery
had definitely been added since she left. Papers were scattered over the floor. She didn't remember those, either,
from before. Part of the evidence, she presumed.

As they approached the room where she'd awakened,
she balked, couldn't make her feet take the final steps.
"Please, can't we just leave," she pleaded once more.

Ignoring her plea, Michal turned to Thomas. "Stay with
her," he ordered.

She watched, her heart racing, as Michal shoved the
door inward and entered the room. Thomas stood a few
feet away as if fearing, like Raoul, she might cost him his
life, as well, if he got too close.

The seconds turned into minutes and still she gleaned
nothing from the hushed conversation in the room. Ami

prayed with every ounce of strength she possessed that they hadn't found something in the room that would contradict her story. Surely Tanner would not be so careless.

Carlos hated her. He would like nothing better than to nail her. She could imagine him on his hands and knees going over every square inch of the place looking for clues against her. She trembled. God, how much more of this could she stand? She closed her eyes and tried to slow the drunken 'round and 'round sensation in her head. She summoned the image of her son and focused on him, pushing away all other thought. He was all that mattered.

"Ami."

Her eyes opened to Michal standing in the doorway, looking directly at her. Before she could dredge up a proper response, he had taken the few steps that yawned between them.

"I want you to come into the room and look closely at this man. Tell me if he is the one who hurt you."

Panic broadsided her. Man? What man? Her gaze flew to the open doorway. Carlos and three other men were crowded around someone seated in a chair. The image of the man tied to a chair in the cellar flashed through her mind. That scene had resulted in death. Not again. Who...

Surely it wasn't the man who'd actually inflicted her injuries. Tanner wouldn't have left him to face certain death. Though the idea wasn't completely without appeal, she didn't want to be responsible for his death. Michal, without question, had murder in his eyes.

Her mind whirling with confusion and fear, Michal ushered her into the room. Carlos and the others parted, revealing the man tied to the chair.

For one long moment Ami was unable to speak. He was tall and thin, Libyan maybe. She peered into his dark eyes and saw the fear there.

"This man," Michal explained, "is the leader of a sub-versive group who has made more than one attempt on my life. According to witnesses, his people moved into this place shortly before we arrived. Carlos has reason to sus-pect they have had someone watching for our arrival." Michal turned to her then. "Now, tell me if this is the man who hurt you and I will make him pay."

Dead silence fell over the room as all present awaited her response. She thought of Raoul and how he had died to provide an excuse for her stupid attempt at escaping. How could she have ever believed even for a second that she could escape this nightmare? Now this man was to die, too.

She couldn't do it.

Not even to save her own life.

She shook her head adamantly, ignoring the resulting pain. "No, it wasn't him."

The pent-up breath the man exhaled echoed in the oth-erwise silence.

Carlos looked ready to throttle her...or worse. Michal appeared taken aback and Ami felt certain she had just signed her own death warrant.

"Look again...more carefully," Michal urged. "Are you certain?"

With no other option, Ami did as he instructed. She looked at the man and surmised from the swelling of his face and the blood leaking from his busted lip that he'd already paid a hefty price for something he hadn't even done.

"No," she said firmly, determined not to be responsible for another man's death. No matter what kind of extremist or terrorist he was, she would not be his judge and exe-cutioner. "It's not him."

Michal peered deeply into her eyes for what felt like an eternity before he turned to Carlos. "Let him go."

"What?" Carlos bellowed. "We cannot—"

"Release him," Michal ordered. His attention shifted to the prisoner. "Tell your people that I am far from finished. I will not forget this transgression. Nor will I overlook another."

Glowering at both her and Michal, Carlos did as he was ordered, cutting the man free then jerking him to his feet. "Go!" He pushed the man toward the door.

Ami recoiled as he staggered past her, at once relieved and fearful. He collapsed against the door frame and didn't appear able to go farther. She'd been right. Carlos had already worked him over considerably.

"Get him out of here," Michal ordered, his patience at an end.

Carlos grabbed the man by the scruff of the neck and dragged him to attention. "What are you waiting for, imbecile? Get out!"

When Carlos would have shoved the prisoner through the door the man twisted, his right hand snagging Carlos's weapon from his waistband.

Ami's breath left her in a whoosh and the scene lapsed into slow motion. Displaying surprising strength, the prisoner shouldered Carlos aside and leveled the barrel of the weapon on Ami. "American whore!" he screamed.

Michal dove in front of her.

A blast exploded in the room as Ami hit the floor hard on her backside, sending pain piercing through her.

Another blast splintered the air.

The prisoner dropped the gun and crumpled to the floor. He lay facing her, his sightless eyes unblinking.

She blinked, stunned.

People scrambled around her. Muffled voices. She

couldn't understand...couldn't make out their words. Could hardly hear at all. She turned to see...

Michal.

He dropped to his knees.

Carlos and Thomas instantly appeared on either side of him.

Ami struggled to her feet, scarcely noticing the detonation of agony that accompanied her every move.

She pushed her way between the men hovered around Michal.

Bright crimson spread across the fabric of the white shirt he wore, the spot widening, plunging toward the center of his chest.

Blood.

He'd been shot.

Nausea roiled in her stomach. The room spun. And then the lights went out.

CHAPTER TWELVE

JACK WAITED IMPATIENTLY at a table for two on the terrace outside Café Marly. He didn't care that the chic French restaurant sat beneath the arcades of the Louvre overlooking the majestic pyramids of steel and glass, or that tourists strolled through the courtyards with properly awed expressions. He only cared that his appointment was late.

The waitress stopped at his table once more to see if he needed anything else, but Jack waved her off. The last thing he needed was more caffeine. Or a flirtatious waitress looking for a roll in the hay with an American businessman. Ordinarily, Jack would have considered that a good thing, but there was nothing ordinary about the situation.

The events of the past twenty-four hours had convinced him beyond a doubt that Ami Donovan was in over her head.

Arad had taken her for medical attention, indicating that he had accepted her story. According to Fran Woodard, who'd stayed behind to monitor the situation, Arad's men had discovered the planted evidence.

Jack massaged his temples, but produced no relief for the insistent throbbing there.

Preston Fowler was already in Paris and had agreed to meet with Jack for a status briefing. Jack was pretty damned sure he wasn't going to want to hear what he had to say.

"We'll have to make this quick," Fowler said, appearing out of nowhere and snapping Jack back to the here and now. "The American ambassador moved our meeting up so I don't have much time." He hefted his portly frame into the delicate chair on the opposite side of the tiny table and scanned the terrace for the waitress.

"Hello to you, too," Jack rumbled.

Fowler gestured to the waitress and indicated that he would have the same as Jack, a high-octane espresso. Then he settled his irritated gaze on his subordinate.

"Be thankful I was able to fit you in at all," Fowler said crossly. "My schedule is tight. I have to be back in the States by morning." He leaned back in his chair, ignoring its creak of protest. "What is it that couldn't wait until the regularly scheduled briefing?"

Jack pinned him with a gaze he hoped relayed the urgency of the situation. "We have to pull her out."

Fowler laughed outright, oblivious to the indignant stares cast his way at the outburst. When his amusement died, a mixture of anger and impatience replaced it. "Tell me you didn't drag me over here for this worn-out tap dance."

"She was almost made," Jack said, his own temper flaring. "Arad is far too suspicious of her already." He shook his head. "This latest setback is only going to increase the risk to her. She won't be any use to us dead."

The waitress stopped at their table before Jack could say more. She served Fowler and sashayed away. Jack was forced to wait out Fowler's preoccupation with the woman's swaying hips before he could continue.

"You have to let me pull her. I think—"

"You're thinking," Fowler cut him off, his attention swinging back to the discussion, "with your dick instead of your brain."

"She won't last—"

"And as far as this latest close call goes, the way I hear it, she brought that heat down on herself."

Jack's spine stiffened. "Who told you that?" There were only three people besides him who knew what had really gone down.

"Patterson and I go way back," Fowler said bluntly. "He told me about her little escape attempt." His glare turned as hard as flint. "Didn't you make it clear to her what she had to lose?"

Something snapped deep inside Jack. Some boundary that had heretofore kept his emotions in check when it came to his profession. But this time was different. This time it was personal. He hadn't saved her life two years ago just to watch her die now.

"Let's say we get really lucky and somehow this assignment is successful," he said tautly. "Any of Arad's men who survive will kill her. Even if she's fast enough and cunning enough to get away, she won't last twenty-four hours. Arad is too popular among his peers and those who support them. Once that world knows he's dead and that she had something to do with it, she won't stand a chance against the wave of vengeance that will be unleashed. She won't be safe anywhere on the planet. Even terrorists have their loyal followings."

Fowler leaned forward. "Who do you think you're talking to, Jack?" There was no mistaking the underlying fury in his tone. "I know the reaction projections just as well as you do, maybe better. It's the only way. We haven't been successful in our attempts to turn one of his men. She's the best shot we've got. We *all* want him dead. What part of that don't you understand?"

Jack clenched his jaw and reached for calm. It wasn't to be found. "When did we stop caring about the cost? There was a time when we didn't sell out our own."

Fowler simply looked at him in that arrogant manner that was apparently prerequisite to the position of deputy director. "Think about it, Jack. Things have changed. We don't do business with terrorists anymore. We squash them. Any way we can. In this case, she's our ace in the hole."

Something about the way Fowler looked when he made that last statement or maybe the overconfident, condescending tone of his voice, brought a new kind of clarity to the situation. Realization sent dread washing over Jack.

"You set this whole thing up," he said, scarcely believing the words even as he uttered them.

Fowler snorted haughtily. "A little slow on the uptake, are we, Jack?"

Before Jack could roar with the indignation exploding in his chest, Fowler went on. "We needed Arad taken out of the picture. You had her stashed away, under the watch of that damned pricy shrink we keep on the payroll, why not use her? What do you think? That we're in the business of baby-sitting?" Fowler huffed with self-righteous indignation. "She's an asset. We use our assets, otherwise we dump 'em. The plan was perfect." Fowler chuckled at his own ingenuity. "We knew Arad had a weakness for her. All we had to do was expose her in such a way that suspicion wouldn't be aroused. The assassination attempt on one of Peres's old friends was the perfect solution."

Rage erupted inside Jack. "You son of a bitch," he hissed.

Fowler's expression turned lethal. "I'd watch my step if I were you, Jack. You're already skating on thin ice. As I said, we don't keep assets that lose their value."

Jack's secure cellular line vibrated. He snatched it from his jacket pocket and answered the call before his baser instincts could take over completely. The way he saw it, he and Fowler had nothing else to discuss and killing him was against the rules. Nothing he could say or do at this point would make a difference. Ami was in too deep. Too vital to the ultimate goal.

"Tanner."

"Jack, there's been a development."

Fran Woodard. His heart rate kicked into overdrive. "Is she all right?" If Arad had learned the truth…

"It's not our girl," Fran assured him. "It's Arad."

An altogether different anticipation surging inside him, he demanded, "What happened?"

"Carlos picked up one of the scumbags from that extremist group we framed. Apparently things got out of hand and Arad was injured."

Shock quaked through Jack. "Is he dead?" Relief edged into the fringes of his anticipation, renewing the hope that Ami might just survive. If Arad was dead, he could pull her out. The hesitation on the other end of the line went on for a beat too long, crushing the hope that had sprouted. "Dammit, Fran, *is he dead?*"

"I don't know," she admitted reluctantly. "They rushed him away. There was a lot of blood."

"Where is he now?" Jack should get back there, be close by. The flight took only—

"They're at the clinic—the same one he took Ami to just a few hours ago. I've given them an hour, but no one's come out yet. It doesn't look good."

That butcher shop scarcely met the most remote definition of a medical clinic. If Arad needed surgery or a blood transfusion, he was a goner.

"I'm on my way."

"Wait."

His pulse pounding out his tension, Jack's brow furrowed against the pressure as he waited for Fran to tell him what the hell was going on. He should have stayed. But when he'd learned Fowler was in Paris, he'd hoped to talk him into aborting the mission. He clenched his teeth against the rage that rose all over again when he considered what Fowler had done behind his back.

"They're coming out."

Jack stilled completely, even his heart seemed to stop beating, his nerves felt raw with frustration...with anticipation. He wanted this over. He wanted Ami safely reunited with her child and hidden away from harm.

"Arad's alive."

The two words deflated his hopes like a players strike right before baseball season. He muttered a curse.

"He looks like hell, if that makes you feel any better," Fran added. "They're loading into two cars. Patterson and I'll be right behind them."

The airport, Jack knew already. Arad would want to get back to his estate. The fortress he called home. The only place on the planet he felt truly safe.

And once he was back there, Jack could do nothing but wait.

Ami was on her own.

MICHAL DID NOT BREATHE easy until he reached his home.

His shoulder hurt like hell, but he would live. The most important thing was that Ami was alive and safe for the moment. He downed his whiskey, numbing the pain a bit. How long would she be safe here? How could he allow the possibility of another incident such as the one that had taken place in Tripoli?

He could not. It was that simple.

She was soaking in the tub now, relaxing the soreness in her muscles where the bastard had beaten her.

Her reluctance to identify the man who had harmed her

nagged at him. Whether it was the man Carlos had killed or another of his group, Michal did not care. They were complete scum. Anti-Israeli as well as anti-American. Still, because she was so upset, he had been willing to give the man his freedom, mainly, he admitted, so that he could take Michal's warning back to his people, and the bastard had tried to kill her.

He poured himself another drink and downed half of it. He should have killed him and been done with it. But he had allowed emotion to get in the way. A nearly fatal mistake. His gaze tracked Carlos's pacing. He had more to say on the subject, of that Michal was certain. But he restrained himself out of a respect that lessened each day.

"Speak your mind, my friend," Michal told him, his pain nicely numbed with the heat of the liquor flowing in his blood.

Carlos pulled up short and glared at him. "You almost got yourself killed." The muscles of his face worked with the rage simmering inside him. "Because of *her*. I told you." He took two steps toward Michal's relaxed position in a wing chair. "She betrayed you once. How can you be sure this was not an elaborate setup?"

Michal shook his head. "You are wrong, my friend."

Carlos flung his arms in the air as if beseeching a higher power for guidance. "They have never before made a move so bold," he argued. "And this story of hers as to how she escaped. I do not believe this." He moved his head side to side for emphasis. "She would not have escaped those animals. She is too helpless for such a fearless feat."

That was the part that nagged at Michal the most. This Amira was far too vulnerable and terrified of his world. Still, in her desperation perhaps she had been merely lucky.

"She escaped." Michal's gaze latched onto Carlos's. "That is all that matters."

He threw up his hands again. "You are under a spell," he shouted. "She is using you and you are too blind to see it."

Michal set his empty glass aside and pushed to his feet. His shoulder throbbed in response. It was a damn good thing the bullet had gone straight through, missing anything important, including bone. There had been lots of blood and there would be plenty of pain, but nothing worse.

"You make many serious accusations," Michal said quietly, his tone laced with a lethal quality for good measure. "Do you have evidence to support this assertion? And what is it she would hope to gain by using me or setting me up? She has asked for nothing."

Carlos looked too smug. Michal's instincts pushed through the haze of alcohol and stood at attention.

"We both know that she betrayed you before."

Michal didn't bother commenting. It was as Carlos said. But that was the past, this was now.

"I have been watching her closely."

Tension slid through Michal. Carlos was no fool. But Michal did not like the idea of him *watching* her. "And what have you observed?"

"Nothing. She remembers nothing of the past, she does nothing." He splayed his hands in confusion. "Nothing."

"What is your point, Carlos?" Michal warned, his patience at an end.

"My contacts in the village tell me that there has been CIA activity." Carlos cocked his head and said the rest with far too much pleasure. "It started about the same time she arrived."

A new kind of tension wormed its way into Michal's

already rigid muscles at that news. "What activities have your contacts reported?"

"Only that a man—an American—has been asking questions, hanging around, watching, pretending to be a tourist."

"This man," Michal prodded, "what does he look like?"

Carlos shrugged. "The description is vague. Dark hair. Tall. Lean."

Michal filed the description for later use. "But you have no direct link between Amira and the CIA or this man you believe to be CIA?"

Fury erupted in Carlos's eyes once more. "What will it take to convince you? You are not thinking straight? Raoul is dead! You were almost killed. If you do not get rid of her, she will be the death of us all!"

Michal advanced on him then, going toe to toe, eye to eye so there would be no misunderstanding. "This discussion is over. If—" he continued when Carlos would have argued "—you broach this subject again, I will consider it an outright act of insubordination."

Deep, dark red rose from Carlos's neck all the way to his forehead, but, to his credit, he remained silent.

"You will keep me informed as to any further CIA activities in Marseilles," he added in case there was any question. "Unless, of course, you no longer wish to pursue this working relationship. Am I clear?"

The standoff lasted all of ten seconds.

"You have made yourself crystal clear."

Carlos walked out of the room as if all was understood, but Michal had the distinct feeling this battle had only just begun. He hoped for Carlos's sake he was wrong. His gut told him that the issue went far deeper than Ami's presence.

Whatever the case, if the man forced his hand, it would not bode well for him.

AMI GINGERLY DRIED her body. Every reach, every bend, was agonizing. When she'd swabbed herself dry as best she could, she wiped the foggy mirror with the towel and studied her reflection. Most of the swelling had gone down in her cheek, but the bruise was an ugly shade of yellowish purple.

Varying shades of purple and green dotted her arms and sides. The worst of which was where the jerk had kicked her in the ribs, fracturing one, making even a deep breath uncomfortable. At least she could hear again. The proximity of the gun blasts had all but deafened her.

Ami closed her eyes and braced herself against the basin. The events of the past thirty-six hours shook her to the very core of her being. She was certain she had never known such brutality. She flinched at the memory of that gun barrel aimed directly at her face. It was insane. Michal had given that man his freedom and he'd used it to try to kill her.

Michal had explained that the group the man represented hated Americans in particular. To die while attempting to rid the earth of one made him a hero.

Ami shivered. This was crazy. She wasn't indifferent to the happenings in the world. She watched CNN from time to time. But seeing it flash across a news screen and living the actual events were two entirely different things.

How could people live this way?

She had seen Michal murder a man with her own eyes. She'd witnessed his cunning when they had traveled to Libya. There was no doubt in her mind that he could be incredibly ruthless when he chose to be.

But he had saved her life.

He'd stepped in front of that bullet with no consideration whatsoever of his own survival.

It didn't take a rocket scientist to figure out that he had released the man in part to appease her.

And it had almost cost him his life.

She shuddered when the pictures flashed one after the other through her mind. Blood…there had been so much blood. She'd seen blood before. She was a nurse, for God's sake! But this had been Michal's blood. An inch or two lower and slightly to the right and he wouldn't have survived.

No amount of training or experience as a nurse had prepared her for that moment. Even the remote possibility of his dying had been more than she could bear.

How could she hope to follow through with Tanner's plan?

Her hand went to her stomach and she pressed it there, trying to quiet the anguish twisting inside her. He was her child's father…the man she loved in spite of all she knew about him.

Hurt tore through her. There was no way to win. No matter what she did, someone would lose. If she refused to follow Tanner's orders she would never see her son again. God only knew what would become of him. Foster homes…adoption. She couldn't be certain Robert would take care of him once he'd moved on to another relationship.

If she did as Tanner told her, she was effectively thrusting a knife into Michal's back.

Either way she was probably going to die.

Hot, salty tears rolled down her cheeks, but she made no sound. Her throat had closed with hurt. She didn't want to die. Michal dying was an even more devastating thought. But the most horrible part of all was never seeing her baby again. She closed her eyes and summoned the memory of his sweet baby scent and his chubby arms and legs.

What she would give to hold him just one last time.

"Let me help you."

Ami's head came up and her breath left her at the sound of Michal's voice. Instinctively she covered her nude body with the towel she'd abandoned on the basin.

"I didn't hear you come in," she said, embarrassment flushing her skin.

"You were deep in thought," he agreed. He touched her and slowly tugged the towel away. She shivered. He'd seen her nude before...but she felt somehow vulnerable this time. The pained look on his face as he surveyed her various bruises made her heart contract.

"Is the pain tolerable?" he asked softly as he picked up the wrap for her ribs.

She nodded, too uncertain of her voice to speak.

"I'll take care of this." He reached around her, his body brushing hers, and wound the bandage around her torso.

Her respiration grew rapid as his long, strong fingers moved over her skin. She watched him in the mirror, her heart fluttering wildly in her chest. He was so beautiful. She knew with every fiber of her being that Nicholas would look so very much like him.

For one long moment she could hardly restrain the urge to tell him about his son. To share that blessed gift with the man who had somehow broken down her every defense with the same ease and boldness that he had saved her life.

She bit back the words. To tell him would be to sentence her son to this survival-of-the-fittest, kill-or-be-killed existence. She couldn't...wouldn't do that.

The tips of his fingers grazed the underside of her

breasts and she gasped. He froze, his gaze colliding with hers.

"Did I cause you pain?"

She shook her head. "I just…" She moistened her lips. Why lie? "You touched me and…" She had to look away from that penetrating gaze. "You made me want you."

He tucked in the end of the bandage, the corset-like wrap pushing her breasts high, the pebbled peaks confirming her admission. Slowly, stealing her breath once more, he trailed one finger over the swell of her breasts, first one and then the other and the dip in between. "I want you, also," he murmured, then leaned down and pressed a kiss in the tender valley he'd teased. "But I won't risk causing you discomfort. I can wait until you're well again."

Challenge stirred. She inclined her head and studied him. "And what about you? Don't we need to wait until you're healed, as well?"

A wicked grin tugged the corners of his lips upward. "Nothing short of death could stop me from making love to you." His gaze roamed the length of her nude—save for the bandage—body and he growled his approval. "However, you must rest now. I will have to be satisfied with merely lying beside you." He picked up the gown she'd tossed carelessly across the bench and lowered it onto her as she lifted her arms. The silk slid down her arms, over her breasts and hips, to swirl around her thighs. He admired the fit, not bothering to hide his approval or his need. When he would have turned away, she stopped him with a tentative hand on his muscular arm.

"Michal."

He looked back at her, the desire in his eyes very nearly undoing her all over again. "Yes."

"Thank you for saving my life."

He looked at her so intently, as if he were trying to

see inside her, to read her thoughts. A twinge of fear pricked her.

"Saving your life was like saving my own."

With those words he turned and walked away.

Sealing her fate by claiming one single thing: her heart.

CHAPTER THIRTEEN

MICHAL LISTENED to the church bells clang, inviting those within hearing distance to come and observe their Sunday-morning Christian ritual. He wondered if they knew that an infamous terrorist loitered nearby...close enough to touch any one of them.

Close enough to rain down more deplorable acts of inhumanity than their small minds could possibly fathom. The mere mention of his name elicited utter fear in the strongest of men. He was the Executioner. He loved only one thing—money. And his only loyalty was to himself.

That was the sacrifice he had made for his country. But the events in Tripoli had made one thing very clear. He would not sacrifice Ami, not in word or deed.

This morning he would initiate the required action, discover the price of her freedom.

Ron Doamiass mingled among the crowd gathered outside the sixteenth-century chapel, speaking to first one and then another as if he knew them personally, which, of course, he did not. A master of public relations, he moved farther and farther from the fringes of the milling throng smiling and offering pleasant greetings like an eager politician.

Admiring the beauty of the gardens, he eventually moved toward the reflective pond and Michal's position amid the nearby thicket of trees.

"You risk a great deal calling me here again so soon," Ron admonished sagely.

"You are here," Michal returned just as sagely. "I am obviously worth the risk to your safety as well as my own."

Ron's usual amiable expression hardened slightly. "I am here because you are a friend, not because I am your superior."

Touché, Michal mused. "Well, as my friend I sincerely hope you can answer my questions."

"First you will answer mine," he countered. "What happened in Tripoli?"

"The mission was a success." Michal leveled an unyielding gaze on his. "What else do you need to know?"

Ron did not appear pleased with his attitude. That was good, because Michal was far from pleased himself.

"Your work was sloppy this time and you were injured." Ron looked pointedly at Michal's right shoulder, though the bandage was not visible beneath his shirt.

Michal expected no less. Ron had eyes and ears everywhere. That was part of his job. Part of the way he kept Michal alive when others plotted against him.

Silence thickened between them for a time. Impatient for the truth, Michal demanded, "I will know the whole story about Amira. I believe there are things you have kept from me. I will know what they are and the reason."

Ron averted his gaze, something he rarely did. His straightforward manner had always been one of the traits Michal respected most about him. "You ask a great deal." Ron looked over his shoulder at Michal. "There are some things that even I don't have clearance for."

Michal cocked one eyebrow. "I have faith in you. You will overcome that mere technicality." He shook his head then, mulling over the inconsistencies he could no longer deny. "Something is not as it should be. This is not the same woman I knew two years ago. There is…" He searched his mind for the right words, but could not assimilate the proper definition for his instinct. "Something is very wrong." He pounded his fist against his gut. "I feel it too deeply."

"She suffers from amnesia, no?"

Michal huffed a breath of impatience. "It is more than that." He considered what Carlos had told him. "Some of my men have picked up on CIA activity in this very city." Michal looked directly at Ron. "Do you know anything about that?"

The CIA usually kept the Mossad abreast of any activities near one of their ongoing missions. But then again, Michal's cover was so deep he doubted anyone in the CIA even knew about it—anyone other than the director himself.

Concern pleated Ron's brow as he considered this turn of events. "I will look into this matter." His gaze settled on Michal once more. "As for the woman, I'm sure the depth of her amnesia is the reason she appears so different from before."

Michal shook his head thoughtfully. "It is much more than that. She is softer somehow…nothing like before."

Ron looked away again, but not before Michal saw the flash of guilt in his eyes.

"You know something," Michal growled under his breath. "I will not allow harm to come to her, so don't bother issuing such an order. Whatever it is you are keeping from me, I must know it. *Now.*"

Ron sighed, his shoulders slumped, another uncharacteristic reaction. "My orders were not to pass along this information for fear that it would prevent you from remaining focused on your assignment."

"What information?" he demanded, sick to death of someone else making decisions about his life.

"While she was away," Ron confessed reluctantly, "she bore a child."

Michal blinked. "A child?"

Ron nodded. "A boy. His name is Nicholas. He is sixteen months old."

Michal didn't have to consider the dates involved, he instinctively knew the child was his. The nudge in his gut evolved into a tautness in his chest. "She didn't tell me." Lines formed along his brow, bearing out his confusion. "Does she remember having the child? Surely she has not forgotten that she gave birth." The whole idea shook him. Amira was a mother.

He was a father.

"She has spent the past two years living with a man— a psychiatrist who treated her briefly for the amnesia. He has provided a home for both Amira and the child. He cares for the child now."

Something savage broke loose inside Michal. He wanted to tear this man apart with his bare hands. He wanted to shake the truth from her...make her admit to her treachery.

"She had no memory of you," Ron reminded him, obviously reading his mind. "She was discovered wandering in a park with no money and no memory at all. This man took her in, cared for her and the child that was born a few months later." When Michal would have roared against the logic of his words, Ron added, "He did so despite the numerous times she turned down his proposals of marriage."

Was that supposed to make him feel better? She lived with the man—slept in his bed—but refused to marry him?

"I can't tell you more for that is all I know," Ron said wearily, his concerned gaze searching Michal's face. "But if there is more, I will see what I can uncover. The CIA activity is likely unrelated, but I will verify that, as well.''

Michal had a feeling that he'd only agreed to dig deeper into the situation because of the profound way this meager news had affected him.

He had a son.

A son he had never seen.

''Before you go back to her with anger in your heart,'' Ron suggested quietly, ''consider how helpless she was. She had nowhere to go, no one to turn to. She did the only thing she could to survive…to protect her child.''

''My child,'' Michal argued, an unfamiliar mixture of emotions building inside him. ''My *son*.''

''As true as that is,'' Ron reminded him gravely, ''what does she do now to protect herself and her child? Has her situation truly changed?''

His friend was right, Michal realized.

Survival would be of great importance to her…she surely wanted to return to her child.

Michal's child.

AMI WAS STILL damn sore this morning. She took her time dressing, dreading another day of endless worry. How could she betray Michal? Cost him his life? As he'd promised, he'd held her last night, held her close, made her feel safe in spite of all that had happened.

But how would she ever get back to her son?

She twisted her hair up and pinned it out of her way. She couldn't deal with it this morning. She'd stopped counting the days since she'd held her child. Tried with all the willpower she possessed to block his sweet face from her mind.

It hurt too much.

She closed her eyes and forced back the emotions. Courage was what she needed right now.

Courage and a miracle straight from God.

A little coffee would help her immediate discomfort, she decided with overwhelming resignation.

She peeked into the corridor. Usually when Michal was out of the house, which was rare, she stayed in her room. She'd had more than enough excitement for a dozen lifetimes. If she stayed in her room she was unlikely to see or to hear anything she shouldn't from any of his men. Especially Carlos.

The great room was empty, which meant Carlos and the men must be outside or in the cellar. She shivered as she considered what they might be down there doing.

If someone had told her one month ago that she would be experiencing all that she had in the past two weeks she would have laughed at them, insisted they were crazy. That she may have lived this sort of life in the past she couldn't remember was ludicrous. She was not like these people.

Guilt stabbed her for lumping Michal in with the rest of them. Somehow, despite all that she had witnessed in his presence, he was not like the rest of his men. She knew it deep in her heart. The heart he now owned.

She groaned and dragged open the refrigerator door. She had to eat. Though she had no appetite. She had to stay healthy…had to be ready for anything. Nicholas needed her; she had to find her way back home. There had to be a way.

She poured a glass of milk and grabbed a banana from the bowl on the table. Barefoot, she padded into the great room to enjoy the view. It was about the only pleasure she had these days. When the memories of making love with Michal abruptly filtered through her mind, she shivered.

Forcing her attention back to nourishment, she consumed the milk and the banana and decided she should have gotten two. When she would have headed back to the kitchen for another piece of fruit, the sight of a car winding up the long drive jerked her back to the window. It wasn't the military-style Hummer that Michal used, or any of the other vehicles she had seen on the estate.

Setting her glass and the empty banana peel on a nearby table, she eased back a step out of sight of whoever was approaching. When the car stopped, the driver's side door opened and a woman wearing an elegant hat—the kind one wore to church on mornings like this—emerged.

Ami frowned, studying her movements as she made her way to the front door. A soft-sided briefcase in hand, she wore a fashionable broomstick skirt in a deep gray and a flattering double-breasted matching jacket. A frilly white collar flounced around the neckline, but the down-turned brim of the tasteful hat partially shielded her face from view. Ami wondered vaguely why Carlos or one of the others hadn't interceded by now. There were always guards outside monitoring the grounds. Still, the well-dressed lady forged fearlessly ahead, climbing the steps as if she were on a mission of supreme importance.

Two things struck Ami simultaneously. Judging by the briefcase and the woman's manner of dress, she decided she must be on some sort of religious mission, a door-to-door evangelist maybe. At the same time she wondered if she ran out the door and dragged the woman back into her car, could they make it away from the house before being shot?

The woman's knock on the door snapped Ami from her fleeting fantasy.

She stood stock-still as the knock came again. No one stormed up the cellar stairs. No one came running into the room from some other part of the house. Nothing.

Anticipation soared through her. This could be her chance. The reminder of what had happened during her last escape attempt had dread, as well as the milk she'd drunk, curdling in her stomach despite the seed of hope sown by the anticipation. She couldn't just stand there. Ami moistened her lips and summoned her courage. She walked straight over to the door, held her breath and pulled it open. No alarm sounded. She frowned, remembering the security system.

Before she could ponder that oddity further, recognition slammed into her.

Fran Woodard stood on the other side of the threshold, a pleasant smile stretched across her Katharine Hepburn good looks. "Good morning, ma'am," she said in a strong Southern drawl that startled Ami almost as much as her unexpected appearance. The woman she'd met before had spoken alternately with an authentic French accent and a vague Midwestern twang.

"What're you doing here?" Ami demanded, glancing quickly around her. Her heart thundered into overdrive, pushing a new blast of adrenaline through her veins and an unholy fear up her spine. Maybe the alarm was silent…most systems had that option, didn't they? If Carlos or one of the others discovered this woman here—

Fran made a magnanimous gesture with one hand. "Darling, I'm a member of the Texas Christian Ambassador Program and I'm here to save your soul." She kept that brilliant smile pinned in place as she added under her breath, "Invite me in."

Ami jerked at the fiercely muttered order. She nodded and quickly stepped back. "Please," she said, a little too loudly, a little too stiffly, "won't you come in?"

"Don't overdo it, honey," Fran chided softly.

Ami nodded again, the movement spasmodic. "I'm not

sure your program is for me.'' Her voice quivered just the slightest bit, but she did manage to keep her own smile plastered in place.

''Well, dear, there's a place for everyone at T.C.A.P.'' She reached in her case and withdrew a brochure. ''We believe that all people are God's children.'' She eased closer to Ami and opened the brochure as if to show off its colorful pages. ''Arad has a mission in two days,'' Fran whispered, nodding and pointing to the pages as if that were the subject of their hushed conversation. ''Tanner has all the specifics already. All you have to do is lay low and then insist on going with Arad. Keep him distracted. Our people will take care of the rest.''

Ami's heart beat violently. The blood roared deafeningly in her ears. This was it…her last chance.

''I can't do this,'' she admitted in a rush, despite her fear of what the admission would cost her. She couldn't. She simply couldn't do what they wanted. Tears filled her eyes and she prayed this woman would somehow understand. ''You have to help me,'' she pleaded, desperation mounting. ''I need to get back to my son.''

Fran's smile sagged just a fraction and the subtlest shift in her eyes told Ami that she sympathized at least to some degree. ''They're going to kill him,'' she whispered gravely, confirming what Ami already knew. ''There's nothing any of us can do to stop that. His number's up. They need him out of the way for whatever is next on the agenda.''

Ami clamped down on her bottom lip to hold back the cry of anguish that burgeoned in her throat. There had to be a way to save him. She grabbed onto her courage with both hands. ''I won't help them do it. I can't.''

The older woman's eyes searched hers for two long beats. ''Well,'' she finally said beneath her breath, ''I won't tell anyone if you don't. Do what you have to.'' She folded her brochure and manufactured that ten-thousand-watt smile once more. ''I'm so sorry to hear that, sugar,'' she said with an exaggerated sigh. ''We all turn to God sooner or later.'' She moved toward the door. ''Thanks so much for your kind hospitality.''

Ami followed her onto the portico, uncertain what to do next. Would she tell Tanner that Ami had refused to co-operate? What about her son? ''Will you be back?'' she asked, her voice shaking now. ''What will they do?''

''I'm afraid I won't be back this way, dear,'' she said with exaggerated regret in that *Gone With the Wind* voice that would have made Scarlett herself proud.

Ami shook her head, unbearable desperation sucking at her ability to stay calm. ''What about my baby? I don't know what to do? Michal can't be what they say he is.''

''Your child is safe,'' Fran said quickly, glancing covertly from side to side. ''As for the other.'' She reached into her briefcase and pulled out a black, leather-bound copy of the Bible. ''Study it, darling.'' She thrust the book at Ami, smiling widely again. ''There's nothing better for the soul.'' Her gaze latched onto Ami's. ''Read Revelation 19:11. The truth is there…seek and ye shall find.''

Ami stood rooted to the spot, too stunned to call out after her as she hurried away, too afraid that Carlos would be standing right behind her to move. She clutched the Bible close to her heart and prayed that Fran Woodard would stand by her word and keep her secret.

Ami couldn't betray Michal.

''What the hell are you doing?''

Carlos jerked her back across the threshold, peering out, instantly noting the car leaving a trail of dust as it sped down the long, curving slope.

A new kind of fear roared through Ami's veins. She

stared up at the evil man manacling her arm and saw the sheer hatred in his eyes.

"A missionary," she stuttered. "She...left me...this." She held out the Bible, her fingers suddenly ice-cold.

The rest of the men filed out of the kitchen and into the entry hall where she and Carlos stood.

Ami looked from him to those passing through on their way to the great room and realization hit her like a physical blow. Carlos and the others—all of the others—had been in the cellar. With Michal gone there was only one reason why he would rally the men into a secret meeting.

"Planning a little coup?" she said, her tone openly accusing as fury replaced the fear she had felt only seconds before.

"Shut up, whore!" He shook her hard, sending a shard of pain through her middle, then kicked the front door closed, no doubt for deafening sound effects. "I have only one plan."

Uneasiness slid through her again.

He yanked her closer and sneered down at her. "Getting the truth out of you." He glared at the others. "Make sure the security system is activated this time, you fools."

Leaving the rest of the men standing there in stunned silence, Carlos dragged her into the kitchen and shoved her against the table, sending a chair toppling over. Trying to catch herself, the Bible slipped from her hand and flew across the floor. She prayed Michal would return. Carlos had been looking for an excuse to hurt her...he would use the woman's visit as the reason.

Ami braced herself against the table, buying time as she desperately searched for a weapon within reach. She suddenly wished there had been a weapon tucked in the Bible that Fran had given her. Her jaw hardened and a zing of something like anticipation went through her, awakening a primal survival instinct. She couldn't just let him kill her, she had to stop him. Her gaze landed on the only thing within reach.

Before she could grab the coffee mug abandoned on the other side of the table, he jerked her around to face him. "Who are you working for?" he demanded, his fingers biting into the flesh of her arms.

She cried out before she could stop herself. Her pain only fueled his bloodlust. "I don't know what you're talking about." The anger she'd enjoyed froze into absolute fear.

"You are working for someone." He shook her harder. "I know it."

She couldn't stop him. He was going to kill her. His intentions were clear in those evil eyes. He'd swear she'd tried to escape again. Tried to run away with the missionary. The weight of defeat had her sagging in his grasp.

She was dead.

"Carlos."

He whipped around at the sound of the male voice, his ironclad grip still firmly shackled around her arms.

Thomas stood in the doorway looking sorely uncomfortable and uncertain of his next step. "What are you doing? Michal will be—"

"Get out!"

Thomas retreated half a step at the force of the words.

In one lightning-fast move, Carlos pulled his gun. "Get out or join her."

Thomas backed fully away from the door. "It is your mistake to make," he muttered as he moved from the kitchen as quickly as possible without turning his back on the madman waving the gun.

Carlos's fingers were suddenly around her throat. "Now, tell me who you are working for." He pressed the tip of the gun barrel to her temple and cocked it. The definitive click echoed through the room so loudly she flinched.

"I don't know what you mean," she choked, his grip nearly cutting off the air to her lungs.

And then he did, that steel grip tightening until she couldn't breathe at all. She struggled against him, the renewed instinct to survive stronger than the defeat dragging at her. She clawed at his face relentlessly despite the weapon pressed against her temple. If she was going to die, she would damn well make him remember the deed. Determination solidified inside her…she'd leave evidence of the struggle so Michal would know that Carlos had had his hands on her when he'd killed her.

Carlos laughed at her, a cruel, sinister sound, and loosened his grip just enough for her to gulp in a lungful of precious air. She was certain it had nothing to do with sympathy and everything to do with prolonging the torture. He flattened her against the tabletop, his lower body pressing into hers. Her eyes widened in a new kind of terror when she felt the telltale bulge of arousal.

Oh, no.

Please, God, not that.

He laid the gun next to her head on the table and ripped open her blouse with his free hand. She whimpered and tried to push him away, to fight him off.

"Perhaps you require this kind of persuading," he suggested hatefully, grinding his pelvis against hers.

She tried to scream, but his fingers cut off the air to her lungs once more.

A calloused palm closed around her breast. She twisted away from his touch, nausea spewing into her throat. Vicious laughter emanated from his chest, adding depraved music to his sickening touch.

He reached for the waistband of her pants. ''Show me, bitch, what power you hold over the great Michal Arad.''

An explosion rent the air. Something splattered over the table beyond her, spewing tiny droplets over her.

A look of startled amazement claimed Carlos's face for a split second before he collapsed heavily atop her.

Gasping for air, Ami shoved him off and scrambled away from the table.

She slipped and fell to her hands and knees, her gaze glued to what remained of the back of Carlos's head.

Her throat burned...her skull throbbed...her sides ached. Tears scalded her eyes and cheeks. She scrubbed the tears and the blood from her face.

She had to think. She had to get away. Had to run...the other men—

The sound of footsteps approaching jerked her gaze upward.

Michal.

She wept, the anguish pouring out of her in soul-shaking sobs.

He offered his hand, gently helping her to her feet.

She went into his arms, unable to stop the tears. Tears for the child she would never see again...tears for the man whose life she could not save...

Nothing she could do...

Tanner had been right...there was no way back.

CHAPTER FOURTEEN

MICHAL STARED down at her. He wanted to rant at her. To demand answers. But his heart would not allow him to press her under the circumstances. He glared at Carlos's motionless body. The traitor.

But then, what did he expect in this world of murder for hire?

Squashing all emotion so that he could do what must be done, he offered his hand. Shaking, she took it, and he assisted her to her feet. "Go to your room."

She wiped at the tears dampening her face with the backs of her hands and nodded mutely before fleeing the scene of betrayal and death.

Michal leaned down and picked up the Bible lying sprawled on the floor. Had one of his men brought it here? Frowning, he skimmed through its pages before setting it aside on the table. He wanted answers. Carlos's treachery he had suspected for weeks now, was not surprised to see it reach fruition. The others, however, were a definite surprise.

Leaving the dead traitor where he lay, Michal stalked into the great room expecting to be met with drawn weapons and suspicions.

"I tried to stop him," Thomas said quietly. "But he was intent on interrogating her."

"Interrogating her?" Michal demanded, his tone as deadly as the weapon he still held in his right hand, the barrel still warm from his recent kill. "You call his actions 'interrogation'?"

Thomas shrugged but remained silent.

Michal scanned their faces, making direct eye contact with each one of them in turn. "Is there anyone else who would wish to *interrogate* me?" He pressed them with a long, hard look, ensuring they understood the depth of his fury. "For if you question Amira, you question me."

Not a single word was uttered in defiance of his statement; nor was any move made to overtake him.

"A good man," Michal said then, "is dead because he chose to betray me. If any of you—" he surveyed face after face once more "—prefers to take your loyalties elsewhere, then do so. I will not tolerate disloyalty."

"We are with you," the Spaniard said. "Carlos tried to convince us that you had grown weak, but we did not believe him."

"I only have one question," another said as he settled onto one of the sofas. "How are we going to split Carlos's cut of the Libyan mission?"

The room burst into laughter, shattering the formidable tension in a heartbeat. Whatever Carlos had hoped to achieve had vanished just as quickly as he had.

"I can assure you," Michal said with a smile, his relief complete now, "all will be satisfied."

More laughter punctuated the promise.

"Thomas." Michal turned his attention to his most trusted man. The only one in the group who had even attempted to stand up to Carlos. For that, Michal was grateful. "Take two men with you into the city and see if you can find the dark-haired man Carlos spoke of. If he is truly with the CIA I want to know about his business here." He shifted his attention to the Spaniard now. "Take care of Carlos. Already the stench of his deceit pollutes the air.''

With a single inclination of his head, two more of his men joined the Spaniard in his mission.

Satisfied that all was as it should be, Michal left the men to their tasks.

The stunning revelation he had learned from Ron shook him once more. Why had she not told him about the child? How could she lie with him and keep that life-altering secret to herself? He considered that she had lived with the American, the psychiatrist, for two years without full commitment. Anger burned low in his belly at the thought of her with another man.

Was that what she was doing here? Holding back on him? The possibility that the CIA had had someone close by since he brought her here twisted in his gut. Could he have allowed her to fool him yet again? Was everything— the two long years of separation, the amnesia, the vulner- ability—all an elaborate set up to finish what she'd started?

Maybe he was wrong about her. She might not be vul- nerable at all. The woman who had fooled him once before might simply be a talented actress.

For that matter, perhaps Carlos had been right on that score.

Perhaps Michal was under a spell.

AMI STRIPPED OFF her torn blouse and stuffed it into the trash basket. She stared at her reflection in the bathroom mirror and winced at the red welts left by her attacker's strong fingers. She shuddered when she thought of Carlos lying dead on the floor in the kitchen.

How many people had died here?

She trembled and chafed her arms against the chill of fear. Would she be next? She hadn't missed the fury in

Michal's eyes. Did he somehow see her as responsible for Carlos's death? She had caused Raoul's. She stilled, searching her emotions, attempting to separate fact from presumption. Was her presence what had made Carlos start undermining Michal's authority?

Closing her eyes, she forced away the thoughts. This was crazy. All of it!

Why hadn't she grabbed Fran Woodard by the arm and rushed to her car the moment the woman arrived?

There had been time. Of course she hadn't known that then, but there definitely had been. No one had been watching her. They had been too busy being brainwashed by Carlos. Dammit. She could have escaped…could have been rushing toward the American embassy this very moment. That is, of course, if Fran had gone along with the idea. Though Ami had seen definite sympathy in her eyes, the woman was CIA…she would probably have told her the same thing Tanner had: she had no choice but to stay and finish this.

She flattened her palms on the rim of the basin and sighed in self-disgust. She wasn't cut out for this kind of business. She didn't know how to seize an opportunity and make the best of it. At least, not these kinds of opportunities.

Pushing away her worries and uncertainties for the time being, she trudged to the armoire and dragged out a new blouse. Any moment now Michal would come into the room demanding answers. For whatever reason, he was angry with her. She had to deal with him first, then she could mull over the worry that Fran would most likely tell Tanner she had no intention of helping them kill Michal.

She pressed her forehead against the cool, wooden surface of the armoire and battled the emotions that threatened to well inside her all over again. She couldn't think about her baby right now. She absolutely would not admit defeat. She would find a way to get back to him. But she would have to do it on her own.

An urge to tell Michal about his son, to share that wonder with him, clutched dangerously at her heart. But she couldn't do that. To tell Michal about Nicholas would be to sentence her son to this life.

That, above all else, was the one thing she was infinitely certain she could not do.

When the door to the bedroom opened, she stood in the middle of the room waiting for whatever was to come.

Judging by the intensity in Michal's eyes, he was still plenty angry.

"Did he hurt you?"

She shook her head. He had, actually, but not the kind of hurt she felt certain to which Michal referred. She massaged her throat, subconsciously contradicting her response.

He paused only inches away and tugged her hand from her throat. "You will have more bruises," he commented, surveying the red welts on her flesh.

She nodded. "Thank you for stopping him." It sounded lame in afterthought, but she was immensely grateful for what he'd done. Her fate had already been decided by Carlos.

Michal's gaze zoomed in on hers like twin piercing laser beams. "Carlos believed you were hiding something." He inclined his head and studied her eyes, her face, more closely. "Are you hiding anything from me?"

She tamped down the automatic need to stiffen, to avert her eyes. He was watching for those very warning signals. "No." The word didn't come out quite as firmly as she would have liked, but she'd gotten it past the constriction in her throat. That was something. Her heart knocked brutally against her rib cage. He knew something. She was sure of it.

There was no way to know which of her secrets he'd uncovered. If she gave away the wrong one...

"Why do you still question me, Michal?" she demanded, hoping to shift the context of the discussion. She lifted her chin and glared at him defiantly. "If you suspect me of some deceit, why didn't you let Carlos do what he would? Surely he would have extracted whatever truth you believe I'm hiding."

Fury flashed in those midnight-black eyes. "Answer the question. Do you or do you not have something you wish to tell me?"

Though she could not recall anything about her life before two years ago, other than the dreams of her with this man, Ami couldn't imagine that she had ever used her body to keep herself out of trouble. She had lived, until quite recently, in a very safe environment with a man who believed women to be equal to men in every way. She had a respected career as a nurse and she was the loving mother to a toddler. An ache pulsed through her when Nicholas's face filtered through her mind.

The very idea of whoring herself to achieve some cause...of setting up a man for betrayal...of betraying her own father, was utterly alien to her. It simply couldn't be possible. The events she had witnessed the past two weeks were like scenes in some action-adventure movie or high-tech video game. None of it felt real.

But it was.

She looked deeply into Michal's eyes. And she had to do whatever it took to stay in the game.

No, she didn't want to help the CIA or anyone else harm Michal.

No, she couldn't bear the thought of being responsible, directly or indirectly, for anyone else's life.

But she was damn sure going to take responsibility for her own survival.

In this game, she was on her own. There was no way forward, that she could see, and no way back.

There was only now.

And right now she needed Michal Arad to need her. She wanted him to trust her whether she deserved it or not. Most of all, she longed to live at least two more days...time enough to figure out how to accomplish the two most important missions of her life.

She must find a way to get back to her child if only for a moment. To hold him just one more time before she died.

But first, she had to figure out how to save Michal's life without alerting the CIA to her new stand.

And all of that hinged on one person. Fran Woodard. If Fran warned Tanner, Ami was doomed.

For now, though, she had a more pressing matter to which to attend.

Earning Michal's trust again now that he'd had to kill his right-hand man for her.

"I have nothing to hide from you," she told him in the most sensual tone she could muster with the image of death still indelibly seared in her brain.

Something like regret flickered in those sinfully dark pools focused solely upon her. Fear that she'd somehow said the wrong thing made her heart stutter. But she couldn't stop now.

"You pulled me back into a world of which I have no memory." Her gaze locked fully with his, despite the worry that he would read the confusion and fear churning inside her. "You tell me all the despicable things I did before and how a good portion of the world, including you,

have reason to want me dead. But you allow me to live.''
She tried without success to shake off the surreal quality
that very nearly overwhelmed her. It all felt so impossible...but it was real.

He was real.

And he held the power over her very existence.

''And still you question me?'' She turned her back on
him, praying her ruse would work to divert his focus.
''What makes you any better than Carlos?'' she added for
good measure as she folded her arms over her breasts.

She heard the raggedness of his breath as he exhaled.
Afraid to even drag in a breath of her own, she held absolutely still and waited for his reaction.

''I trust that you will tell me anything you believe I
should know,'' he said finally, his tone gentler now but
laced with a definite defeat that she would never have associated with the dangerous man known as Michal Arad.

Facing him once more, she struggled to read his eyes,
but they quickly shuttered, refusing her access to his true
feelings. Her chest felt suddenly heavy with sadness then.
This was his world...a world of kill or be killed...of dis-
trust and constantly looking over one's shoulder. As much
fear as he could inspire in others, he was just a man, sen-
tenced to a prison of living for the day with no promise
of tomorrow. For that, she wept inside, her heart squeez-
ing, bleeding for him. She suddenly wanted to know all
she had forgotten about this man. Where had he come
from? What had happened in his life to shape him into the
ruthless killer he was today? She resisted the urge to shake
her head. Not totally ruthless, she argued with herself.
There was a human compassion in Michal Arad that none
of the others with whom he associated possessed.

That was the part that attracted her to him.

The part that promised hope.

"There is one thing I'd like you to know," she said as she reached for the buttons of his shirt.

He stilled her hands by covering them with his own. Her gaze bumped into his and she saw resistance there. He didn't want to be seduced. Here was a man accustomed to doing the seducing. Well, this time it was going to be different.

"And what is that?" he asked cautiously.

She twined her fingers with his and moved closer still. "That I need you more than I've ever needed you before." She pulled his hands down to her waist and settled them there so that she could return to the task of releasing the buttons of his shirt. It startled her to realize just how true the words she'd spoken were.

She did need him.

And, as crazy as it sounded, he needed her.

She touched the bronzed skin revealed as his shirt, free of the buttons restricting it, gaped open. Her breath caught and heat instantly shot her internal thermometer into the red.

"I killed a man for you today and I would do it again if necessary. But I do not take death lightly. Do not play games with me now, Ami," he whispered savagely, his hands tightening on her waist.

Hearing him call her Ami instead of Amira sent a thrill through her. But it was the ferocity of the fire in his eyes that undid her the most.

"Michal." She took his handsome face in her hands and was caught off guard all over again at how very much her son looked like him. "This is not a game." She pulled his mouth down to hers and whispered, "It's very, very real."

She pressed her lips to his and kissed him with all the desperation exploding inside her. The exotic taste that was purely Michal assaulted her senses, weakened her knees. He pulled her closer, sensing her need for support.

"I don't want to hurt you," he murmured between kisses.

She pulled back just far enough to rip open his shirt and bare the rest of that amazing chest to her. "What about you?" she asked, then nibbled his full lower lip. "I wouldn't want to cause you discomfort, either."

He didn't bother answering with words. Instead, proving his physical prowess in spite of his injury, he lifted her, taking most of her weight with his good arm, and carried her to the bed.

For a long while they simply stood there, next to the enormous bed still rumpled from the previous night's tossing and turning, and stared into each other's eyes. There was so much she wanted to know...to say...to believe. Words would never be enough to convey what she felt at that precise moment.

When they could no longer bear to merely look, they undressed each other slowly, the urgency taking a back seat to the more tender emotions neither of them could deny. Her blouse floated down to the floor. Shoes were kicked aside. His trousers as well as her slacks joined the tangle of attire scattered around them.

All that stood between them was the sheerest, most intimate of fabrics and soon those were gone, as well. The white bandage was stark against his dark skin, a startling reminder of how he had risked his life for hers. His broad shoulders looked powerful enough to hold up the world and she was so glad he carried the weight of hers for she was incapable of that enormous feat just now. The marvelously sculpted width narrowed into a lean, ribbed waist. The beat of her heart increased to a rapid staccato as her gaze moved over his well-endowed manhood and down those long, heavily muscled legs. Every part of him was perfectly formed.

She looked up into his eyes once more and found the same appreciation glimmering there that she felt. Her stomach tingled with the knowledge that her body pleased him, as well. She'd left off the bandage to support her ribs this morning and now she was glad for it.

Suddenly those strong arms wrapped around her and snuggled her body close to his. The nudge of his sex sent all sentimental thoughts and sensations scurrying away; there was only the undeniable need to have him buried deeply inside her.

He lowered her to the tousled bed and settled on all fours above her. Slowly, one lingering kiss at a time, he loved every welt, every bruise, every scrape on her flesh. Each flick of his tongue and tease of his lips sent shower after shower of heat and desire cascading along every square inch of her. That wicked mouth brushed the silken curls of her mound and she cried out with the intensity of it.

He parted her thighs and continued with his sensual torture. Using his tongue, his teeth and his lips, he suckled, nibbled and laved her to the very edge of orgasm. She wanted to beg him to stop, to plunge into her, but instead she urged him on, threading her fingers into this thick, dark hair, arching to meet him. One long finger slid inside her, making her feminine muscles contract wildly. She moaned her approval.

Another finger slipped inside, circled and rubbed. With two fingers deep inside her he suckled the budding part of her sex and sent her completely over the edge. She tensed as every sensory perception froze then focused entirely on that one part of her as wave after wave of sweet satiation flooded her. Her body grew limp with the heat of it.

She locked her legs around his and urged his hips toward hers. She needed him inside her now. To finish this the right way. Still, he held back; instead, taking more time to lave and suckle her breasts. Her fingers bit into his muscled arms, her hips rose to find fulfillment, but he denied her.

She was ready.

Michal peered into the blue eyes that had gone almost navy with desire. Lust glazed those wide depths, and it pleased him greatly to know he had taken her there. Her body arched like a bow once more, seeking to become one with his, but he held back, needing to see her like this a moment longer. To know, at this precise second, that she was completely his, body and soul.

The truth she had denied him only made him want her more. Common sense told him he shouldn't trust her if she refused to tell him about the child, but her desperation made him understand. He knew desperation. Fool that he might be, he was certain he knew her.

She was his once more and that was all that mattered.

If he died tonight, having her at his side would make it worth the price.

With that thought he thrust fully into her hot, welcoming body. They cried out together and raw, primal pleasure quaked through them. He trembled and so did she.

His body burned with the need to spill his seed deep inside her…to make her with child again…to share every step of that momentous occasion with her this time.

Her hips rose to meet his every thrust, her gaze locked with his and in that moment of completion, when both their bodies reached the ultimate pinnacle, he knew that whatever happened tomorrow, tonight and the woman in his arms were all that mattered.

THAT NIGHT Michal made love to her twice more. Cocooned in his arms, Ami slept deeply, her body sated from their lovemaking. He held her tightly as if he feared she might somehow slip away during the night.

She dreamed of their time together before. Their love-making. The night Nicholas was conceived…on the eve of that dangerous mission.

She moaned, pushing away the next images that surfaced, but she couldn't stop them. They tumbled in one over the other, dampening her skin with sweat…making her heart race…

HE WAS ON HIS KNEES. *His olive skin and dark eyes contrasted sharply with his graying hair and his gauzy-white robe. Her gaze jerked back to his chest. The knife had been plunged deeply into his chest; blood soaked rapidly across the front of his white robe.*

The pain in his eyes as he looked up at her shook her. "W-why?" he croaked.

She stared into those anguished eyes with no emotion except relief and then, suddenly she knew…

She stumbled back a step, her head shaking with the realization forming in her brain. Her eyes connected fully with his and she whispered, "Daddy?"

AMI BOLTED UPRIGHT in the bed, her lungs heaving against the lack of oxygen. She blinked in the darkness and the dream shattered into a thousand screaming pieces of agony.

Michal moved up beside her in the darkness, his arms going around her, comforting her.

"Are you all right?" he whispered hoarsely.

No.

Her heart thundered hard, but failed to send enough oxygen to her brain to ensure its proper function, leaving her unable to form the single syllable required to articulate that one word out loud.

She wasn't all right. She would never be all right again. She'd killed her father.

CHAPTER FIFTEEN

MICHAL WATCHED Ami sleep the next morning for a while longer before he left her. Part of him wanted to hold her again and to hear her cry out his name in that sweet, melodic voice caught in the throes of ecstasy, but she had hardly slept at all after the nightmares. He didn't have the heart to wake her now that she appeared finally to be resting peacefully. Though he'd held her and crooned to her until she dozed off once more, her bits and pieces of sleep had been riddled with more nightmares. She had sobbed, crying out frequently.

I didn't know. I didn't know.

Whatever demons had haunted her, they had been relentless. None of her mumblings had made sense. The one phrase was the only string of distinguishable words.

When he considered all that she had been through since he'd dragged her back into his world, he supposed that was completely understandable. Even if she never fully remembered her past, her time with him had given her numerous events to evoke future nightmares.

She was right in that regard, he admitted. He had pulled her back into his world. Selfishly. But, had he not, the people of his own homeland would have hunted her down and executed her for the murder of Yael Peres. She had been much safer with him than left on her own.

Still, the regret he suffered was great. The idea that his son was left without his mother for all this time ate at him like a cancer. He longed to know the child, but she had chosen to keep her secret. Hurt arced through his heart. He told himself again it was fear that kept her quiet on that score.

He hoped his emotions had not blinded him once more to the possibility of betrayal.

Michal closed his eyes and exhaled wearily. He was so very tired of this life. Every minute of every day was filled with the possibility of instant death, with the threat of betrayal from those closest to him.

But the killing was the worst. It never ended. There was always a new name added to the list. An endless roster of Who's Who among the soon to die.

It was no wonder Ami did not want him to know about their son. Look what he had to offer an heir.

Money, certainly. Money tainted with the blood of a hundred men. An infamous name synonymous with death. His son would never know that he had served his country...that Michal Arad was, in fact, a hero.

No one would ever know.

Sick to death of the self-pity session, Michal pushed to his feet and left the room quietly so as not to disturb Ami. Strong, bitter coffee was what he needed now. He and his men had to be ready for tomorrow's quest.

Another name on the list.

More money in their pockets, which kept his cover intact.

One more chink in his conscience. He feared that very soon he would have no conscience at all. That he would truly become like those he executed.

He paused, one hand on the carafe. He glanced at the place where Carlos had fallen less than twenty-four hours ago. Perhaps he was already like them.

The telephone rang, tugging him from the disturbing thought and thrusting him into yet another.

His gaze went immediately beyond the door to the place where he kept the telephone hidden. He'd tucked it away and rendered useless the one in the bedroom after Ami's arrival. Since he rarely received calls, its presence had gone undetected. Michal's orders came directly from Ron, never by telephone or any other means that could be monitored or traced.

Setting the carafe aside, Michal moved toward the sound, ticking off the names of the handful of people who knew the number.

This could not be good.

He opened the door to the sideboard that served as a liquor cabinet and pulled out the base, quickly picking up the receiver just prior to the fourth ring.

He muttered a frustrated French greeting, one he and Ron had agreed upon if the use of a telephone were ever to become necessary.

The men who weren't on guard duty were still in their respective rooms. The three on duty were roaming the grounds. Despite that measure of leeway, he took no risk that he would be overheard.

"Napoleon is in the house."

Michal hung up without responding, his heart kicking into high gear. There was no need to respond. The message was definitely from Ron. The code phrase precise in its meaning: Short fused orders awaited him in the usual meeting place.

This was the highest priority call. Anything but an outright emergency would have been handled in person at the usual time and meeting place.

Depending on the nature of the order, tomorrow's mission might have to be put on hold.

Before leaving the estate, Michal awakened Thomas and stationed him outside Ami's door with strict orders not to let her out of his sight.

Thomas had always deferred to Carlos's lead, partly out of fear, partly from necessity. But that was over now. Thomas was Michal's new right-hand man. He had not grown so cold as Carlos. Like Michal, Thomas killed only when necessary. That, Michal decided, would be a change for the better.

RON WAITED for Michal near the chapel, careful to stay out of sight since there was no church service this day. Meeting on Sundays had worked well so far. Risking a daylight rendezvous at any other time was dicey at the very least. Even in a city the size of Marseilles strangers behaving covertly were noticed in this time of heightened security all over the globe.

One look at his old friend's face and Michal knew that something more than simply new orders had brought him here today. Anticipation knotted in his gut.

"You have orders for me?" Michal inquired in the same way he always did.

"It's a trap."

The weight of Ron's words settled heavily onto Michal's chest. He didn't have to ask to know to whom he referred.

"There are reasons she doesn't remember her past."

"What reasons?" Michal moved closer so that he could see every nuance of his friend's expression when he spoke.

"Two and one half years ago Amira Peres was abducted from her university dormitory in the United States," Ron explained. "She was a second-year medical student whose mother had recently passed away. She had reportedly suffered from bouts of depression for quite some time. Apparently her mother was the only family she had. Her grandfather, a former ambassador to Israel, had died ten years prior, as had her grandmother."

"What about her father?" Michal wanted to know. "Where was he during this time?"

Ron scanned the area before continuing. He was more than merely concerned about being seen in the usual sense. Michal had a feeling he wasn't supposed to be passing along this information at all.

"Amira's mother and father separated when she was only five years old. She had not seen him since that time. He had, apparently, been cruel to her mother and she had chosen to avoid him at all costs."

Michal ached for Ami and all she had lost. She must have felt so alone. "Is that why she chose to have him murdered?" He could understand how that kind of loss, combined with the depression, might have driven her to act in such an extreme manner.

Ron considered his words for a moment before continuing. "This next part," he said grimly, "could get us both killed."

Michal's instincts moved to a higher state of readiness.

"The CIA and our own people had decided that Peres must be stopped. He continued to secretly support anti-American groups, undermining the sometimes tenuous but forever necessary Israeli-American relationship. He had to be stopped. But, understandably, someone else had to take the blame."

Michal had known that part. "What is new about that?"

"We couldn't do it, of course, not officially," Ron explained, looking suddenly uncomfortable.

Michal shrugged. "That is why the order came to me."

"But first, you needed someone who could get you close enough to him."

A frown worked its way across Michal's brow. No, that wasn't right. He had met Ami first...then...

"The CIA sent her to me," he guessed, the full impact slamming into him at once.

Ron nodded, his face grim. "They abducted Amira Peres and brainwashed her into thinking she was this non-existent Jamie Dalton. Then, after they'd messed up her head completely, they trained her as a field operative. When she came to you, she truly believed she was Jamie Dalton portraying Amira Peres."

So, their former relationship hadn't been real. That realization shook Michal when he'd felt certain nothing else could. It had all been lies...the betrayal had been deliberate from the beginning.

"Michal," Ron placated, "she did not know what she was doing. They set her up just as they set you up."

"And did you know?" Michal roared, every muscle primed and ready to hit someone...to do some kind of damage to relieve the raging emotions erupting inside him.

"No." Ron looked straight at him. "You can't believe I had anything to do with this."

Michal looked away, though he felt certain that his friend spoke the truth. Ron might omit as required, but he would never lie to him.

"There is more," Ron said.

His fury momentarily on hold, Michal turned back to hear the rest, though he could not see how it was possible to top what he'd already learned.

"When the hit went down, Ami was captured. A CIA agent named Jack Tanner risked his life, as well as his career, to rescue her before she could be executed for the murder of her father. He had her memory erased using some experimental technology and left her in the care of the psychiatrist who worked from time to time for the Company.''

That news quelled Michal's fury and at the same time sent jealousy coursing through his veins. ''Who is this Jack Tanner?''

''The CIA operative your man discovered hanging around recently.''

It wasn't necessary for Ron to explain what that meant. The possibility that the CIA was once again using Ami was too great to ignore. Every instinct told him that she was innocent, that she didn't know she was being used. But he couldn't be absolutely certain.

''She has asked for nothing nor has she attempted to persuade me to track down anyone.'' Michal shook his head, it didn't fit together properly. ''If what you're suggesting is the case,'' he offered, certain it couldn't be, ''who is the target?''

Ron looked directly at him. ''The target is you.''

AMI STOOD BENEATH the hot spray of water and tried to wash away the tension…tried to erase the images that, once unleashed in her head, would not go away.

Yael Peres had been her father.

She swallowed tightly and squeezed her eyes shut to block the picture of him staring up at her…asking why?

It couldn't be right. There had to be a mistake. How could he be her father and she not know it until after she'd had him killed?

She leaned her forehead against the cool tile and allowed the hot water to sluice over her back. She tried sorting the myriad emotions whirling inside her, but gave up when she couldn't determine where regret ended and bitterness began. She didn't understand the feelings. Couldn't remember why she would experience them. Had she hated her father that much? Did it have anything to do with her mother? A mother she couldn't remember any more than she could her father.

Forcing the troubling thoughts away, Ami summoned the sweet memories of the last night she'd spent with Nicholas. Their bath together. Rocking him to sleep, softly singing his favorite lullaby.

The hurt started way down deep, climbing up from her belly, twisting inside her chest until it lunged into her throat, forcing a sob from her.

Somehow, for reasons she couldn't remember, she had choreographed the murder of her father and the simultaneous betrayal of her lover, the father of her child.

Michal was a fool for trusting her.

She straightened, her eyes going wide with a new terror. All this time she'd worried about her son and the kind of life he would be exposed to were Michal to learn of his existence.

What about her?

Could she really be certain that Nicholas was any safer with her? What day—what hour—would her murky past come back to haunt her again? Who was to say that she hadn't committed crimes much worse than even this? That she had been at work, away from her son, when the last run-in with her past took place was no guarantee she would be the next time.

How would she ever walk down a street with him at her side, or get into a car and start the engine with him tucked into his car seat without worrying that some past sin of hers might catch up to them both?

Fury tightened her jaw. There was only one way she would ever know the whole truth. She had to force Jack Tanner to tell her everything.

She had to know or her son would never be safe.

After her shower Ami dried her hair and slipped on a pair of jeans and a ribbed-knit blouse. There were thin, elongated bruises on her throat, but she didn't care. She was thankful to be alive. Extremely thankful considering what she now suspected. She needed to talk to Michal. She saw no reason not to admit what she had remembered regarding Yael Peres. Maybe he could shed some light on the fragments of recall.

When she walked into the great room, she pulled up short at the sight of his men gathered around him. Michal stopped speaking and looked directly at her.

"I'm...sorry." She glanced around the room, unable to ignore the unexpectedly thick tension. "I'll talk to you later."

"Now is fine," Michal said, stopping her before she turned away. He said to his men, "We will resume this briefing after lunch."

Ami glanced out the window, only now realizing it was past noon. She'd slept much later than she'd thought. But she'd needed the rest. The nightmares had haunted her relentlessly through the night. Even after Michal had made love to her, draining her physically, satisfying her so deeply that sleep had come swiftly.

But it hadn't lasted long.

It warmed her now to think of how Michal had held her through those endless hours of tortured dreams.

She managed a shaky smile for the men that filtered past her out of the room. Without Carlos the entire atmosphere was different...for the better.

Michal approached her with slow, deliberate strides, her heart reacting in spite of her numerous troubles. How was that possible? she mused. No matter what happened, somehow he always had that effect on her.

"I asked you last night if there was anything you needed to tell me," he said, his voice cold and hard.

She blinked, certain the ice she saw in his eyes was her imagination. "I remember." As if she could forget.

Silence lengthened between them for a second that turned to ten before he spoke again. "I will only ask you this once."

The arctic blast that accompanied his words had her stumbling back a step. "I don't understand...what is it you think you need to ask?"

The same old fears plagued her all over again. Had he somehow discovered Nicholas? Had someone told him about the woman who'd visited yesterday?

"Has anyone from the CIA contacted you since I brought you here?"

Bingo. She stiffened before she could stop herself. "Who?" Her voice sounded strained to her own ears and she couldn't stop the trembling that traveled through her body like the rumble of a quake beneath the earth's surface.

He moved closer still and repeated through clenched teeth, "The CIA. You worked for them once before, are you working for them again?"

She blinked twice...three times. "I...I don't understand. Why would you think—"

"It is not what I think." He took her by the arms and shook her hard, forcing her gaze to meet his. "It is simply a question. Has *anyone* from the CIA contacted you in any manner?"

Her head was moving side to side before she even realized her mind had formed some sort of response. Lying was her only protection in this case...wasn't it? Could she tell him the truth? Right here? Right now? Would it matter?

"Since you are having difficulty with your memory," he said with the same kind of bitterness he'd worn like a shield when they'd first met just over two weeks ago, "you will let me know if your answer changes."

He sidestepped and walked past her, leaving her standing there ready to crumple with the anguish bursting inside her.

He knew. And she sincerely doubted he would ever trust her again. That nothing she could do would buy his confidence.

Now, even if she tried, she would never convince him that she wanted to help…that she couldn't bear the thought of losing him.

She was the enemy…again.

AMI LAY IN BED alone that night.

Michal had avoided her all afternoon and evening. And then tonight he had opted not to sleep with her. She assumed he had taken another of the rooms or maybe the couch.

She eased over onto her side and struggled with the tangle of emotions pulling her first one way and then another. One moment she was certain she should have told him the truth, the next she was just as convinced otherwise.

Two days, Fran had said.

That meant tomorrow. That's why Michal had been meeting with his men. Some sort of new mission was happening tomorrow and that's when the CIA planned to strike.

She turned on the bedside lamp, threw the covers back and climbed out of bed. How could she lie there and sleep knowing what might be in store for him come morning?

But what could she do? How could she stop it? She

couldn't. Fran had said his number was up. That it was going down.

Revelation 19:11.

It wasn't until that moment that Ami remembered the Bible verse. She hurried over to the table near the bed and opened the top drawer. The black leather-bound Bible that Fran had given her was there where Ami had put it when she'd noticed it in the kitchen after lunch. After Michal's complete about-face where she was concerned. She shivered at the remembered iciness he'd emanated. Even his posture had been cold and unyielding, brutally so.

She quickly flipped through the pages until she located Revelation, the final book of verses. She slid her finger down the page until she came to Verse 11 of Chapter 19.

And I saw heaven opened, and behold a white horse;
and he that sat upon him was called "Faithful and True"
and in righteousness he doth judge and make war.

Ami shivered as she read the words once more. She considered each part alone, then the verse as a whole. What did it mean? Fran Woodard was too smart to drop a clue that meant nothing at all. There had to be some connection to the mission and/or to Michal.

But what?

She read the verse again.

Okay, the white horse. That generally denoted goodness. The rider was called "Faithful and True," that definitely was good. In righteousness he sat, judged and made war. That was the part that she didn't fully understand.

Was Fran somehow trying to make her see that what the CIA had in store for Michal was necessary? Did she mean that Jack Tanner judged rightly? Or the CIA in general.

Did it even have anything to do with the CIA?

Ami hugged the Bible to her chest and did the only thing she knew to do.

She prayed.

CHAPTER SIXTEEN

DAWN HAD SCARCELY climbed the treetops when Ami was roused from her bed and told to be ready in fifteen minutes. She pushed off the covers and sat up, struggling to think past the fog in her brain.

Another sleepless night had rendered her sluggish and barely able to form a coherent thought, much less deal with what the day would bring.

Fear shuddered through her.

She had prayed last night until she'd exhausted herself.

Still there was no divine epiphany.

No strike of inspiration.

Just a hollow sense of defeat.

By the time she was ready to go, Michal and his men were already climbing into the Hummer. Only three men accompanied them this morning, Thomas, the Spaniard and Kolin.

Ami tried not to read too much into the fact that the usual number wasn't on board for this mission.

Michal had done this numerous times before, she reminded herself. He knew what he was doing.

Besides, what good would it do her to suggest otherwise? The few words he had conveyed to her were cold and unfeeling, leaving her to struggle with the hurt as well as the fear for what was about to happen.

After what felt like an eternity on the road, they stopped in a small village and picked up different transportation.

This time they loaded into separate vehicles, both Jeeps and more than a little rugged-looking.

To her surprise, Michal had insisted that she ride with him. The others rode together in the second Jeep. The journey took them through the low-lying yet steep hills above the rich vineyards of wine country. To the west, across fertile plains, the Rhone flowed. The beauty of their surroundings did little to slow the pound of anticipation inside her. She tried to turn it off. To focus on anything else, but it kept breaking through the surface. Emerging with renewed intensity each time.

"Michal," she began, desperately seeking a way to warn him that he would trust.

"This man—" he reached into a folder between their seats and withdrew a photograph and handed it to her "—will die today," he told her frankly.

Startled, she stared at the picture of the man. He was thirty to thirty-five, she guessed. Tall, thin with angular features. He looked ruthless.

"He sells arms and various other items from our friends in the former Soviet Union." He shrugged nonchalantly. "He has made himself quite a reputation in the past six months. But recently he auctioned a small stock of weapons-grade plutonium, which garnered some ill-will toward him from those who deal in that particular merchandise on a regular basis."

Ami stared at him, wondering why he was telling her all this and at the same time relieved that he was even speaking to her. She couldn't say how much time she had left, but she had to try until the very last. When she opened her mouth to speak, he continued.

"The price I was offered to execute him was very high." He glanced at her. "More than ever before."

The fact that his fee was higher than usual only heightened her already monumental anxiety. Didn't he see that there was something wrong with that picture?

He maneuvered along the back road that wound through the pine and oaks soaring on the lower slopes as they climbed upward. As he spoke, he continuously surveyed his surroundings to ensure that they were not being followed. "I will be ridding the world of a serious threat and getting paid at the same time." He laughed, but the sound held no humor. "They call me a murderer and yet I wipe evil from the face of the planet. How ironic is that?" He laughed again and shook his head.

"Michal—"

"When this is over…" He cut her off again, unable to bear whatever excuses she intended to give for her affiliation with the CIA, for her lies, and for stealing his heart once more. His words drifted off as reality crashed headlong into him again. She'd refused to tell him about their son, obviously considering him unworthy. Perhaps he was.

All this time his superiors had insisted that the role he played as the Executioner was far too important to risk. They needed him to stay under just a little longer. His cover would not be jeopardized under any circumstances. And yet, the CIA was plotting his assassination and no one had warned him. He had, obviously, outlived his usefulness.

Each time he was ordered to kill, they told him that his impressive record made his performance unparalleled. No one had gotten this deep and accomplished this much.

Not once had they told him that when it was over he would be terminated for fear that their ruthless tactics would be discovered. No one could ever know that the Mossad had sanctioned Peres's murder.

Ron had risked everything to warn Michal that today was the day Michal Arad, the Executioner, was to die.

Amira Peres would take the blame, as she had for the death of her father. An old lovers' quarrel, people would say. Michal's assets in the numbered account would be seized and put to good use in fighting terrorism in his homeland. That was supposed to make him feel better. But who would ever know the real story?

"When this is over—" he repeated, getting his thoughts back on track "—you will need to keep moving until you've found a safe place to relocate. Take this." He passed a small folded paper to her that contained the banks and account numbers he used. All his assets had been transferred in such a way that, without the account numbers, no one would ever locate them. He was one step ahead, just barely.

"There is enough money there to take care of all your needs for a lifetime." *And for my son,* he didn't add. He fought back the agony of realizing he in all likelihood would never know his son. But, if he did not survive this day as so many hoped, he had to be certain she and the boy were cared for. Even if she had chosen not to tell him about his child. That wasn't the child's fault. It probably wasn't even Ami's fault. Her mind had been tampered with, there was no way to know the full extent of the damage. She might never regain all that she'd lost.

"Why are you telling me this?"

It only took one look into her eyes for him to know that his coldness toward her had hurt her deeply. His pride had kept him from making amends with her last night. Had kept him from her bed.

Now he regretted that.

But it was too late for regrets.

"I'm sending you away," he said bluntly. "This life is too dangerous for you."

His words stabbed deeply into her heart. "Why now?"

What had he learned to change his mind? To set him on this course? Somehow he had discovered that she was involved on some level with the CIA, but why didn't he just tell her what he knew? Why all the secrecy?

Realization dawned.

He knew he was going to die.

The coldness might very well have something to do with his suspicions about her, but it could also be related to what was about to come.

He was disengaging emotionally, even going so far as to prepare for her future financial well-being. She looked down at the folded piece of paper in her hand. He wanted her to be safe and cared for whatever happened to him.

The Jeep stopped and Michal climbed out before she could think of the right words to say to keep him from going. She wanted to physically restrain him, to hold him back from danger. But she knew that would be impossible.

He offered her the perfect out. Her freedom as well as the money for Nicholas and her to disappear.

But her son would never know his father.

She would never again know his tender touch.

She watched as Michal walked toward his men. Did the others know, as well? Was that why only three men had accompanied him?

She had to do something. She couldn't just sit here and let this happen. But what could she do? She glanced around at their hilltop setting. Trees provided ample camouflage from the valley below. Was Jack Tanner here watching? Would he know if she made some move to warn Michal? Would he see that she never found her son again if she didn't obey his original orders?

Dear God, what did she do?

After a few minutes of discussion, Thomas trotted back down to the Jeep where she waited.

"Michal asked me to take you back to the village. He—"

He was sending her out of harm's way. Fear slashed through her, sending her pulse into an erratic rhythm, blotting out whatever else Thomas said to her. She couldn't let Michal walk into this deathtrap. She had to do something. She thought of what he'd told her about the man he was supposed to execute. An evil man...one who sold weapons of mass destruction. She shuddered. Michal was right, he really was ridding the earth of evil.

...the rider of the white horse judged and made war...
...Faithful and True...

Suddenly she understood.

The Bible verse had referred to Michal.

Fran was letting her know that he wasn't the bad guy he portrayed. Somehow, and Ami could only guess at how, he was working for the good guys. A knight on a white horse making war on the side of truth.

Despite Thomas's protests, Ami barreled out of the Jeep and ran toward Michal. She would not let it end this way. She had to help him. She had to tell him everything.

"Michal!"

He turned just in time for her to skid to a stop without slamming into him. He glared past her in Thomas's direction, clearly not pleased with his failure to get the job done.

"I can't let you go until I've told you everything," she said in a rush, her voice breathless.

He gestured to his men and they moved on without him. To get into position, she assumed. Thomas returned to the Jeep to wait for her.

"I don't have time to—"

"Your son's name is Nicholas," she blurted, her heart too full to wait a second longer. He had to know. She *needed* him to know. "He looks exactly like you." She smiled, remembering her baby's sweet scent, his wobbly walk and his constant jabbering. "I would look at him sometimes and wonder if the dark man in my dreams was his father." Her gaze locked with Michal's, and somehow the ice there melted just a little. "And he was. That man is you. When we made love that last time...before...I got pregnant. When we made love the first time after you brought me back here I knew it was you. A part of you was always with me."

Michal was still reeling from her words about their son when she rushed on.

"You were right. The CIA did contact me." She shook her head shamefully. "They've been using me...or trying to since this whole crazy thing started with the shooting of Nathan Olment." She looked directly into Michal's eyes and told him the truth he already knew. "They wanted me to help them set you up for assassination. It's supposed to happen today." She blinked back the tears shining in her eyes. "But I couldn't do it. I told them no."

That part was news to him. With every fiber of his being he wanted to believe her, but remembered betrayal held him back. "Why would you do that?" he asked cautiously, determined to have solid evidence of what she appeared to be professing.

"Because I'm in love with you and you're the father of my child. I don't want you to be hurt."

Her arms went around him and she hugged him with all her might. "I love you, Michal, please don't go. Let's just get out of here."

He pulled away slightly, his eyes searching hers for any hint of deceit. He found none. "How could you love a man who kills for money...who martyrs whatever cause offering the highest price?" His breath stilled in his chest as he waited for her reaction to what she surely considered the truth about him.

She melted against him, the heat of her body warming the cold that had settled over him forty-eight hours ago. "Because I know you're not what you seem." She lifted one delicate shoulder in a shrug. "I know you're the rider on the white horse."

Need, desire and love—definitely love—welled inside him, bringing the sting of moisture to his eyes. He had no idea what she meant about the white horse, but he understood perfectly the rest of her words. Pulling her to him once more, he kissed her with all the emotions churning inside him.

"Go," he said, pulling back before it was too late. "Thomas will take you to a safe place."

She shook her head. "I'm not leaving without you."

He set her away from him. "You must."

"They're going to kill you! You can't go through with this," she pleaded, tears sliding down her cheeks.

If Michal did not survive this day, he would carry this moment in his heart to whatever reward or punishment lay in store for him. She was willing to risk everything to save him. Ron had told him how the CIA had threatened to keep her child from her if she did not cooperate.

"I cannot abort this mission," he explained as Thomas made his way back to their position. "It's too late."

Thomas urged her to come with him, but she resisted. "It's only too late if you let it be."

"The decision is made," Michal said more firmly. "Thank you for telling me about my son."

He walked away then, knowing Thomas would not allow her to follow. It was time for him to be in position. The hit was a relatively simple one.

The complexity lay in what came after that.

He was not afraid of death…but he did resent its source under the circumstances.

But it was past time this life was over…well past time.

AMI WATCHED him move out of sight…nothing she could do to stop him. She'd told him all that she knew and still he'd maintained his course. A sob knotted in her stomach as Thomas drove away. Fear that she would never see Michal again quivered inside her. Her heart squeezed painfully.

Would she ever know who Michal Arad really was?

JACK WAITED for Fran to reach the rendezvous point. He glanced at his watch. The final mission of the Executioner was about to go down.

One way or another Jack had to see that Ami didn't get caught in the aftermath as was planned.

But he couldn't do this alone.

Fran parked her ancient Audi near his rental and quickly emerged from the car. In four long strides she stood face-to-face with him.

"Why'd you move the time up?" she asked, taking a look at her own watch.

"I need your help."

A well-honed guard slipped into place, concealing whatever she might be thinking. "The last time you needed my help you almost got me killed."

She didn't have to remind him of the incident. He'd hoped she'd forgotten that by now. Jack had been new to the Company back then. Things were different today.

"It's important."

Fran cocked an eyebrow. "I can see that. You wouldn't have called otherwise. What is it you need me to do?"

"I don't want Ami to take the fall for this," he said,

knowing that what he was about to ask her to do risked not only her life but also her career. Something he was fully prepared to do, but Fran was nearing retirement, she might feel entirely different about the situation.

She looked at her watch again. "It's a fine time to make a decision of that magnitude. What did Fowler say about it?"

Jack had known Fran long enough to surmise that though she was clearly suspicious, she wasn't opposed to a change in plans. She would have balked at the first suggestion otherwise.

"Fowler doesn't know," he stated flatly, not bothering to pretty it up.

She didn't look surprised. "Well, he always was a stick in the mud when it came to human needs and basic emotions."

Ire kindled low in Jack's gut. "This isn't about emotion," he protested, setting her straight. "This is about what's right. She's already sacrificed far too much. It isn't right to take anything else. I want her back with her child. I want this nightmare over for her."

"What about Arad?" she countered. "Doesn't he deserve a reprieve, as well? Let's face it, the past three years haven't exactly been a frolic through a rose garden for him."

"That's out of my hands," Jack snapped.

Fran nodded sagely. "I see."

She was enjoying the hell out of this. Well, Jack didn't have time to amuse her, nor did he give one shit if she derived pleasure from his squirming. "Look," he pressed. "We have to move now. Are you in or out?"

She propped her elbow on her arm and tapped her cheek. "What's it worth to you, Jack? I can always use a field supervisor in my pocket."

"Now, Fran. I need a decision now," he growled.

She grinned. "I'll take that as a yes." She angled her head toward her antiquated Audi. "Let's get going before the concept becomes moot."

As usual Fran could always be counted on for a quick analysis of the situation.

They had to get to Ami now…before it was too late.

CHAPTER SEVENTEEN

MICHAL PAUSED before climbing into the Jeep. He stared back at the villa some twenty or so yards away. Even the air around it seemed to still. He surveyed the hillside to which they would retreat, and then the grounds surrounding the villa once more.

"Something is wrong," he said, his tone matching the somber mood that had abruptly settled over him. More wrong than his men could possibly guess.

This was the defining moment.

"What is wrong?" the Spaniard demanded. "The *bastardo* is dead and the electronic transfer is complete. We have confirmation. Nothing is wrong," he insisted, clearly ready to leave the scene of their most recent kills.

Michal shook his head. "We can't take that risk."

"What risk?" Kolin prodded.

He wanted to get the hell out of here, as well, Michal would wager, but his years of experience over the other man's would not allow him to so easily dismiss the possibility Michal had suggested.

"I have to go back in." Michal did an about-face and started toward the villa.

"What the hell are you doing?" The Spaniard moved in front of him, blocking his path. He glanced up the hill, scanning cautiously. "We must get out of here. You know that, Michal. Going back inside is not necessary."

"Mother of God," Kolin swore between clenched teeth,

his gaze fixed on the second story of the grand villa. "Someone's in there." He pointed to one window in particular. "I saw him in the window."

The Spaniard threw his hands up. "We have accomplished our mission. It is time to go. Whoever else is in there is none of our concern," he persisted.

"Go," Michal said to them, his full attention locking onto the second story. "I will tie up this loose end and meet you in Marseilles."

"How—"

Michal cut off whatever else Kolin intended with a look. "Go *now*. Wait for me in Marseilles."

"This is *loco!*" the Spaniard snarled before double timing it toward the Jeep. He didn't like what Michal was about to do, but he liked the idea of hanging around to watch even less.

Kolin reluctantly followed.

Michal didn't look back. Not once. He strode quickly to the villa and disappeared inside.

Looking back would not have fit the character of the ruthless Executioner.

Michal Arad never looked back, he moved forward constantly. Always accomplishing his goal.

He had never failed.

Not once.

Fifteen seconds after he passed through the arched portal that separated the courtyard from the shadowy interior of the villa an explosion shook the very foundation of the massive structure. Glass and bits and pieces of decor burst from the windows…the doors, spraying down a lethal rain of razor-sharp edges and spearlike material. After a moment's groan, the walls fell inward, burying all that was inside.

The Spaniard and Kolin watched from the safety of the

hillside. They had scarcely chugged up the road half a mile when the unexpected tragedy struck.

The two men exchanged looks of sheer terror and then the Spaniard floored the accelerator.

Getting the hell out of here was their only priority now. The import of the news they carried would reach the farthest corners of the globe before the sun set.

The Executioner was dead.

THE HOUSEKEEPING CART stopped near Room 214 and the maid rapped on the door.

Thomas cautiously pulled the door open, but only a fraction. He had no intention of letting anyone get close to Ami. Michal had given him specific orders that her safety was to be considered above all else.

Unlike his predecessor, Thomas would not fail.

"What do you want?" he demanded of the maid before she could articulate a syllable.

"Yours is the only room on the floor I have not cleaned," the woman said in French, her abuse of the language making him wince. "My work is not complete until I have cleaned *all* the rooms," she added with a stubborn tilt to her chin.

Thomas didn't want anyone else in the room, but he supposed this was necessary. He grunted an affirmative she would understand as he pulled the door fully open.

Ami lifted her head from the pillow when she heard the squeaky wheels of the housekeeping cart. She'd heard the voices, but the words hadn't really registered. All she could think about was Michal. Why hadn't they heard something already? How long would it take?

She worried and worried about what was the right thing to do, and in the end, when she'd realized that she actually had only one option, it had been too late.

Her head felt swollen and achy from her hours of sobbing. And far too heavy to hold up. When she would have collapsed back onto the pillow her gaze collided with an all too familiar one.

Fran Woodard was the cleaning lady who'd just weaseled her way past Thomas.

She fiddled with her supplies, smiled and shared a secret wink with Ami.

Hope soared inside her like a rocket taking off. Fran hadn't given up on her, after all.

She had to be here to rescue Ami.

Her hopes crashed and burned like a doomed airliner. But what about Michal?

Utter fear slammed into her then. Had the CIA been watching, witnessing her full confession to Michal?

That was it, she realized with rising dread.

Fran was here to kill her.

Ami shifted into an upright position, preparing to run like hell if Fran came near the bed.

But she didn't. She flitted around the rest of the room, dusting, rearranging, tidying anything that looked out of place. Finally, Thomas resumed his seat on the sofa and his captivation with the news. He didn't have the vaguest clue what hit him when Fran brought the ceramic table lamp down onto his head. She then brushed her hands together and said, "Well, that's that."

Ami leaped from the bed, her destination the door.

Before she could make heads or tails of the cleaning cart's sudden shaking and shifting, Jack Tanner emerged from it. One look at Ami was all it took for him to know total hysteria had hit.

"We're here to help you," he said quickly, stepping into her path when his sudden appearance failed to do more than slow her down.

"Get out of my way," she yelled, shoving him as hard as she could. She wanted to scream at him for what he had allowed to happen. She wanted to demand answers. But there was no time. Michal might need her. She had to get back to him.

"I've got your son…" he began.

She barreled into him with the full force of her weight. "You bastard." She lashed out. "Haven't you done enough already? What else do you people want?" She stood there, directly in front of him, her whole body shaking with emotions too strong and too numerous to name.

He reached for her, but she stumbled back from his grasp. "It's not what you think."

"I know what *it* is," she snapped. "You want both Michal and me dead."

"We're wasting time," Fran put in, tapping the watch she wore on her left wrist and looking pointedly from Tanner to Ami. "Nicholas is waiting."

Ami swiveled toward the woman, ready to tear into her, as well. "How could you taunt me that way? I thought you understood—"

Fran cocked an impatient eyebrow. "I do. Now let's get out of here before sleeping beauty over there wakes up and we have to do permanent damage."

For the first time since she'd recognized the CIA operative, Ami realized she was serious about helping. "My son is here?"

The mere idea sent warmth and relief flooding through her, weakening her knees, very nearly overwhelming her.

"That's what Jack has been trying to tell you," she said succinctly. "Now, let's get a move on."

At the door Ami hesitated, she looked straight into Tanner's eyes and demanded the truth. "What about Michal?"

For two excruciatingly long beats Tanner didn't respond, then he made her worst fears a reality.

"He's dead."

THE JOURNEY to the basement was made in a kind of shocked silence. Ami didn't speak, she scarcely breathed. She was capable of nothing. Tanner, with one arm around her shoulder, ushered her forward as necessary, forcing her legs to make the required movements.

Michal was dead.

Nicholas would never know him.

And somehow, even though she didn't fully understand it, she was partly to blame.

She had been the bait, of that she was certain now.

She didn't need Tanner or Fran to spell it out for her. In two years they had not been able to bring him down, but once they'd brought her into the picture, the feat had proved painfully simple.

A shudder worked its way through her when she considered that the whole Nathan Olment thing could have been an elaborate setup. Tanner had told her she was one of theirs. Had she simply lain dormant—a sleeper, so to speak—until they needed her back in action?

None of it mattered now.

It was too late.

Michal was dead.

Tears rolled down her cheeks and she attempted to console herself with the realization that she was finally going to see her child again. But even that left a gaping wound in her heart.

Tanner stopped next to a long black SUV and opened the rear passenger door. "We'll—"

The tip of a gun barrel suddenly pressed against his temple.

Ami gasped.

Tanner froze.

Fran had taken a position, her legs spread wide, her gun held in firing position and aimed directly at the interloper.

Michal Arad.

"Let her go," Michal said harshly, his weapon cocked and ready to fire.

"I thought you were dead," Tanner argued, a frown creasing his brow as he attempted to reason the situation.

"Obviously you were wrong," Michal countered hotly. "Now, let her go."

"You don't understand," Tanner hastened to explain, "we're taking her to her child."

"Drop the weapon, Arad," Fran suggested. "Don't make me do something we'll both regret."

He looked at Fran then. "This has nothing to do with you. It is between him—" he jerked his head toward Tanner "—and me."

Fran shrugged and lowered her weapon. "You're right."

Tanner gaped at her. "What the hell—"

"Let her go," Michal repeated, halting whatever Tanner intended to rant.

"They used him," Fran reminded Tanner. "He didn't deserve a termination order and you know it." She said the last with more ferocity than Ami had heard her use before.

Tanner had known Michal wasn't a bad guy? Shock radiated through Ami all over again. That meant the CIA knew…

Clearly recognizing when he was outnumbered, Tanner released her. Ami went immediately to Michal. She thrust her arms around him and held him close, determined to hear for herself the steady beat of his heart.

"Before you die," Michal said to Tanner, "you will tell Ami all that you and your people did to her."

Fran leaned against a nearby car. "Might as well get comfortable. This is going to take a while."

Too thankful for Michal's safety to care one iota about the rest of the conversation, Ami clung to him, sending up silent prayers of gratitude.

"Tell her," Michal ordered savagely.

Startled by the savagery in Michal's tone, Ami shifted her attention to him and then to Tanner. Anticipation spiked. He was finally going to tell her the truth. She could see the defeat in his eyes.

Her disbelief growing with every sentence he strung together, Ami listened as Tanner described her innocuous life as a med school student. The loss of her mother and the long-standing, deep-seated dislike for her father. Then, visibly reluctant, he told her the rest. The way her cover as Jamie Dalton had been initiated. The whole crazy scheme. Down to the fact that he had known she was alive all along, had been the one to rescue her.

When at last he'd finished, Ami did the only thing she could. She slapped him hard. Wanted the sting to go on and on until the quake shook loose some sense of compassion in him.

What he'd done had been wrong.

But it was over now. If what he'd told her was true and he'd brought her baby back to her, she could forgive him most anything.

"Where's my child?" she demanded, ready to do him bodily harm yet again.

To his credit, he didn't step back. He took it like a man. "Get in." He tossed a challenging glare in Michal's direction. "You, too. I'll take you both to Nicholas."

Michal inclined his head toward Fran. "She will take

us to my son. The only place you're going is to hell." He tightened his grip around his weapon.

"Wait!" Ami pulled back and peered up at Michal. "He only followed orders. Killing him won't make any of this right." Her voice grew even more pleading then. "I just want to see my baby."

"Besides," Tanner put in, "the two of you need me."

Michal made a sound of disbelief. "And how have you reached that ridiculous conclusion?"

"I can sink your files. As far as the CIA will be concerned, neither of you will ever have existed. Only a handful of people will know and even they won't be able to prove it."

Michal didn't bother to tell him that Ron Doamiass had already taken similar steps within the Mossad. Michal owed him a great deal. A debt he would never be able to repay. As far as the world knew, Michal Arad was dead. Ron had risked his career as well as his life to set up that very scenario. That it was witnessed and survived by two of Michal's men had been the pivotal strategy.

Yet, on some level, Michal knew that Tanner spoke the truth. The history of Michal and Ami would be best served if it no longer existed in any government agency.

"Who will ensure that you—" he glanced at the attractive older woman who had allowed him to make his case without interference "—and you keep this secret?"

"What was your name again?" Fran quipped.

"Your son is waiting," Tanner reminded him, uncertainty as to his own fate hovering in his expression.

A single beat passed before Michal lowered his weapon.

Tanner's relief was palpable.

In less than half an hour Tanner drove into the parking lot of a small dry-cleaning business. He looked from Michal in the front passenger seat to Ami in the back, her hand already rested on the door latch. "Fran will go in and bring him out."

When Michal would have protested, Tanner reminded him, "We don't need any more people than absolutely necessary to see you alive at this point."

Seeing the reasonableness in his assertion, Michal allowed the woman to emerge from the SUV and go into the rundown shop.

Two minutes later she opened the rear passenger-side door and handed Ami a large bundle of squirming arms and legs.

Michal's heart seized.

This was his son.

Her smile trembling on her lips, Ami pulled back the soft blanket and revealed the child's expectant face. Michal's breath evacuated his lungs in one blast.

This was his son. His every feature was just as Ami had described—a mirror image of his father.

"Michal." Ami turned toward him and offered the child to him over the console between the seats. "Meet Nicholas, your son."

Michal took the child in his arms, his heart swelling with equal parts pride and love. The child wiggled and squirmed, but did not pout up and cry. Awe paralyzed Michal's ability to speak or to even think.

But words were not necessary.

He had all that he had ever wanted within his reach.

EPILOGUE

SIX MONTHS AFTER holding his son for the first time, Michal had settled his family in a small, quiet village in a country where terrorism was an unfamiliar term rather than an everyday affair. A curiously sheltered environment where time seemed to have stopped at a better place.

Ami pressed a kiss to the top of Nicholas's head as he scrambled down from her lap to play with his father on the beach.

She laughed and clapped at their antics as they rolled and wrestled on the warm sand, the ocean lapping nearby.

Though months had passed, Michal knew that she still struggled with some aspects of the past she had not been able to fully recall. The steps that had been taken to erase her memory had left some parts irretrievable. But she was coping, one day at a time.

Tanner had been true to his word, as, of course, Ron had been. Not a single shred of evidence existed supporting Michal's or Ami's cases.

With new names and a low-profile life, there was no reason to ever suspect anyone would learn the truth.

Their son kept them busy by day and making love filled their nights. Michal could not be happier.

His life was at long last complete.

Ami watched the two men in her life frolic on the beach. She loved both of them more than any words she knew could convey. Still, she tried every day to get the message across in all that she said and did. She had learned first-hand that life was not to be taken for granted.

The past seemed a long ways off now. Though the nightmares still surfaced once in a while, for the most part she had accepted that she would never remember everything.

And as long as she had Michal and Nicholas, nothing else mattered.

Well, except for maybe one other thing.

When Nicholas had tired and his father had tucked him in for an afternoon nap, Ami knew it was time to tell her secret.

Michal hauled her up against him and pressed himself intimately to her. "Shall we get an early start?"

She heaved an exaggerated sigh and wrinkled her brow into a frown. "Really, Michal, you are scandalous."

He nuzzled her neck. "It is my one downfall," he whispered against her skin, the vibration of those masterful lips sending pleasure straight to her bones.

"First." She wriggled away from him. "There's something I have to tell you."

He dropped onto the sofa and pulled her down into his lap. "Speak, woman, I have other things on my mind."

Judging by the fullness of his arousal, she felt certain this was so. Though she'd like nothing better than to crawl between those sheets with him right this moment, they had to get this out of the way first.

"We're pregnant," she announced without further ado.

It took a moment for the words to fully assimilate in his brain. Michal stared at her blankly for two beats before realization struck.

His dark eyes gleaming with excitement, he folded his strong arms around her and held her close to his heart. "A girl, I predict," he said with complete confidence.

She wouldn't admit it just now for love or money, but she had a feeling he was right. "And just how can you know that," she teased.

His wide smile was more beautiful than any she had ever known the pleasure of laying eyes on. "Because this is what I have wished for."

"Do you always get what you wish for?" She felt herself holding her breath as she waited for his answer.

His expression turned somber then. "I wished that you would be returned to me."

The sweetness in his words tugged sharply at her heartstrings. "Who am I to argue with destiny?" she mused, her gaze drifting down to those perfectly formed lips.

"Enough talk." He covered her mouth with his own and slowly but surely proceeded to show her that wishes really could come true.